"Robin D. Owens...provides a wonderful, gripping mix
of passion, exotic futuristic settings and edgy suspense."
—*New York Times* bestselling author
Jayne Ann Krentz on *Heart Duel*

"Like a well-played symphony,
Guardian of Honor resonates in the hearts of those
fortunate enough to read it."
—*Huntress Reviews*

"Fans will gobble up *Guardian of Honor* and still be
hungry for more."
—*The Best Reviews*

"Robin Owens blends medieval history, a richly layered
magical world and fine characterizations to weave a
spell-binding story in *Guardian of Honor*."
—*BookLoons*

ROBIN D. OWENS

SORCERESS OF FAITH

LUNA™

www.LUNA-Books.com

LUNA™

First edition February 2006

SORCERESS OF FAITH

ISBN 0-373-80221-8

Copyright © 2006 by Robin D. Owens

This edition published by arrangement with Harlequin Books S.A.

® and TM are trademarks of Harlequin Books S.A., used under license. Trademarks indicated with ® are registered in the United States Patent and Trademark Office, the Canadian Trade Marks Office and in other countries.

www.LUNA-Books.com

Printed in U.S.A.

ACKNOWLEDGMENTS

The Usual Suspects:
Kay Bergstrom (Cassie Miles), Liz Roadifer, Janet Lane,
Sharon Mignerey (www.sharonmignerey.com),
Steven Moores, Judy Stringer, Anne Tupler,
Sue Hornick, Alice Kober, Teresa Luthye,
Peggy Waide (www.peggywaide.com), Giselle McKenzie

To Kay
Who encouraged and supported me from the
beginning and continues to do so—
my stories would be so much less without you

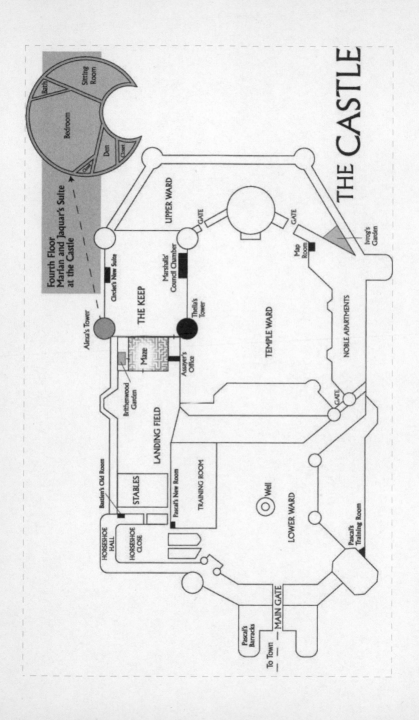

THE CASTLE

Fourth Floor
Marian and Jaquar's Suite at the Castle

Bath
Sitting Room
Bedroom
Den
Closet
Closet

UPPER WARD

Alexa's Tower

Cinder's New Suite

THE KEEP

Marshalls' Council Chamber

Thella's Tower

GATE

Ivrog's Garden

Map Room

GATE

Assayer's Office

TEMPLE WARD

NOBLE APARTMENTS

Maze

Brithenwood Garden

LANDING FIELD

GATE

Bastien's Old Room

STABLES

HORSESHOE HALL

HORSESHOE CLOSE

Pascal's New Room

TRAINING ROOM

Well

LOWER WARD

Pascal's Training Room

Pascal's Barracks

MAIN GATE

To Town

I

Boulder, Colorado
Late spring, early morning

She was running, running, running. Marian wished the passages were narrower, twistier, because the thing that chased her was huge and deadly. With each breath putrid air seared her lungs. The cavern's corridors oozed slime.

She stumbled, clutched the plastic ball holding her hamster close. Looking down at her cross-trainer shoes in horror, she saw the laces were untied. She always tied them in perfect double bows.

A vibration hit her back. The monster's breath. Stitch cramping her side, she used terror for a burst of speed and reached narrow upward stairs. Fresher air, laden with blood instead of poisonous acid, fouled her nostrils. She climbed, thinking the thing behind her could flow up the stairs. It wanted her blood, her guts, her brains.

Bumping from side to side, scraping skin raw, protecting her pet, she jumped up the steps and burst out onto a wide ledge of rock. With agility she didn't know she had, she pivoted, avoiding the edge, hit the cliff face. Leaned into it. Gulping night air, she felt the thing brush past her, and fall screaming.

She couldn't stop herself from looking down. Saw something worse than the huge shattered body of the monster that had hunted her. Her younger brother Andrew was surrounded by chanting black-robed druids who looked like death personified. Some of the druids held scythes, some gongs, some chimes.

Prone Andrew was, more pale than he'd ever been in life. Shrieking, "Nooooo!" she put the ball between her feet, lifted her arms as if she could call thunder that would set his heart to thumping again, push his blood; lightning that would nail his soul into his body, fire the spark of life.

A wet chuckle came next to her, freezing her blood. Slowly she turned her head to see a cowled figure with gleaming red eyes, a face not quite human but which might have been a man's, once. He opened his mouth wide, and it got larger and larger, ready to swallow her whole. She raised her hands, fingertips arcing blue fire—

Marian Harasta jolted from the dream, covered in clammy sweat. Morning light streamed through the high windows of her garden apartment and she gasped in relief.

Before she could exhale, the chimes sounded, rippling through her nerves and echoing in her mind. Then the gong reverberated, arching her body off the bed. Her vision blurred and distant chanting rushed in her ears. She was bowed for one long moment before she fell back onto the bed, panting.

First the nightmare. Now the sounds. For the past months, dreams and auditory hallucinations had peppered her life— sleeping and waking. She steadied herself with even breathing. She would figure out what was happening to her. She'd had a full physical the week before, and a psychological evaluation, too. And she was perfectly fine.

The strangeness had started with sounds, then the dreams, then an itchy feeling as if she were a butterfly escaping from a constrictive cocoon, ready to stretch her wings. The notion was more than a little scary because her academic career was on track and her life tidy and under control. Except for Andrew, her half brother with progressive-remitting Multiple Sclerosis.

Brrrrinnng. The telephone. She flung off her covers and stumbled from bed, staggering to the phone charger on the kitchen counter. She had to blink a couple of times to read the caller ID. Her mother, Candace. Hell. The relationship with her mother, too, was out of Marian's control. She let voice mail answer.

Marian wiped her face on the sleeve of her flannel nightgown, pondering options to understand, then fix, her problems. She couldn't discuss this with her academic professors of Comparative Religion and Philosophy, or her advisor sheparding her through her doctorate. Her university profs would not understand. She didn't want any oddness attached to her spotless reputation as she planned on a professional career.

Since the problem wasn't physical or psychological, she'd considered psychic phenomena. Since she'd been fascinated by alternative spiritualities for years, she thought she might find help there.

She'd examined all the notes from all the classes she'd taken outside the university—New Age classes that fed her thirst for knowledge—searching for answers. Somewhere there was a solution for what plagued her and she *would* find it.

As she padded to the bathroom, she checked on her hamster, Tuck, curled in his cage in the alcove. A half-chewed piece of carrot was within paw reach. All was well in his small world.

Marian only wished it were the same for her. She worked hard to keep her life in order, and usually succeeded, but lately...

In the shower as water slicked away sweat, she decided to call Golden Raven. The lady leaned more to Native American beliefs than Marian did, but she was more open-minded than many and would listen without judging. She might know of instances similar to Marian's experiences. That would be a good step in controlling the weirdness that had invaded her life.

"Yes," she muttered as she dressed for her work-study job. "I need Golden Raven." She went to the telephone. Should she call Golden Raven or Candace? Glancing at the clock, she thought it might be too early for Golden Raven. If Marian didn't phone Candace back, her mother's mood would turn nasty and her demands would escalate. Inhaling deeply, Marian called the residence of Candace's sixth husband, a mansion in an old, upscale area of Denver.

Candace's tone was sharp. "Well, Marian, it's good you called." Papers rustled in the background. Since Candace didn't launch into speech, Marian figured her mother was multitasking.

Excellent. Maybe they could get through a conversation without damaging each other. "What do you want, Mother?" asked Marian.

"Hmm? Oh, yes, Marian. You must come down here to Denver for a fund-raiser tomorrow night, Friday, 7:30 p.m. Cocktails and dinner."

"Why, Mother?" Marian was deeply entrenched in academia now; she'd never be a person who could enhance her mother's status in any way. Thank God.

Candace heaved an exasperated sigh. "Trenton Philbert III remarried a month ago. A woman who runs one of the largest occult shops in Denver. Why he married such a *creature,* no one knows. I just learned he and his new wife will be at the benefit. Trenton dotes on the woman and his contribution is necessary for us to meet our goal."

Ah, various cities competed to raise the most money and Candace intended to prove she was the best. Candace continued, "So I need to keep his wife happy to keep *him* happy."

Instead of zooming in on the woman like a barracuda.

"I can't imagine that anyone would have any idea what to say to her." *Creature* was still in Candace's voice. "Then, I thought of you, of course. With all your…experience in that area."

Sounded like Marian attended seances and channeling every night.

Hooking up again with the Denver New Age community might not be a bad thing. In one way, Marian could even convince herself that her company would be beneficial for the unknown woman. And there were some good, kind people in Denver society that Marian would like to see again. Too bad her mother didn't happen to be one. Despite her methods, though, Candace was great at raising money.

"I don't think so, Mother."

"I can make it worth your while," Candace continued.

Marian waited for the bribe. Bribes sometimes worked. Marian had to know more about the situation to figure out whether the favor was worth whatever Candace was offering.

"I know you're studying too hard. Having the rest of your college fund would make life easier."

In Candace's mind, Marian was always studying too hard. Candace didn't understand that learning was a pleasure. Though she understood that knowledge was power, at least when it came to playing the Denver social game, using secrets.

"Marian, did you hear me? I told you that I could release the last of your college fund."

Good bribe, and if bribes didn't work, Candace used the threat: Withholding her college fund now, Andrew's welfare when he'd been younger. He was twenty-four, four years younger than Marian. She'd tried to take care of him, since Candace was uninterested in her son.

"I'll think about it," Marian said.

"I need a commitment," Candace snapped. "I'll call Andrew. It may take some doing on his part, but he'll come."

"No, Mother, I don't want you bothering Andrew."

Candace ignored her. "Of course he'll come. The Colorado Charities Fund disburses money to the Multiple Sclerosis Foundation of Colorado. I always have an advantage when campaigning for the Chairmanship of the Fund drive—with poor Andrew being afflicted with MS, and at such an early age, too."

Fury veiled Marian's vision in a red haze. Good thing that the phone was industrial strength; otherwise it would have crumbled under her grip. How Candace could think of her own son that way...

"Andrew is a person with a challenging disease. Don't define him as a victim."

Candace sniffed. "Believe what you want. Now, about the fund-raiser, tell me whether the weather will be clear."

Heat crept up Marian's neck. She'd always had weather-sense. She shifted and felt the connection to Mother Earth, one reason she loved the garden-level apartment. "Clear and cool," she said.

"Good. Your drive down from Boulder should be fine, then."

Rubbing her forehead, Marian said, "I'll be there."

"I thought so, and bring that delightful Professor Wilse with you."

Marian shuddered at the thought of Jack Wilse. *Mistake.* She admired his body but deplored his values. He'd manipulated and used her, too, before her mind got her hormones under control. It was inconceivable to her now that she'd had a brief affair with him. "He won't be coming with me."

"Marian, you can't attend alone! How will it look? Speaking of looks, you *have* used that exercise club membership I bought for you so you'd lose those extra pounds, haven't you?"

"My weight is my own business." Candace would continue to comment on it anyway. "I *will* be coming alone—or not at all. If you want me there, deposit the rest of my college fund into my account and e-mail me the details." Marian hung up.

Mistake. She'd allowed her mother to manipulate her. Would she ever learn? But this time, she'd gotten the last of her college fund. With chilled fingers she reached for her appointment book, flipped to the end where she'd listed her five-year plan. She inserted Friday's date as the day she'd receive the money that would set her free from her mother, and launch her fully on her career path. Ahead of schedule, but right on track. She wouldn't allow anything or anyone—especially her mother—to control her again. Her own mistakes might be bad, but they were *hers*. Hers to learn from.

She felt as if she'd been stung, and poison was spreading through her system. Like so many times before in her life. That's what happened when you were raised by an unevolved Scorpio.

Grumbling, Marian stalked through her living room. A book from the bookshelf-lined walls thumped to the floor. She stopped and stared. There was a gaping hole on the second shelf where she kept her Wiccan books neatly alphabetized by author.

She swallowed. Even before she picked up the book, she knew what it would be: *Craft Your Own Ritual*, by a well-respected Wiccan. It was the third time this week that volume had fallen from the shelf.

As usual, the crisp pages fell open to a full-moon ritual. Rising anxiety made her pulse race. She closed her eyes and colors swirled behind her eyelids, followed by a flash of the image of Andrew from her nightmare.

Her eyelids flicked open. Her chest tightened. All the recent coincidental signs pointed to her conducting a full-moon ritual. Marian glanced at the yearly moon phase chart she'd framed. Full moon tomorrow night, Friday—the same night she'd agreed to attend Candace's benefit.

A knock came at her door and a tingle ran up her spine. She pushed aside the curtain draped over the apartment door's small window, looked out. Golden Raven stood on the threshold. She smiled until the lines deepened around her blue eyes and framed her mouth. Beyond her was an old van packed full of boxes, ready for a long trip.

With a sigh, Marian opened the door.

"I heard you call me," Golden Raven said.

Jaquar's Tower, Sorcerers' Mue Island, east of Lladrana
Late spring, that same morning

Jaquar stood naked in the alcove that held his magical supplies and looked into the round ritual room of his tower. A faint blue-green steam eddied and flowed along the lines of the pentacle carved into the stone floor. His shoulders tensed at the thought of plane-walking—leaving his body behind to float astrally through different layers of existence. He was a Circlet—the highest rank of Sorcerer—of Weather Control and plane-walking, but he'd been focused on the second craft for the past three weeks.

Putting off the moment when he'd have to look in the Enhanced Mirror, the last step before the ritual, he turned back to the work counter and set his hand on the upper leaf in a huge book.

He'd made the book himself. Each sheet was a non-physical plane he'd traveled. Sheets were arranged in the same layers as the planes themselves. A being existed on many planes, but a good plane-walker like himself could separate himself from his body and explore one layer at a time.

The leaf he'd turned to was the plane he'd visit. One of seething, low emotions—evil emotions only. A plane for monsters, not humans. But he was tracking a monster. The monster that had killed his adoptive parents three weeks ago.

A chime notified him that the ritual should be started within the half hour. Jaquar inhaled deeply and went to the left end of the narrow alcove. There he unfolded the three-paneled mirror. To ensure he didn't get lost amongst the planes, he had to know himself, and for that he used the mirror.

He scanned his physical appearance. He was taller than the average Lladranan male, had filled out in maturity. His strong body appeared nothing like that of the abandoned street boy Simone and Torrence Dumont had found and raised. But the awful inner loneliness of the boy before he'd known them filled him now. He'd once thought he'd never feel that desolation again.

His body showed a few childhood scars. His eyes were still the hated deep blue that made him an oddity in a brown-eyed culture. Some ancestor had not been Lladranan.

He'd lost weight since the deaths of his adoptive parents, but not so much that it would compromise his strength. His black hair touched his shoulders and looked limp, not as shiny as it should. The silver streaks denoting Power had visibly spread over the past three weeks as he'd searched for the evil thing that had killed his mother and father. Both had been powerful Circlets, yet the horror had sucked them dry of magic and energy and life.

As Jaquar had searched the planes for the killer, he'd grown in magical wisdom and Power, discovering new layers. These new planes would be valuable in tracking the horrors that invaded Lladrana.

The northern magical boundary of mainland Lladrana had been failing, gaping open so that hideous evil creatures could slither through to prey on the people. First the smaller horrors would cross, such as armored snippers. Then the greater monsters would attack in groups—renders and slayers and soul-suckers. And the sangvile. At the same time, frink-worms had started falling with the rain, affecting even the Tower community's islands.

The horrors had never reached the Sorcerers' town of Coquille-on-the-Coast where his parents had lived until Jaquar had led the sangvile there. He had answered the Marshalls' call for a Sorcerer, given them information, then left. The sangvile had attached itself to the flying horse he'd ridden from the Marshalls' Castle to his parents' house. He'd left the deadly thing there, unknowing. Just two weeks past, the key to restoring the magical boundary had been found—too late for his parents.

He met his own hollow gaze in the mirror. "Mental," Jaquar said. The reflection in the mirror changed and he saw the white sparkling of his brain, the waves of strong mental energy. The rhythm of his energy was good. His mind was clear.

"Magical," he ordered. The mirror showed his Power radiating out in colorful bands from his body. Lladranans tended to judge magic by the tones and tunes it made, but the mirror reflected it visually. There were no breaks, no streaks of blackness. His Power had never been stronger. Good.

Jaquar hesitated. "Emotional," he whispered, and saw his body shrouded in grief. Fury and vengeance glowed red in his eyes and heart. Not good. But he wasn't going to travel to any plane that needed lighter, more uplifting emotions.

He'd be able to find that ugly lower plane easily, blend in, cruise through it.

"Spiritual," he said. Again the darkness, nearly smothering the gold aura tracing his body. Ragged spikes showed how his spiritual health fluctuated. Perhaps when he'd destroyed the sangvile he would make an appointment with the Singer for a personal Song Quest. A Song Quest would tell him how best to manage his grief and guilt. Later.

"Physical." There he was again, face strained, changed since his adoptive parents had died. He recalled his last leave-taking with his adoptive parents, no more than a month ago. *Parents,* they would have corrected him, not "adoptive parents." They'd been right in that as in so many other things. Though they hadn't birthed him, had only taken him off the streets when he was eight, they'd been his parents.

His last memory of them was as they laughed at some joke his father had told just before Jaquar left their home. They were framed in the golden light streaming from the doorway of their house. His mother, round of face and body, leaning into his father, the aura of love radiating from her....

Just the moment before, her sweet breath had caressed his cheek as she'd kissed him farewell. Her scent had wound around him—the flowery herb fragrance that had been his comfort from the moment she'd claimed him as her own.

His father had hugged him hard, as always, and Jaquar had felt the strength of Power and body that had always meant love and safety.

No more. Ever. All because of him.

He had brought their evil killer to them. The odd boy they'd saved from the streets had ultimately led their deaths to them, far before their time.

"Off." His image faded and he was glad.

Unhurried, he walked to the pentacle, closed the circle with a hummed note, and settled into a soft pallet in the center to begin his quest to find and destroy his parents' slayer. He sang.

When the Songspell ended, his astral shape slipped from his body with an easy pull and a tiny "pop." Hovering over his physical form, he felt light and free.

He stayed in the same physical plane and rose above his Tower, his island, to orient and anchor himself. As was customary, his was the only Circlet Tower on the island, and the island itself was small. Most circlets lived on their own island in the Brisay Sea, east of Lladrana. He'd wanted one only a few miles from Coquille-on-the-Coast where his parents lived so he would visit them often.

On the physical plane, the sangvile had two forms: one, a black spiderweb, and the other, a manlike dark energy. Its rudimentary, *nasty* emotions were that of an evil predator. As strong as it was now, if spread out in spiderweb form, it would cover a house. The man form would be a giant.

The monster had gloated over the pain and fear it caused, laughed in malicious glee at its feast of Circlets and their Power. Those tainted emotions had leaked through several planes and led Jaquar to it. He had found the horror too late to pin it down, set it ablaze and watch it die.

Below, he saw his Tower, round and of red stone, with a flat roof and a walkway around it; Mue Island, looking like the blunted top of an archery arrow, slightly southwest of Coquille-on-the-Coast. He drifted even higher, until he could see most of Lladrana, the rocky hill where the Marshalls' Castle sat—in the middle of Lladrana, far from the ocean, east and north of Coquille-on-the-Coast. He tugged on the cord between his astral self and his body. It held firm.

Then he plane-walked, searching for the sangvile.

He passed through several known planes to reach the one he wanted, tuning himself to its unique vibrations. Only on this plane could he pinpoint the hideous energy of the sangvile.

And there was the monster that had slain his parents. And Jaquar lusted to destroy the sangvile with all the fierce desire within him. Here, the sangvile was a gliding black smudge.

Jaquar was back on the hunt. Though this lower emotional plane was a gray nothingness, Jaquar could dimly sense the geography of the physical plane below, where the sangvile roamed. Here, the image of the sangvile was a gliding black smudge, traveling northwest from Lladrana. Jaquar followed.

No sights; worse, no sounds. The dreary atmosphere made his emotions all the more powerful.

The sangvile moved. Geographic familiarity, physical reference points, were gone. The sangvile was far outside the borders of Lladrana, flying north with information and energy and magic to give the Dark.

Jaquar's astral self followed. As a mind-shadow, Jaquar had no eyes to weep or voice to scream his grief. The emotions that gave him the strength and cunning to track the beast scoured him, made him vengeance incarnate. He would kill the servant and destroy the lord. No price was too high to pay.

The thing hesitated in flight, then lashed out with a black-energy tentacle. Jaquar ducked, drew back. Was it aware of him? Aware of something as predatory as itself, as ruthless?

Coalescing into a streak of dark lightning, the horror sped up. The monster was near its…nest?

Ahead, the grayness of the ethereal plane changed. In the distance was a black point. Jaquar sensed something huge and vile and pulsing.

2

In front of Jaquar seethed a mound of evil so dark that it swallowed all light, all energy. The sangvile rounded itself into a ball and arced downward into a hole of red, with tentacles of gray and acid green and black. The mound radiated a loathsome, diseased feeling that seemed to coat Jaquar with slime.

The place was inimical to all humans. And it was hungry.

No price was too much to pay to avenge his parents.

Jaquar flung his astral-self into it.

And hit a magical shield. Rebounded, stunned and aching.

He spent his rage battering the magical barrier with all his might, all of himself. He shifted to planes above and below and struck the shield time and again, then returned to the first plane.

Jaquar Dumont. A sneering voice resounded in Jaquar's head along with a hideous clash of notes. He stopped his fruitless assault. Hovered. Wondered whether to reply, if acknowledgment would make him vulnerable.

The great Jaquar Dumont, bastard with tainted Exotique blood, the voice continued, and Jaquar realized it *was* human—and male.

A human Sorcerer consorting with the horrors and monsters that invaded Lladrana? Had Jaquar been in his physical form he'd have been sick with revulsion. Did Jaquar know the voice? He didn't think so. He did sense the Power of the Sorcerer. The Sorcerer was nearly a Circlet—but he wasn't the true and ultimate evil. The man served another.

The Sorcerer laughed at Jaquar. *So, you have found us, but only on this low plane. You cannot break the Dark's shield, nor harm this nest. No Sorcerer or Sorceress of Lladrana can.*

Come out and fight! Jaquar threw the mental call to the human.

The Sorcerer snorted. *If and when I exit our nest it will be with an army, or allies so strong that no one will be able to stop us.*

All of Lladrana will fight you! Jaquar shouted, trying to pierce the shield with Mind and Power alone. Futile.

More sneering laughter. *The Marshalls have discovered how to raise the magical barrier against us. But in two weeks they have not done much. The Marshalls are few and slow. The boundary still has many gaps.*

Wild shrieking came from the human. If he'd been sane at one time, he wasn't now.

Gathering himself into a spear of Power, Jaquar arrowed to the red maw-gate of the pulsing mound. And was flung away.

The sangvile is safe from you, as are all the servants I control. You will never be able to pass the shield on any plane. No Lladranan with Power can breech this forcefield. No Lladranan can hurt this nest. The voice insinuated into Jaquar's mind as he continued to batter at the gate. *Since you loathe the sangviles so much, I will set more upon Lladrana. Soon. Aimed at Circlets.*

Despairing, Jaquar continued the assault until his energy faded and he had only enough strength to return home. He awoke hours later, body stiff, psychically blind since he'd abused his Power. With croaking voice, he dismissed the magical pentacle.

Jaquar staggered to his desk and fell into his chair, ready to record all he knew of the sangvile, all he'd learned in his pursuit. His face was colder than the rest of him. He lifted his hand and touched his cheek. It was wet.

Boulder, Colorado
The same morning

Marian froze. "I didn't call you."

Golden Raven raised little penciled-in eyebrows and pushed by her to enter the apartment. "I heard you." She tapped her head, glanced around and took a seat on the couch.

"I find that very strange." Just as odd as everything else that was happening. Marian shut the door.

Golden Raven wore tight jeans and shirt that did nothing for her heavy figure. But unlike Marian, Golden Raven accepted her body. "I know you do, but just listen. My vision was of you and a young man who looked a great deal like you—except he had black hair instead of your red."

Andrew. Marian had never told Golden Raven about him. Marian had met a lot of frauds while taking New Age classes, and Golden Raven wasn't one of them. The woman was a brilliant forecaster.

Tilting her multi-shaded blond head, Golden Raven surveyed Marian's apartment. "Very much like you, Marian. Books, papers, everything too neat and tidy. Still striving for perfection, I see."

"Golden Raven, I'm running late for my job—"

"Our paths are not the same, but I had to tell you of the vision before Wood Elk and I left for the West Coast." She looked at Marian, eyes narrowed. "You have a great deal of intelligence, and more—just plain *magic* in you, right beneath the surface. But you dabble. You don't commit yourself to freeing your powers."

Marian wasn't accustomed to teachers berating her. She stood stiffly beside Golden Raven.

"You dabble, not taking what you learn seriously. Yet I feel a brilliant spark within you, humming just under your skin." She tapped Marian's chest above her breasts. "Strong magic."

"Golden Raven, it would be interesting if that were true. But—"

"You feel your psi powers trying to break free and even now reject them. I *heard* you calling me this morning—can you deny *that?*"

"No." But she wanted to. On the other hand, she'd always had an internal push to find...*something*...ever eluding her. Could it be magic? Could she have strong psychic powers? She'd only been aware of her weather sense and her connection to Mother Earth.

Golden Raven grasped Marian's arm, then stilled, her eyes going blank and unfocused. "The full moon. Tomorrow night." Golden Raven sucked in a breath and stepped back from Marian, breaking the physical connection. She shook her head, then met Marian's eyes. "I don't know what it means. I can't tell you. Except that this full-moon ritual is very important for you. It will be life changing. For you *and* your brother."

Her words were as fearsome as Marian's nightmares, and

seemed just as real. Believe, or not? Golden Raven had mentioned Andrew again, the bait Marian would always swallow.

She said steadily, "When I said your name this morning I wanted to ask if you knew others who had had experiences like these I've been enduring."

"Your psi potential demanding to be fulfilled. Do the ritual, find one who will help you direct it. As for your brother, he is linked to you and I believe he will be…greatly affected in a good way by your psi development." She opened her mouth, then shut it and shook her head again. "No, I should not tell you, even if I could. I'm sorry, Marian. I must go now, and Blessings upon you." With a little duck of her head she turned and left the apartment. The door clicked shut behind her.

Marian barcly saw her go as emotions churned inside her. She needed another shower, although a hot bath would be better to banish the sudden chill.

She might have shrugged off the continuing auditory illusions, might have ignored Golden Raven's advice to find another teacher. Might have continued to "dabble" in New Age spirituality on her way to receiving her doctorate. But she would never ignore any threat to her brother. Andrew was the person she most loved. She'd do the ritual tomorrow night.

She'd anger Candace by not appearing on demand, couldn't in good conscience take her mother's money when she wasn't going to follow through on the favor of the fund-raiser. That meant putting her career on hold, getting a job—leaving her college fund with her mother. Marian squared her shoulders. So be it.

If a full-moon ritual was important to understand the

strangeness happening to her and if it could help Andrew, she'd do it. And take it seriously, by God—or by All the Powers that Were.

Lladrana
The same day

Jaquar had just finished recording his journey in his lorebook when a crackle of lightning had him jerking his head to the crystal sphere on his desk. He flicked it with his fingernail, *ping*, and accepted the sending of another Circlet.

Cloudiness filled the crystal, then dissolved to wisps. Two people finished the Songspell that allowed them to communicate with Jaquar and stared out at him. A shaft of pain speared through him. Jaquar was accustomed to speaking only with his parents this way, and they would never sing to him again.

Chalmon Pace and Venetria Fourney—on-again, off-again quarreling lovers—gazed at him. They both bore the mark of great magical Power, thick streaks of silver at both temples in their otherwise black hair.

The last Jaquar had heard, Venetria had been backtracking the sangvile. She'd lost an aunt in Coquille-on-the-Coast.

"Bad news," Chalmon said gruffly.

Jaquar grunted.

"Venetria's information, compiled with what I've gleaned from the oldest lorebooks, tells us that the appetite of the sangvile is exponential." He cleared his throat. "And it prefers those with Power. The monster is directed at us, the Circlets of the Tower Community."

With stiff lips Jaquar said, "We lost eight strong Sorcerers and Sorceresses in Coquille-on-the-Coast. That can't be allowed to happen again."

The other two nodded. "We agree," Chalmon said. "We must protect ourselves from this horror. We're sure you are right—the sangvile followed you from the Marshalls' Castle."

Jaquar laughed harshly. "I thought it was too weak to attach itself to me. I thought it would hide and garner strength in the Castle. Instead it knew I could lead it to a richer feast later." He didn't think he'd ever forgive himself for that. "You said its hunger is exponential?"

"Yes," sighed Venetria.

"It's back at its master's nest." The words pulled jerkily from Jaquar, he didn't want to think of his journey to the red maw, his vain assault, the gloating triumph he'd sensed. Nevertheless, he told Chalmon and Venetria.

They were both pale when he finished.

"It's coming back, and not alone," Venetria whispered. "More than one sangvile?"

"Yes," Jaquar said. He'd be ready for the horrors, and he wasn't averse to attacking. "We need more to find the nest, to understand what this 'master' is and how to battle it. I'll organize the effort."

Chalmon frowned. "I don't know—"

Jaquar gestured, stopping Chalmon's protest. "I've lost the most. Isn't that the Tower Community tradition? The one who is most passionate gathers Powerful Circlets of the Fifth Degree and directs them?"

The two looked at each other again.

"We're all concerned with the defense of Lladrana and now finding the master who directs the monsters to invade," Chalmon said.

Smiling coldly, Jaquar said, "If anyone wants to challenge me for leadership, I'm available."

Venetria dipped her head. "So noted."

Chalmon shrugged, turned the subject. "No Sorcerer or Sorceress could pass. No Lladranan with Power could breech the shield. That means we use someone from the Exotique land. Someone for the Tower community. Our Exotique."

"We could ask the Exotique Alyeka," Venetria said.

"She's one of the Marshalls. We can't be indebted to them. We'd lose our independence," Chalmon snapped.

"Summoning our Exotique is already planned," Jaquar said.

"The master said, 'No Lladranan can harm the nest,' as if just the presence of one who is *not* Lladranan can hurt the Dark."

"A natural weapon," Chalmon breathed.

"Think what she'll be like when she's trained!" Venetria said.

Jaquar said, "The Summoning Song will bring to Lladrana a person who will work well with us."

Venetria sucked in a breath. "Yes, but she must be strong if we are going to send her to the nest."

Jaquar said, "Any Exotique the Marshalls can contact will naturally be strong. As eldest and most powerful of the Tower, I believe Bossgond sent the Marshalls a list of the proper qualities." Jaquar felt his mouth twist. "Bossgond didn't notify me, but I received an acknowledgment from the Marshalls."

Frowning, Chalmon said, "Bossgond didn't tell me, either. It is time he breaks this hermit existence."

"I'm sure he'd be glad to hear you tell him so," Venetria said sweetly.

Chalmon continued. "The Exotique must be well-trained before we send him or her to this master you discovered, Jaquar. He or she must at least be trained enough to report what is found in the nest."

"We may not have that luxury," Jaquar said. "Not if the maw spews out more sangviles, as well as the other horrors—the slayers and soul-suckers and renders."

"And dreeths." Venetria shivered. She'd barely survived a battle with one of the winged lizards.

Chalmon scowled. "Yes, we must be prepared to sacrifice the Exotique, for the good of Lladrana, for the planet Amee herself. Knowledge is more important than one life. If worse comes to worst, we could attach a reporting orb to her and send her with a destruction spell—perhaps she'd be able to untie that weapon knot you have."

"I would go myself, if I could," Jaquar said.

Venetria looked at him sharply. "You are the best planewalker. You already tried. Do you think the shield applies to all planes?"

Again Jaquar's laughter was bitter. "It applied to as many as I could reach within the limits of the spell—twenty or so. I'm not sure exactly where or what the physical location is, but it's big."

Making a note, Chalmon said, "Other things to research—the shield, whether it is only magical or is physical also. Where the nest could be. When the Exotique comes, I'll train him or her."

"No! If she's female, like the last one, she will want a woman as teacher!" Venetria said.

"The new Exotique is mine," Jaquar insisted.

Now Chalmon barked laughter. "All of us will want to work with someone so Powerful. This is exactly why we need the Marshalls to Summon her. We don't work well together." He shot a glance at his lady. "Sometimes not even those who are intimate with each other."

Jaquar's heart tore. His father and mother had been an excellent team, stronger together than apart. Perhaps that's what had drawn the sangvile to them.

Chalmon and Venetria sniped at each other, then Chalmon faced him.

"We'll call a Gathering for tomorrow at the Parteger Island

amphitheater to discuss all this," Chalmon said. "I'll move the process along."

Venetria sent him a fulminating glance, then looked back to Jaquar. "What is the Marshalls' price for the Summoning?"

Jaquar said, "I promised them objects, not favors. Some books, most of which are duplicates in *all* our libraries. Whatever magical weapons we have. Old battlespells."

"A price easy to meet," Chalmon said.

Venetria nodded. "Yes. I think I only have two weapons in my Tower—what of you?"

"One," Jaquar said, but it was an incredible one, something that perhaps only an Exotique could handle.

"I have four," Chalmon said.

"Of course you must pretend you're the best," Venetria said. And then they were arguing again.

"I'll coordinate with the Marshalls as necessary in the days to come," Jaquar said. He wouldn't lie to the Marshalls, but he wouldn't welcome them unless he had a use for them.

With thumb and forefinger, Jaquar tapped the crystal and Chalmon and Venetria disappeared. An hour later he had sent the contract and books as first payment to the Marshalls for the Summoning.

Then he crossed to his armchair and sat again, letting the soft, old leather settle around his body. He wondered if the other Circlets had forgotten one very important thing, and if they had, whether he could take advantage of it.

The Singer, the Oracle of Lladrana, had prophesied that the next Exotique would be best suited for the community of the Tower. The Singer had also told them of the time of the next Summoning—when the Dimensional Gates between Lladrana and the Exotique land aligned. The Marshalls knew this. It was tomorrow night.

In all the history of the Tower, the Sorcerers and Circlets had never come to an agreement in a day. Chalmon was too optimistic. He wouldn't be able to forge a plan amongst all the individual personalities of the Tower.

Jaquar sank back into his chair to sleep. It would be a long time before he could face his bedroom adorned with the quilt his mother had made and the landscapes his father had painted.

He would not argue with the rest of the Sorcerers and Sorceresses at Parteger Island, had no intention of compromising. The Exotique was his. For knowledge. For vengeance.

Colorado
The next evening

Power hung in the air like a fine mist ready to condense into dewdrops. It shimmered with every ripple of chimes, every strike of the gong—the music only Marian could hear, had heard for the past month. Now the sounds reverberated in a pattern that set her nerves humming as she finished taping a ten-foot red pentagram on her living room carpet.

She took a shaky breath as she connected the last line of the star-shaped pattern and sank back on her heels to calm her excitement. She wiped her damp palms on the sweats she'd put on after her bath. Biting her lip, she examined everything again. She'd had to scramble to craft the ritual, to get the herbs and tools. There'd been no time to practice.

No negativity, not now. No doubts. So she shoved them aside.

Soon the exact moment of the full moon would finally come and it would be time to act. To perform a ritual that would bring great change into Andrew's life and her own. To ask for what she wanted most, a miracle—a healthy brother.

In order to clear enough space to tape the pentacle, she'd

had to stack books around the edges of the room, evidence that her hunger for knowledge had burgeoned until it was nearly a craving. She felt like the Chinese Dragon, ever pursuing the Pearl of Wisdom. Someday she'd find just the right knowledge that would make her whole, or set her free: the key to herself.

Marian stood and put away the tape. She checked the alcove where her hamster Tuck sat blinking at her in a corner of his plastic cage. He seemed to feel something unusual, too, since both his cheek pouches were huge with food.

"Nothing to worry about, Tuck." She smiled at him, then rubbed her arms. Crossing to the door of her garden-level apartment, she pushed aside the small curtain over the door's window to look out. Twilight was falling.

Hands on her hips, she scanned the rest of her preparations; her altar was fine, the notes for her ritual were on her PDA in the pentagram. A small spiral of smoke from the incense burner twisted, sending lily-of-the-valley scent through the room. The smoke sparkled silver.

Marian blinked, narrowed her eyes and stared. The glitter in the powder shouldn't carry up into the smoke, and she thought she'd seen a flash for an instant. Maybe. Maybe not. Tonight was a night for stretching all she was, experiencing all she could.

With a sigh she looked at her gray sweats, still wavering between doing the ritual in a gossamer crocheted cotton broomstick gown or nude. She should be less self-conscious, able to accept her plumpness as pleasing.

Just as she was about to shuck her sweats for the gauze dress, the telephone rang. She glanced at the clock and bit her lip. It was only an hour before the full moon and she'd wanted to be at the climax of the ritual when that occurred. She debated answering the call. Hesitated. Then she ran across the living room floor, hopping over the star-points to reach the kitchen and pick up the telephone.

"Hey, sis." Andrew's light voice floated across the line, and she smiled.

"Hey back."

There was a heartbeat's pause. "Is everything okay there? I had a feeling…" he said.

"Everything's fine." She eyed the red-taped pentagram on the floor.

"Candace isn't giving you grief over anything, is she?" Their mother had asked Andrew at the age of four not to call her any variation of "Mommy."

"She wanted me to attend a benefit tonight, but I…wanted to study." She *was* studying, learning.

Andrew groaned. "Yeah, the Colorado Charities. Sent her a check for them, and one for the Multiple Sclerosis Foundation of Colorado, too. She didn't say thank-you, but I believe she was pleased. I don't have much contact with her anymore. Might be better for your mental health if you backed away, too."

"I will, soon," Marian said.

Andrew's snort came through the phone line. "Wrong. You're always trying to reconcile with her. It's a girl thing. Or maybe it's just that you think a perfect life should have mother-daughter happiness. Too bad your dad didn't leave you as well off as mine did me—you wouldn't be at her beck and call over that college fund."

He didn't offer her money from his trust fund, and Marian was glad. "How are things going with you?" she asked.

"I get it, previous subject closed. I'm doing good, sis. Turned in the new game project today and I'm going off on sabbatical." He paused, then words rushed from the phone. "I'm in remission right now, but—uh—I've had a few incidents—"

"Andrew!" Fear spurted through her.

"—and I want to try out that program we talked about last year, the one set on Freesan Island in the San Juans. Sort of a retreat, and they want us to minimize contact with outsiders. The codependency thing, you know."

"Andrew!"

"So I won't be available or calling you for about six weeks."

"Did you do another check on these people? The system?"

Andrew laughed. "You always have to be in control, sis. Not an issue I've ever had."

No, Andrew had always been at the mercy of his condition, his workaholic father and a series of stepmothers, most of whom found him distressing.

He continued. "The camp's A-Okay. I know you're frowning—"

The warmth in his voice almost made her smile.

"But they aren't after my money and won't sell me to labs for experimentation," he said. "Dr. Chan recommends the program and you know how much we both trust her. I also had my financial advisor and my private investigator check it out."

"They'll be careful with you?" *Oops.* "Tuck worries about you." Now she knew he was rolling his eyes.

"*Sis!*" A slight pause. His voice deepened. "I'm a man. I know how to work around my health issues. I plan to live life, not merely exist."

"All right, all right. You have my blessing. Go and enjoy yourself." She didn't know why those phrases rolled from her lips. But they both knew the day-to-day risk he lived with.

"Hey, I was the one with the funny feeling, not you. Make sure Tuck takes care of himself. Oh, and you take care of yourself, too. Uh—by the way, will the weather be good?"

A familiar *feeling* whispered through Marian. "It should be pleasant but cool to start off with, then showers. Take your rain gear."

"Will do. Love ya. Bye." He smooched into the phone and hung up.

When Andrew left Colorado for California, he'd made it clear that he wanted to live as much as he could on his own. He wanted *her* to pursue her studies in Boulder as she'd planned, so she'd made herself let him go. He had been as desperate to live independently as she had been. Currently he had a housekeeper, a nurse who specialized in caring for people with MS. The matronly woman had separate quarters in his home. Andrew had a car and driver.

Their sibling relationship had actually improved. If he wanted her with him, he knew all he had to do was call.

Tuck rattled in his cage and brought her back to the moment. She studied the pentagram and found her pulse thumping fast. Andrew had phoned just before the ritual. Surely that was a bit of magic in itself. Further, he was trying another new program—could this ritual influence that? She didn't want to think about what Andrew would do when the disease became more debilitating.

Andrew's telephone call had thrown Marian's timing off. She'd have to hurry through the first part of the ritual, use her notes on her PDA. Not perfect. Perhaps she should delay the ritual until next month? She wanted to, to ensure it would go more smoothly, but she dared not.

She walked around the star to her bedroom, stripped out of the soft cotton pants and shirt and folded them. Then she freed her still-damp hair and fluffed it, enjoying the feel of the strands as well as the slight tugging on her scalp as she ran her fingers to the shoulder-length ends.

Returning to the living room, she lit the candles, drew the

outer circle, summoned guardian spirits. Palpable energy charged around her. The chanting she'd heard in her dreams sounded as if it came from her stereo, until she couldn't tell if it was real or only echoed in her mind.

At the last minute, on impulse, she put the plastic ball with her hamster into the center of the pentacle, too. After all, when Andrew's and her own life changed, so would Tuck's, even if he only dimly sensed the alteration. He was an essential part of her life, so he should be included.

She stepped into the center of the pentagram and lifted her voice in counterpoint to the music. Lightning flashed. Incredible. Nothing like this had ever happened before. Energy raced through Marian, making her feel powerful, like a goddess, and she laughed. A bright carnelian-red ribbon of light unrolled, then curled around Marian and Tuck. She stared at it in disbelief.

She grabbed Tuck's plastic sphere. With one small tug, they were swept through a hole, like thread through the eye of a needle.

Power spiked and whirled and changed. She lost her connection with Mother Earth. That deepest connection she'd felt all her life, snipped.

They were somewhere else, in a wind-whipped corridor of dust brown. A corridor to where?

Tuck's ball was torn from her grasp and she screamed. She looked, listened, reached with all of her senses, flailed arms and legs and couldn't find him. He'd been her companion for two years. She cried and grieved.

Adrift and alone in pummeling, whistling winds, she felt terror rip through her. Felt no links to anything. Not the earth, not the trees, not the moon or stars. All that she'd recently realized had spoken to her of her place and her life had vanished.

She reached mentally, emotionally for Andrew. Screamed and heard silence again.

Nothing.

3

She found herself on a cold floor.

Marian didn't believe her senses. It felt as if she was on stone, not the threadbare carpet in her apartment. The scent of the room changed from lily of the valley to jasmine and sandalwood. As she inhaled, the air felt more humid. The space around her seemed larger, sounds echoing.

When she heard ragged breathing not her own, she squeezed her eyes shut, sure she was dreaming. Maybe experiencing out-of-body travel, though that had never happened before. She *must* be safe in her apartment. She didn't want to think otherwise.

People started talking—not in English but in what sounded like mangled French. As part of pleasing her mother, Marian had learned French and spoke it like a native. This wasn't true French. She thought her heart would jump from her chest it pounded so hard. This couldn't be happening. If she kept her eyes closed, it would all go away and she'd be home and safe and never dabble with magic ever again.

With one singing ripple of chimes, her whole body arched involuntarily. Despite her will, her eyelids flew open.

A circle of faces peered down at her, all slightly Asian in appearance with dark eyes set in golden-toned skin. Marian gaped. An older woman with golden streaks of hair at each temple and compressed lips held up both hands palms outwards.

"Vel coom," she said.

With only a little deciphering, Marian translated the word into "Welcome." She wasn't sure what to do. She still couldn't connect to Mother Earth, let alone Andrew. Of course this whole thing could be a hallucination, or worse, madness.

What should she do?

"Vel coom!" the woman shouted, gesturing for Marian to get up.

Why didn't the woman help her? Marian squinted and saw flowing lines of—energy? electricity? the Force? between her and the circle of richly robed figures. There were at least sixteen people surrounding her, evenly spaced along the large circle, pairs dressed alike. Swords were sheathed at their hips. From what she could see, the figure on the floor beneath her was a huge pentacle—a star in a circle—larger than hers, about fifteen feet.

She licked her lips and felt the dampness. The floor was cold flagstones under her, not carpet. Her breath caught in her throat as her mind spun with possibilities that she really didn't want to consider, sorting and analyzing. Her brain told her she wasn't on Earth, and she was in the midst of strong magic.

And she was lying in a big circular stone room, with wooden rafters and high windows around the top.

She wanted to think of anything except that she was in a different place. Naked.

Just the thought of her nudity made her flush—probably from her toes to her hairline.

The people continued to stare.

Since it didn't look like they were going to approach, it was time to put reality to the test and rise and—she gulped—pretend she wasn't ashamed of her body.

Marian stood with shoulders back, hips tucked, stomach sucked in, hoping her blush wasn't as red as it felt. Keeping within one point of the star, she walked about five feet to where the others stood, outside the circle of flowing red energy-lines. Visible magic. If she weren't so scared, she'd be impressed. Everything looked fascinating, *would be* fascinating, if she could engage more of her mind than her emotions. But dreams ran on emotions. This had to be a dream.

Her brain said it was, but her senses contradicted that notion. Her emotions spiraled out of control until she controlled the panic gritting her teeth. *Act logically! Observe, at least.*

The women were all as tall as she—at least five foot eight—the men taller. They all had black hair, dark eyes and golden skin—and silver or golden streaks of hair at one or both temples.

Marian pointed to a gray cloak a woman wore and made the motion of swirling it around her. Unfortunately, in response to her actions most of the men's gazes locked on her breasts. She wanted to melt into the floor.

Marian cleared her throat. Was this real? Why were so many people here if she'd only needed one teacher? "Where? Um— when? I don't know— May I have the cloak, please?"

The woman who'd spoken earlier stared at her, frowning.

All she wanted to do was find a corner and hide. That

thought reminded her of Tuck and she forced back tears. He was gone. What chance did a hamster in a plastic ball have in the winds of that corridor?

This experience had already cost her more than she'd expected, Tuck.

But she'd stood around long enough. She'd act as if this was real, try and figure out what was going on, get her act together. Be bolder, take action. Take control.

Ka-Boom! Thunder rattled the silver gong at the edge of her vision. The gong responded with a low echoing tone. A flash of light blinded her. Heat and vibration struck her, sent her flat to the pavement again.

She blinked but could not see. She rolled to her side.

Arreth! The word rang strange in her head, but the image of herself, still on the floor in the point of a carnelian-red pentagram, teased her mind. *Stay?* Cloth brushed against her ankle—someone was in the pentacle with her!

Swords rasped from scabbards.

A scream bubbled from her lips but emerged as a weak cry. So much for being bold. She'd try again in a minute. Strong fingers curved over her shoulder, squeezed in simple comfort, almost she thought she heard a tune. She sat up, choked, coughed. The hand moved from her shoulder to her nape, patted her upper back, then left, taking the funny music in her ears with it.

Arreth. Stay, the masculine voice whispered in her mind. Telepathy. She believed in magic, sort of, she'd just never experienced *so much* of it.

Then his hands closed around her upper arms, and she was lifted and pulled back into the center of the pentagram. Her ears rang. Again the hands fell from her and the music stopped.

Her vision began to clear. Beyond the afterimages of floating neon blobs, she saw the rich robes of those surrounding her. They held swords pointed at the man standing beside her.

But their gazes slid over to her. She got the idea they were fascinated by her pale skin that turned pink, red, then back to white.

She blinked, then looked up at the man. He was about six foot four. His face was broad at the forehead, with wide streaks of silver at both temples, emphasized by the golden headband he wore. His lips were full and mobile and dusky. He smiled down at her and offered his hand. She met his eyes. They were deep, deep blue in a tanned face.

A jolt of prophetic foreknowledge sizzled to her center. Uh oh. *Major, major MISTAKE!*

This wasn't her teacher. This was her doom.

The wide eyes of the Exotique woman drew Jaquar. They were a lighter shade than his own and for the first time in his life he found blue eyes beautiful.

A flicker in her gaze and the Power pulsing around her were signs she was experiencing a vision. His touch on her mind was too superficial to share her natural melody, but it was sweet.

The Exotique's full mouth lured him as much as did her soul-tune. He shook the sensual thought from his head, strove to ignore her nudity. She looked delicious, but he had a use for her and it wasn't as a lover. Still, he smiled his most charming smile, hoping she'd trust him.

When he'd touched her, a lance of pure desire from their mingled energies had shot straight to his groin. *No.* Despite what his body wanted, he could not allow himself even affection for her. If he had sex with the Exotique, there was a chance they'd bond. He couldn't risk that. She was the weapon of vengeance he'd set loose on the Dark like a blazing arrow. For his own peace of mind, he dared not become attached to her.

"Jaquar Dumont," Swordmarshall Thealia Germaine said flatly from the circle of Marshalls surrounding them, obviously unhappy that he'd shown up uninvited.

He paid little attention to the Marshalls, watching as his Exotique crossed to the pentacle, squatted and touched the flowing magical red lines. Sparks flew, and she recoiled.

Standing, she slowly extended her arm through the barrier of magic. It didn't hurt her. Jaquar let out a relieved breath. The Summoning had worked, bringing an innately powerful mage from the Exotique land to Lladrana. A woman whose power would be potent here.

She tugged on the gray cloak of one of the female Marshalls. With raised eyebrows and a smile, the Marshall gave it to the Exotique. She donned the cape, then looked around, very serious, examining the circular Temple, scrutinizing the altar with the rainbow crystal lamps that also served as chimes, and the huge silver gong beside it.

With narrowed eyes, she gazed at him and where he stood in the center of the pentagram, the place of Power. She gestured for him to move away. Demanded something in a language close to, but not Lladranan. "Leave…go…home."

Jaquar smiled and shook his head. She scowled and marched back to stand in the center of the pentacle with him, muttering what seemed to be her own words of Power. But they would do no good. The Marshalls had closed the hole between worlds.

She was still close to him and Jaquar had trouble ignoring her softness, warmth and unusual fragrance. Her nudity under the cloak was impossible to forget.

"Dumont!" Thealia snapped. "We did not expect anyone to use this pentacle today except the Exotique. You of the Tower should leave the *entire* Summoning to us."

He inclined his head and took the offensive. "Greetings, Swordmarshall. We of the Tower Community thank you for this Summoning. However, we thought Exotique Alyeka would be leading this ritual." He was friends with the other Exotique—he might have been able to persuade her to release the new lady into his care.

"The Singer foretold that the second Exotique is to bond with someone here and it should not be Alyeka. She should not be present. Even *she* listens to the Singer, now."

"Ah," Jaquar said, smiling and gesturing to himself. "Well, I am here and the lady can come with me." Time to get out of here, before any other Circlets showed up to try to take the woman for their own apprentice. He'd paid for the Exotique, now he should take his prize and leave.

He strode to her and curved his right arm around her. The quiet notes stringing between them deepened and took on a richness. The Exotique took a step away, but stumbled, so he kept his hold. Her blue eyes narrowed and her mouth thinned. Her innate, powerful magic flared and set the gemstone lamps on the altar chiming. She stared at them and shivered.

Bong! The gong thundered, announcing another presence traveling into the closed sphere of the pentacle.

Venetria materialized inside the star, along with a pile of books and two magical weapons. She glared at Jaquar. Though his ears still rang with the sound of her arrival, he heard her shouting.

"Jaquar Dumont! You will not claim this Exotique as your apprentice. Doubtless she will relate better to a Sorceress." Venetria tossed her head, gave the woman one quick, penetrating look, then offered her hand to the Exotique.

Eyes wary, the woman touched Venetria's fingers. A clash of tones echoed in the round Temple as the women's hands met. Venetria dropped the Exotique's hand, flicking the incompatible energy from her fingertips, then converted the gesture into a wave as she spoke to the Marshalls.

"The books you requested—the ancient spellweapons at my disposal, and instructions to use them."

Clang! This time the altar crystals rang and the sound ran around the outstretched steel of the Marshalls' swords in a bone-shivering scale.

Inside the pentacle, the two women stumbled against Jaquar. Chalmon appeared in the north point of the pentagram.

Jaquar set his teeth, shouldered Venetria aside and steadied the Exotique, enduring the sensual and powerful string of notes rapidly deepening into a melody. They were already forming a connection.

Chalmon glared at them. Beside him was a stack of books and four weapons.

"This is ridiculous," Swordmarshall Thealia said, sheathing her broadsword. The other Marshalls followed suit. She studied the gifts in the pentacle and her smile was as sharp as her sword. Her lip curled. "I see that those of the Tower are cooperating as usual, which is to say, not at all."

Jaquar grasped the Exotique's arm. "As you can see, our energies do not clash. I sent payment for the Summoning yesterday. On behalf of the Tower, I again thank the Marshalls." He glanced at Venetria and Chalmon, who stood in opposite points of the star. "I claim this Exotique woman as my apprentice."

Chalmon scowled. "No."

No price was too much to pay to find and destroy the master and avenge Jaquar's parents. "Then you challenge me. Tests of Power or a duel of sorcery. The Marshalls can set up a procedure and officiate."

Swordmarshall Thealia made a disgusted noise. Chalmon stiffened in outrage.

The Power in the pentacle was incredible, radiating from four strong mages. Jaquar sensed that the Exotique was merging all the energies, changing them until they melded into a single Powersong that he could use easily. She was inherently a strong Sorceress. He couldn't wait to mold her raw power into focused magic.

Sunlight shafted through a high stained-glass window, framing the voluptuous woman by his side in a pointed arch, painting the pale skin of her face, hands and feet in jeweled colors, illuminating her like a fine vellum manuscript. Her aura glowed vibrant silver and turquoise, indicating strong and unusual Power. The tune between them was distracting. She was beautiful beyond compare in body and spirit.

A pity she might have to be sacrificed to stop the sangviles from leaving the Dark's nest.

Time to leave. Jaquar looked around the large round stone room of the Temple—at the Marshalls who seemed to be communing and approaching a decision; at Chalmon and Venetria who stood in the pentagram with him and the Exotique woman, but in opposite points; at the Exotique herself who appeared less dazed.

Definitely time to go. He began gathering Power.

Bong, Bong, Bong! Suddenly the ringing of all the glass in the room—from the windows, the storage crystals in the rafters and chandeliers, the chime crystals on the altar—resonated through his head.

A few seconds later his ears stopped buzzing and he saw the oldest and strongest Sorcerer of them all, Bossgond, holding a satchel. Chalmon went to Venetria, protectiveness radiating from him.

Jaquar's stomach tightened and his lips pulled back from his teeth in a silent snarl as he anticipated failure. There was no way he could best Bossgond. Disappointment seared him. He wanted the Exotique, he had plans for her.

What Bossgond's plans were, he couldn't imagine.

The greatest Sorcerer wore a stained, shabby robe that didn't disguise the sticklike, knobby bones of his body. His full head of hair was golden except for a small streak of black in the middle—denoting his great Power.

He put his satchel down. Ignoring the rest of them, he bowed slightly to the Exotique, then touched his fingers over his heart. "Bossgond," he said in a deep, rich voice that sent a small hum through the gong.

He took two steps and held out a swollen-jointed hand. She placed hers in it. A white flash of their auras merging sent a single, resonant note from the silver gong. The Exotique blinked, then her lips curved. The Song between the old man and the young woman must be comforting to her.

Jaquar ground his teeth. His prize was slipping from his grasp.

With gentleness and grace the old man raised the Exotique woman's hand to his lips, then loosed it. Jaquar wondered what sort of music had spun between them—notes, or more. Then he remembered the songs that had linked him and his parents, resonant from the moment they'd found him. He'd been their apprentice, too. Grief gripped him. To distract himself, he watched the Exotique.

Standing close to Bossgond, the Exotique was his height.

She wet her lips, then placed her hand above her breasts and said, "Marian."

It was a good name—a name everyone could pronounce, unlike the first Exotique's, *Alexa*. Jaquar wasn't the only one who released a soft sigh.

Bossgond reached down and took a large crystal orb from his satchel. He sang two notes and color whirled inside it, forming a picture.

The scene in the sphere-crystal solidified into Alf Island, Bossgond's home, and his tall, stately white Sorcerer's Tower. A small image of Bossgond walked with Marian, obviously instructing her. Marian was dressed in a beautiful velvet robe and carried a staff of deep mahogany inlaid with twining silver and gold leaves.

Then the image turned to night. The tower's outer wall disappeared, showing the top ritual room as dark; the level beneath was Bossgond's suite, lit with mellow crystal lights. He worked at a desk. The next floor down was richly appointed for a woman. Papers, books and jars of herbs cluttered a beautiful desk. Marian sat at it, looking intense. Her staff leaned against the wall, glowing the same deep red as her hair.

With a hum from Bossgond, the scene inside the globe faded. He set it back into the satchel, then spoke one carefully pronounced sentence. It wasn't in a language Jaquar knew.

Marian did. She smiled at him. A sincere smile. She looked around the room, her expression turning wary. She nodded stiffly to Chalmon and Venetria. Marian studied the Marshalls who stared back at her but she didn't move from the center of the star or indicate she wanted to be with them.

Jaquar thought she meant her glance to slide over him, but it snagged and they gazed at each other. Her blue eyes held intelligence, focus, determination. She would have been perfect for him—no, for his purposes. No chance of wresting her from Bossgond, even if she'd been willing.

The old Sorcerer looked at Marian and repeated his line.

"Yes," said Marian, and it was close enough to the Lladranan *ayes* for Jaquar to know she agreed.

Bossgond turned to the rest of them. "The apprentice, Exotique Marian, is coming with me. I anticipate that she will graduate from apprentice to scholar in two weeks."

Venetria gasped. Bossgond sent her a chill look and she made a strangled noise. Chalmon set an arm around her shoulders. Now they looked like a couple again.

Bossgond met Jaquar's scrutiny. "Does anyone here in this Temple challenge me?"

4

Silence filled the Temple at Bossgond's words. The old man grinned. "I didn't think anyone would want to engage in a sorcerous duel with me." He held the gaze of Swordmarshall Thealia. "Please open the pentacle so the others can leave."

Swordmarshall Thealia drew her baton from her sheath, stepped to the Power lines and sang an opening spell. The flow of Power bent back on itself, allowing egress from the pentacle to the rest of the Temple.

"Clear out of the star and circle," Bossgond ordered.

Chalmon strode out, head high, body tense. Venetria followed, and from the sour look on her face as she glanced at the new Exotique, Jaquar knew she recalled that Marian's energy didn't mesh well with hers.

Neither Chalmon nor Venetria had suffered anything except a little scraped pride from this debacle. Unlike himself—his plan was a shambles.

Bossgond stared at Jaquar and raised an eyebrow. "Go," he repeated.

Slowly, Jaquar complied.

"We would like the additional books and weapons," Thealia said. "The Summoning was not as hard as that of our Exotique Marshall Alyeka, but it was done at our risk and with our Power and in our Castle Temple."

The old man inclined his head. "Agreed. If the Tower Community was disorganized enough to pay you three times, then you should take advantage of it."

Jaquar stood outside the circle and watched helplessly as the old man handed Venetria's and Chalmon's offerings to the Marshalls. He'd wanted to ensure the new Exotique was trained in plane-walking, focus her studies on what he needed her to do, and what she would have to learn to make the journey and, if possible, return.

Thealia glanced dubiously at the six weapons. "All the spell-weapons of the Tower Community were promised."

"I have no weapons." Bossgond stared at Jaquar. "I trust you will ensure the Marshalls receive the remaining payment from the rest of the Towers." He examined the two swords, three knives and a pair of gauntlets the Marshalls claimed from Venetria and Chalmon. "I believe the last inventory of all the Towers stated we had twenty weapons."

So the old Circlet had been studying the reports after all, just not commenting.

Swordmarshall Thealia laid a hand on her baton of Power.

Jaquar nodded shortly at her. "As Bossgond says, I'll ensure the delivery of all the weapons, except..." He glanced from Bossgond to Thealia and swept a quick look around the rest of the Marshalls. "I was gifted a knot-weapon when I raised my Tower, too powerful for me to handle." He grinned with all his teeth. "Should you wish to send someone for that weapon, I'll be pleased to relinquish it."

"Not me," said Bossgond.

Thealia fingered the end of her baton but stepped back. "I'll discuss it with Marshall Alyeka. We know nothing about knot-weapons."

Bossgond reconnected the pentacle's Power lines with a small wand of polished turquoise. He raised his head and sniffed, as if testing the flavor of the Power. "Very good," he said, raising the Exotique's hand to his lips.

After he'd finished the elegant gesture, Bossgond placed Marian in the center of the pentacle and began the chant that would whisk them from the Castle Temple to the pentagram in Bossgond's Tower on Alf Island.

Marian listened to the old magician sing what she thought was a spell. It was amazing. She drew the cloak around her. Her hands and feet were cold. She'd agreed to go with the old man and it looked like she was going by magic.

Still, she could feel the pressure of energy, magic, whatever, gathering. Was there any chance that it might send her back home? Was this a dream about how to find her teacher? She'd like to believe it, but the bruises she had on her body ached with all-too-real pain. In an hour or two the marks would show on her skin.

With every moment that passed, Marian felt her hope fade that this was a dream.

She looked at the oldest mage again. She should have been watching her new teacher all along, paying attention to what he was doing, but there was too much going on. And he'd made it clear he would be her mentor, she'd learn. She hoped.

"I would be honored to teach you to use your Power," he'd

said. The cadence of his words had hummed through her, feeling *right*. She felt inherently she could trust him, unlike everyone else in this place. There was a smoothness of the energy of his intentions toward her that didn't come from anyone else in the room.

Every other person who had touched her had *snags* in their Power flow toward her that she'd recognized as self-interest, specific goals in their minds as to how to use her. Bossgond hadn't.

She understood now that the circle of people who'd brought her to this place were called Marshalls. She'd picked that word up. She'd always been a quick study and didn't think the language would pose much of a problem, especially since it was close to French.

The Marshalls still ringed the pentacle, grouped in pairs and watching with interest. Since they'd been chanting when she'd come here, they had to be the ones who'd burdened her life over the past month. Their music was unique. The crystal lamps made of great gemstones and arranged in the colors of the chakra were the chimes she had heard. And she knew the sound of the silver gong.

Yet she didn't feel at ease with those pairs dressed in matching colors, clinking with chain mail under their rich robes and carrying weapons. She didn't care for this enormous, echoing Temple. Something about the atmosphere raised all the fine hair on her body.

Then there were the other magicians. The handsome Jaquar scowled at her from outside the pentagram, almost vibrating with intensity. Oddly enough, she could hear a stream of melodious notes coming from him and it lured her. *No. Absolutely not.* That wasn't right. She trusted her instinctive impression of him as someone who could harm her deeply.

These people seemed to use music in their magic, but it was

still difficult to believe that the trickle of tunes she heard from them was anything but her imagination.

She usually soaked in and analyzed everything around her, but all the new experiences demanded that she shut down the overflow of sensory information for self-preservation. She stepped closer to Bossgond.

Marian clutched the cape. The lining was soft and warm. She swayed to the chant. Bossgond had a fabulous voice. She'd enjoy listening to it, learning from him.

Slam! The huge door to the Temple hit the stone wall and a small woman shot into the room, followed by a big man who was reaching for her.

"Alexa!" the man called.

Unlike everyone else, the woman was pale-skinned, with a white scar on one cheek, short in stature, and though she had silver hair, she appeared young.

The Marshalls started to surround her.

"Wait!" the woman called. In English.

Bossgond gripped Marian's upper arm hard and sped up his chant, the rhythm now almost syncopated, making her dizzy with the energy surrounding them.

The Marshalls' protests drowned out most of the woman Alexa's words. Marian heard, "Wait! I came as soon as I could. You need to know, you're in Lladrana—"

Magic coalesced around Marian and Bossgond, a huge pressure of Power. She tried to take a step forward, but was held in place by an invisible force.

"Can I go home?" Marian cried, straining to hear.

"Not yet," Alexa called.

"How soon?" Marian yelled.

Alexa shrugged. "Maybe a month!"

Marian bit her lip. What if Andrew returned earlier or had

an exacerbation during his retreat? She could lose him! She would definitely lose her college fund…and her job.

What should she do? What *could* she do?

Her ritual had been in part to find help for Andrew. These people might be able to cure him. She'd just have to find the information and get back to him fast.

The man who'd followed Alexa plucked her from an irritated circle of Marshalls. Holding her protectively, he ran with her to the edge of the pentacle.

Alexa met Marian's gaze. "Make sure you ask about Pair-Bonding. And the Snap!"

Bossgond intoned, *"Vont!"*

The room disappeared. Vertigo hit Marian, and in the next instant she fell onto a thick rug into which was woven a red pentagram.

"Gagghhh," she croaked. Brilliant. Wonderful impression to make on her teacher—and now the man whose power she was under.

Surely she could beat him physically if she had to, couldn't she? Heaven knew she had heft.

But he sat next to her, watching with concerned eyes, then stooped and brushed back her hair. Then he took her hand and helped her up with unexpected strength, banished the flowing energy lines around his pentagram with a whistle. Then he led her to a soft chair that looked a lot like a fancy outdoor lounger. A series of velvet pillows was attached to an adjustable wooden frame; the back was set in a reclined position and the footrest was elevated.

Marian sat, leaned back and arranged the cloak in folds around her. She'd kept a good grip on the front since receiving the cape and it had only flapped open a little now and then, but had saved her modesty.

In Lladrana.

Alexa had called it Lladrana. Who was she, and why wasn't *she* the one helping Marian?

Bossgond, who'd gone to a sink on the far side of the Tower, came back with a goblet of water. From the sprig of leaves that floated on top she guessed it wasn't just water. She picked the greenery out of the cup and sniffed. Minty. She dropped the leaves back into the drink and, keeping her eyes on the old man, swallowed a bit.

He smiled in reassurance, took the cup from her, drank some himself and handed it back. Had she looked that suspicious?

Bossgond went to a large cabinet and opened it. Out floated a sphere the size of an exercise ball. Large and blue-green-brown, it rotated slowly. Marian's stomach tightened when she realized it was a globe, but that the oceans and continents were unknown to her. She looked away.

"Amee," Bossgond said.

First things first. Finding out how time passed on this new world was of the utmost importance. All around her and through her, magic surged like electricity. She should be able to master it and use it to help Andrew, but how much time did she have?

She stood and moved closer to the globe, saw three large continents and a countrylike portion outlined in black.

When the globe completed one full rotation, she said, "One day." As it continued to move, she ticked off the days on her hand.

Feeling a little foolish, she continued with her mime. She drew a pentagram, then sat on the floor. "Earth!" she said.

With skinny little brows raised, he said, "Exotique Terre."

"Terra." She nodded.

His eyebrows rose higher. "Exotique Terre."

Marian sighed and repeated, "Exotique Terre." With whooshing sounds and wide gestures, and more noises to indicate the gong and chimes and chants, she acted out her trip to Lladrana.

Then she went to the globe again and counted days as it rotated, tilting her head in a question. Was any of this getting through?

Bossgond frowned, then crossed his tower room to more shelves and cupboards. He returned with a crude globe of Earth, about five inches around. When she took the heavy ball of metal, she sensed someone from her own world had made it. The echoes of the Song of Mother Earth lingered. She could do better.

Narrowing her eyes, she concentrated, reaching deep inside her for the Earth-song. While she was at it, she visualized the continents and oceans as best she could. Not well enough. She closed her eyes and thought of space shots of the earth, radar and Doppler weather maps, especially of the United States, and Colorado.

The metal in her hands warmed. When she opened her eyes, the globe looked a lot better, the land masses and oceans well-defined. She scowled at the eastern coastline of the United States. Something was definitely off there; Australia and Asia weren't as sharp as on a regular globe. Not perfect. Her shoulders slumped.

Bossgond's bony fingers closed over her shoulder and squeezed. Catching her gaze with his own chocolate-brown one, he gave a little bow. "Thank you. You have increased my knowledge of Exotique Terre tenfold."

He was trying to drive another point home. She was well aware of a teacher's body language. Cradling the Earth globe in the crook of his arm, he touched the much larger orb with his index finger.

"Amee." He glanced at her, eyes piercing. "Thay parfay."

Ah, the words were close enough to French. The image of planet Amee wasn't perfect.

So he could sense her emotions, or perhaps he just read her dissatisfaction with her construct in her face.

She sighed.

Bossgond released the Earth-globe and it hung next to the large one of Amee. Earth rotated slower, in sync with Amee's days and nights. Amazing that the days were the same—or perhaps this was an alternative earth—but with different continents? Maybe all the planets with similar rotations were reached by one dimensional corridor....

Marian's head hurt. She had too little information for hypothesis, and so much was happening.

All the tension in her body at the thought of being trapped here and Andrew worrying himself into seizures released in a long shudder. Weary, she swallowed hard, walked stiffly back to the lounge chair and sank into the pillows, closing her eyes.

When she opened them, she gazed up at Bossgond, feeling lost. He urged her to drink more of the herbal liquid, and she did. Her stomach calmed.

Bossgond touched her shoulder. "Marian," he said. Tapping his chest, he said, "Bossgond."

He was encouraging her, emphasizing how much she'd already learned. That she was learning with every breath, with every glance.

He took her hand and linked their fingers. She sensed great age. Vitality, isolation.

Looking down at their hands, she saw a white aura, heard

chords forming into a song. He smiled, and she found herself smiling back. Bossgond patted her hand and rose.

He went to the pentagram and fished out the large crystal ball from his bag, then returned. With a little tune, mist swirled inside the sphere, then solidified into the image of the handsome magician who'd first entered the pentacle with her.

"Jaquar Dumont," Bossgond said.

Marian remembered the older woman who'd spoken for the Marshalls calling him that, in flat tones. *Jaquar.*

"Chalmon Pace," Bossgond said, and the other mage's face replaced Jaquar's.

He looked like a pompous associate professor, ever conscious of his status and sure of his worth. Still, there was something in his eyes that made Marian think he could be a good friend. His image faded.

The female magician appeared in the sphere. "Venetria Fourney," said Bossgond.

The strikingly beautiful woman was easy to recall. They'd both received shocks when the woman touched her. Marian rubbed her fingers and grimaced at the memory. She'd liked the look of Venetria, but since they'd shocked each other and Bossgond and she meshed, if the conflicting energy was any indication, they wouldn't work well together.

Marian caught her breath as she reran the thought. Wasn't she being cool and analytical about all these strange and wondrous things? Perhaps it *was* a dream. When she went to bed and woke up, maybe everything would be fine. Tuck would wake her up in the middle of the night by running on his wheel or rattling in his cage, rearranging his hoard....

Right now, all she knew was here. She licked her lips. Marian wondered about Alexa. She'd liked the look of her better than the rest. Marian tapped the ball with a fingernail.

"Alexa?"

The woman's image formed. To her surprise, Marian saw the small figure dressed in jeans and a down parka with knit hat, scarf and mittens, trudging through snow in the mountains. She recognized the parka as one she'd admired in a local boutique. Colorado? Was Alexa from Colorado, too? Excitement flooded Marian and she nearly missed seeing Alexa enter a silver arch.

Several seconds later, the woman appeared in the same pentacle as Marian had, except that the energy lines of this one glowed green.

Her parka was ripped, her hat gone, and her hair was brown. Not silver, as Marian had seen. Something had turned Alexa's hair silver since she arrived. Some experience here in Lladrana.

Jaquar wanted to leave the Temple, fast. Since the Marshalls were dismissing the pentacle, none of the Circlets would be able to leave that way.

His mind raced, considering plans to retrieve the new Exotique. He ignored Chalmon's and Venetria's recriminations. Unlike them, he had friends in the Castle.

He also ignored most of the Marshalls. Jaquar immediately went to Bastien Vauxveau, who was talking to his wife, the Exotique Alexa. Jaquar tapped Bastien on the shoulder. "Come along, I have some propositions. One for you and one for Alyeka."

Bastien turned to Jaquar with gleaming eyes. "We'll be glad to negotiate." He sent a glance to the other Marshalls. "They don't need us."

Alexa sighed and spoke in heavily accented Lladranan. "I got here too late."

"You weren't supposed to interfere at all," Bastien scolded.

"I don't mind flouting the Marshalls, but the Singer knows what she's doing and she said not to take part in the Summoning."

"Huh," Alexa said, glancing around as if she was afraid the Singer was watching. "We weren't part of the ritual, but I did want to help her understand. It was miserable for me." She set her mouth and swept out of the Temple.

For a small woman, she moved fast. Jaquar thought her locomotion might be aided by her great Power. Alexa wanted to hurry, thus the Song swept her along.

When Jaquar exited, he stopped under the Temple's portico to let his eyes adjust to the moonlight. It was a beautiful spring night and the Marshalls' Castle looked magnificent, as always. But Jaquar sensed a distinct change in the atmosphere since he'd last been here. At that time, under all their trappings of Power, the Marshalls had been fearful. The magical boundaries of Lladrana were falling and the Exotique they'd Summoned to reverse this had just left. They'd discovered the sangvile in their walls.

Just that easily, remembering the sangvile dimmed the evening for Jaquar. Alexa, who'd been waiting for Bastien and him, put a hand on Jaquar's arm.

"I heard about your parents." She pronounced every word carefully, clearly. "I'm sorry for your loss."

Jaquar grunted.

Bastien threw an arm around Jaquar's shoulder, squeezed and let go. "You have propositions for us?"

If he wanted vengeance—*justice,* he'd need help from these two. He twisted his mouth into the semblance of a smile. He must not have done too well, because Alexa took a step back and her hand fell to the Marshall's baton she wore on her left hip.

Jaquar switched his gaze to Bastien, who was shorter than

he and more solidly made. "You have the best stable of flying horses. I want a volaran, preferably one you raised from a foal." It seemed he'd be doing a lot of traveling and volaran-back would be the easiest, least energy-consuming way.

Now Bastien clapped a hand on Jaquar's shoulder. "We'll deal."

"And I want to talk to Alyeka about the new Exotique...." Jaquar noted Alexa's scowl at the word and corrected himself. "Marian. I want to consult Alyeka about *Marian*."

Alexa sent him an approving look. "Let's discuss this in our suite," she said. With a whirl of blue-green robes she took off down the cloister walk.

Renewed hope filled Jaquar. He wasn't finished yet. Somehow he'd get the woman back.

5

Marian awoke to the sound of waves pounding against rock, different from her white-noise machine. Opening sleepy eyes, she stared at a rounded stone wall—not white plaster. She shot up in bed and memory rushed back. She was not home in her apartment, not in Boulder, not in Colorado, not in the United States of America. She wasn't even on Earth—she reached for that basic connection…and felt nothing.

She'd had no nightmares, but shivered as she recalled the ones she'd had in the past month. The druids could have been the Marshalls. Other parts of those dreams could happen here on Lladrana. Could they possibly have been more than dreams—like a foretelling of the future? Fingers clutching her blankets, she stared around her.

A beautiful, stained-glass partition showing flowers in a meadow stood a few feet from the end of the bed. To her right and left, the stone wall curved out of sight. She was in a tower room of the Sorcerer Bossgond.

"Lladrana," she whispered, and the word seemed to sink down, down, echoing through the floor, through the two stories beneath her, into the ground—and sent a resonance back. The faint, broken notes of a beautiful, sad melody rose to strum in her mind like a sobbing violin. She shook her head, but the song remained, hovering in the back of her brain.

Inhaling deeply, she tasted the faint tang of salt, and noted the waves again. She was on an island. Beyond the glass partition she saw bright sunlight from the windows on the far tower wall. She'd traveled through a wind-whistling space, but not outer space—another dimension?

Her stomach rumbled, and she focused on her hunger…and finding a bathroom. Last night she'd merely stumbled into the room, found the bed behind the glass partition. Letting the cloak drop where she stood, she had crawled under the covers. She'd shivered, then visualized heat surrounding her body and it had happened. Magic? Maybe.

She hopped from the bed and her feet sank into a luxurious rug of jewel-toned colors. The long gray cape she'd borrowed from one of the Marshalls who'd summoned her lay like a dark cloud against the carpet. She frowned as she picked it up. Though it had braided frog-fastenings all the way down the front, she didn't consider it viable clothing, but since it was all she had, she swirled it around her, pushed her arms through the slits and looped the frogs. Feeling a little better—and warmer—she noticed shelves on the far side of the bed where a stack of clothes were folded. She'd investigate later.

Though the glass partition didn't rise as far as the stone ceiling, it ran along this portion of the tower ending at the wall to her right. To her left, there was space enough for a doorway. When she walked around the partition, she saw that the bedroom was approximately a third of the whole room. The other two-thirds looked like a study, except for a small, carved wooden closet protruding halfway down the round wall in front of her. The closet door faced her. She hurried to it, opened the door and sighed in relief at the sight of an old-fashioned toilet with the tank near the ceiling.

When she was done, she left the closet in search of a sink and found multiple ones behind the closet. On the far side of the sinks was a counter that held glassware, like an old alchemist's setup.

Then came the door to the stairway and, after the door, a huge desk. Shelves lined the room, except for the three large window embrasures and a fireplace. A small grouping of two chairs and a love seat sat in front of the fireplace close to the stained glass.

It was charming, but not home. How long would she be here? She only wanted help for Andrew, then she'd leave.

A horn blew and Marian jumped. Bossgond's voice came to her. *Breakfast and lessons in fifteen minutes.* None of the words were hard, so she grasped the meaning and hurried back to the clothes shelves in the bedroom.

She touched the yoke of a royal-blue velvet garment, then lifted it and found herself holding a long gown with embroidered yellow birds. It seemed to be her size.

Additionally, she had a green dress, a maroon one and a black gown—all with little yellow birds and narrow three-quarter-length sleeves.

Though the blue robe had looked and felt heavy when she held it, the minute she put it on it seemed like gossamer. It molded around her breasts and lifted them, and Marian squeaked in surprise. Built-in magical bra! This would take some getting used to. The gown sent warmth to her skin—reflecting her own heat?

Marian looked dubiously at the one pair of footwear on the floor, tucked under the lowest shelf. They appeared more like pouches to put over her feet than actual shoes. Picking them up, she found they had soft leather uppers and springy insoles. When she turned them over she saw a material that looked like fine scales. Snake? *Dragon?*

Anyway, they looked far too big for her, and the uppers stuck up in folds. She couldn't see any laces.

Bracing a hand against the wall—it was warm to her touch—she slipped on one of the shoes. It felt lined with fur and she hummed with pleasure at the soft silkiness. Then the pouch tightened, molding to foot and ankle. She tottered, stumbled, took a few steps to regain her balance and fell onto the bed. She stared at her foot. Not only had the slipper conformed to her body, but it had turned the same color as her gown and now had little yellow birds all over it. She wiggled her feet—one shod, one bare. The one with the shoe felt better. Magical shoes.

Her heart jumped. What if she couldn't take it off? "Off!" she ordered.

Nothing happened.

She hooked her thumbs inside the shoe and pushed down. The shoe slid off her foot, tickling her sole, and plopped to the floor.

All right; one of them could come off. But if she put on both, would she dance to her death? There were plenty of folklore stories about shoes and mutilation, like Cinderella.

For a moment she just stared at the shoes, realizing that she was in a place far, far different from home. That it seemed somewhat like Earth accentuated her shock—she judged this place by Earth experiences, concepts, standards, and they might not apply. Any move she made, thinking she knew the outcome, could be wrong and lead her to her doom.

She fell back on the bed, hands over pounding heart, touching the cloth that seemed like velvet but could be anything—fur, skin, *plastic wrap* for all she knew. Even her senses could be lying to her. Perhaps nothing here was real.

And if she continued to think that way, to challenge everything—her senses, her mind, her experiences—she'd go mad. To her horror, tears dribbled from her eyes.

This should be such an incredible, fascinating experience for a true scholar! A whole new world to learn, a new aspect of her own self—and magic!—to explore and master. She should be thrilled.

Instead, she wanted to curl up into a fetal position and pull the covers over her head.

Bossgond was waiting for her. With breakfast. Even the thought of food couldn't move her.

She was flipping out over a pair of shoes.

They were magic shoes.

Now her nose was clogged. She'd need to go to the toilet closet and get some tissue-stuff she'd found there. It was in a roll and had felt like regular toilet paper. She'd just used it, not scrutinized it. Who knew what it was?

Was she going to let panic over the thought of a new world, a *magical* world, paralyze her?

Wrong question.

The right question was, How *long* was she going to let panic paralyze her?

Marian had always thought of herself as willing to learn new things, explore new ideas—perhaps she'd even been snobbish about that quality. In fact, she was a coward.

But her full-moon ritual had been about discovering why

she'd experienced odd sounds and nightmares. Now she knew. Golden Raven had said she'd meet a teacher. She had. Now she had to figure out how all this could help Andrew.

"Marian." The rich, deep voice of Bossgond seemed to echo around the room. It certainly reverberated inside her mind. She turned her head to see a tube running down the wall next to her bed, with a flared opening like a trumpet.

"Marian, the oeuf is cooling."

She struggled to one elbow, then the second. "I'm coming," she replied in French—the language she'd been speaking for hours now—except for that tiny exchange with Alexa.

Alexa! While wallowing in her own fear she'd forgotten Alexa—someone who'd already come from Colorado, had experiences she could share with Marian. She was pitifully grateful that she didn't have to take everything on faith, walking into a fog without a clue as to the landscape around her. Alexa would help her. Marian was not *alone*.

Just the thought of the other woman energized her.

"I'll be right there," she called out to Bossgond, a Sorcerer who would teach her magic.

She stretched, feeling her muscles pull, feeling something inside her that had been squashed and cramped, unfurl—a butterfly-breaking-open-her-cocoon feeling.

She would practice *wonder*, learn all she could of magic, in relation to herself and to Andrew. He'd expect her to live life in the moment, wring everything she could out of each experience, good or bad, not worry about being in control or making mistakes.

So she put on the shoes and forced herself to admire the feel and look of them. Then she marched to the toilet closet and took some tissue and blew her nose, washed her face with water from a tap.

Then she went out her door to find out if "oeuf" meant egg.

She ascended the stairs to Bossgond's quarters one floor above her own. When she reached the door there was something like a harp hanging on it. She pondered for a moment and decided it must be a doorbell or a knocker. Running her thumbnail over the strings released a ripple of sound that echoed through the tower and plucked a couple of strings inside her, too—excitement and anticipation.

Bossgond opened the door, wearing a short tunic that showed his bony knees, a large yellow bird embroidered on the front. The garment was cut so full that it hung on his slight frame. He stood aside and Marian entered.

His space looked much like hers—windows letting in spring sunlight, shelves all around the room, a desk, bathroom closet and a partition hiding the bedroom. But it was as warm as a summer's day—and the warmth felt more natural than the central heating she was used to at home. Perhaps it was the humidity, or the scents the air carried—fading spring blossoms and the start of summer.

The word *oeuf* meant omelette—a mild cheese omelette along with croissants and hot chocolate with whipped cream. They ate at a table near his fireplace. The fire flickered rainbow flames and Bossgond let her watch them, examine the room and eat in peace.

When they finished, with a wave of his hand the dirty dishes disappeared. If she were on Earth she could have marketed that for a fortune—but where did the dishes go, and would they return? If they returned, would they be the *same* dishes, but clean? How clean would they be? Would bacteria still live—

Bossgond chuckled. "I see many questions in your eyes," he said, enunciating each word.

Marian nodded and he nodded back. Apparently that was the same, too, nodding as agreement.

He rose slowly and his joints popped. She frowned. He could make the dishes disappear but had trouble rising? With motions and two or three attempts at rephrasing the question, she made herself clear.

"I have great Power," he said, rubbing his fingers together in a gesture like the one that meant "money" back home. "And my will and the Power make magical tasks easy, but my body is old and physical tasks are not easy."

Marian wanted to know how old he was, but it was rude in her culture to ask and she didn't know the rules of this society. She just looked concerned and nodded again.

He pointed to the center of the room where three thick oriental-looking rugs were layered. Huge pillows lay atop them along with several small tables that held objects: odd bottles— and were those wands?—and a couple of knives.

Marian hoped the knives were used ritually and practically, like in Wicca, and not for bloodletting and sacrifice. From the corner of her eye she studied Bossgond. She could take him in a physical fight, but if he used magic she was sure she could be bound and gutted in the blink of an eye. She shuddered.

The old man chuckled again and went to lower himself to the rugs. He sat cross-legged, palms up on his knees and sent her a quizzical glance.

She squared her shoulders. There was nothing she could do this minute except scream and fight for her life if he meant her harm. So she sank down across from him. To her amazement, her gown needed no adjusting: it flowed out of her way when she sat.

"First we'll determine how strong your Power is and whether you will be a good apprentice for me," he said, lifting his arms shoulder height, hands angled up as if pressing against an invisible wall. "Do as I do."

Marian mimicked him, putting her hands up. There was enough space between them that they had a few inches between their hands and didn't touch.

Bossgond hummed, and invisible pressure against her palms snapped Marian's hands back to her shoulders. He smiled, but kept the pressure steady.

Magical arm wrestling? Marian narrowed her eyes, sucked in a deep breath. She felt her own will, and something else—Power?—surge through her body, tingle through her hands, leave the hollow of her palms to push against his, be stopped against a barrier.

She concentrated, found a pool of energy within herself, drew it up and sent it out in a ragged stream against his Power. His hands trembled. Marian set her teeth, visualized a river of force inside her, welling up from the deep pool, turning into a torrent pouring from her hands to crash against Bossgond's wall. His hands snapped back to his shoulders.

Looking surprised, he frowned, then pushed back at her. She kept the Power steady against the strong force of his for what seemed an eternity that drained her and started her panting—perhaps only a minute. Then she slumped back against the pillow. Bossgond's Power followed her, taking her breath, then vanished.

"Extraordinaire," he said.

She heard his voice around buzzing in her ears. Gentle, inexorable fingers clamped around her wrists and brought her upright again. Her lungs pumped and the dress seemed to soak up her sweat and release a floral scent. Huh. Wriggling her legs and bottom, shifting her shoulders, she stared at the man from under lowered lashes.

He was inscrutable. Like a certain little green, pointy-eared Master of the Force.

Her own personal taskmaster. Great. She knew now that she hadn't given the green guy's students the sympathy they had deserved.

"Next test," Bossgond said, raising his hands, palms vertical again.

Marian didn't think she could twitch a finger, but managed to tilt her hands up from her wrists.

"To see how well we will do as Circlet and Apprentice," Bossgond said.

Marian suppressed a grimace. She knew the word "apprentice." It made her feel like she was ten again—maybe younger, just starting elementary school—though, she *was* a beginner at magic.

She didn't even have the basic socialization of any child brought up in this culture—what constituted rules of magic?

But Alexa seemed to have managed a position of high status, and in a relatively short a time, if Marian's recollection of the coat Alexa had worn in the vision was right. It was last winter's jacket, so she would have purchased it no earlier than the fall....

A sting against her palms brought her back to find her teacher frowning at her from under silver eyebrows. Her cheeks flamed. She'd let her attention wander! Oh yes, just like a kindergartner. Heat flushed her neck, too. She'd disappointed a prof—not good. She prided herself on being an exceptional student.

So she dipped her head in apology. *"Excusez moi."*

Bossgond nodded solemnly. "Attencion," he said.

She nodded again, kept her gaze fastened on his face, her mind on what would come next. Her stomach tightened. She hated pop quizzes. How could you get a perfect score without practice?

"Follow me," Bossgond said. He moved his hands far apart, cocked his head.

Intent on him, she moved her hands apart, too. Then he began gesturing, doing odd things with his hands, arms, face.

Marian mirrored him, watching. Finally, he returned to his original position.

"Now you move and I will follow," he said.

This was the strangest activity Marian had ever done with a teacher. Tentatively she set her hands together as if in prayer. He did the same. A little bolder, she tilted her head, grinned. He did the same. So they continued, Marian leading, until he said, "Fini."

When her eyes met his, he said, "Now we move together, but neither of us leads."

That sounded very strange. So she watched him and when he moved his hands a little she followed, but leaned to one side, and he did so, too. It was…balance. More than that, it was a connection, knowing how they should move together, and in her mind she began to hear a stream of musical notes weaving into a melody. A couple of minutes later, they brought their hands together, palm to palm, and a huge flare of energy burst from her, dazzling her with its lightning brightness, its orchestral chord thundering in her ears, her mind.

She spun free. Suddenly she was looking down on her body, hand-to-hand with Bossgond, in a round tower room. Then she was in the room above them, where she saw the star pentagram that had brought her. She rose above the tower to see a large island, the green coast of an unfamiliar land, then drifted even higher until she saw how the world curved.

Free.

Terrified. There was nothing to hold her here—no bond with this planet, this land. She still couldn't feel any link to Earth or Andrew, and wherever that corridor was that she'd entered Lladrana from, it didn't seem to be a physical place she could find.

Marian floated, unable to control her magic that had pushed her from her body. The Power was so strong she was unable to move her spirit-self even a smidgeon.

A slight breeze could blow her away.

6

Bossgond's strong hands squeezed hers. "Come back!" His resonant voice trembled through her wavery self and she plummeted into her body. She clung to his hands, stared at his homely face with her physical eyes. Her body trembled.

"You have returned," Bossgond said. "Good." He separated his fingers from hers one by one and stood up stiffly. "I will get you hareco—a drink to help you settle."

Leaning back on the huge, firm pillow that braced her, Marian hoped it wasn't some pitiful herbal tea. Good black tea would be nice, or—

She smelled it. Coffee! And she murmured a prayer of thanks. Bossgond handed her a mug and she inhaled the fragrance. Hot, dark coffee. She drank greedily, while he sipped from a matching mug. The pottery had a big yellow bird emblazoned on it, but she was too shaken to ask about the icon.

"Your first lesson will be in grounding." He frowned, and

the small black streak in his golden hair seemed to darken, or perhaps the rest glowed.

Marian pressed her lips together. She understood what he said well enough, and she wasn't that much of a kindergartner that she didn't know what "grounding" was—making sure you were solid in your body before doing magic.

Keeping her voice even, she set aside her mug and said, "This will be hard. I do not have a link—" she hooked her two index fingers together "—to Amee. My link to Exotique Terre is broken." Her chin wobbled at the thought. She grabbed her mug and sipped again—something she could understand, coffee.

Bossgond patted her shoulder awkwardly and took his place again. "From my observations, it seems as if Exotique Terre has little magic," Bossgond said, as she drained the last, lovely gulp from her mug.

Exotique Terre was what he'd called the globe of Earth the night before. Marian didn't know what to say, so she shrugged.

"A Power like yours would not have been so stifled, so bound until it struggled to get free, here on Amee." The old man's tone was laced with disapproval of her previous world. "You are far beyond the age of the standard Apprentice." He snorted. "But perhaps it is good that you are an adult. I have little patience."

He'd been fine with her so far, but she sensed she was a novelty to him.

The meaning of his words sank in. "From your observations? You can see into my world?"

"Indeed," he said, and waved to something that looked like an enormous set of binoculars on a stand, aimed at a series of mirrors that reflected infinitely. She couldn't figure out how the device worked, didn't know if she dared to ask to see her old world.

She yearned to know that Andrew was all right.

Bossgond came and took the empty mug from her, offered his hand to help her up. As she took it, the song between them uncurled again. He nodded.

"We have a small bond, which will grow. It is good."

After she was on her feet, he released her. "Come, we must remedy your lack of a link with Amee as soon as possible." He held out his hand and a walking stick flew into it.

Marian gulped.

Nodding to the table holding the wooden wands, he said, "Choose a walking stick."

His words made her uneasy, but she walked to the table and picked up each in turn. The dark red one felt the best, as if it were an extension of her arm. She repressed the urge to wave it and say "abracadabra" or "kalamazam." Instead she handed it to Bossgond.

He grinned in satisfaction and said, "Staff!"

The wand grew into a walking stick as high as her head— looking like a rod or wand from a tarot deck.

Bossgond handed it to her, and when she grasped it this time, a low note sounded and the thing vibrated. Small twigs appeared, then sprouted greenery, then ivy twined up the staff, spreading silver and gold leaves. She stared at it open-mouthed, and again her memory was prodded—by the vision Bossgond had shown her in his crystal ball when they'd first met. She'd had a staff just like this. No wonder he smiled— either he'd foreseen this, or he had deduced her Power correctly. What else wasn't he telling her?

Many things, she thought. The old sorcerer wasn't revealing anything he didn't want her to know, and he probably thought she knew more than she did. Her ignorance would impede them both.

He took her hand and led her to the stairs, and they wound their way down the tower to arched, double wooden doors. Marian watched intently as he slid the bar on the door to the side and into iron brackets attached to the stone wall. She'd be getting more than magic lessons, more than the sociology of a new culture—she'd learn more about architecture, too. So much to learn! It excited her.

Bossgond shoved open the door and they walked out into a small area paved with large gray flagstones, then into springy green grass. The wind whisked their garments around them, tugged at Marian's hair. He set a hand on her head and said, "Alam," and her hair settled around her head. Neat trick, but she rather missed the fingers of the breeze caressing her scalp.

The sunlight was yellow, clouds wispy white against a sky not quite as blue as a Colorado spring sky. Marian shifted her shoulders as she saw forested hills rolling to the horizon. She was used to a view of the Flatirons and Rocky Mountains. She was accustomed to a campus full of buildings, professors and students, not a lonely island tower with one brilliant Sorcerer.

Bossgond pulled on her hand and they circled the great tower, over bony rock, slippery moss and sweetly scented grass, until they were almost halfway around. He stilled, closed his eyes, cocked his head, then opened his lids and nodded once. "No one watches."

That was good to know—another trick Marian would like to learn. A person couldn't depend on atavistic itching between the shoulder blades. Bossgond squatted, gestured to her to do the same, then indicated the top of a stone at the bottom of the tower wall that looked well buried. He licked his finger and wiped off some dirt, and Marian saw a tiny outline of a bird. Bossgond's heraldic bird—she'd figured that much out. He whispered a word that was taken from her ears by the wind and a cube of moss and earth around the stone lifted as if cut. Another sighing two-note whistle and the stone removed itself. Bossgond waved for her to look into the darkness.

She had to wait a moment for her eyes to adjust before she could see a rough pyramid point inside the hollow.

"The keystone of the tower," Bossgond said. "The proof that a person has become a Circlet Sorcerer or Sorceress is when they raise their own tower with their Power."

Marian swallowed.

He reached in and caressed the keystone, smiling as if he petted a beloved animal.

Marian thought of her lost hamster Tuck and sniffled. What on Earth—on Amee—did these people do for handkerchiefs? And where would they put them? She hadn't noticed any pockets—but as she thought of them, four flapped against her skin. Interesting.

"If this stone is found and destroyed, my tower will fall. I may or may not be hurt, depending on whether I am in the tower and how much of my Power I have invested in my tower at the time. At the moment you are not Powerful enough to do me harm, and when we Bond by Blood as Master and Apprentice, we will be incapable of harming each other. Any secrets will never be able to pass our lips."

Blood-bond. Right. The idea should have deterred her, but it didn't. Blood played a large part in various cultures' rituals to symbolize a connection between people. She considered it a small price to pay for knowledge.

"You understand?" asked Bossgond.

Marian nodded, tucking the information and ramifications away to consider later. She reached in and touched the keystone. A little current ran through her—not soothing like her connection to Mother Earth had been—and she twitched. She couldn't imagine grounding herself with this rock; there was too much energy.

Bossgond sighed, shrugged. "Not a good stone for you to link to." With a wave of his hand the tower stone and the cube of sod settled back into place, looking as if they'd been undisturbed for centuries. "This is my Tower on Alf Island. But it is not the first Tower. We will walk to old Mortig's Tower. Perhaps that will be better for you."

They set off briskly and a minute later Marian bumped into a sizzling invisible barrier. She yelped and jumped back.

On the other side of the…forcefield, Bossgond smirked at her. Then he stepped up before her, touched his index finger to the barrier and "cut" a door for her. She lifted her chin and swept through past him.

"When we bond you will be able to enter or leave at will. I will also show you the courtesy portal for well-intentioned visitors."

After a quick walk away from the sun—west, then—of about a half hour, they reached the remnants of tower walls about five feet high. Bossgond showed her the hidden keystone to this, too. She started to touch the thing and electricity zipped between her fingers and the stone, shocking her. She fell back on her bottom with an outraged cry.

Bossgond creaked a laugh, helped her up, dusted off her seat and strode off in another direction. As they walked, Bossgond told her about his island.

He had demonstrated the strongest Power in several generations when he was a youngster and had piqued the interest of the Powerful Mortig. The choice of islands was always given to the most Powerful first. Bossgond had held Alf Island for many years.

Alf was about a hundred miles across and had everything a person would want—fresh streams full of fish, hills, forests, glades. His tower was near enough to the coast and a small harbor to appreciate the waves without being threatened by any flooding or crumbling ground. A paradise to Bossgond.

It sounded pretty good to Marian, too, though she was sure she'd miss mountains.

She thought back to when she'd hovered over the island. The shape was a little like Australia.

After an hour-and-a-half walk they came to a depression in the ground, too close to the rocky edge of the island to be altogether stable. The circle of flat stones was barely visible, but Power still radiated, drawing her.

Bossgond stood back and watched, but she strode to the hidden keystone with confidence. This one didn't vibrate quite right, either, but it felt better than either of the others.

Bossgond shook his head. "You are not of Amee, so no previous keystone will tune to you easily. Perhaps you will find a better place than this as you range the islands. For now, let us do the grounding here."

To Marian's embarrassment, she found herself lying on her stomach, arms angled down a few feet to the keystone. When she curled her hands around the pyramid-shaped rock, Power shot through her, erasing any exhaustion, starting a tingle racing in her veins.

Bossgond sat cross-legged beside her and placed a hand on her back, rubbed it. It felt nice, gentle, avuncular. She closed her eyes and let her mind sink into a quiet pool, only feeling— the warmth of the ground beneath her, the small breeze around her. And with three hummed notes, Bossgond sent her into a deep trance.

Distantly she heard his voice instructing her. Under his

spell, she sang to the stone and it reverberated one note, two, three back to her, and she felt a small tether to Amee.

With a soothing chant, Bossgond lifted her from her trance, brought her into clear-headed wakefulness. Again she felt energized. She laughed in delight at the connection with a world-song again, though this particular planet-melody was heart-wrenchingly sad.

She stood and stretched, limbering up after her time lying so still on the ground.

Bossgond looked at her, then at the circle of grass and stones. Then he gazed out to the sea, his face impassive. "If we do well together and you do not want another island or a manor on the mainland, I will grant you the right to raise another tower on the island." The corners of his lips curved slightly upward. He gestured. "You may choose where you please, as long as it is outside my protective ring around my tower."

The forcefield they'd crossed. She nodded.

His expression turned grim and he raised a finger. "*If* we do well together."

His tone was that of a man who'd been crotchety for decades.

When they returned to the Tower, Bossgond led her back upstairs for lunch. She sat at the table and he set a plate and silverware for them both. Then he put a few empty platters between them. He went to a cupboard and came back with a box.

Taking a crumb of bread, he put it on one platter, then added a bit of dried fruit, a few strings of jerky. As Marian stared, Bossgond passed his hands over the dishes and sang a long Songspell. The breadcrumb turned into a large loaf of bread dusted with flour, the jerky became four thick slices of roast beef, the fruit plumped into apples.

Under Marian's fixed gaze, Bossgond cut a piece of each and put it back into the magical box, then returned the box to the cupboard.

When he returned, he sang a little blessing, then made a sandwich and dug into his reconstituted meal.

Hesitantly, Marian sliced a piece of bread—wishing there was some Dijon mustard—and put a slice of roast beef on it. She took a bite, chewed and swallowed.

The food was plentiful but tasteless. The victuals had to be nutritious because Bossgond was still alive and he'd probably been eating this way for years. No wonder he was so scrawny.

After finishing off an apple and half her sandwich, Marian said, "Don't you cook?"

Sandwich at his open mouth, Bossgond's eyes widened. He put down the bread and meat.

"Do you?" His voice was hoarse, his gaze gleamed with hope.

"Of course."

He stood up so fast that his chair rocked. "Come with me!"

Nearly running to keep up with him, Marian followed him out the door, down the stairs past her own suite and to the level below her room.

Bossgond threw open the door. A gleaming kitchen took up most of the space, along with an empty pantry.

"Cooks were too much bother," he muttered. "I can fish," Bossgond said eagerly. "I can draw a deer to us and butcher it."

Ick. Marian was a civilized supermarket predator; she couldn't imagine such a thing. It was enough to make a person a vegetarian.

She crossed her arms. "I don't intend to be here very long. My priority, and what I want to spend my time doing, is learning from you, not cooking."

He looked torn, then tried a pitiful look, but he was too arrogant to do pitiful well.

"I would, however, supervise a cook." She liked her food, too—all too much.

Bossgond's lower lip stuck out.

"How long has it been since you had a cook?"

"Fifty years," he muttered.

"You need a little pampering. You're too thin, you need good food. You *deserve* it. I'm sure you could afford a cook."

"They are impossible to work with, men or women. They pry. They talk too much. They don't like living on the island."

So he wanted an unambitious introvert who liked solitude. Marian wondered how to advertise the position. "Let me think about this." She wouldn't be able to eat Bossgond's rations for long.

He nodded, but his expression eased. He climbed the stairs back to his chambers with a spring in his step.

Bossgond banished the food and dishes with a wave of his hand, then they both returned to the center of the room.

Scowling, he said, "You plan on leaving soon? We paid the Marshalls for your Summoning."

Marian lifted her chin. "My brother is ill, he needs me. *My* ritual was to find answers to strange things happening in my life and how to help him. I'm hoping that Amee will have information about his disease and how to mitigate it. I intend to take that knowledge back to him. I'll try to repay you."

Bossgond snorted, then studied her with narrowed eyes. "We will speak of this later. First you must study."

Within a few minutes, Marian had mastered the art of grounding herself, and the small, invisible thread spinning between her and the ancient keystone had thickened to a braided strand.

He taught her to light the fire with her mind, to levitate a book, to "call" her walking stick. Energy drained from her with each task, and a slight film of sweat dampened her skin. Her dress gave out the scent of herbs.

Then Bossgond rose and offered both his hands, beaming. "You have mastered the first level of Apprenticeship." He bowed.

Already? She dropped a little curtsy and a bubble of triumph expanded in her chest.

"To celebrate we will have another cup of hareco."

Oh boy, if coffee was so rare that she had to pass tests to get it, life was going to be tough.

He poured them each another cup of coffee and settled into the middle of the room with his mug. He gestured around them. "Survey the room, touch what you like to discover your particular vocation of study."

Marian blinked at him. "How?"

One corner of the man's mouth crinkled upward. "You will know. It will hum in your mind."

Marian had always loved music as much as books, but this aural culture made her feel alien. Still, she smiled, drained the last, delicious sip of coffee and set her mug aside. She looked around.

Bossgond leaned back against the pillows and sipped, staring out the window. Without his penetrating gaze, Marian felt able to act more naturally and to concentrate on exploring the room full of fascinating objects. She looked at the huge binoculars, but didn't cross over to them. When she moved away from the instrument, Bossgond grunted in approval, and she decided to save the binoculars for last if she didn't find anything else that struck a chord.

She scanned the shelves. The books intimidated her a little

since she couldn't read the fancy cursive lettering. She leafed through one and jolted when a couple of the pictures became three-dimensional. Then she put it back with a sigh. She wouldn't be in Lladrana long enough to learn how to read the language. A pity.

For an hour she indulged herself with the treasures crammed on the shelves—boxes and bottles, rugs, goblets and instruments, and art objects of all kinds. She found an elegant, gold-etched bottle that held all the scents of summer, a flying carpet for short trips around the island, models of castles and people and animals. Bossgond only stiffened twice during her explorations: once when she picked up something like a wand, but longer, heavier, and feeling like blood and death; again when she reached a big, open book that looked like new pages had been added.

She moved on to another table with a series of glass jars that looked a little like terrariums, increasing in size from a large mug to a great globe of about two feet. She touched the top of one in the middle and a sharp *ping* sounded in her mind. Static electricity—from *glass?*—shot up her arm.

In an instant Bossgond was beside her. Grinning.

"Very good," he said, rubbing his hands.

Marian wet her lips, stared at the jars. Now that she'd touched one, they all *sang* to her, like a series of glass windchimes. "What does it mean?"

7

Bossgond smiled. "You are a Weather Mage."

Her pulse quickened. "Weather? Are you sure?" She'd always had that odd sense….

He chuckled. "Very sure." Taking the largest globe with both hands, he walked to the conversation pit and set it in the middle. "You must start with this one. When you reach Scholar status, you will be competent in modifying the weather in the midsize jar. Your Circlet Test will be of fire, wind, wave and earth in the smallest jar."

The one with plants and trees and tiny bugs. Marian gulped, knowing instinctively that she could kill them all.

She sat cross-legged in front of the large sphere.

"Look into the glass," he said.

She did and caught her breath. There was a world down there! With continents and oceans, mountains, streams, vegetation.

Bossgond sat behind her, his skinny chest to her back, his legs framing hers. Marian tensed.

He clucked his tongue and placed his knobby hands on hers. His chest expanded behind her as he inhaled deeply. "I was no better than average at this task," he murmured. "But I can show you how to direct your Power. Concentrate on the world below. Do you see the clouds?"

Marian frowned and narrowed her vision, and a portion of one continent seemed to enlarge. "I see...buildings! There aren't really people down there, are there?" Her voice trembled in horror. She couldn't do this, *wouldn't* do this if she might harm anyone! Mistakes would be terrible.

"Look closer," Bossgond said.

Marian did. Concentrating, she focused her gaze until she saw a city of stone and wood, with winding roads to manor houses and two castles on a hill. They were all perfect little models, but they were models—as were the trees and animals. There were no fake people. Her breath rushed out.

"Now, back to where you see clouds," Bossgond said.

She "zoomed out," noted fat cumulus clouds and some wispy ones. She hadn't taken any science courses in years, wished she recalled more about weather. She smiled. Weather, with a capital W, was now her focus of study. She was a potential Weather Magician. How cool!

"We will try to move the clouds." Bossgond's hands tightened over hers. "*Feel* the essence of the clouds, their density and shape."

Was that like the exercise of "be a cloud" that profs in the Drama Department taught? Bossgond's mind led her to a cloud that showed gray at the bottom, yet puffed up white and pretty near the top. It was humongous.

She shut her eyes and focused on sensation. She seemed to

be floating in the sky, but not as she had before, not herself, Marian, but Cloud. She floated stomach-down, and the portion of her body closest to the ground felt heavy and full of liquid. For the first time in her life her ass felt airy. She couldn't prevent herself from thinking of it as a huge billowing cloud, and giggled.

Bossgond hissed. His irritation nudged her, and control of the cloud slipped from her grasp. It rained. Thankfully nothing happened to her real body.

"See if you can move the cloud," Bossgond said, disapproval clear.

She pushed her cloud. Nothing happened, except that she got a visual of her hands penetrating cool air. She tried something different. She was now separate from the cloud and grappled to *encompass* it. With her mind she formed a tiny membrane from air molecule to air molecule of the cloud, then *pushed*. It moved. She pushed again, and it slid rapidly through the air. Having fun, she set her mind against it and shoved. It turned into a streak of white.

"Whee!" Marian cried. She was flying, chasing a cloud.

Bossgond made a strangled sound and fell backward, away from her.

She stopped, withdrew her consciousness from the weather globe and shifted around to see what was wrong.

He was holding his head as if he had a migraine.

"Bossgond?" she asked.

The mage winced. "You are Powerful. I didn't expect you to be able to move the cloud so easily, so fast and far. I never could," he grumbled.

"You have other talents." Marian scooted behind him and started massaging his temples, wondering why she felt compelled to reassure him. He grunted, then sighed with pleasure.

"Of course," he said, but he didn't sound as sarcastic as she'd expected. He huffed out a breath. "You are a naturally gifted student in Power. It happens sometimes, that there are geniuses."

An inner glow of pleasure lit her. Of course, she'd been a professional student all her life and knew she learned quickly...not that this was learning so much as *revealing,* discovering something deep inside her, something she was meant to be.

Bossgond said, "Naturally the Song would bring someone innately Powerful to the Tower Community."

That evening after another mediocre meal, Marian joined Bossgond in the ritual room. He began to Sing the blood-bond ceremony and she joined in when she could. When he picked up a small, sharp knife and strips of linen, she froze. What was she getting into?

Bossgond smiled reassuringly. "We will be bound together for four hours—the correct amount of time for a bond between Master and Apprentice. There are both lesser and greater bonds, depending upon the length of the binding. A Pairing-Marriage bond is a full night and day."

She nodded and tried to relax as he took her arm and shoved up her sleeve, concentrating on something else—like how glad she was that neither of them had drunk a lot at dinner.

His voice deepened with mystery, with mastery as he cut her arm. The pain was slight, but she yelped and stared as he inserted a little tube in her arm. It looked as if he'd encased a whole vein. Then he slit open his own arm and captured a vein.

Exactly how much blood would they be exchanging? This whole thing involved a lot more than she'd realized.

After they were linked, they finished Singing the ceremony, Marian in a low tone, experimenting with using her voice and

Power. Even before they snuffed the last candle, she could feel his blood inside her, weighty with age, with Power, but also… murky.

With his blood came memories, strange and distorted and flickering too fast before her mind's eye for her to catch and analyze them.

As the minutes passed, through Bossgond, Marian's small tune merged with the planet's. Wonder grew inside her.

She found herself panting, and regulated her breath—yoga breaths. Slowly, they left the top ritual floor and descended to Bossgond's study. He'd placed a small desk and chair next to his larger one, along with the big glass sphere that contained Marian's planet.

His mouth moved and a second or two later she heard his distorted voice, not beautiful now, but beating at her ears.

"Study the continents, the contours of the land, and especially the weather."

Marian stared at the sphere, but minutes passed before her eyes focused. She swallowed. Everything was so overwhelming! She chose a cloud—studied it as it floated over the continent, changed shapes, absorbed other clouds and became a weather front. Her heart pounded dully in her chest.

Bossgond fiddled with lenses on his desk. Glimmers of his thoughts came with the flow of memories.

A few minutes after the second hour, Bossgond abruptly quit his work and they went back to the ritual room, where they relaxed in lounge chairs. This was easier, as she didn't have to struggle with the input from his mind as he worked.

Slowly, slowly, without the distraction of her studies or his, relaxing in the chair, Marian regained her equilibrium and could snatch bits of Bossgond's knowledge, process it, understand it. Comprehension of the language came first, and she smiled faintly. Lladranan culture celebrated the Singer—a prophetess oracle—and the Song, what they called the Divine. It made sense that she "heard" the language in her blood, trickling to her brain, opening new paths.

Too aware of her own memories flowing to Bossgond, Marian let Bossgond's most personal ones zoom past her. She knew he'd had two long-term lovers, that the relationships hadn't been totally satisfying. He probably learned all about her mother—and Andrew. Perhaps he could help with Andrew. At least Bossgond now knew how much she loved her brother and why it was imperative for her to return to Earth.

Then Marian "saw" the northern boundary of Lladrana, the fence posts and magical forcefield boundary strung between them. The fence posts blackened and fell, the border gaped. Monsters invaded. Horrible, hideous, *evil*-looking things that brought nausea, so she pushed the thoughts away.

She experienced worms in the rain. Most died when they hit the ground, some tunneled into the earth. Frinks.

Some people opened mouths to the frinks, were consumed by them inside until they turned into monsters within a human skin. Mockers.

From a colorful whirl of views through the binoculars, Marian picked out Alexa—at a graduation, at a funeral, hiking up a mountain trail at night, walking through a silver arch.

Alexa choosing a baton. Alexa in battle—grisly images… Marian shook her head sharply, no! She didn't want to see that. Not now, not yet.

A new fence post—Alexa grinning, holding a helmet under her arm.

Marian herself at her work-study job in the Engineering Department. On a date with Jack Wilse. Talking to her mother. Hugging Andrew.

She pulled her thoughts back to the here and now—to the shrouded room around her, the cupboards that held the globes of Amee and Earth she'd seen the night before. The clock showed three hours had passed and seemed to tick with her heartbeat.

Bossgond made a strangled noise. She glanced at him—a gray tinge had crept under his skin. His breath was ragged.

"I can't bear it," he mumbled. "Your world is too difficult to contemplate. Too harsh."

Marian thought that being invaded by terrible monsters was worse than Denver traffic, which she'd been thinking of. But she reached for the linen strips that bound their arms together.

"No!" Bossgond cried, sitting straight up. "This needs a delicate touch."

She understood him much better now, so she leaned back. As he began to chant over the bindings, her blood slowed and dizziness hit her. He carefully separated their arms. The tubes had dissolved. A hollow sigh of relief escaped him.

After a few more chanting words, his hard fingertip ran up her arm, sealing her wound and leaving cold fire in its wake. Bossgond wrapped one strip along her arm and sang a simple healing tune that made Marian smile. She was feeling sleepier and sleepier. Had Bossgond siphoned her own energy into himself, thinking it was his right as her master? She didn't like that thought or the dark parade that followed. Maybe he'd been acting all day, and now she was about to become a sacrifice. Bad. Very bad. How could she have been so gullible?

Darkness swooped down on her.

Maps tucked under his arm, Jaquar followed Chalmon up his Tower stairs to his study. The other Sorcerer radiated irritation, probably still upset at Jaquar's behavior in claiming Exotique Marian the day before. Or perhaps it was that Jaquar had gathered a circle of Sorcerers and Sorceresses to watch the Dark's nest, and they were reporting to him.

Before Jaquar's parents died, Chalmon had considered himself the leader of their generation of the Tower Community. Jaquar, like most, had gone his own way and done small tasks for Chalmon as requested, and if they cost little.

That had changed. Jaquar had never wanted to be a leader, barely had the patience to deal with the idiosyncrasies of a group of individuals, but he hungered for vengeance.

When they reached Chalmon's tidy study, Venetria rose and came forward. Jaquar sensed she'd been with Chalmon since the debacle at the Marshalls' Castle the day before.

"Salutations, Venetria." He bowed and kissed her hand. "How did you two get here?"

Chalmon waved a hand as if impatient with the question, any small talk. "I bought a coach and Venetria bespelled it to fly. It will be a welcome addition to my household."

Venetria frowned. "It's *my* coach."

"I bought it." Chalmon scowled at his lover.

"But my flight spell is much more costly than the coach itself."

"Why didn't you settle this between the two of you before?" asked Jaquar.

Chalmon reddened. Venetria smiled in satisfaction. "Chalmon was in a hurry to get *into* the coach. All that Power compressed in that pentacle yesterday was so *invigorating*."

Venetria heaved a sigh, which raised her chest. She did have beautiful breasts. Almost as beautiful as the Exotique's, though Jaquar had no business thinking such thoughts.

He strode to the center of the room where a study table and

several chairs sat, unrolled one of the large sheets of paper he'd brought with him and placed it on the table. "This is a diagram and map of Plane Eighteen. I've found it to be the best for observing the nest. The master and monsters don't sense us because it is a few levels more spiritual—more *good*—than what they can achieve."

"They are too destructive for Eighteen?" Venetria asked. "I don't do well in any Plane lower than Twenty-four." She slid Chalmon a glance. "Unless I'm angry at Chalmon."

Jaquar's mouth twisted. "I've reached upward to Eighty-two, as low as Eleven—which is the Plane the horrors use most often."

Chalmon grunted. "Is that other roll level Eleven?"

"Yes." Jaquar moved the first map to one side of the table and set the second down.

As he unrolled it, Chalmon placed a paperweight on each of the four corners and studied the musical notation at the bottom of the chart. His nose wrinkled as if smelling a bad odor.

"Foul," Chalmon said. He tapped the music and a low, grating hum and clashing notes reverberated through the room. Venetria jumped and put her hands over her ears.

"You probably shouldn't have done that," Jaquar said mildly.

Greasy smoke hovered in the air. "You're right." Chalmon scowled. "Now they could become aware of me, might have a direct path here. I'll have to do a Ritual Cleansing." He glanced at Jaquar. "How do you make such maps without alerting the monsters, the Master, the Dark itself?"

"Very carefully." He had no intention of revealing his secrets.

For an instant, Chalmon's face lightened with humor, then he sobered again and nodded to chairs near the fireplace. They were simple and covered in royal blue, Chalmon's color. He waited until Jaquar and Venetria were seated, then said, "I am not comfortable with your previous plan to train the new Exotique and use her to infiltrate the nest."

Relief eased Jaquar's tight muscles. Despite his lust for revenge, he'd had qualm, too, since he met Marian. Her personal Song was so lovely.

Chalmon continued. "I studied the information you sent regarding the recent observations of the Dark's nest. The Sorcerer who was watching last night said there was a great stirring when Marian was Summoned. The Dark obviously knows she's arrived. We may not have time for her full training."

Venetria pursed her lips. "True. I hope Bossgond teaches her rapidly and well."

Chalmon said, "The Sorceress watching the nest this morning stated there has been increased activity, as if more monsters would soon be released." He squared his shoulders. "I contacted the others. We—the group of us—agree that we may have to move faster than anticipated."

Anger stirred inside Jaquar. "Sounds as if you were busy during my trip from my island this evening."

Eyes steely, Chalmon said, "From the Power I felt surrounding the Exotique, she is strong enough and *Exotique* enough to penetrate the magical shield keeping the rest of us at bay."

"I want her trained up to Circlet status first," Jaquar insisted. "It would be foolish to throw away such a fearsome weapon as Marian without learning all she is capable of." He stood and paced. "Has it occurred to you that the Master is baiting a trap? And he wants us to do just as we planned—send the new Exotique Marian to her destruction instead of guarding her and using her? She's Powerful and could be the worst danger to him if she develops into a Circlet, unites us and fights with us and Exotique Alyeka."

Chalmon shifted his shoulders. "That may well be true, but I'm sure she could hurt the nest, and you saw what *one* sangvile did. Its damage is exponential. If the Master releases several—"

"We are *watching*. We will know when the horrors leave the nest maw. We know how to defeat all the monsters we've encountered so far, including the sangvile, including the dreeth. I do not want to act in haste!"

Venetria and Chalmon exchanged glances.

"We should definitely spend more time with her and learn her Powers before we solidify our plans," Venetria said. She grimaced. "I suppose we should visit Bossgond."

"He'll probably be having many people dropping by—Circlets of the Tower and Marshalls, too. Nothing will stop Exotique Alyeka from greeting another from her old world." Jaquar smiled as he recalled the small woman's excitement the previous day. "And since Alyeka doesn't fly well, her husband, Bastien, will bring her. As a black-and-white, Bastien has a wide streak of curiosity himself."

Jaquar chuckled. "Yes, Bossgond's Tower may become a busy place. Enough to make him cranky. I plan to go see him and Marian myself."

Venetria and Chalmon watched Jaquar leave. As they stood at the top of the tower, Chalmon's fingers tightened on hers, his profile went stern. The Song between them was rough and uneven as their thoughts and desires conflicted. As usual.

"I didn't ask to be jolted out of my complacency and into the knowledge of great danger."

She jerked her hand from his and turned away from the window. "I'm sorry I burdened you when my aunt died, made you face what the sangvile could do to us," she said stiffly. "I must go." She'd wanted to stay, had felt protected and warm here, even though his furnishings were not to her taste. He'd never noticed that, of course. She digressed from the topic he'd introduced, but she didn't want to think about what plans he might propose.

He grasped her, both hands on her shoulders. "Jaquar is deviating from his original tune in this."

"Easier to consider harm to an unknown person than someone we've met."

"A very beautiful woman who has an intriguing Song. Who he held in his arms, who spun notes with him even during a short interval." Now Chalmon gazed beyond her. "But if Jaquar retreats from this plan, I will not." His hawkish stare met hers again, pinned her. "What of you?"

"I don't know."

Marian woke at the feel of a cool, damp, herbal-scented cloth wiping her face. Bossgond stared down at her, concerned.

"It's only been a few minutes, and is still evening," he said in a raspy voice. "Let us adjourn to my chambers."

Testing her arms and legs, Marian stretched. Her limbs worked fine, though her insides felt a little hollow.

She took Bossgond's hand and rose, stood a moment, but no dizziness occurred. Smiling at her master, a man whose bark was worse than his bite from all she'd learned of him, she went with him back down to his study.

It seemed even more comfortable since Marian had experienced the Power it had taken to raise the Tower, the money—known here as zhiv—to furnish it.

Attentive, Bossgond settled Marian in the nest of pillows in the center of the room, then brought her coffee. She'd discovered through their bonding that coffee wasn't rare—not as rare as tea—but Bossgond considered it a treat.

He sat opposite her, his wrinkled cheeks faintly flushed. "We *are* bonded, but not as deeply as usual between Master and Apprentice. To compensate for my failure to complete the full bonding I will show you something special tomorrow morning."

Marian stared at him, recognizing that his self-condemnation at such a "failure," wasn't attractive. He'd done his best, hadn't he? They *did* have a bond, a Song, and it felt strong to her. He'd done neither of them harm. In fact, harm to him had been averted, since the strangeness of Earth had threatened his sanity. Yet he expected her to condemn him? She didn't know what to say.

He waved a hand irritably. "You may go."

So she curtsied and left. Head crammed full of the day's experiences, she wound down the stairs thinking that she should keep a journal. She entered her room in full dark, but before the door closed behind her, a soft light flickered on.

A lantern atop the large desk glowed—bright on the first blank pages of an open book. Marian's mouth dropped open, but she was too tired to make a sound, too weary to mess with the feather pen sitting in the pretty gold-edged glass inkwell.

Instead she went behind the stained-glass partition to her bedroom and removed her clothes and shoes, folding her dress up as she'd found it. Not a wrinkle or a speck of dirt marred the cloth. On one of the lower shelves she found a pile of pale gowns that looked like nightwear, and drew one on, sighing with tired pleasure as the soft material whispered over her skin. When she climbed into bed and found the sheets warm, she chuckled. Magic could provide incredible luxury.

Trying her own Power, she said, "Lights out," and smiled as darkness enveloped her loft.

Just before she fell asleep, a thought occurred to her: all her skill in being able to shape weather would not help Andrew.

In the morning Marian found a little golden tattoo of a bird on the inside of her left wrist, but no other scar. When she tried to converse with Bossgond at breakfast, he replied in grunts, and she decided he was naturally a grumpy old man who'd tried to tone down his manner for the past couple of days. She much preferred his slight deception to her mother's hypocrisy. They ate another bland cheese omelette and coffee.

She must remember to get them a cook.

After breakfast her heart pumped hard as he gestured to the oversize binoculars—the ones he used to watch Earth. They had their own stand of polished brass. The instrument itself was of copper-inlaid brass and shone—obviously Bossgond's pride and joy. The eyepieces were the right size; it was the other end that held great lenses, each about three feet in diameter.

Bossgond went to the stand and adjusted gleaming gears. "I've been observing your Exotique Terre for half a year now—as soon as a Circlet reported that destiny tunes indicated more Exotiques would be Summoned."

"Oh?" Marian encouraged.

"Then the Marshalls Summoned the first Exotique as expected, to keep and train as one of their own, and indications appeared that we, the Tower Community of Circlets, should accept the next Exotique as one of us."

He was leaving a lot out, Marian was sure, but right now all her attention was focused on the binoculars. She bit her lip, waiting impatiently.

Bossgond tapped the fancy brass instrument. "This is still focused on your former abode. See for yourself."

8

Careful not to joggle the binoculars, Marian bent to peer through the eyepiece.

Her breath caught as she saw the gray carpet of her apartment, the taped red star. The incense smoke had long since dissipated, but the little power-light for her sound system was still on. Her PDA was in the middle of the pentacle.

Drawing back, she nibbled her bottom lip, glanced at Bossgond. "I know it's been only two days, but my brother is very sick. Could I check on him?"

He stared at her in silence, and she wondered how much he'd received and understood about Andrew. She kept her eyes on his. She wouldn't back down. Bossgond's eyes narrowed.

"How far away is your brother?"

Marian spread her hands. "Across the country from me. My home is in the middle of a great land mass—"

Bossgond nodded.

"—and my brother is on the West Coast." What was that island's name? She'd researched the program when Andrew first considered it a year ago. Freesan!

"You know the geography of your land and where to find him?" Bossgond's eyes shifted, and she sensed excitement flowing from him. He'd have someone to help him tour Exotique Terre.

"Yes," she said.

He pointed to a couple of great gears with knobs and calibrated markings. "This will distance you from the scene, and this gear will bring you closer."

One eye at the lens, Marian turned the biggest gear. Her living room shrank and was replaced by her apartment building. As she kept turning, she saw her street, the city, the state. It was brown—much drier than Lladrana, even in the spring. With a gentle touch she angled the viewing field until she saw northwest Washington State, moved the binoculars again to focus on the many islands. Freesan was small and undistinguished—long and narrow. She recalled that the center sat on the north end of the island. Finally, she found the main structure. She zoomed in, but couldn't see Andrew. A fine tremor started within her.

"You are blood. Think of his Song," Bossgond murmured near her ear.

That didn't help. She hadn't ever noticed a Song coming from Andrew. She set her teeth, drew in a deep breath. Her magic was strong here in Lladrana. If she couldn't hear him, perhaps she could sense him or see his aura—or something. She mentally *reached* for Andrew, visualizing him. For a moment she touched him, then lost him. She muttered under her breath, *reached* again—and there he was! Quickly, with fumbling fingers, she narrowed the scope of the binoculars and saw him. Her heart clutched. She hadn't seen him for a couple of months and his recent exacerbations had taken a toll. He was very thin, as if his will sustained him more than his body.

Bossgond nudged her aside, but kept a hand on her upper arm as he looked through the binoculars. "Ah yes, I hear your family melody."

He did?

He glanced up at her and clucked his tongue. *"Listen!"*

So she did, with her heart and imagination, more than her mind, and caught a brief series of notes. She *did* hear that while her own portion of the twined melody was strong, Andrew's was arrhythmic and missed beats.

"He does well," Bossgond said. "He is active."

The old man stepped aside, allowing Marian to peek again, and she saw Andrew laughing in a group as they picked up packs and walked from the building.

"That is enough," Bossgond said, drawing her away. "You used much Power for this session, but the worlds of Exotique Terre and Amee draw apart, and every day it will cost more energy to view. You have much to learn, and need your strength to do so."

"I want to check on Andrew at least once a week."

Bossgond raised his brows. "We will discuss a price for this."

"How about finding and supervising the cook, as we spoke of?"

His eyes went calculating, as if pondering whether she could survive in his culture, outside his Tower. She wondered, too, but she'd think of something.

"Very well," he agreed.

Light-headed with relief, she took a couple of paces to the wall and leaned on it.

Bossgond smirked. "You don't know how to restore your Power yet." Then he bent and adjusted the gears. "They are focused on your former rooms again. 'I am a Circlet, behold,'" he said.

He whistled—sharp and nearly at the edge of her hearing—and made an intricate, swooping gesture. Then he held her PDA in his hand.

Marian gasped.

He bowed, grinning, and offered it to her.

She snatched it from his hand, clutched it to her chest. "Thank you."

"You are welcome," he said austerely. "Consider it payment for my failure last night to complete the blood-bond to its proper strength."

"You retrieved my…little machine book. Could you possibly find my pet? He was lost in the corridor when we came here."

She thought of a pocket in the green gown she wore and one appeared, perfect to hold the PDA. She put her possession—her only possession from Earth—into the pocket.

Waving her hands, she tried to describe Tuck. "He's a…a mousekin in a clear ball."

Bossgond shook his head. "The corridor between worlds is inexplicable. The winds can be absent or like a hurricane. Monsters…"

"No!"

"I saw you come through, but only glimpsed your pet at that time. I have not seen him since. The binoculars are not designed to explore the corridor. I'm sorry."

Marian bit her lip. "Thank you, anyway."

At that moment all the chimes in the open window sounded.

"Visitors come." Bossgond scowled.

"A boat?"

"No." He flicked his fingers to the window. "Go see." He looked as if he suppressed a smile…at her expense? She crossed to the window.

A flying horse carrying two people circled the Tower, then descended to land in front of the main door. Marian found herself leaning out of the window to stare at the Pegasus. It was the most beautiful creature she'd ever seen, and she'd never been a girl fond of horses. But this beast was different. It glowed with magic.

"Hey!" someone called. "Hey, Rapunzel, Rapunzel, let down your hair!"

Marian choked and tore her gaze away from the winged horse to narrow her eyes at the small woman at the bottom of the Tower. Alexa—the other Earth woman, the first Exotique in centuries.

"Will that grumpy old man let us in?" Alexa called, and Marian was torn between laughter at Alexa's words and surprise that they'd both called him the same thing.

"I'll ask," Marian shouted back in English, then turned to Bossgond. "Will you allow Alexa to visit?"

"I let the volaran through my shield, didn't I?" he snapped, and Marian sensed he'd learned enough English from her to know "grumpy old man." She flushed but didn't apologize.

"I have not spoken with the Exotique Swordmarshall Alyeka yet." With little grace, Bossgond tromped down the circular stairs, grumbling under his breath.

Marian followed, excitement fizzing through her. When they reached the bottom of the stairs, Bossgond ordered, "Light." The lowest round chamber, which Marian hadn't seen before, lit with a mellow glow.

The room was so beautiful that Marian gasped: the walls were paneled in rich wood, carpets covered the stone floors, two large fireplaces with sculpted marble surrounds held crackling fires. Several tapestries hung on the walls. There were no windows. A defensive measure?

Ripples of sound came from the entry doors—a scale rising and falling, rising and—

"Will you stop that!" Bossgond yanked open one side of the doors, letting late-spring sunlight flood into the room, and faced a woman smaller than he. Alexa.

She wore thick tights and a tunic that came to mid-thigh. And chain mail, with sheaths for sword and her wand—baton. Grinning at Bossgond, she said, "Shalutashuns, Bossgond."

Marian realized several things all at once: Alexa was about Marian's own age, small for an Earth woman—about five foot even—and very small for a Lladranan. And she had a terrible accent.

"Shalutashuns, Marian," Alexa said, sounding drunk. She sighed and switched to English. "It's the accent. I'm not good at languages and Lladranan still tangles my tongue."

"Kind of you finally to visit me," Bossgond huffed. "I'm only the most Powerful Circlet on Amee."

Alexa blinked at him. Her next words were carefully pronounced. "I had no idea you wished to see me. You could have invited me, or come to the Castle."

Bossgond drew himself up so he could tower over the smaller woman. It didn't faze her. "I do not travel."

"Huh," said Alexa. "Sounds like you were just as interested in me as everyone else in Lladrana and irritated because I didn't come and satisfy your curiosity." She grinned widely. "As a matter of fact, I'd never heard of you until a couple of days ago."

He narrowed his eyes and looked like an evil mage. "Th-those arrogant Marshalls. Those impertinent younger Circlets…" he sputtered.

"I'm sure you're right." Alexa nodded. "Sometimes prying information out of them is like pulling teeth."

He looked horrified.

Alexa glanced at Marian. "You think they use that idiom?" she said in English.

"It doesn't look like it. I think you've shocked him to his core."

"Hmm. I haven't had any dental problems since I've been here." She ran her tongue around her teeth. "I wonder what they do. I hope it's better than on Earth. I hate dentists."

"How long have you been here?" Marian asked.

"Nearly three months. The weeks and days are about the same as on Earth, you know."

"Yes."

Alexa heaved a sigh. "I suppose we'd better find out what you know and what you don't."

"A good idea."

"You must have a million questions."

"Somewhere around that."

"Did the feycoocu come with you?" asked Bossgond.

"What?" Marian didn't catch the word.

"Fey-coo-cu," Alexa said slowly. She fingered the baton sheathed at her side. "She's my sidekick." Alexa grinned. "A magical shapeshifter."

Marian stared. "If you say so." But a little thrill went through her.

Alexa laughed. "Yep, we have plenty to talk about." She turned to a simmering Bossgond. "I am not proficient on volaranback. My husband brought me. The feycoocu accompanied us in her hawk form."

"Husband?" Marian asked. "Did two of you come from Colorado?"

"Nope, I met him here." Alexa shifted, flushed slightly. "I know it's been quick, but you know that old saying about extreme circumstances and love. You don't get any more extreme circumstances than these on Lladrana." All humor left her face, and she rubbed at the scar on her cheek. "Let's walk and talk."

"I think we'd better," Marian said, swallowing apprehension. On the whole, she'd been treating this lightly, but there was no denying that if a bunch of people summoned you from another world, they were probably desperate and wanted something from you.

Alexa made a half bow to Bossgond. "May I visit with your Apprentice, Circlet Bossgond?"

He nodded regally. "Send the feycoocu to me if you see her. I have never met one." His lip curled. "And if you don't see her, I will talk to your Pairling. I've heard he is a black-and-white. We need to study those unfortunates more."

"I'm sure he'll be glad to let you examine him," Alexa said dryly.

"Pairling?" asked Marian.

"Husband, partner." Alexa frowned. "Isn't there a word 'shieldmate'?"

"Yes," Marian said.

Alexa nodded. "Then he's my shieldmate. We fight together."

A chill slithered down Marian's spine and she glanced at Alexa's sword out of the corner of her eye. It appeared well used, with plenty of nicks on the fingerguard. Marian couldn't imagine fighting with a sword or shield. A hint of the dreams she'd had at home drifted through her mind. She'd fought, though, with magic. This was feeling more and more ominous. She ran her hands up and down her arms.

"You may go, Apprentice," Bossgond said in a tone he hadn't used before with her.

She stiffened and frowned at him. But that made her think, too. Alexa apparently was a Marshall, which Marian had deduced was a powerful elite. *She* was stuck as an Apprentice.

Alexa jerked her head to the door. "You should have seen the horrible Tests the Marshalls put me through the minute I arrived," Alexa said under her breath.

She shuddered, and Marian knew the woman was utterly sincere.

Marian followed her. "Bossgond showed me an image of you walking in the mountains. Colorado?"

"Yes."

"You had brown hair."

Throwing open the door, Alexa stepped into the sunlight. It gleamed on her silver hair. She looked back at Marian. "It was one of those turn-white-overnight deals. The night I came."

"Really?" Marian's mouth had dried. As she went through the door she welcomed the cheery warmth of the sun.

"Yeah, and my eyes deepened in color, too," Alexa said, her curled fingers showing white knuckles as they clasped the top of her baton.

The door slipped from Marian's grasp and slammed shut.

Alexa smiled at Marian and switched to English again. "You know your way around here?"

"Not much."

Chuckling, Alexa said, "It's only been a couple of days since you arrived—but I'm sure they've been jam-packed with experiences."

"Oh yes," Marian said fervently. "I remember a nice forest path and a peaceful meadow a few minutes away—will that suit?"

"For sure." She tilted her head. "I'm connected mentally to my husband, Bastien. He's giving us privacy and hiding from Bossgond. He says he'll talk to the old mage when he's ready."

Marian led the way from Bossgond's Tower. They paused at the forcefield for Marian to open a "door" for Alexa. Outside Bossgond's sphere of influence they stood in the sun and studied each other.

"I like the looks of you," Alexa said.

Marian felt relief from an anxiety that she hadn't known she was feeling. "I like the looks of you, too."

She held out her hand and they shook, then Alexa turned Marian's arm over to see her wrist. Alexa's eyes sharpened.

"You've blood-bonded with Bossgond?"

"Yes, as Master and Apprentice." Marian pouted a little.

"Won't be long until you're a Circlet," Alexa said casually, confidently. "The Song only Summons the best."

Marian liked her more and more.

Alexa held out her left arm and pushed her sleeve up, showing her own tattoo: crossed wands. One was green with flames coming out of the top, the other black with silver twined around it. "This is my Pair-bond with Bastien—it's a blood-bond, sex bond, love bond. We haven't had a formal ceremony—like a wedding—the full binding—yet, though. We're both a little nervous about that."

Then she flipped open the short sheath and drew out the green stick shown on the tattoo. It looked like jade.

"It's my baton—do you want to see it?" The offer was cheerfully made, but her gaze watchful.

As soon as Marian touched the cool jade, a hard shock

jolted up her arm. She hung on as the energy—Alexa's energy—whirled through her, then settled, itchy, under her skin. As she stared at the baton, carved figures appeared, and the flames at the end danced.

Alexa's eyes widened and she nodded incisively. "Good. I thought you might be able to handle and use it. My husband, Bastien, can hold it for a couple of minutes, use it once, but that's all. It's good to know that you could wield it in an emergency."

"What emergency?" Marian said faintly, her stomach tightening, watching mercury flow viscously in a glass tube under the flames.

"On the battlefield, if I fall," Alexa said.

Marian dropped the baton. Alexa caught it—or rather, it flew into her hand. Marian stared at the woman, fit and strong, with the scar running down her cheek and somber eyes. Alexa heaved a sigh.

"I was afraid that they'd leave this to me. That miserable old man. But maybe you won't be fighting. Many Circlets don't." She shrugged, but her voice was faintly condemning. "Let's walk and talk."

"I'm not staying here. I have a life back home."

"Which is?"

"Boulder."

"Ah." Alexa's smile was quick and charming, but she covered the ground rapidly. "Thought I pegged you for an academic."

"I'm working on my doctorate in Comparative Religion and Philosophy," Marian said stiffly.

Alexa halted in the small meadow. A couple of large rocks graced the center, looking like seats. She turned to Marian and tapped herself on the chest. "Swordmarshall Alexa Fitzwalter, Esquire, Attorney at Law."

"You're a *lawyer?*" It was the last thing Marian would have guessed.

"Was." Alexa hitched herself up on one of the rocks and wiggled to get comfortable. "Nice seat, warm from the sun." She smiled serenely at Marian. "Now I do all my fighting on a battlefield, not in a courtroom." A shadow lingered in her eyes.

Marian wasn't ready to hear her story. She had to make something else very clear, first.

"I'm not staying. I can't. I have a life I must return to."

Alexa lifted her chin. "I have a life I crafted here."

"I have a brother with MS."

"Oh, I'm sorry." Alexa held out her hand, and Marian took it—this time a sweet comfort flowed between them.

"It's progressive regressive MS, so it comes and goes. I'm hoping to find a cure to take back. Maybe I can become Powerful enough to cure him with magic?"

Alexa just shook her head. "I'm not sure how healing magic works here. I've seen great wounds healed." She grimaced. "But it usually takes more than one person and some serious spellchants. For a disease, I just don't know."

"My mother is back home, too," Marian said. She ran her hands through her hair as she took the rock seat next to Alexa. It felt as if many had sat there before—to talk, to eat, to watch the stars at night.

They sat in silence for a moment before Alexa spoke. "I suppose you'll return to Earth when the Snap comes, and stay. To be honest, I don't know how much of our magic here will translate to magic there." She waved a hand. "I never made it all the way back home during the Snap—"

"The Snap?" Marian asked.

"I'll tell you about it later."

Marian sighed. "All right."

Alexa's hazel eyes appeared greener. "I didn't have any family at home, nothing much to go back to, not compared to what I have here." She shrugged and her smile quirked. "Though a vision I saw indicated I'd become a federal judge if I went back."

Marian didn't doubt it. The woman was walking determination.

"I can't stay," Marian said. "I can't leave my brother."

"All right. But I'd better tell you what's going on, anyway."

"That's a very good idea."

9

"Let me tell you why you were Summoned," Alexa said.

"As long as you don't expect me to stay," Marian cautioned.

"Too bad. Lladrana needs all the help it can get, and I can tell by your aura that you'd be *a lot* of help." Alexa slipped from her rock to sit on the sun-warmed ground.

Marian did the same and tried not to think about bugs.

Her expression completely serious, Alexa said, "The fact is, Lladrana is in deep trouble. There are monsters invading from the north." She shot Marian a glance. "I'm not talking about other people with differing belief systems, but real, live, evil monsters. The Lladranans usually call them 'horrors.'"

Bossgond's images of monsters came to Marian.

Alexa frowned. "Watch." With a sharp indrawn breath and narrowed eyes, the air between them hazed. A huge, vicious-looking creature hulked into view. It had long, sharp teeth that dripped saliva. Curving, knifelike claws extended from its lifted forepaws.

"Render," Alexa said. She kept the image up and rotated it, until Marian had to swallow hard.

The second monster was worse. Bigger even than the render, it had putrid yellow fur, horns and spines along its arms, head and back.

"Slayer. It can shoot the spines. They're poisonous, of course."

"Of course," Marian said faintly, wondering if she was turning a shade of green.

The slayer vanished and a third horror appeared. Worse. This one had lizardlike gray skin, a round knobby head with burning red eyes and a hole for a nose. Each shoulder sported an arm and two tentacles with suction cups.

"Soul-sucker," Alexa said. "But it really just drains your life-force." She waved a hand.

Just? Marian thought she squeaked, but Alexa showed no evidence of hearing her.

The next horror that appeared metamorphosed between two shapes. A black weblike substance and a dark manlike thing with rudimentary head, arms and legs.

"It has a penis, too," Alexa said unsteadily. "Sangvile. One tried to rape me as it sucked my Power from me."

The thing turned its head and its burning gaze struck Marian like a blow.

This vision disappeared once quickly, as if Alexa didn't like remembering it. Marian couldn't think how anyone could survive an attempted rape by the hideous being.

"Dreeth," Alexa said on a sigh, and something Marian recognized formed. At her exclamation, Alexa smiled.

"They look like pteradons, don't they?" Alexa said.

"More like a quetzalcoatluses with big bellies."

"Quetzalcoatlus. That sounds like the Aztec god."

"Yes, they were the largest of the flying dinosaurs." In her studies, she'd found that many cultures had stories of dragons.

"Okay. They're dreeths here, as big as a house. A couple of them nearly fell on me as they died. Bad," Alexa said so casually that Marian stared at her in pure amazement.

She sorted out the implications. "You battle these things?"

"Pretty much every week." Alexa stroked the scar on her face.

Marian couldn't imagine it. "You?"

Alexa met her gaze with fathomless eyes. "The Marshalls Summoned me to be one of them, the best magical warriors in the business." She shrugged. "Like Joan of Arc."

"Must have been a shock."

"Yeah. In Denver I'd taken one personal defense course from the free university, several years ago. Big change in lifestyle." Now she smiled. She waved a hand down her body and suddenly Marian saw a rope of purple and silver. The link throbbed with life and vibrated with a pretty melody. "But I'm well compensated. This is my bond with my Shield, Bastien. As for financial reward, I have wealth and an estate—you'll get your pick of land, too, if you stay. And Bastien—" she grinned "—he's rather like a certain rogue mercenary with a spaceship in the movies." She sighed. "I miss the movies."

"You—they—the Marshalls, don't expect me to become one of them, do they?"

"Nope. The Marshalls Summoned you for the Tower Community, the Sorcerers and Sorceresses—the major ones are called Circlets." Alexa grinned again. "No wonder they reached Boulder. Mostly scholars, I think. Though Jaquar is one prime man."

Marian hadn't forgotten the hunk who'd appeared in the pentacle with her.

"He's had it rough, lately, though. The sangvile ate his parents."

"Ate his parents!"

Alexa waved her hand. "Okay, to be exact, the sangvile drained his parents of their Power, turning them into husks that crumbled into gray dust."

That didn't sound any better.

"He's really grieving. I'm sorry for that," Alexa said quietly. "I know what he's feeling."

Not wanting to think about the man or his hurt, Marian said, "So the Tower Summoned me."

"The Tower had the Marshalls of the Castle Community Summon you," Alexa corrected. "The Circlets do not play well together."

"What do they expect me to do?" Marian asked plaintively.

"I don't know. But there's plenty of work. The Marshalls are just dealing with the monsters as they invade. That doesn't address the underlying problem of where they're coming from or why, or how to stop them."

Another image coalesced between them, this one of a topographical map. "The country of Lladrana. Note the northern border," said Alexa.

Marian studied it. Bright yellow glowed at points, and between the lights wove a blue line.

"Magical fence posts and shield along the boundary," Alexa said, explaining further Marian's vision from Bossgond. She always preferred the maximum amount of facts, and appreciated Alexa's visit. "The old fence posts were wearing out, the shield failing, and the Marshalls didn't know how to make new fence posts or power the boundary. That was my task."

"Sounds incredible."

"Yup, but I did it." Alexa beamed with pride. "Now we know how to create fence posts and the boundary, but it isn't easy or quick. You can see we still have big gaps in the border. Thus the continued fighting—building up the army, which consists of Marshall Pairs and Chevalier Pairs—Chevaliers are like knights, or singletons. We're equal-opportunity employers. There are fifteen Marshall Pairs now."

"So few!"

Alexa glanced at her. "There were six when I came a couple of months ago. We're ramping up as fast as we can. But we lost three Pairs before and during the first big battle."

There wasn't anything Marian could say. She stared at the tiny glow of the fence posts and boundary line. So fragile to keep a land safe. Magic and muscle, physical courage and a willingness to fight were the only weapons being used to defend Lladrana now.

"It sounds to me," Marian said carefully, "as if the Lladranans are missing a lot of knowledge."

Nodding approvingly, Alexa said, "That's right. They'd depended on the boundary for centuries, killing the monsters as they straggled over or through weak points. The Lladranans didn't find their enemy, learn its flaws, formulate a plan to defeat it, or destroy the threat once and for all."

Marian closed her eyes. "That's exactly what must be done."

"Yup," Alexa said with an exaggerated Western twang. She stood and brushed off the seat of her pants, but since the leather looked as if it would deflect an oil well, no dust or grass had stuck to her. Old habits, Marian mused. No matter that she'd become integrated into Lladranan society, much of Alexa would always be pure Earthling.

She held out a hand to Marian. Marian put hers in it, her

fingers far larger than Alexa's. With a smooth pull, the smaller woman drew Marian easily to her feet.

"Um, Marian." Alexa colored.

"Yes?"

"I think it would be good for both of us if we—uh—had a closer connection so we could call each other mentally if need be, for instance."

"A blood-bond? Like I have with Bossgond?"

"Yes."

"About that bond with Bossgond. Do you think it was the wrong thing to do?"

Alexa shrugged. When she met Marian's eyes, hers were serious. "I've relied heavily on my instincts here. I think it might serve you well to do the same. After all, the Song sought you out, so you have what is needed to mesh with the Tower, to stay here on Amee."

She lifted her hand before Marian could speak. "I know, I know, you need to get back to your brother, but I have the feeling that the Song—that's fate, God, Goddess, whatever—doesn't make mistakes, and it chose you." She hesitated. "Be careful of the Singer—the oracle—though. She's a sneaky old witch."

Apparently having said all she was going to on the matter, Alexa withdrew a wicked-looking dagger from her boot. She turned over her left wrist and nicked the vein, then glanced at Marian. "You ready?"

No. But she held out her arm anyway.

Alexa was quick and careful. The knife had little bite. Marian watched blood well from her wrist. Alexa took Marian's arm and held it against hers.

A wash of visions flowed from Alexa to Marian—recent ones of battles on Lladrana that caused Marian to sway in horror, but mercifully they flashed by.

There was Alexa hearing the same gong and chimes and chant as had Marian. A lovely blond woman dancing in the sunlight down Denver's 16th Street Mall. Graduation from law school. Classrooms. Alexa growing younger in a series of foster homes. Each picture brought a spurt of emotions—terror…grief…triumph…resignation.

Marian's sight dimmed. Her knees collapsed and she was on the ground again. She flung out her left hand and it hit Alexa's rib cage.

"Oomph!" Alexa protested.

"Sorry," Marian said weakly.

"No problemo." Alexa sounded as dazed as Marian herself. "Didn't expect this to be so strong. I saw your brother, Andrew. You love him very much."

"Yes."

"Your mother would never take care of him."

"No."

Alexa sighed. "Can you see yet?"

Marian blinked. Everything was cloud-thick gray. "No."

"Neither can I. Guess since we're not doing anything, I'll tell you about the Snap."

"That would be good."

"The Snap is when Mother Earth calls you back—"

"I've lost my connection with Mother Earth." To her horror, Marian's voice rose.

"Well, I never knew I had a connection until I got here," Alexa said. "I thought I'd lost it, too, but it *did* pull me back. I'm sure somewhere you still have a link to our home planet."

"Go on."

"It's hard to describe—a pull. More, it's a choice—stay or go. Like I said earlier, I was given visions of what my life might be if I went back, but I never actually left Lladrana. I could have, if I wished—just wished to be back, I guess. But by that time I'd made a life here. I had too much emotional commitment to Bastien and the Marshalls and Lladrana to leave Amee."

Before Marian could ask questions, a man's honey-smooth voice purred, "Well, well, well. Look what I've found, beauties basking in the sun. I wonder what I'll do with them."

Terror froze Marian. She was blind, helpless.

"Bastien, that's not funny. You're scaring Marian," Alexa said.

There was an instant of silence.

"My apologies, Marian," said the man. He was closer now—on the other side of Alexa.

"Salutations, Pairling." His voice crooned now, full of tenderness and love.

Marian still couldn't see the outer world, but a beautiful glow came from her left side. Her tense muscles relaxed. Then she chided herself. Knowing Alexa as she did now, if there'd been danger, the woman—blind or not—would have been up and swinging.

"I'm having trouble seeing or moving, Bastien." Alexa sounded very drunk—her bad Lladranan accent—and pissed.

"Always impatient."

Alexa snorted. "As if you aren't."

"Hey, another person is here who needs help," Marian said.

"Ladies, join hands and I'll aid you in clearing out your systems of the aftereffects of an ill-prepared blood-bond. Pairling—" his voice lowered dangerously "—I don't suppose you researched the blood-bond before you did it with Marian?"

Another silence. Then Alexa said, "Uh, no. It came to me that it would be good to have a blood sister. I *like* Marian. I thought it would be best for everyone—for Lladrana, even—

if we blood-bonded." She spoke faster and faster, slurring her words, as if trying to convince them all of the impeccable logic of her impulsive act.

"Somehow I think Marian would have researched the blood-bond before initiating it," Bastien said, humor in his voice.

Marian groped for Alexa's small hand, found it, squeezed.

"We're in this together," Alexa said with dignity, and Marian wondered which "we" she meant.

Marian had no intention of staying in Lladrana, despite Alexa's yearning for a sister-friend. Then she felt a pulse of clear, bright silver—Bastien's energy to Alexa, thundering through the smaller woman, then rolling into Marian. A flash enveloped her. When it faded, she could see deep blue sky with fat white clouds.

She turned her head to check on Alexa, but her gaze went straight to the man. Alexa had called Jaquar a prime man, but this one exuded charm and virility from every pore. His hair was striped black and white and the murmuring sound coming from him was like nothing Marian had heard in this world. Bossgond had said something about his being a "black-and-white," and...

"Unfortunate?" she whispered, incredulous.

Alexa grinned. "Yeah. He really looks unfortunate, doesn't he?"

"He looks like a bad boy to end all bad boys." He was a rogue to the bone—with or without a spaceship.

He winked at her. "Actually," he said, grinning at her with too much devilment, "I'm better with volarans."

Bastien had read her thoughts, and she picked up images of winged horses from him. She'd been contemplating sitting up, but remained still. All the new input was beyond her.

Alexa jumped up and into the man's arms. From there she

looked back at Marian. "Your initial questions answered?" she asked Marian in Lladranan.

Marian's mind was unfortunately blank. She should have a thousand more questions, but none surfaced. "I suppose."

"Anything else you need right now?"

Only one thing came to the forefront of her mind. "We need a cook. Someone who'll get along with the grumpy old man, doesn't like to socialize and would love to live on an island."

Alexa nodded. "That shouldn't be a problem. I'll find someone for you. I have connections in Castleton."

Bastien squeezed her and whirled her around in a circle. She shrieked.

"If you think you're going to Citymaster Masif alone, you're wrong," Bastien said. His voice was steady despite his exertion. The man was buff.

Marian managed to rise somewhat gracefully, curtsied to the both of them, then left Alexa and Bastien to their pastoral idyll, feeling a little melancholy. The woman had certainly landed on her feet—though there was that comment about falling in battle. Perhaps she wasn't much to be envied after all.

Angling off toward the ocean so as not to intrude, Marian considered what she'd learned. At least she could still go back, with the Snap. She hoped fervently that she could return to Earth before Andrew got worried. She could check on him through the binoculars, and if she had the Power that everyone thought, that she *felt*, she'd discover the knowledge to help him *and* force her return before he was finished with his retreat.

She was listening to the ocean, absently watching spray as the tide pummeled fierce rocks, when she stumbled into it. A tide of full orchestral sound flowed over her, heavy on the strings. She stopped. She stood in a large glade, green with grass. The sky seemed bluer, the clouds whiter, the view of the ocean perfect. She turned in place. The panorama was exquisite.

Her heart thudded with recognition. *This was her place.*

She acknowledged the thought, then added a caveat. This *could* be her place, the location where she'd build her Tower, *if* she stayed in Lladrana. But she wouldn't.

Though the world tempted her. During her time with Alexa, Marian had sensed that the Swordmarshall had a great need to be useful, contribute meaningfully to society. The idea echoed in Marian.

And there was the fabulous magic. If she stayed, she could become a Circlet at controlling the weather. Was that cool, or what?

But not at the cost of losing Andrew. She could never live with herself if she turned her back on him, chose this place instead of him. An inner, awful trembling came at the thought.

So she determinedly left the glade and went on.

As she drew up to the front of Bossgond's Tower, she saw a large frog sitting on a paving stone in front of the door. Maybe it was a toad—she didn't recall enough biology to distinguish them. It was green and about a foot long. Big, dark eyes watched her.

"Well, look at you." She smiled. She liked frogs.

"Ribbitt."

"You *do* know that you're blocking my way to the Tower?" she said, feeling a little like she was in a fairy tale.

"Ribbitt."

Laughing, Marian said, "I hope you don't expect me to kiss you." There was something intrinsically beautiful about the frog.

No, it said in her mind.

"Excuse me?" She didn't believe she'd heard it.

You do not have to kiss me. I wanted to see and speak with the new Exotique. I am a feycoocu.

Marian stared, mind scrambling, though she recalled Bossgond and Alexa talking about the magical being.

I am Alexa's companion.

That reassured Marian a little, so she let her shoulders relax, closed her eyes and sighed. So many new things! Something to learn every minute.

When she opened her eyelids, a fairy the size of the frog perched on the door lintel. Marian stared. "You're not a frog."

No, and I am not really a fairy. I took that image from Alexa's mind and yours. You have a different idea of fairies, though. She glanced at her gossamer wings, the long black hair that floated around her and her sparkling light-blue dress. She smiled in satisfaction. *Good, I am not all pink. Being pink was a pain.*

She sounded like Alexa. Marian grinned.

You are very Powerful.

The fairy's changing eyes mesmerized Marian. She fell into the gaze and was caught in a cloud, between dimensions, then abruptly landed with a jolt. She shook her head and blinked.

You will do. The feycoocu's voice appropriately sounded like windchimes. She launched herself from the door and pirouetted in the air. *You will do very well. But it would be good if you had a companion.*

Marian swallowed. She wasn't sure that she could deal with a magical sidekick. "You?"

No, I love Alexa and will stay with her. The fairy's smile bloomed, dazzling Marian. *But you have just taken care of that matter yourself.*

"What?"

Instead of answering, the feycoocu gestured and a small

golden sphere appeared to hover between them. *Take this and feed it to him.*

The thing plunked into the hollow of Marian's palm so heavily that it drove her arm down and she staggered under the weight. By the time she'd braced her wrist with her other hand and lifted both hands to waist level, the fairy had transformed into a hawk and was flying away.

"Wait, what—"

Look for him in the place that called to you. Feed him the walnut. She paused, turning her head back, and speared Marian with a bright, glinting gaze. *I am Sinafin. Guard my name, but call on me if you have need.* She zoomed out of sight.

Marian opened her hand. The heavy thing did look like a golden walnut.

A companion. Andrew? The place that called to her—the meadow near the rocky beach with spraying surf. She ran, slowly and awkwardly due to the great weight of the magical nut. When she reached the meadow above the rocky beach, her breath came fast and raggedly.

There, in the middle of the meadow, was Tuck in his ball.

10

Marian sprinted to Tuck, who sat in his plastic hamster ball in the middle of the green glade that had tempted her to stay in Lladrana.

When she reached him, her legs simply collapsed. She thought she whimpered at the sight of her pet. He'd pulled an orange wildflower blossom through one of the plastic slots and sat, munching on it. In the bottom of the ball was a small hoard of nuts and raisins, and a bit of dried-up carrot that had been in his cheek pouches.

He wasn't lost. He wasn't dead. He looked as fat and sassy as ever. Gently moving the ball until the door was at the top, she lifted off the lid, reached in and drew him out. Putting him against her face, she sniffed the unmistakable odor of hamster and cedar chips, felt the softness of his fur. It stuck to her cheek, to the track of her tears.

She sat cross-legged and set Tuck in the folds of her skirt.

He looked up with bright eyes and continued to eat, apparently happy to stay put. She could have sworn he smiled. Though he was a nocturnal animal, she supposed the circumstances—the trip through the corridor—how had he made it here?—the new world and the food kept him interested enough to stay awake.

Marian heard herself croon his name. "Oh Tuck, oh Tuck." He just ate on.

With a little shock, she realized she'd dropped the walnut. Looking around, she didn't see it; it hadn't made a hole, and didn't glow or anything. She bit her lip. The feycoocu had insisted that she feed Tuck the magical nut, but what would happen if she did? Would Tuck acclimatize better?

Could Sinafin be trusted?

Looking down at the small, new cut on her wrist where she and Alexa had shared the strange sensation of mixing blood, Marian sent her first telepathic message. *Alexa, can you hear me?*

Yes came the immediate response.

Marian received the vision that Alexa and Bastien were flying back to their estate on the mainland.

Though she didn't need to speak aloud, Marian wet her lips. *Can Sinafin be trusted?*

There was a pause. *Sinafin can be trusted to do what is best for Lladrana,* Alexa replied.

That didn't help much. But Sinafin *had* approved of Marian, and had wanted her to have a companion.

Alexa said, *Sinafin says that the walnut will not hurt Tuck. It will make him better.*

I lost it. I dropped it when I saw Tuck, I think.

If you have a connection, you might be able to draw it to you if you visualize it.

Marian stroked Tuck, but he still seemed happy to stay in her lap. In fact, he'd curled into a ball to sleep. She closed her eyes and formed an image of the walnut.

A spurt of surprise came from Alexa. *So Sinafin took it. I never thought of it after my first night here.*

What?

It's an atomball.

Something in the tone of Alexa's thoughts sparked unease in Marian. *Is it dangerous? Sinafin said to feed it to Tuck.*

She heard Alexa's sigh in her mind. *Just be careful. Call it slowly. Think of it rolling to you.*

Marian did, and felt a pull at her mind as if a thread were attached to a ball she was rolling toward herself. A moment later, something tapped the sole of her foot. It was the atomball. *Now* it glowed. *I have it. Thank you, Alexa.*

Glad to be of help. Do you need me to stay in contact?

Marian wanted to say yes, but decided it was cowardly and an imposition. *No.*

Feel free to yell if you need help, Alexa said.

That's what Sinafin said. Thank you both.

Don't thank her until everything is all over, Alexa said dryly. *She has her own agenda.*

Marian swallowed. *Thank* you, *then.*

Bye, said Alexa, and the telepathic connection went still.

With both hands, Marian scooped up the golden walnut. It was the size of a real walnut, but she didn't know how she was going to convince Tuck to eat it. She shifted her legs so she could put the walnut on her dress against the ground instead of in her lap, and set it next to a sleep-snuffling Tuck.

He unrolled. His ears perked up. The hamster crawled over the walnut several times, from several directions, then bit in and gobbled greedily. The nut disappeared into Tuck at an amazing rate. She thought she heard him burp, but hamsters didn't do that. Then he looked up at her and blinked his black eyes, wiggled his nose and curled back up to sleep.

Marian stayed in the meadow for a long time, petting Tuck with one finger. Both the lovely wildflowers and the animal soothed her. The quiet seemed almost luminescent as it sank into her bones.

When she lifted Tuck, he felt slightly heavier, but nothing like the golden-walnut atomball. She'd have to fashion a cage—Bossgond would help, she was sure. She put Tuck back in his plastic ball, set the lid atop the ball but did not screw it closed, and rose.

She could see Bossgond's Tower from here, and walked back to it, musing that she now had three things from her old life. Tuck, her PDA, and a clear, plastic hamster ball. Life was odd.

Bossgond awaited her, arms crossed, frowning—until he saw the ball and Tuck. Then the gleam of a true scholar lit his eyes. "What's that?"

"This is my hamster, Tuck, and his vehicle."

"Vehicle?" Bossgond reached for it.

Marian slipped Tuck from the ball and cradled him in her hands. He didn't stir. She handed the ball to Bossgond.

"I met the feycoocu," she said casually, but kept a sharp gaze on the old Sorcerer.

All his attention focused back on her. "Yes? What did it look like?"

Marian started to correct him—to call "it" a "she"—then decided against it. "First a large frog, then a fairy."

"Fascinating."

"She told me to feed Tuck—" Marian lifted the hamster for emphasis "—an atomball."

Bossgond took a couple of steps back, glanced a little nervously at Tuck. "An atomball? Where did the feycoocu get an atomball? What did it look like? I've never heard such a thing."

"Tuck ate it," Marian said.

Eyes wide, Bossgond jerked his chin at the stairs. "Let's go up to my suite. I want to study this."

The day had faded into evening, and the moment they walked through the door, inside lights flared on. They were set in torch holders, but obviously magic, glowing like the natural light of the sun. Bossgond strode to his desk and placed the clear plastic hamster ball on it.

"This is a very interesting substance," he muttered, tapping at the ball. "Not glass."

"No." Marian studied Tuck, beginning to worry. He was so still, but his small back still rose and fell with his breathing. "I need a cage for Tuck."

Bossgond waved a hand and a low cabinet door opened in the wall. Marian went over and bent down, then sighed. It appeared to be an old aquarium. Tuck wouldn't like it. He preferred a nice plastic cage with many toys and tubes.

Bossgond assigned Marian some "basic" lessons and spent the evening studying the plastic ball and sleeping Tuck. He'd sworn not to hurt either one.

After she'd demonstrated to Bossgond that she could ground herself, call fire and cause a bean to sprout, he allowed her to work with clouds in the weather globe. It thrilled Marian to play with the clouds. She couldn't create them, or make them rain, but she could push them around the globe and form images in them—they wisped, then billowed into castles and dragons and a huge tree—the world tree. Every culture had a symbol for the world—a globe, a serpent, an egg, a circle, but Marian had always liked the world tree the best. With a glance at Bossgond, she wickedly made a caricature of the man, then his Tower.

Finally she got bored with her limitations and interrupted him as he was tickling a sprawled Tuck's belly. Marian had the idea that Bossgond was imagining the hamster's anatomy.

Alexa's description of the Snap earlier in the day bothered Marian. She needed more details. "Alexa told me of the Snap today."

"A very interesting phenomenon, the Snap," Bossgond said, staring at her, fingers pyramided, tips tapping. He nodded once. "It is an event. The Exotique land will bring you back to it."

Marian blinked. It was that easy? Just wait and she'd be returned automatically? That didn't seem right. She shook her head. "I felt the loss of my connection with Mother Earth." Her chin wanted to tremble so she set her jaw. "It's gone." *It hurt.*

His fingers continued to tap. "Very interesting information." He looked at her, then reached out and picked up a sheet of paper and a writing instrument. He made a note. "Perhaps, then, the Snap is not a link to your planet. Perhaps this is an effect of the Dimensional Gate."

Now he tapped his lips with the pen. "No Circlet is currently studying the Dimensional Gateway, or Corridor. We will have to rely on lorebooks about the topic." He made more notes. "The closest thing the Tower Community has to experts on different dimensions are me and…Jaquar Dumont, the planewalker." He looked up from his pad at her.

She knew the name, knew the man. The great-looking guy who'd tried to claim her first. She suppressed a shiver at the memory of her reaction to his touch—the searing certainty that somehow he was her doom. Fate, and not a nice one.

Bossgond grunted as he studied her expression. "We won't speak of him now."

Marian straightened. "*You're* my teacher."

"That I am."

"When does the Snap occur?" She yanked the conversation back to the topic.

"It is individual to the person."

Marian narrowed her eyes. "Someone must have kept a record, studied it."

"Someone did."

She released a pent-up breath. "May I have the record, please?"

He turned to her with raised brows. "I don't think the records we have on the Exotiques and the Snap will illuminate you, but I will give you the *Snap Lorebook*." With a sly smile, he snapped his fingers and a piece of paper appeared between them.

"That's it? The *Lorebook?*"

"Yes. An Exotique usually works with the Marshalls. The last one before Alyeka was Summoned for the Singer and the Friends of the Singer."

That was the prophetess, the spiritual basis of Lladrana. "So?"

"So Exotiques have not been of a bent to record great details of the Snap, or their passage to Lladrana. We Circlets must extrapolate. Alyeka has provided the most detail of the experience. I trust you will report your passage also."

"Of course." She went and took the sheet from him. It was hardly more than a list.

It was the first "reading" she'd attempted since she'd bonded with Bossgond. She had hoped it would be as easy as absorbing the language. It wasn't. The alphabet was subtly strange, not quite the Greco-Roman alphabet.

Bossgond indicated the writing at the top. Squinting a little, Marian could make out the name "Thomas Lindley," a range of dates and a phrase.

Bossgond's finger underlined the phrase. "Two weeks," he said. The words appeared a neon white in her mind, then reshaped into English, then returned to Lladranan.

Okay, reading would be more difficult and take time...but if she was patient, the words and meanings might come to her.

"Thomas Lindley, two weeks," Marian repeated, moving her fingers under the words. To the right of the time was a word in red. All down the list the last word was in red or blue. It looked as if three-quarters of the words were blue, one-quarter red. Marian indicated the word. "This means?"

"Returned," he said gruffly. "Thomas chose to return to the Exotique land."

Marian's pulse picked up. "There's a choice." Alexa had said so, but Marian needed—emotionally more than mentally—to have it confirmed.

Bossgond angled his head to stare into her eyes. His own were dark pools of brown-black, expressionless. "The individual chooses to stay or go. This list is currently arranged according to the length of time between Summoning and the Snap." He pointed to the last name on the page, about halfway down the sheet, "Jessica Smith." His finger hovered over the time-period column. "Seven years, three moons, twelve days," Bossgond read.

"Seven *years!* The Snap took that long for her? Why?"

"No one knows."

The last word for Jessica was "Stayed." Marian imagined so. After seven years a person would have a whole new life.

"Time passes the same," she said.

He patted her shoulder with a knobby hand. "As far as we know, yes. Our time units are nearly the same, also. Perhaps because our lands are close to each other along the Dimensional Corridor."

He flicked a finger at the names and they rearranged themselves on the sheet. "Now the names are arranged according to most recently Summoned person."

Excellent.

At the top, Marian read, "Alexa Fitzwalter," scanned over to the far column and saw the blue word "Stayed." She was the latest Exotique. After her was Thomas.

Marian scanned the list. "The Snap usually occurs between a week and six months." Six months was too long for her to wait. If she wasn't back by the time Andrew checked with her—probably as soon as he finished with the retreat—he'd move heaven and earth to find her. She didn't want to contemplate how her loss might affect him, emotionally and physically.

She took the sheet of paper. It felt slick and repulsive and she gasped, letting it fall. Bossgond smiled humorlessly. "Parchment, made from a slayer."

Marian recalled the yellow-furred creature with poisonous spines.

Bossgond picked it up and placed it back on the desk. "I know that Alexa told you of Lladrana's—and Amee's—peril."

For comfort, Marian retrieved Tuck from Bossgond's desk. He snuffled a little. Cradling him in her hands, she met Bossgond's eyes seriously. "You know of my brother Andrew and his circumstances. I *must* be back home in a few weeks. I want you to promise me that you will help me return, if my Snap doesn't occur before that time."

Bossgond's lips tightened. "I don't know of anyone who has returned to Exotique Terre under any circumstances other than the Snap."

Marian nailed him with her gaze. "You are the oldest, most Powerful Sorcerer of Lladrana. You can see my abode through your binoculars. Both Alexa and I have passed through the Dimensional Corridor, so we can visualize it. She understands my situation and will help me return. Among the three of us—and anyone you think might help—I should be able to go back."

He looked pained. "You won't change your mind?"

"No. My brother's health is at stake. He is my greatest priority."

Bossgond rose and paced to the black-shrouded binoculars and back. "I will do my best, but Lladrana needs you."

Marian heard more than that from the melody linking them. *I need you.* Had he already become attached to her? That was so sweet. She must admit that she'd already developed an affection for him, as well as respecting him.

"Very well," he said. "I will request the Friends of the Singer look through their Lorebooks and Oracle Archives for any information regarding your brother's disease, as well as requesting all data from the Tower Community. Occasionally we have had Sorcerer or Sorceress Medicas. I will contact the Chief Medicas attached to the Castle, the Cities and the Seamasters. If there are instances of people who have or had your brother's disease, I will learn of it, along with all treatments or cures."

Unexpected tears stung her eyes. "Thank you." But she was afraid to hope.

"We are blood-bonded, as are you and Alexa. Though it has never happened, perhaps you might be able to return to Amee."

She didn't think she'd ever abandon Andrew, even if he were in perfect health, but Bossgond seemed to expect something from her. "Perhaps. I *was* conducting my own Ritual at the time the Marshalls Summoned me. I might have adequate Power even in Exotique Terre to come back here."

He nodded briskly. "The Marshalls' Power and ritual coincided with yours. Your Power is raw and untaught. But by the time I finish instructing you, you could be our first Interdimensional Traveler."

A gleam entered his eyes, and Marian got the sinking feeling that he had a new career goal for her.

Oddly enough, obtaining her doctorate and starting on an academic career—once her heart's desire—now seemed flat. What teased her mind, plucked at her emotions, was the idea of becoming a Circlet Weather Sorceress and raising her own Tower. She knew exactly the place where she'd build it, too—in the green glen that called to her. She suppressed a sigh and refrained from shaking her head. She couldn't figure out how she could get everything she wanted.

"It has been a long day for you," Bossgond said. "I think you should retire and rest."

His gaze slid to the binoculars again, and Marian sensed he wished to pursue his studies alone. Would he check on her apartment? He now had Andrew's coordinates—would he watch Andrew? Could Bossgond possibly learn how to help Andrew by observing her brother?

"I am tired. Tuck and I will go to bed now." On impulse, she kissed Bossgond's wrinkled cheek. "I could ask for no better teacher." She thought she saw a tinge of red under his golden skin.

"Perhaps you'd rather have Alexa as your mentor."

Marian laughed. "I think she is an excellent Swordmarshall." And would have made a hot-shot attorney. "But I don't think she has the patience to be a good teacher."

He smiled faintly as he took her arm and walked her to the door.

"Besides—" Marian stopped "—she is very busy—fighting. She said some Sorcerers and Sorceresses fight, too?"

"That was true of the last large battle, when Alexa requested help from the Tower Community." He waved a hand. "Jaquar Dumont organized our contribution. At that time the fence posts were still falling and no one knew how to make new ones. The magical shield along the north boundary of Lladrana was failing. A large number of horrors had massed to invade."

Marian's imagination painted a vivid picture of the conditions.

Bossgond finished, "So some of the younger Sorcerers and Sorceresses used their Power in battle."

Marian's admiration for Alexa increased. She'd literally saved the country—how had she felt as Joan of Arc? Marian wanted to know the woman better.

Another wish that would not be fulfilled.... Time was too short for everything Marian wanted to do, to learn, to explore.

"But during the battle, Exotique Alyeka discovered how to create the fence posts." Bossgond looked grim. "Every Sorcerer and Sorceress of the Tower made twenty copies of the information as to how the fence posts are made, how the border shield is energized. We sent Lorebooks to every contact we had in the other Communities. The knowledge will *never* be lost again."

"A very good thing," Marian said quietly.

"Essential." Bossgond opened the door and ushered her out with a small bow. He hesitated, then said, "Sleep well, and the hamster, too."

Marian smiled. "We will. Sweet dreams."

Bossgond looked a little startled, and Marian went down the stairs, smiling. It was good to surprise a teacher now and then—keep him on his toes.

* * *

The next morning, Marian awoke to a small squeaky voice calling, "Here's Food! Here's Food!" She blinked and struggled from sleep, and the words went on and on. Cocking her head, she realized the voice was close—coming from the table she'd brought into her bedroom.

Coming from Tuck's aquarium.

A shiver feathered down her spine. Time to brace herself for more magic.

Slowly she walked over to the glass cage. Tuck rose and placed his little pink paws on the glass. He smiled.

He was not just a hamster anymore. She didn't know what he was, but she knew he'd changed—become a companion to her.

"Hello, Tuck," she said.

"Hel-lo, Here's Food." He beamed. "Hun-gry."

11

Marian stared into the old aquarium. Tuck had just spoken to her in squeaks she could understand! She blinked. "My name's Marian."

"Here's Food," he said.

Glancing at the corner of the cage where he kept his food, she saw his hoard wasn't as large as he preferred. She left the bedroom for the "kitchen" area of her circular loft and pulled out a small bowl of nuts and dried fruit that Bossgond had given her. Taking the handful, she went back to the aquarium.

"Here's food," she said, and stopped to listen to her own words. Tuck associated her with food, with those words. No wonder he called her that.

She shrugged and put the handful of food in his cage.

He hurried over and began arranging it, eating an especially tasty piece now and then. She stood and watched. A few moments later he was done. Then he paced the cage. She'd lined it with shredded paper. "No fun," he said.

The hamster had vocal cords. She wondered if she would ever be able to study them. Then again, she didn't know what human vocal cords looked like, and there were plenty of other topics that demanded her attention.

He squeaked, "Out!"

"If I let you roam, will you stay, or run off so I will never find you?"

He scrabbled against the glass. "I will stay in this place."

"This room," she said firmly. "No crawling down any pipes, wiggling into any holes in the floor or walls and not returning." She shook a finger at him, even as she wondered if he could understand her. *How* he could understand her. Only one answer occurred.

Magic.

Tuck wrinkled his nose. "Bad house. Want new one."

It might be interesting to make him a little house, without a cage. She'd feel better if he were off the floor, but he climbed well—a low table would be fine.

"Out! Out! Out!"

"All right!" She scooped him up and placed him on the floor. She'd really have to learn to mind her step. He had only roamed her apartment in his ball. "Do you want your ball?" Bossgond still had it.

Tuck ran under the wardrobe. Gleaming black eyes peered out at her. "No."

Marian sighed. "All right, but be aware that I might not see you, so you have to be careful underfoot."

"Yes. More food. *Soft* food."

She smiled, figuring "soft food" meant a bit of cheese or egg or fresh vegetables. "I don't have any here. I'll check with Boss-gond." She headed for the speaking tube.

"Old man teacher," Tuck said.

"Yes."

"He smells funny."

Marian stopped at the edge of the stained-glass partition and looked back into the bedroom. As she watched, Tuck appeared, crawling up the far side of her bedspread to explore her bed. He sat, Buddhalike, in the middle of her bed, paws clasped.

"Smells funny how?"

Tuck sniffed. "Mostly big sweet smell, then man smell, then old smell."

"Ah."

The hamster blinked at her and smiled. "You smell sweeter."

To her amazement, Marian found herself dipping a curtsy, smiling herself. "Thank you, Tuck."

"More food."

She laughed. Cocking her head, she quieted her thoughts to sense Bossgond. His thoughts sparked, indicating he was awake.

She went to the tube and spoke into it. "Tuck and I are hungry."

Bossgond grunted. "The oeuf is ready. You can share it with him."

Marian grimaced at the thought of the tasteless omelette. "We'll be right up." She hurried to wash and dress, then picked Tuck up from her bed.

"Shoulder," he said.

Looking at him askance, she said, "Are you sure? I don't want you to fall."

"I will not fall."

Marian shrugged, then made a note not to do that when Tuck was riding her shoulder. She set him on her right shoulder and winced as his sharp little claws dug through the material.

As she ascended the stairs at a quick pace, Tuck kept steady, and she knew they were both pleased at this new way of transporting him.

When she entered Bossgond's chamber, the first thing she noticed was his crystal ball flashing a rainbow of colors.

He followed her gaze, sniffed in disdain and snapped his fingers. "Requests to visit. Or demands. I do not want to see people, and I want *you* to concentrate on your training before satisfying others' curiosity."

"Alexa came yesterday."

"That was different. I had not met her."

His curiosity had needed to be satisfied, and not only regarding Alexa. Marian knew he'd wanted to meet Sinafin.

Bossgond studied Tuck on her shoulder. "Is that a safe way for the hamster to travel?"

"Yes," Tuck squeaked.

The old mage froze, his eyes sharpening. "It speaks."

"*Me!* You talk to me. And I am a he."

Bossgond swallowed. "He knows grammar."

Marian gave a nervous laugh herself. "I think it must be the atomball. He's sentient."

"What is sentient?" asked Tuck.

"You think," Marian said.

Tuck grumbled. "Of course I think."

She shared an amazed glance with Bossgond. He narrowed his eyes, and Marian lifted her left hand to curve it protectively over Tuck. "No dissecting!"

Bossgond looked affronted as if the idea hadn't crossed his mind. "Of course not. The longer we have him to study— hmm—as your companion, the more we can learn of him, of the atomball. It must have been the atomball that made him intelligent—but how the atomball…" Bossgond shook his head. "I had a few notes on this atomball. The Marshalls made it as a Test of Exotique Alyeka's Power. So twelve Marshall minds might have imprinted it—four of those people are now deceased. I believe both Alyeka and the feycoocu transformed the thing. Now it has been eaten by a hamster. Very interesting." He looked distracted and headed for his desk, instead of the table where two cheese omelettes sat.

"Food!" cried Tuck.

Before Marian could stop him, he scrabbled down her dress, snagging his claws in the embroidery, which she watched reweave itself. He hopped to the floor and ran to the dining table, up the leg and onto the table to sit on a plate and shovel egg into his mouth.

Ick. Despite the fact that she knew the food wasn't very good, Marian hurried over and cut a quarter of the omelette for Tuck, saving the rest for herself. She recalled where Bossgond kept the extra plates and the coffee. She poured a mug for herself and one for her teacher, giving him the coffee, omelette and a fork and napkin as he sat at his desk.

While he ate absently, she sighed and returned to her place, wondering how long it would take Alexa to find a cook for them.

After breakfast, Tuck explored Bossgond's room and the old mage requested that she take the largest of her weather terrariums down to the lowest floor and work with it there. Marian did as he asked.

When she'd actually settled into the luxurious room, she found herself smiling at having such rich surroundings. Better than the best home office she'd ever seen. She allowed herself another cup of coffee, then began her lessons.

Bossgond had printed instructions for her. Just reading was a lesson in itself. Following his directions was even more fun. Today she practiced stirring the wind and waves in preparation for making clouds.

She'd mastered Wind—the scudding of the clouds around the enclosed environment, little breezes that ruffled the tiny tree forms and slapped up waves. She'd even managed a little hurricane in the ocean and a tornado on land.

Now she studied Water. When Bossgond wasn't looking she'd tried a little Tide and flooded most of her seacoast. Then, of course, there was no way to hide her mistake.

He'd snorted with laughter, made her do her Wind exercises again, and commented that she'd better not try Lightning without him—she could take out the Tower. Abashed, Marian had agreed.

She was slightly distracted whenever Tuck skittered across her line of sight. Joy and affection welled in her at the thought of having him back—and as more than a pet. Whether he could be a real companion she didn't know, but she enjoyed seeing him explore, and listened with half an ear to his squeaky comments. "Good smell, here!" "Nice hole." "Stone too cold on paws here. Stay away."

With incredible effort she visualized raising minute droplets of water from a river and bay—she discovered she didn't have the energy to handle a whole ocean, she had to limit herself geographically. A good education, including basic science, had saved her from lectures by Bossgond on how water became clouds. He'd seemed impressed, but had grumped off to his own desk.

Marian was muttering to herself, lowering the temperature so the droplets might coalesce, when she became aware of someone looking over her shoulder. More than one someone.

She lost control of her condensation and the water fell back into the sea. Turning, she scowled—and found herself looking at the other two who'd appeared in the pentacle when she'd been Summoned. Searching her memory as she nodded to them, she recalled their names. The woman was Venetria and the man Chalmon.

The way they stood together, it seemed they were intimate—but she knew each had wanted to claim her as an Apprentice. Relationships must get as tangled here in Lladrana as they had among scholars at the university.

"Salutations," she said, now knowing why she was using the ground-floor parlor for her experiments. Bossgond had anticipated the advent of other Circlets. He wouldn't have wanted to show them into either her or his working space.

They'd come to check out the new kid on the block, she supposed. Only natural, but it ate into her time. For an instant her gaze went to the door that was open on the pretty spring day, but no shadow of sexy Jaquar announced him. Just as well—she hadn't forgotten that touch of warning.

"Salutations, Marian," said Chalmon. He held out his hand, and Marian recalled that she hadn't touched him. Jaquar—a cascade of notes; Venetria—a clash of chords; Bossgond—a streaming tune.

Carefully she put her hand in his. There was a tiny shock and a little hum between them, as if he could become a friend—but only a friend.

All three of them relaxed. Marian sensed Venetria had been prepared to be jealous, and Chalmon had been unsure of what he truly wanted from Marian, but now was willing to settle for what had naturally occurred.

Marian released his hand, gestured to the open door. "Shall we walk?"

Venetria cast a nervous glance at the stairs winding up the Tower wall. She licked her lips. "Will Bossgond mind?"

"I'll tell him. We're blood-bonded," Marian said.

The other two exchanged glances, and irritation rose in Marian that she wasn't conversant enough with the culture to understand nuances.

"I would like to walk and talk," Chalmon said, with a half bow.

Bossgond, Marian sent mentally, *I am taking a break. Venetria and Chalmon are here and we will stroll along the meadow path.* She wasn't going to lead them to the place that resonated to her. Their inherent formality kept her at a distance—of course, anyone seemed more formal than Alexa and Bastien.

Bossgond replied telepathically. *Good, get them out of my Tower. I don't want to talk with them. And,* he added with a cackle, *this will allow your coastline to dry out.*

Please watch Tuck, Marian said stiffly.

An absent grunt came from Bossgond.

Chalmon nodded to her practice sphere. "Your Power is for weather?"

"Yes."

"Jaquar," Venetria muttered under her breath.

Marian looked at her quizzically and the other woman flashed an insincere smile. "Jaquar Dumont also has that Power. No doubt sometime in the future you must study with him."

Her expression went blank, and Marian sensed she hid something. She sighed and led the way out of the Tower.

The day was beautiful, spring edging into summer. The scents particularly pleased Marian—crisp sea breeze, flowers, grass. She'd miss the freshness of unpolluted air when she returned to Earth.

Breathing deeply, she smiled.

But the other two wore all-too-serious expressions.

"You know why you were Summoned to Lladrana?" asked Chalmon.

"Not specifically," Marian said. "Swordmarshall Alexa dropped by yesterday and told me I would be working with you of the Tower Community, but no one of this Community has stated why you requested I be Summoned." Of course, it had been only three nights and two-and-a-half days, and Marian had her own priorities.

Chalmon cleared his throat. "Much of the knowledge regarding the Dark that invades Lladrana has been lost over the centuries." He waved a hand. "Since the magical fence posts and borders protected the mainland, we of the Tower Community focused on our own studies."

Marian supposed that was the rationalization all the Circlets were using to explain their inaction.

Venetria took up the story. "Then the fence posts fell. The monsters invaded the mainland and Alyeka was Summoned. She convinced Jaquar and some of us to fight. More terrible horrors invaded—dreeths—" Venetria put a hand to her throat "—then the sangvile." Her lips quivered. "The sangvile ravaged a town where many Sorceresses and Sorcerers lived—Coquille-on-the-Coast. I lost an aunt."

A cold chill raised the hair on Marian's neck as she recalled Alexa's image and story. Venetria's aunt might have been about the same age as Marian's mother.

Stepping closer to Venetria, Chalmon wrapped an arm around her waist and looked directly at Marian—and she saw cool determination, perhaps even the edge of fanaticism. "More sangviles may return. We must stop these evil beings."

So now that the Tower Community was actually threat-

ened—Marian hadn't forgotten that the sangvile targeted
Power users—Circlets would actually bestir themselves to
contemplate the problem. Sounded a lot like the scholars of
her own world. But Marian didn't think Alexa had had much
of a choice in ignoring the problem, and now it appeared Marian would be integral to the Tower's effort.

"Alexa was Summoned to fight? Why did you Summon
me? What do you want of me?" she asked. When both pairs
of eyes shifted away from her, a cold feeling spread along her
spine to her gut.

"We want you to learn. Then you will be able to help," Venetria said gently, still not looking at Marian but at the path
through the serene forest.

"And what is my compensation?"

"Learning for learning's sake. Making a world safe—" Chalmon's voice rose.

"It's not my world."

Venetria stopped, so Marian and Chalmon did, too. Venetria said, "You can raise your own Tower and teach students,
if you want. Also, as a Summoned Exotique, you receive an
estate and a certain amount of zhiv." She waved her hand. "We
have islands to spare, and will collect jewels to ensure you live
well."

"This is not my place. I will not stay. I have a sick brother
I must return to. *If* you can find me a cure for his disease, I
will do what you want." As soon as the words were out of her
mouth, she felt infinitely reckless. But it would take a miracle
to cure Andrew.

Chalmon frowned, absently took Venetria's hand and kissed
the back of it, placed her fingers on his arm and began walking again. "A Circlet Medica is rare. One has not raised a Tower
for over two centuries."

"Pity," Marian murmured. "I will, of course, learn all that I can, but when the Snap comes, I will return home. And you still haven't given me any details of what is expected of me. Nor has Bossgond. Hard to fulfill a goal if I don't know what it is."

Again Chalmon cleared his throat. "We are still formulating a plan to fight the Dark."

"Who is 'we'?" asked Marian.

"Chalmon, myself, Jaquar, some others." Venetria made a moue. "Planning will take some time—now all you must do is learn." She looked at the pretty meadow ahead of them and sighed. "Truly Alf Island is graced. Spring has barely touched my own island of Zi."

"What are your specialties?" asked Marian. Perhaps she could figure out what they might want of her from what they studied.

"I am studying cold," Venetria said. "Ice. I was able to freeze the thin membranes of a dreeth's wings. In battle—" She choked.

Marian had a flash of the horror from the waves of fearful memory coming from Venetria.

"I study the pulses of the world core and the intervals between them," Chalmon said.

They walked for several seconds in silence while Marian thought, shuffling his words around until they might make sense. There was a faintly patronizing smile on Chalmon's face when she said coolly, "So how have the pulses and intervals been? Weakening? Slowing?"

He stopped, eyes widening. "How did you know?"

Marian shook her head. Another scholar blinded by the intricacy of details and failing to see the whole picture—the forest for the trees.

Staring at her, he muttered, "You are bright. All the more reason...for you to progress quickly."

Venetria stepped up to Marian, linked arms—and neither

of them were shocked. Pondering it, Marian thought Venetria had dampened her personal magnetic field.

"A very valuable insight," Venetria said, lifting her chin arrogantly in Chalmon's direction. "Another reason to consider our options when planning."

Chalmon's eyes narrowed. "How did you guess that Amee's Song has diminished?"

Marian raised her brows. "Not a guess, a deduction. I've heard *two* World Songs." And despite all the harm humans had done to Earth, it was strong and intense and Powerful compared to Amee's.

"Humph," Chalmon said. Then he turned on his heel and headed back toward Bossgond's Tower. "I've discovered all I need to know about you."

Marian didn't follow him and neither did Venetria. "How nice for you," Marian said.

He shifted. "Do you have anything you wish to ask us?"

"A fair trade, do you mean?" Marian said.

Lips pressed together, he nodded.

"How kind of you to ask. Yes, Bossgond and I need a cook."

Both of them looked at her with surprise.

It was good to surprise colleagues, too—let them know that she'd soon be a force to be reckoned with.

They walked back to the Tower in a not-quite-comfortable silence that Marian refused to break. She'd wanted to meet more Circlets—and still did. There must be more compatible people for her, those who could grow into friends. Naturally, the image of Jaquar popped into her head and she strove to keep from coloring. She could share commonalities with him, but he struck her more as "lover" than friend. If she ignored a vague warning and let herself get involved with him…

When they reached the Tower, they saw Bossgond talking

to a little glass orb as he watched Tuck roll around the flag-stones in his hamster ball.

As soon as Tuck saw her through one of the slits he attempted to roll to her—and the ball lifted slightly from the ground to glide.

He squeaked angrily. "Out, out, out. *Nasty* ball."

Marian wrinkled her nose. It was cloudier than before, which meant Tuck had peed in it.

As Bossgond disappeared into his Tower, she ran to meet Tuck.

"The grumpy old man would not let me out! I am *not* a dirty animal. I tried to go through a slit, but—" His words were more like high-pitched squeals in her mind than real verbalization. He stopped and stood, nose twitching, pounding the ball with tiny clenched paws.

"I'll get you out. Just a minute," Marian soothed. She bent down and unscrewed the cap. Ick, eau de hamster.

She tilted the ball and Tuck bulleted out to roll in the sweet grass, then moved onto a clump of wildflowers.

"Throw it away, away, away!" demanded Tuck. "Out of that mean old man's reach."

Chalmon and Venetria stared at him. Marian didn't like the look in Chalmon's eyes, even more detached and examining than Bossgond's.

With two fingers Marian sailed the lid away like a Frisbee. Then she pulled back her foot, called on her Power and kicked the plastic ball. It made a satisfactory *crack* and flew out of sight. "It's gone."

Tuck ran back to her, smelling much better. He scrambled up her dress and into her pocket, hiding in embarrassment.

Marian aimed a cool glance at the pair of Circlets and smiled superficially. "Nice meeting you."

Chalmon half bowed, Venetria half curtseyed, amusing Marian. Apparently her status wasn't high enough to rate full honors.

As soon as Marian entered Bossgond's Tower, Chalmon started off in the direction of the strange orb that Exotique Marian's creature had been in.

"What are you doing?" Venetria asked, hurrying to keep up with him.

"An experiment, a trial run," he said. "We've hypothesized from what the Master told Jaquar that even the essence of an entity from Exotique Terre could harm the Dark's nest."

"Ah!" Venetria said, excited. "In that odd sphere is the essence of an entity of Exotique Terre."

"I'm sure we can find a way to send it into the maw as a weapon—observe whether it can truly penetrate the shield and, if so, what result it might have on the nest."

Venetria frowned. "We don't know where the nest is geographically, on the physical plane. We only know it isn't near. So we must transport the sphere on an etheric plane and fire it from there. That will take great, great Power."

Chalmon stopped and looked down. The ball lay at his feet. It wasn't as odoriferous as it had been. He hooked a finger in the opening and lifted it. Cracked but whole. "The orb is made of a strange substance that is very light."

Feeling as if she was already several paces down a slippery path leading to immorality, Venetria whispered, "How can we do this?"

"It is time to replace observers loyal to Jaquar with those who respect me more. With the aid of many, we should be able to accomplish sending this sphere into the Dark's nest."

She stared into his brilliant, glittering eyes. "I meant how can we consider sending a *person* into the Dark maw?"

His mouth tightened. "We need the knowledge. She can harm it, stop it from spewing out more horrors, more sangviles."

Shaking her head, Venetria said, "You are becoming someone I'm not sure I know."

His voice was tough. "I am refining down to the man I must be in dangerous circumstances. We cannot do *nothing*. We must act."

"At the expense of a woman's life?"

Chalmon started back to the landing area where they'd left their volarans. He sent her a glance, one side of his mouth lifted in an attempt at a smile. "She is very strong. She could destroy the nest and survive."

Venetria snorted. "You say that to pacify me. I'd rather wait, let the Exotique develop into her Power."

"Who knows how long that will take? And she does not wish to stay here. We need to know what happens in that nest. The more knowledge we have, the easier it will be to defeat the mind behind all this—not only the horrors, but the Master and *his* master." He stopped. "I am proceeding with this plan, Venetria, and nothing you can say will stop me."

"But why?"

His eyes fastened on her. "For you."

For the rest of that day and the next, Marian waited for the third Sorcerer she'd previously met to show up. She braced herself to see Jaquar. Surely now that she'd gained her balance in this new world—and had Tuck—she would find that her initial response to him was exaggerated by circumstances. He'd be attractive, of course, but no more so than any other man. In the back of her mind, she fretted about that vision she'd seen when they'd touched. She didn't recall the images that had flashed before her eyes—just the feeling of overwhelming danger.

Exactly the way she wanted to feel for a hunk. But better that than making a mistake and injuring her pride or her heart later. This time, of course, she'd be cool, knowledgeable, graceful.

But he didn't come.

Since Bossgond loaded her with work, she let her expectation of meeting Jaquar fade. She received the idea from Bossgond that she moved rapidly from one level of spells to the next…and the next. For herself, the lessons seemed to open someplace in her that inherently knew what to do, what to say, how to form her spell tunes, whistles and chants for the best results. Some of this was her training, but most of it sprang from her irregular studies of New Age beliefs.

By the middle of her second full week, Marian worked in all three of her "terrariums." Oddly enough, she was most proficient with Lightning and electrical storms. There had been no scary "incidents."

Bossgond had allowed her a brief look at Andrew one morning, but when she'd come up the next day for breakfast, he'd covered the binoculars. He told her there would be no more viewing by them both. He would watch and report, but the Power to coordinate so they both could look through the binoculars was draining energy they needed. Marian glared at him but said nothing.

One morning during her third week on Lladrana, the bells from the harness of a volaran rang near her windows, and Marian rushed to one, hoping Bastien had brought Alexa to visit.

Jaquar rode a black volaran with small white spots. The Circlet *was* sexy. Every time she saw the man, he was more attractive. Marian snorted. She couldn't afford to fall for him.

"Marian!" Bossgond's irritated voice came from the trumpet tube next to her desk.

"Yes?"

"That boy is here. He has good intent toward me so he just flew through my shield—"

A knock echoed like thunder through the Tower.

"Ever since I took you as an Apprentice, there's been no peace. You'd think if people saw that a door didn't have a harp, they'd know they weren't welcome," Bossgond grumbled. He'd taken the door harp off several days ago.

"I'm not answering it," Marian said, and got an immediate image of the old man's ears perking up in interest.

"Why not?"

"Because I had a vision when we first met."

"Ah! That has happened in the past with those who were Summoned for the Tower. Visions upon their arrival. What was it?"

Marian sighed. "I can't recall. Too many experiences since then have piled on top of that memory to remember it clearly. I just know he's *Trouble*."

"Hmm," said Bossgond, sounding more cheerful. "I've changed my mind. I want to talk with the boy."

12

Marian wanted to argue with Bossgond about admitting Jaquar to the Tower, but Bossgond appeared at the door to the stairs from her suite, opening it.

"Coming?" he asked, eyes bright with curiosity.

"Yes." Marian shifted her shoulders. A tingle had run up her spine to lodge itself at the back of her neck. For the first time, she realized that there was no mirror in her outer room. There was a small one that showed her face in the bedroom of her loft, but nothing else. Bossgond had plenty in his chambers, but they were for magical work.

She looked at him. He was neat and tidy in a midnight-blue tunic that looked brand-new, but only his clothes seemed ageless. He was ugly. Cute ugly, like a bulldog puppy, but it was no wonder he didn't hang mirrors around.

With lagging steps, she followed him down to the bottom-floor parlor.

Jaquar stood there. The sight of him—tall and well built and handsome, with those wide streaks of silver over each temple and the blue, blue eyes—sent hormones zinging through her veins.

She caught him staring at her, and a whispered tune fluttered between them.

Marian had learned enough to know that this could mean real trouble. Best she stay away from the man. So she moved from the stairs and put a wingchair between them.

His eyebrows rose, but his attention turned to Bossgond, who watched them both with a sly smile. The old mage held out both hands, wrists straight and palms up.

Jaquar glanced at Bossgond's gesture and his lips tightened. Marian realized she'd noticed his full mouth, and tried to gather a little shield around her that might block out the string of notes between them. It didn't work.

Carefully Jaquar placed his palms on Bossgond's, overlapping the older Sorcerer's hands. Jaquar jerked, and Marian saw the flash of energy between them, the blending of auras.

"I see I made a mistake years ago," Bossgond said. "Your parents requested you spend some months under my tutelage, and I was too immersed in my own studies and declined. But you would have been an excellent student and would have helped me, and would have gained your Circlet status earlier." Bossgond sighed gustily and dropped his hands. "That's in the past."

"You have an Apprentice of your own." Jaquar inclined his head to Marian. "Marian."

She nodded coolly. "Jaquar Dumont."

"She won't be an Apprentice for long," Bossgond boasted. "I'll have her a Scholar by the morrow and a Circlet by the end of the month."

Jaquar looked surprised. "Indeed."

Marian's stomach churned. Tests ahead. She wished she hadn't known, and wondered if there was any mention of Testing for Scholar in her books upstairs—if she could find the notes and prepare somehow.

"Come upstairs to my suite," Bossgond said silkily, like a spider to a fly.

Jaquar eyed him warily. "Why?"

Bossgond snorted. "Because I want to speak to you alone."

Marian gripped the back of the chair. "You could talk to him here."

Waving her suggestion away with an impatient hand, Bossgond threw them both an admonishing look and started up the stairs. "Come, Jaquar."

The younger man made a half bow to Marian, then followed Bossgond.

Bossgond's voice floated down. "Marian, I want you to rearrange the western coastline of your continent in your planet ball, generate a force-three storm, then bring the sphere upstairs to us. Jaquar should see the results of your lessons with me and your level of expertise."

Her pulse pounded in her ears. He'd just assigned her two huge tasks and expected them to be carried out quickly! More, she would have to gather the storm, then hold it as she walked from her rooms to his. She calculated—it was a trip up twenty stairs. If she took it slow and breathed properly she might be able to do it.

"Oh, and we will be talking in the ritual room at the top of the Tower," Bossgond said.

Her hands fisted. She couldn't make another twenty stairs, a full two stories, could she?

She heard Jaquar's grunt of surprise. Something in the sound sent adrenaline coursing through her and she set her teeth. She didn't have any time to waste. Everything she had must be focused on her task.

She didn't want to fail the old Circlet. More, she didn't want to fail in front of Jaquar. A woman had her pride. Even though she'd been here only two and a half weeks, she refused to fail.

For a moment she just stood, jaw clenched, then she heard a scrabbling noise and found Tuck sitting on his fat rump on her desk. He stared at her with wide black eyes, his paws clasped together. "I will help!"

She deliberately relaxed her mouth, rolled her shoulders and eyed him. No doubt many people would dismiss the aid of a small rodent, no matter how magical, but Marian just nodded gravely. "Thank you." Who knew what an animal who ate an atomball could do? Best to stretch his abilities as much as her own. Her pulse jumped at the thought that he might not want to return to Earth with her—something she didn't want to think about, couldn't think about, right now.

Walking over to her desk chair, she settled into the fat cushion that was beginning to take on her form. She looked at Tuck. "How do you want to help?"

He chittered a few seconds—his thinking sound, she'd learned—then said, "I will keep you calm."

"Keeping my hands from shaking as we take the terrarium up to Bossgond will be a great help. Thank you."

His nose wiggled. "I need food," he squeaked slyly.

With a chuckle she scooped him up, rubbed him against her cheek, then set him carefully down. "Come back to the desk when you're done eating," she said absently, already focused on the planet globe, parting the clouds to see the coastline. She took a moment to loosen her muscles, inhaled deeply and placed her hands on each side of the two-foot terrarium.

Frowning, she nibbled her lower lip as she considered how extreme the alteration to the coast should be—or rather, how little alteration she could do that would be acceptable to Bossgond. The real test was gathering the storm and holding it so it didn't break apart or go inland before she reached the two Sorcerers.

From what she'd experienced on Lladrana, equality of the sexes was close, but some men would always innately believe that strength made them superior to women.

Not Bossgond. He was an intellectual snob. As long as a person had Power, they were respected.

Jaquar intimidated her because he was a Circlet, intelligent, handsome…and very attractive.

There was that warning she'd received when they'd first touched. Perhaps she could recall the brief vision if she touched him again….

"Four minutes, Marian," Bossgond said through the speaking tube.

Marian jolted—stared down at the west coast of the continent in her terrarium. Concentrating, she delicately warmed the globe, causing the polar ice cap to melt. It took time and mental effort, but better that she be late arriving than not get her project done.

Melting the ice cap raised the water level of the ocean and changed *all* the coastlines of her continent, but she was following the rules. As she watched the ice liquefy, she let out a slow and steady breath, blowing at the terrarium. She used this to symbolize a rising wind—energy she sent to stir the air and whip up the seas until a force-three storm whirled in the ocean, sucking in clouds and water.

She moved a little faster and harder than she'd thought, and the storm whirled apart. Teeth clamped again, she struggled to keep the energy steady, growing, spinning the storm off the coast.

A few seconds later she heard a squeak and automatically angled her foot and leg so Tuck would have easy climbing. He hurried up her gown to her shoulder, then placed a tiny, clawed paw on her neck. The paw was cold.

But it calmed her. Since most of her mind was engaged in her task, she didn't hold back when Tuck's energy touched hers—a burst of light on her shoulder, stronger than she'd expected, a tiny rush of tuneful notes.

"Sinafin is teaching me," he said.

Her attention almost wandered. She kept it steady, forced extraneous thoughts from her mind.

"She says when you raise your Tower, I might become a feycoocu."

No! Marian would not listen. "Are you *trying* to distract me?"

He squeaked a chuckle. "Payback for all those times I rattled in my cage and needed food and you were *studying*." He sniffed, then licked a drop of sweat that had beaded around her hairline.

"Time to go," she said.

Slowly, slowly she stood, lifted the planet globe.

It tipped.

She righted it, expelled a shaky breath. Dropping it would be disastrous.

With tiny, cautious steps, mind on holding the storm, tension settling between her shoulders, she moved from the desk to the door. And stopped.

She'd have to separate some energy from the storm to open the door latch, or shift the globe to lie along an arm, use her left fingers to push the latch…

"I will open the door," said Tuck.

It flew open and slammed against the hall wall. His whole little body felt warm—with embarrassment?

"Thanks," Marian croaked.

Male shouts came from above. Jaquar's "No, I won't!" startled her, and the planet globe joggled. Marian gasped, struggled to keep the storm steady. She pursed her lips in irritation that the men couldn't leave her to do her work in peace.

Her head ached as she climbed the stairs; her arms tensed with the strain. The forty steps seemed interminable, draining. Her whole body trembled and she panted by the time she reached the ritual room.

Again Tuck handled the door. The harp strings sang, the latch slowly compressed, the door inched open.

When it was wide enough for her to walk through—a graceful glide was beyond her—she carried the terrarium in, looking only at her planet, ignoring the men except as shadowed bulks she had to negotiate around to reach a waist-high table near the pentagram rug.

"Let the storm go, Marian, but no destruction to the land or trees."

That would mean keeping the Wind and Lightning in the sky or moving the storm farther out to the sea. Marian clenched her fingers around the glass. Sweat trickled from her temple and was absorbed by her hair.

She couldn't do it. She was going to fail. The storm started slipping from her grasp, moved quickly inland, and lightning struck just outside the city in forks that would soon ignite trees—her anxiety fueled the storm. If she wasn't careful, there'd be an earthquake, tornado *and* tidal wave. Heat crawled up her face.

Her neck strained as she angled her head to focus on the planet ball. For an instant, she thought she'd grabbed control. Then the outside of the city went up in flames, and a few seconds later the tidal wave put out the fire.

"Very impressive," Jaquar said.

She bit her lip. She wanted to shut her eyes, or cry, or scream. Maybe even all three.

Gasping in a breath, she relaxed her hard, frozen grip on the glass, finger by finger, cleared her mind of outside distractions and sent calm through herself *and* the ball. The damage had been done. She'd averted an earthquake, but the city model was in ruins.

As far as she was concerned it had been a pop quiz, and she *hated* those. She'd had no time to prepare. If she'd known in advance, she could have practiced. The wind peaked again and she forced her thoughts away from self-recrimination to slowly heat the land and dry it.

"Now restore the coastline to its previous form that you showed me this morning," Bossgond ordered in a steely voice.

She almost lifted her eyes to stare at him. He must be kidding—or she wished he was. But his energy beating at her was stern, forceful.

She had no energy to do the task he required. Another failure loomed. Her dress stuck to her, then released the scent of fresh flowers, and she flushed again—they knew she sweated. She snatched at the heat of her body for energy and re-formed a third of her coastline.

Now she was cold, her knees trembling. She'd fall down soon.

"Sunlight," squeaked Tuck in her ear. His fur was warm by her neck. He was the best male in the room, no question.

Good idea. She lifted the globe and paced to a patch of sunlight slanting through a tower window. The warmth felt good on her back, more, it gave her energy. She thought she could *feel* it sifting through the ends of her hair.

Collecting threads of Power from the sun's warmth, the light that surrounded her, she visualized the strands braiding into a rope. A link from the sun through her, to her hands, to energy forming inside the planet ball.

She hummed low, under her breath, then a little louder as Power crackled between her hands, became a pressurized force that reclaimed land from the ocean, solidified it, carved it into its former configurations.

Again her dress released fragrance, but Marian barely noticed it. She was concentrating on her world, the eastern coast of *her* continent. She sculpted a cliff here in the north, making it more sheer, a rocky outcropping appeared in the south. She re-formed the caves and arches she'd enjoyed creating— why had she done that? It was fierce, intricate work. Finally the last rock jutted from the sea.

With the realization that she was through, her hands turned slippery, weakness threatened. She couldn't drop the sphere! No! Hastily she tottered back toward the table to put the terrarium on it. The glass slid from her hands and landed with a *clank*. But nothing worse happened.

She let her knees fold and she sank to the floor. Not caring about appearances, she wiped her sleeve across her forehead. Only then did she turn to look at the men.

They were inspecting her planet.

"What say you, Circlet Jaquar?" Bossgond's voice held a note of challenge.

"It's a little too pretty. Obviously made by a woman," Jaquar said.

Tuck ran down her gown to her lap, down her dress to the

floor, crossed to the table and swarmed up the carved leg. From there he jumped for Jaquar's hand and hung on with all four teeth.

"Yow!" Jaquar shook his hand. Tuck bit deeper, then was thrown off.

Marian instinctively reached out—a small ball of golden yellow coalesced around Tuck and brought him to her. She held him in one palm and stroked him with an index finger.

"How dare you hurt my friend!"

Jaquar smoldered at her. "Whatever it is, it attacked *me*." He fashioned a bandage around his hand. "Bad bite."

"Rodent teeth are quite sharp. They grow continually, you know."

Jaquar's eyes flashed with pain and anger as he turned to her. He swore hot and long, but since Marian didn't know any of the words except *merde*, she just smiled blandly.

"What *is* that thing?" asked Jaquar.

She lifted Tuck and stroked her cheek with his small body. "*He* is my friend."

Jaquar snorted, narrowed his eyes. "I wouldn't have thought it had the brain power to understand me—but it did, didn't it? It's sentient, and has the beginnings of a personal Song."

"Tuck—that's his name—ate an atomball."

Jaquar's eyes rounded, his stare fixed on the hamster. "Remarkable," he murmured.

"Let us return to the point, Circlet Jaquar. Do you agree that Apprentice Marian has passed her Testing to become of Scholar status?"

Shaking his head, Jaquar tapped the glass. "She didn't make Circlet level. Her control was poor."

"But she *did* succeed in her Tests to name her a Scholar."

Jaquar sent her and Tuck a hard gaze, cradled his hand. "It's only been a little over two weeks since she arrived!"

"Time is not relevant. Power and mastery of her art is. She passed the Scholar Tests."

"Yes," Jaquar agreed reluctantly. "She is no longer a mere Apprentice."

Giddy delight filled her and Marian was glad she was sitting. Her muscles were relaxing so much that she might flop to the ground. That would not be very graceful, but she was so happy, she didn't care.

Bossgond inclined his head to Jaquar. "We agree she is of Scholar status, then." Her teacher looked down at her. He was a short man, but seemed to loom over her. "Marian, you will go to the hot spring baths in the lowest level of the Tower and cleanse yourself while I prepare the Ritual from Apprentice to Scholar."

She stared. Tuck ran from her hands up to her shoulder, then said, "Let's go, let's go, let's *go!*" He patted her face with tiny claw-tipped paws that snapped her from her amazement. She blinked, nodded and rose stiffly to her feet. Tuck hung on to her gown.

Hesitating at the door, she looked back at the men. Bossgond was placing a light wooden altar in the center of the star, intent upon his work. Jaquar met her gaze from under lowered brows, his blue eyes brilliant. From the tune linking them, she sensed frustration, but pride in her, a touch of incredulity that she'd already become a Scholar.

She dipped a half curtsy and left the ritual room, then hurried to her own chambers where she took a towel, her favorite soap that smelled of lavender, and a clean gown and underwear to put on. When Alexa had offered to have someone make bras and panties for Marian, she'd jumped at the offer and the garments had arrived a few days later. Now Marian had enough underthings to last out her stay. She kept the bras just in case her magical robes failed.

Though she yearned for a long soak in the hottest pool, to reflect on her Tests and what she should have done better, Marian bathed quickly but thoroughly in the coolest pool— she had no wish to appear lobster-red before the men—and dried and dressed in panties and robe. She was pleased that she wasn't out of breath by the time she climbed the five stories.

The room was lit by indirect sunlight and candles when she entered. Bossgond stood in the top point of the star, wearing a golden robe that matched his hair. Jaquar stood to the south, between the two lower star-points, and had changed into a maroon robe. Both robes were tied with belts of string and had no ornamentation. They both wore embossed golden circlets around their foreheads.

Bossgond bowed to Marian, Jaquar did the same. With a dull, silver-handled knife, Bossgond indicated to Marian that she should stand at the left point of the star, the east.

The incense was strong, and mixed with her triumph and relief and exhilaration. She was giddy. Giggles caught in her throat. She'd done it! She'd passed her Apprentice tests and become a Scholar, on her way to being a Circlet. She felt prouder than if she'd aced her doctoral dissertation. She wondered if she'd get a robe with a hood— Marian shook the fuzzy thoughts away. She swayed. Narrowing her eyes, she stared at the scented smoke filling the ritual room. Was that what made her feel dizzy? Blinking hard, she turned her head to Bossgond. He stared at her with an avuncular expression.

She glanced at Jaquar. His eyelids were lowered so that only a deep-blue glint showed. A flush showed under his skin, and his mouth curved. He looked as if he was admiring her.

Tuck squeaked loudly in her ear. His claws dug into her neck and the sharp pain focused reality around her.

"She is here, she is here, she is *here!*" Tuck's high, piping voice hurt Marian's ears.

A neon-purple bat swooped through the window.

Marian blinked.

It hadn't swooped through an *open* window.

The bat zoomed around the Tower room, dizzying Marian again. She couldn't watch.

Very good, Sinafin broadcast mentally. Everyone turned to her. The magical shapechanger stood by the planet globe in fairy form. Leaning toward it, she stared inside and nodded. *Very good, indeed.*

"You are here!" Tuck hopped up and down on Marian's shoulder.

Vaguely she recalled that he'd said something about becoming a feycoocu like Sinafin. Marian wanted to lift her hand to him, catch him close to her heart and keep him, protect him from any major change. Any *further* major change. But her limbs were too heavy. Was it the incense?

She stared fixedly at Sinafin, seeing a huge golden aura surround the fairy, mirrored in small glitters that floated in the air of the chamber.

Sinafin flew from the table to perch on Marian's other shoulder. She was lighter than Tuck. The hamster scrambled around her neck to meet the fairy.

Turning her head, Marian watched as Tuck held up bloody paws to Sinafin.

You have blooded the new Sorceress. Good, Sinafin said approvingly. Dipping her head, the fairy lapped blood from Tuck's paws. He did the same.

Blood. *Her blood,* Marian thought. Eeeew.

13

Sinafin sent mentally, Bossgond and Jaquar, let us proceed with the ceremony raising Marian from Apprentice to Scholar. I will witness for the Marshalls, since Marian will be working closely with Exotique Alexa.

Marian stood at the altar, Sinafin on one side of the platform, Tuck on the other, Jaquar watching from the eastern star-point. Bossgond gave her a chilled golden goblet with thick yellow liquid she was supposed to drink.

Marian eyed it warily, but whether it was the smoke from the incense or the aftereffect of her Tests, her mouth was dry and her thirst horrible. So she braced herself and glugged.

It was the best orange juice she'd ever had, and she coughed to cover her nervous giggle.

So many strange events—like the ceremony—and so many familiar things used in different ways—like the orange juice. She'd congratulated herself on being flexible, on going with the flow, but now wondered if that had all been a lie and she'd wake up crazed one morning from the stress of it all.

Before she could grab on to the thought, Sinafin was brushing a kiss against her cheek and it felt suddenly as if she were drinking a mimosa.

It is done! Sinafin said, a big smile on her fairy face. Marian sensed the feycoocu spoke only to her. *An Apprentice could not have handled any trouble, any fearsome magics aimed at her or demanding responsibilities. But you are now a Third Degree Scholar.*

Oh yes, there were certainly things to be wary of, and one of them fluttered just beyond her nose. Marian hadn't forgotten that Alexa had said the shapeshifter had her own agenda.

"I don't know what you are talking about," Marian said stiffly to the fairy.

There are five degrees of apprenticeship and scholarship that you must master before you become a Circlet. You are already a Third Degree Scholar. It is good.

Marian licked the last traces of the juice from her lips and gave Sinafin a hard look. "What about the rest—the trouble, fearsome magic and demanding responsibilities?" She didn't mind the last, but the first two were definite causes for concern.

"Time for you to discard the old robe of apprenticeship and don the new one denoting a Scholar," Bossgond said, a proud note in his resonant voice.

That dragged Marian's attention away from Sinafin. Bossgond held up a robe—this one with a new symbol on it, an open book with a whirlwind coming from the pages. And the symbol was stitched around the hem and the ends of the sleeves. Marian liked the symbols, but would have preferred to have chosen her own icons.

Then his words sank in. She was supposed to strip? Here? Now? *In front of everyone?*

Tuck, of course, had seen her naked both lately and when he was a mere hamster. And of the beings in the room, he was the only one she felt comfortable seeing her naked and vulnerable. How could she bare herself to everyone's—to Jaquar's—stare?

Bossgond shook the robe impatiently. "Come, Marian, undress that I might robe you."

"Couldn't you just *give* me the gown?" She reached for it, but he whisked it away, narrowing his eyes.

Alexa, too, has a problem with nudity, Sinafin announced to them all.

Heat crept up Marian's neck, her face.

Alexa, too, does this changing-color thing, Sinafin transmitted.

Grim, Marian snatched off her gown and dropped it to the floor, then grabbed at the new dress Bossgond held, missed. It was already too late to be ladylike, unconcerned and dignified.

He stared at her panties. "You aren't naked under your robe!" he said indignantly.

Alexa, too, wears such strange garments, Sinafin chirped.

Marian wanted to strangle the little being.

"Nice," rumbled Jaquar from somewhere at Marian's left.

Of course she hadn't forgotten he was there. She leaped at Bossgond, wrenched the new dress from his grasp and pulled it over her head.

When it slipped down she felt respectable again. "Is the ceremony now over?" she asked.

Bossgond huffed, then went to the altar and picked up a long, sharp knife. He dipped it in a bowl of earth, then water, held it over a flame, then incense. The Sorcerer chanted as he did so, words stirring the air.

Marian stared in horror. Surely she wouldn't be cut or branded! Why hadn't he told her he'd—

He took her left wrist—the one both he and Alexa had cut—and laid the flat of the blade on her arm, beneath the tattoo that had appeared on her arm after she and Alexa had blood-bonded—a crossed wand and jade baton.

But the knife was warm, not hot, and when he lifted it there was a small red triangle.

"When this fades, you will be a Circlet," he said. Then he nodded to Jaquar. "She is your pupil, now, formally under your care and protection."

Marian yelped as if the knife had burned her. "What?"

No one answered her, they all concentrated on finishing the ceremony. A moment later Bossgond, Jaquar, Sinafin and even Tuck clapped their hands once. The sound echoed like thunder through the room.

"It is done," Bossgond said.

This time Marian believed it. The room dimmed, then brightened.

Bossgond addressed Jaquar. "Teach her Weather but *not* plane-walking. Her bond with Amee is not strong enough to keep her here rather than lost in the planes. I will speak to both of you each evening. Separately."

Jaquar's face turned impassive. He jerked a nod at Bossgond.

A sound like a foghorn came. *That's the boat with the cook,* Sinafin said.

"Stay in the pentagram, Marian. Jaquar, join with her and I will send you to Mue Island," Bossgond said conversationally.

"No, wait—" Marian objected.

"Will you help me, feycoocu?" asked Bossgond.

Yes.

"I'll send your volaran home, Jaquar," Bossgond said.

Marian didn't see him, but Jaquar moved behind her, wrapped his arms around her waist. "We're ready," he said.

Tuck ran to her and crawled up her dress to a low pocket.

"No, I'm not ready," Marian said crossly. "What's going on here?"

"I'm a Weather Sorcerer, Bossgond isn't. He can't teach you what you must learn." Jaquar's breath ruffled her hair and Marian shifted away. His arms tightened.

He was too close. Too…dangerous. And though she didn't experience the same flash of foresight she had now as when they'd first met, warning bells rang in her ears.

She wanted to change her major.

Marian and Jaquar arrived in his Tower with a soft *pop* of displaced air. Marian stumbled, but Jaquar held her and she didn't fall. She was all too aware of his fast heartbeat. From the trip? Or from proximity to her? She'd like to think the latter, but didn't flatter herself.

As soon as her balance was steady, she pulled away and his arms dropped from her. She strode across the parquet floor.

"Don't cross the circle!" he ordered.

It didn't seem smart to breach magic. She'd already walked down a star-point and was near the circle that surrounded the pentagram. She crossed her arms, turned back and scowled at him.

"I didn't agree to be your student."

He raised his brows. "I didn't ask that you be my pupil. That was arranged by Bossgond and the feycoocu. Two beings who should not be crossed." His hand dipped to a pocket near his belt. He withdrew his fingers, holding a stick slightly larger than his hand. With a flick, the rod lengthened and thickened until it was a seven-foot staff of smooth and gleaming white-gold. Atop the staff was a *real* miniature cloud that wisped and flowed with the currents of air in the room. Or maybe from Jaquar's emotions. It was looking like a thundercloud.

Excellent trick. Marian tightened her jaw to keep her mouth from falling open. She itched to examine the wand up close. How would it feel to keep a cloud in your pocket? To what use could you put such an item? The notion captivated.

He tipped the staff to the star-point to her left. A *crack* and flash of lightning and the whole pentacle smoked gray, then turned into a silver pattern inset in the floor.

"This is my ritual room. Let's descend to my study. I have my Scholar planet spheres in storage there. You can use them. Today I'll want to judge the scope of your Power. If you are as well versed as Bossgond believes, we can start your practicum outside tomorrow."

She could feel her eyes round, her heartbeat rushed loud in her ears. Outside—that meant with real weather. Wind. Clouds. Ocean. Thunder. She focused on the cloud hovering atop his staff.

He chuckled. "Bossgond said you were particularly adept with Lightning. But we will start, as always, with Wind and clouds."

"Of course," she said, trying to be calm.

A rustling came from her gown and Tuck popped his head out of the pocket. He fixed his eyes on Jaquar. "I am hungry."

Jaquar scowled, cradled his hurt left hand against his chest. "What are you doing here, *mouse?*"

Tuck issued a miniature growl she'd never heard before. "I am Marian's companion. I am a hamster," he squeaked. "I eat nuts, and fruit and *atomballs.*" It sounded like a challenge.

Jaquar blinked, then he flung back his head and laughed.

"So you do." He set his wand aside to stand by itself and

snapped his fingers at Tuck. "Come here so I can meet my guest and provide for him well."

Tuck narrowed his eyes, cocked his head. *Take me to him, please.*

Marian started at the tiny voice in her mind. Tuck's voice. She froze. Another thing that was far out of her experience. Having a magical shapeshifter from another world, or an old Sorcerer speak to her mind-to-mind was far less shocking than hearing her hamster. Blindly, she reached into her pocket, closing her fingers gently around his soft fur and sturdy little body. She cupped her hands so he could sit in them. As she walked to Jaquar, Tuck rode as if he were a king. King of the hamsters?

Incredible.

She stopped within a couple of feet of Jaquar, eyeing him warily. He scrutinized Tuck, who wore his hamster-Buddha aspect. Tinkling music emanated from him. She almost expected Tuck to spout wise instructions.

"May I pick you up? I'll be careful," Jaquar said to Tuck.

"Yes," Tuck said.

Jaquar slid his hands under Marian's. A ripple of hot notes licked between them. Jaquar's deep-blue eyes met hers and they stood, linked by music and warmth and gaze. The world, even Tuck, seemed to fall away until only Jaquar mattered.

Tuck nipped at her right index finger and Marian gasped, jerked and spilled the hamster into Jaquar's steady hands.

Even as she stepped back, Jaquar was lifting the hamster to eye level, studying him.

"I'd like to see all of you," Jaquar said, and turned Tuck to look at his belly, check his ears, even look at his back end under his stubby tale. Then Jaquar peered at the hamster's ears and eyes. "Not a mouse, not a rat," Jaquar murmured. "Could you open your mouth?"

Marian said, "Bossgond has representations of Tuck, perhaps even of his internal organs and skeleton. I'd prefer you ask Bossgond for the *Hamster Lorebook* instead of prodding Tuck."

Jaquar didn't look at her but raised his eyebrows. "And what would Master Tuck prefer?"

Tuck preened. "Food," he said.

Laughing again, Jaquar said, "We'll get some for you." He placed Tuck on his left shoulder, took the staff and strode from the pentacle to a door in the far wall.

Unlike Bossgond's Tower, Jaquar's was octagonal. Marian wasn't sure what that said about him. From what she'd read, when a Sorcerer or Sorceress raised a Tower, it came from the image of the "perfect" Tower in their mind. So did the shape indicate that the man had many angles?

"I don't have any food in this room. Let's go down to my study." He opened the door, and instead of a hall and stairway winding around the full building like Bossgond's, Marian saw a tiny circular stair built into its own round Tower, straight up and down. It would be steep.

"Wait," Marian said, staring at the empty center of the circle. She frowned. "Once again I've been transported without any of my belongings."

Jaquar tilted his head. "I have some bespelled cloth you could make into gowns, if you know how."

"I don't." To her dismay she felt a sting at the back of her eyes. She straightened her spine, waved at him to go on.

His face softened. "I'm sure Bossgond will send your things with my volaran."

That hadn't occurred to Marian; she still fumbled with small daily strategies of planning and doing. Irritated at herself, she nodded at Jaquar and said, "Of course." She walked over to the door and waited for him to descend.

"The door will close and lock behind you automatically," Jaquar said, his voice carrying up from the shadowy stairway. "I'm sorry to be discourteous, but I would prefer that I know you better before I give you the Songspell to my ritual room."

"Naturally," Marian said. How could such a thing be discourteous? She hated when people messed with her stuff; it was one reason she lived alone. She reached out and found a pipelike rail against the curved wall. Passing a window, she looked out. Bossgond's Tower had been five stories high, and this one looked to be the same. Was the mass of a Tower also the measure of the Sorcerer's Power? Jaquar's ritual room hadn't been as large as Bossgond's. But it had been more beautiful. Airier, with pairs of long pointed windows around the walls.

Since her new gown lifted itself from her feet, keeping her from tripping, Marian had no trouble with the stairs, except that they were in such a small space. Claustrophobia had rarely bothered her before, but perhaps that was another change. She seemed to metamorphose daily, perhaps even moment to moment, as if she unfurled and tried new butterfly wings.

The pleasant fancy kept her mind occupied until she reached the lower floor of Jaquar's study.

She entered to find this room was much like the one above, with pointed-arched floor-to-ceiling windows in every wall, but the chamber was larger by about a third. The octagonal proportions were lovely, though it had fewer shelves than Bossgond's study, due to the magnificent windows. She could see the whole room; it wasn't a partitioned loft with study, sleeping space and tiny kitchen as Bossgond's had been. Again the floor was parquet strips in an elegant pattern.

Jaquar stood at a pretty sideboard, wooden with a top of colorful tiles. One of the tiles glowed red-hot under a teakettle.

Marian's mouth watered. She could almost taste tea—wanted it more than coffee. Tea was a comfort drink.

At a small table next to the sideboard, Tuck sat. "Food," he demanded.

Slanting a glance at Marian, Jaquar said, "Food?"

"Nuts, fruit. A bit of soft cheese. Some grains and greens, dried vegetables and seeds."

With a gesture, a large china bowl appeared on the table with Tuck. It was filled with various nuts, many of which Marian didn't recognize.

Tuck cheeped in delight, hoisted himself over the rim and plunged into the bowl, scattering nuts. Jaquar shook his head and chuckled. "He really did dive into his food."

"Yes." Marian found herself smiling back at him. "He really did."

The kettle whistled and Jaquar poured water into a teapot. Matching mugs sat on the sideboard. He handed a cup to Marian. "Let us sit. The tea will come when it is ready."

She wasn't quite sure what to make of that, but followed Jaquar to a couple of large, soft chairs made of pillows. They were set before windows looking out on a view across the island and to the western ocean, not toward Lladrana. Marian realized from the shine of the floor that he'd moved the chairs to this pair of windows from across the room—and recently. Sensing that it had something to do with his lost parents, she said nothing.

Jaquar sat and stretched out his legs. "Tell me what you want to learn, Marian."

He almost sounded like a departmental counselor. But his voice was too much a tool—even more than a professor's voice was—to belong to a counselor, and she thought he probed more sharply than any counselor would. Less interested in her and her wants and needs than how she might fit into his plans. Her stomach tightened. She hadn't had a return of the strange feeling that he was a dangerous threat, but she wouldn't forget it. Still, there shouldn't be anything wrong with honesty. Perhaps it would prompt him to be open in return.

"I want to find a cure for my brother's disease and take it back to Exotique Terre."

He stared at her in surprise.

"Bossgond didn't tell you?" she asked.

"No." Jaquar's voice was a mere whisper. "You don't intend to stay here in Amee, then?"

She narrowed her eyes. "No. More than that, if the Snap doesn't happen within the next few weeks, I'll be asking for help to return to my home. My brother has a degenerative disease."

"I'm sorry," Jaquar said, and she thought he meant it.

"And what do you want of me?" she asked.

14

Jaquar's eyes widened. He opened his mouth, then shut it, and
his lips shaped a grim line. When he met her gaze, his was
darkly serious. "What do I want from you? I wish you to progress rapidly to Circlet status." A corner of his mouth kicked
up. "Despite what Bossgond says, and your spectacular demonstration of Power this morning, I do not believe that you
learn so quickly."

"Oh? And how long did it take for Alexa to become a Marshall?"

His head jerked back in surprise. "I, uh—" He blinked,
then looked as if he were calculating.

"The Marshalls have Tests, too, don't they?"

"Yes, yes they do." Again he half smiled. "Many would say
they have the hardest Tests in all of Lladrana. Alyeka was
Tested the moment she arrived and had passed by the time she
went to bed. Say, three hours."

Marian stared at him, struggling to keep atop the discussion. She recalled what Alexa had said had happened the first night she was in Lladrana. "But it cost her—her hair turned white."

Jaquar inclined his head. "Very true, and though she became a Marshall at that time, it took her weeks to develop her Power, to become a Marshall in more than title only. I may be wrong, you may be extremely quick." He shrugged. "You *are* more mature than most Scholars who are so innately Powerful."

"I've been told that the…Song…and your Tower Community chose me in some way. That I heard the Summoning and answered it because I fit your requirements."

"Also correct," he said.

At that point, the teapot sailed between them. It went first to Jaquar. He held out his mug and the teapot tipped, pouring a golden-brown stream of liquid into his cup, stopping when it was about a quarter-inch from the top. Then the pot slowly turned, and, as if it were a heat-seeking missile, aimed for the cup Marian held.

Though her hand wanted to tremble, she forced it still while the tea decanted into her mug. "Wonderful." She couldn't help a sigh of pleasure.

Jaquar smiled. "I keep black tea for Alyeka. She has a weakness for it, and apparently it is not as easily available here in Lladrana as it is in your own land."

"That's kind of you."

"Not really. I like her, and she is an excellent Marshall, which means that she can provide us with very interesting items such as dreeth acid sacs."

Marian willed herself not to pale. She nodded.

"And it riles Bastien when a man pays attention to Alyeka. Before she tamed him, Bastien had a habit of irritating people. I am no exception."

Marian wouldn't have called either Alexa or Bastien tame. The teapot finished turning another circuit and settled itself on a small, solid wooden table in front of them. Since the top was heavily scarred as if the table had been used for many purposes, Marian didn't move to protect the surface. Jaquar didn't even seem to notice that the pot might have left another unsightly mark. Sorcerer or not, he was a real guy.

She had let new magic distract her long enough—as it had far too often lately—so she returned to her priority. "Do you know much about diseases or healing? I can tell you my brother's symptoms."

But he was shaking his head. "I am sorry. I have no skill in that area. I cannot help you."

Marian nodded and sipped her tea. Disappointed again.

Jaquar finished his drink, picked up the teapot and crossed the room. She could hear him, but didn't take her eyes off the view from the windows. Green land, a winding stream, the ocean beyond. A lovely view. And nothing like the Flatirons of Boulder or the mountains of Denver. Home.

An odd clatter caught her attention, and she turned her head to see Jaquar pushing a cart containing the spheres. "Why don't they float like the teapot?" she asked.

"Because the teapot is imbued with generations of household magic and is used often. I fashioned these planet spheres a while back in my first year as a Circlet when I wanted to experiment with weather in a controlled environment. When I was done, I removed the energy from them to use elsewhere." He wedged the cart into the space between her feet and the table, then waved a hand. It lowered to angle over her chair like an adjustable desk.

Marian chuckled. No, Lladrana wasn't home, but it continued to be endlessly fascinating. She *could* make a home here—even raise a Tower—if she didn't need to return to Andrew.

"Revive the spheres," Jaquar said.

Though his tones were low and spoken like a request, Marian didn't delude herself. The downtime they'd spent together was finished and he now watched her with the keen gaze of a judging prof.

It was easier than she had anticipated, and obviously far less difficult for her than Jaquar had expected. But the glass and the models—the land and cities and dried plant life—all resonated of Jaquar, and Marian found the patterns simple to work with, as if the man had familiar thought processes. In a few moments, all three terrariums were vivid with "life"—and weather. The smallest jar showed a pretty ocean lapping at newly plumped trees, opening and stretching under bright sunlight and a sky with a few clouds…that spelled *Marian* in English. It was a signature that she just couldn't resist. The middle terrarium was dark with rain and storm. The largest planet sphere had new continents, oceans and trade winds.

Jaquar studied her work from under lowered brows. He lifted his head, shaking it. "Unbelievable."

Marian smiled sweetly.

"We will definitely begin your practicum outside, tomorrow morning."

Tuck waddled up, squeaking something that Marian couldn't understand because his mouth was full and both of his cheek pouches were distended. He looked nearly two-thirds bigger than usual.

"By the Song!" Jaquar said. He squatted. "May I pick you up, Tuck?"

There was mumbled hamster agreement.

Once again Jaquar scrutinized the hamster nose-to-tail,

paying particular attention to his cheeks. "What a remark-able animal."

Tuck smirked.

Jaquar looked to Marian, and for the first time she thought she saw him without any mask. His eyes held a dark shadow, his faint smile had no practiced charm, his whole body exuded interest and attraction.

"A remarkable companion to a remarkable woman."

Warmth bloomed in Marian, both simple and complex. She felt pleasure at the sincere compliment, and a low ache at the magnetism humming between them, all too tempting to act upon.

Tuck wriggled in Jaquar's grasp. "Bed!"

It was too close to Marian's drifting thoughts. She straight-ened. "Yes, what of the sleeping arrangements? I had my own apartment in Bossgond's Tower."

"My Tower is just as well equipped as Bossgond's," he said. He gestured upward. "As you know, my ritual room is the top of the Tower, as is customary. This room is my study." He waved a hand. "It has many windows and great light. I prefer dimness in my personal rooms, so the lower three levels have only a few square windows." He hesitated. "I was quite young when I raised my Tower and gave little thought to having an Apprentice. I have never taken one. But there's a suite of rooms—half the bottom floor—that should serve."

He held Tuck up to gaze into the hamster's eyes. "Do you want to stay with Marian, me, or have a little house here, Tuck?"

"A house!" Tuck squeaked.

Jaquar strode over to a shelf that held an elaborate model about four feet square. The top was a church and attached buildings that looked like a monastery or nunnery. But it was what was *below* the building that fascinated—a series of tunnels and "underground" chambers. Some were stone vaults and paved, others rough caverns. Marian glanced down to the brass plate at the bottom of the model. It read "Portions of the Singer's Abbey."

"Portions?" she asked.

He grimaced. "The Friends of the Singers are the most secretive people in Lladrana. Much to the Tower Community's dismay, we don't have accurate maps or models of the Singer's Abbey. This construct is the best we have."

His gaze met hers and they shook their heads in unison. No knowledge should be hidden. It wasn't right. She smiled, then his lips curved, too.

Tuck squeaked and wiggled. "My house!"

"I think he likes it," Jaquar said. "One moment, Tuck, and I'll take it off the shelf. The model has its own stand that rises from the floor." Jaquar handed Tuck to Marian. The hamster quivered with excitement. Jaquar ran his hand down the carved front support of the bookcase, found a sculpted cloud and turned it. There was a soft *whirr* and a pedestal rose from the floor and sat in one of the octagonal corners of the room.

"That location matches the geographical placement of the Singer's Abbey in relation to the sun," Jaquar said.

Tuck clapped his paws in delight, causing notes like glass windchimes to tremble through the room.

Marian chuckled and walked over to the heavily carved stand that consisted of a bottom, four pillared legs and an open top with inset grooves for the model.

Jaquar overtook them and carefully placed the dollhouse on the stand, then stooped, reached up and hooked his fingers into the bottom of the construct. With a pull, a small ramp descended to the floor. He grunted, then looked askance at Tuck.

"When old Sorceress Entanra gave this to me, neither of us knew why she'd included the staircase." He stood and dusted his hands off. "There are several Lladranan noble families that have a touch of foresight, and she came from one of them."

"Put me down, down, *down!*" Tuck demanded. He obviously yearned to try the staircase made just for him. Marian set him on the floor. He ran to the little wooden ramp and climbed it until he disappeared into the model.

"Entanra was of the Chiladees—Bastien's mother's family," Jaquar said.

Marian shot him a startled glance. "Bastien has the gift of foresight?"

Jaquar grunted as he tested the fit of the model in the stand. It was solid. "No, but his brother Luthan Vauxveau does. You might remember that if you happen to meet him." Jaquar tapped a finger on the chapel. "He's a noble Chevalier with land and volarans of his own, but he's also the representative of the Singer to the Marshalls' Council. The Marshalls usually lead Lladrana—they are the ones who like to do that sort of thing."

"Ah."

"Chevaliers of the Field are our main fighting force— knights who ride horses or fly volarans."

At that point, Tuck popped out of one of the holes in the cavern bottom and wound his way up to a large chamber, sniffing madly all the way and making his usual comments to himself. "This is dusty, no good. Smells like incense here, not nice for food. Where to store the food?" He stopped and turned to them, clasping his paws.

"Thank you, Jaquar. Thank you, Marian. This is a wonderful house!" Then he hopped into a tunnel that vanished into the depths of the model.

Marian frowned. "Is there somewhere we could see the

whole thing if we wanted?" A twinge of abandonment rushed through her.

Jaquar shrugged. "Each side provides a different angle, of course, and if absolutely necessary, the model is constructed in different, interlocking-spell layers and could be disassembled, but I would prefer not to do that. Does having Tuck up here in my study instead of your rooms bother you?"

Marian shifted. "A little." Jaquar's eyes had deepened into sapphire. "I lost him during the Summoning. He was trapped in his ball—his vehicle—and the wind took him away." She choked. "I thought he was dead."

"How did you find him?"

"The feycoocu told me where to look. He was on Bossgond's island."

Eyes widening, Jaquar said, "How did he get there?"

"I don't know." She shivered. "I don't know," she repeated in a whisper. She glanced at the new hamster house. "I asked Tuck, but he only vaguely recalls when he was just an animal."

"Hmm," Jaquar said. "He should be safe enough in the model, and in this Tower. Outdoors is another matter."

Marian fisted her hands. "I don't know if I could lose him now. He's a real companion." She couldn't imagine how hard it would be to leave him here on Amee when she went back. More and more she feared that Tuck wouldn't want to return to Earth.

"Sleep!" came Tuck's high voice, and as Marian turned to look at the model of Singer's Abbey, the light in it dimmed. That gave her a jolt, too. Hamsters were nocturnal, but since he'd awakened after feasting on the atomball, Tuck had become more diurnal. And he had enough Power to dim the light in his own house.

"You worry too much," Jaquar said. He reached out and took

her closed fingers in his large, elegantly long-fingered hands, lifting one of her hands, then another to his lips.

With the brush of his mouth on her fingers, an intricate Song bloomed between them, full-bodied, with a long melodic line.

Marian shivered. Her hands opened and her fingers twined with his. As they joined palm to palm, a current of music twisted between them.

The intensity of feeling, and the orchestral music, built until her every nerve ending shivered.

"Dance with me," he said, voice low.

That was the last thing she'd expected.

Slowly, slowly, he raised her left hand to the top of his shoulder. His smile was edged with challenge and irony—and she sensed he dared both himself and her.

Jaquar's smile looked more ironic than amused. Then he stared down at her. "You're surprised. Odd."

"I'm not used to…to melodies between people."

"But your people cherish music. I know this is so, because I know Alyeka."

"Our…Power…doesn't manifest itself in music." It was all Marian could say. She didn't really know how strong or how pervasive true magic was on Earth. Surely it was secret knowledge, practiced by only a very few.

"Do you dance?" he asked.

With the words came a rush of kindness, interest, attraction from him. She grew light-headed.

"Yes," she said.

He set his left hand on her waist, in waltz formation. Did they waltz here? Did Lladranans bring the waltz to Earth or vice versa? Or did an Exotique learn it and take it home during a Snap?

The music between them surged, developed undertones, harmonies. Jaquar swept her into a waltz, and the only music they heard was that which they made between themselves.

He was graceful, supple, his steps wooing. More than the turns made her dizzy. She'd never felt so womanly, so pretty. Nothing in his gaze, his touch, his aura made her feel too tall, or too plump.

Along with that came another realization—no one on Lladrana had looked at her with critical eyes. Bossgond had studied her work and snorted at her early efforts, but he'd never examined her person with a judgmental gaze.

No one seemed to think she was overweight and out of shape. Her body didn't seem to matter.

She felt beautiful.

And the man dancing with her was achingly alluring.

Her focus changed from herself to *them,* as a unit. The dance.

Their steps matched. His body angled toward her, tempting, his eyelids were heavy over gleaming eyes, his mouth relaxed to show the natural softness of his lips…

With another turn, the scent of him, something male that spoke of storms and windswept cliffs, flowed through her senses. The Song between them mesmerized, was a primal mystery meant to be explored.

Without thought, her body became supple, pressed against his. Her blood heated until she felt flushed, ready, open.

The Song could go on forever and she'd enjoy every moment.

Rhythm and tempo changed, the music became slower, languorous. He led and she followed, her senses filled with the pulse of desire between them, soft air caressing her, embracing her as she danced with him.

Daylight faded from the windows, let in whispering dark, and still they danced, caught in the moment, never tiring, building a strong connection between them.

It seemed like a dream.

Dream.

The word dropped coldly into her consciousness, opened her memory. She'd had many lately. Dreams of the Songs and Summoning, of Power, of doom and death. She stiffened, and with her thoughts, the music spiked harshly.

The expectation in his eyes changed from misty to wary. He slowed, brought them to a stop after a quick whirl, then bowed before her, keeping his gaze on her face. "A lovely dance indeed."

Though his voice was still quiet, Marian could almost hear his defensive shields snapping up.

They stepped apart.

Marian cleared her throat. "It's a very strong Song between us. Stronger than the one I have with Bossgond, even, and we're blood-bonded. No doubt because you're my teacher and I've advanced to Scholar?"

He smiled, and it was empty. "No doubt."

Irritation washed through Marian. He was keeping things from her. She wondered if the same thing had happened to Alexa, and would have bet her doctorate that it had. She'd have liked to ask Alexa, though. Marian had discovered her telepathy didn't reach the Castle from the islands. Where was a good telecommunications system when you wanted it?

But Jaquar had masked his expression and moved to the doorway to the circular stairs. "I think we should survey the small suite at the bottom of the Tower. I haven't been there recently and don't know how comfortable the rooms are."

"Of course." Marian smiled politely. She wanted to talk to

Alexa. Yearned for a telephone, or the crystal ball they used here. Marian wondered who was the Circlet specializing in communications and what they'd charge for making a link with Alexa.

She was walking briskly when she saw something on the floor near the shelf where the model of the Singer's Abbey had been. She didn't know why it snagged her attention, or how she saw it so well, except that it, too, had a Song, and the minute she focused on it, the dark tune came clearly in her mind. As she grew closer she saw an intricately knotted length of six-stranded embroidery floss in ox-blood red. She certainly would have missed noticing it except for the low and slow drumbeats emanating from it.

As she picked it up, her fingers closed convulsively over the floss and drumming poured through her, drowning all her other senses.

Danger!

15

Only the thread in her hand had substance, and the drumming of it eradicated all sight, sound, and even the pressure of the air on her body, the floor under her feet. She hoped she was standing.

She wanted to scream but didn't even know if her mouth opened. A symphony of drums would drown her out.

Don't panic. Panic could only make her situation worse.

Focus!

Feel!

And she did. She felt the tide of her own body moving in counterpoint to the drums.

More!

She felt her Power. Pulling it, gathering the magic, started a warmth in her feet that rose through her, accumulating speed and heat. Her skin felt hot, tight, flushed with the magic she contained. It spread up her neck, finally reached her face and head.

Her ears popped and for a moment she was dizzy enough to think the top of her skull was exploding with heat and light. The drums subsided into a thrumming whisper just above the threshold of her hearing.

Then she heard Jaquar's voice.

"What do you have there?" he asked sharply.

Light painted the insides of her eyelids red and she realized she'd closed her eyes. She opened them and shook her head.

Jaquar stood a pace in front of her. "Can I see what you have?"

Marian blinked up at him. Tension was back in his superb frame, lining his face. "I—" It came out as a squeak lower than Tuck's at his quietest. She tried harder. "I think this fell to the floor when you took the model off the shelf." Relaxing every muscle of her hand, her fingers curled open to show the thread.

Jaquar's mouth tightened. "The weapon-knot."

"Weapon?" Marian asked faintly.

He nodded. "Interesting that you can handle it. I never could."

"What kind of weapon?"

"I don't know. *We*, the Circlets of the Tower, don't know."

"Please explain," Marian asked.

Shrugging, Jaquar said, "As usual, after a successful Tower raising, I had an open house." He grinned. "You get gifts. Entanra brought the model of the Singer's Abbey, and I put it on the shelf. When I started cataloguing my gifts the next day, the knot was here. I didn't know what it was, but I could feel the energy. My parents had spent the night, and Mother realized it was a weapon, but not what sort or how to use it. We sensed its danger. None of us touched it. I never did. Now, there it is, in your hand." He nodded to the thread.

Marian opened her hand flat. She seemed to have mastered the latent energy of the thread. The drums were muffled. The dark-red strands of the floss gleamed wetly, like living arteries. If they'd pulsed, Marian would have dropped them and run screaming from the room. She tried for a casual tone.

"I suppose you untie the knots to loose the weapon."

"Probably, but do you want to try it?"

"No!"

He laughed shortly. "Neither do I."

"Should I put it back?"

Jaquar turned and strode back to the door. He opened it and started down the steps, his voice echoing hollowly back to her. "Do what you please. As I said, I never could handle it. Consider it yours."

Her fingers closed back over the floss. Carefully, she returned it to the shelf.

Jaquar stood at the night-black windows of his Ritual room, the northeastern windows facing the Dark's nest. Marian and the mousekin had retired and now was time for thought—which should have been full of regret, but wasn't.

He'd done it. Despite his original plans, despite all that was wise, despite the vengeance that still raged inside him, he'd made a Song with the new Exotique.

In the weeks since he'd found the nest, with around-the-clock Scholars and Circlets watching it from other planes, they'd only discovered that the place wasn't true north, but northeast. During that time, the Exotique had gone from Apprentice to Scholar with lightning speed. Then, just a few moments ago, she'd strolled to the weapon-knot and picked it up, as easily as if she plucked lint from her gown.

Obviously she was the one to send into the nest, to learn of the monsters and the master and the Dark. To harm it, perhaps destroy it.

A hive of activity seethed around the maw of the nest, as if it would disgorge new sangviles soon. Sangviles that had hideously destroyed his parents, killed exponentially, and threatened the Tower Community.

Yet he had formed a bond with her. Vengeance warred with desire. Not the desire of baseless lust, but of affection mixed with caring.

He'd liked holding her.

He couldn't send her. Not without great preparation, spells of protection, knowledge. Jaquar knew her now—Marian. Not the Exotique, the tool for revenge, but Marian, the eager Scholar with shadows in her eyes from pain for her brother. The woman who had a ridiculous but powerful mousie as a companion.

He'd liked having her hands on him even more than he'd enjoyed holding her. The dance had been wonderful. Inside the moment, his despair had dropped from him until there was only the woman and the emotions she made him feel.

The emotions, the Song that had resonated between them. Affection, desire, even delight in the discovery of one who shared talents and thought processes.

He could not send her to her destruction.

His hands fisted and a great pressure built inside his chest— grief needing to break free. But he didn't know how to release it. It filled him until he could hear it pounding in his ears, stinging his eyes, drying his throat.

Beating at the shields of his emotions.

Fumbling, he opened the latch of one of the floor-length windows, stepped out onto the roof of his study, raised his arms and called the wind.

A gale whirled around him, sucked him up inside it, and he was the strength and the power and the raging of it. The funnel spun him away, shrieking out his rage. Then air whipped his eyes and he laughed until tears ran down his face.

He rode the wind into a storm.

Another awakening in a new place…. The next morning, Marian blinked sleep away, her eyes growing used to the gloom—and the silence. The undertone of the music of the island, of Jaquar's Tower, of inanimate objects still pulsed, but there was no clatter of Tuck. Or of Bossgond.

Or Jaquar—though, as she thought of him she heard notes cascading from above like those from musical strings.

Sighing, she stretched under the quilt. There was a feel to the room as if the season was deep winter—the chamber was warm and dark and cozy, with threatening cold outside. It seemed to have missed rejuvenating spring. Frowning, she tested the whole Tower and found that the "winter" was Jaquar's underlying grief and low-level depression, the "threat" was the sangvile.

She didn't want to remember the image of the sangvile.

And the quiet was too much. So she hurried to the shower cabinet and bathed and dressed. Then she left her rooms for the corridor that bisected the floor, and went to the door to the staircase tower and up.

She learned something immediately. Jaquar's Tower wasn't nearly as soundproof as Bossgond's.

"No! I won't. That's final." His tone was sharp even through the door.

He'd said no to Bossgond. Was the old mage pressuring him again?

"I'll see you this evening, and I'll come alone."

Marian hesitated. Should she strum the doorharp or leave?

"Marian, Marian," squeaked Tuck. He scrabbled on the other side of the door, tiny paws showing under the crack.

"Scholar Marian awaits me. Until later," Jaquar said tersely.

So Marian ran her thumbnail over the doorharp and smiled at the pleasing riff of notes. She wanted to do it again, and recalled how Alexa had enjoyed sounding Bossgond's. Easily amused, we Earth women, she thought with a smile, then looked up as Jaquar opened the door.

He was scowling.

She curtsied. Tuck shot forward and patted her foot in greeting. She scooped him up and put him on her shoulder. "Good morning, Tuck."

The hamster cuddled close to her neck, thrummed against her throat. With surprise, she realized a Song ran between her and her companion now. They'd both progressed in their own way to make one. And it resonated with memory-tones of Earth as well as new and exciting experiences in Lladrana.

Jaquar took a pace back and held the door wide. "Come in. I have reviewed your work in the planet spheres. They continue to progress extremely well. It is definitely time to start your practicum. We will work outside this morning."

Marian raised her brows. "Good morning to you, too." She entered the room.

Color deepened under the golden tone of his cheekbones. He inhaled deeply, closed the door quietly behind her. Then he inclined his torso in an elegant half bow that emphasized his body under the fine cream-colored linen shirt and brown suede trousers he wore. "Forgive me, I was concentrating on work." He gestured her in. "Breakfast is in the hotbox."

Something about him was different. She studied him

closely from under her eyelashes. He was pale, lines of weariness slightly deeper at the corners of his eyes, but his muscles seemed…looser. He no longer hummed with stress. With exquisite care, she sought the tune echoing between them, analyzing it. The edge of his grief was gone, mellowed into resignation. Perhaps the feeling of melancholy would soon fade from his Tower, too. He wouldn't thank her for commenting on either him or his Tower, though.

He led her to the chairs they'd sat in last night when she'd revived his terrariums. When she sat, he placed a lovely black lacquered tray over her knees. The dishes looked like fine china, but the coffee mug was sturdy. On her plate was an omelette—since two sorts of cheese oozed out the end and the top had a sprig of what looked like dill, she could only hope that the meal was more than fuel.

Cautiously she tried a bite, and moaned in pleasure at the delicious mixture of tastes.

That pulled him from his brooding and he actually smiled. "I'd heard that Bossgond's meals weren't too tasty."

"Mmm," Marian said. She didn't want to criticize Bossgond, but couldn't disagree. "I would have liked to interview the cook who arrived, though."

"You can trust Alyeka," Jaquar said.

Marian smiled. "Yes." In fact, Alexa was the *only* one Marian trusted.

Meanwhile, she enjoyed the meal he placed before her and darted looks around his den as he sat staring into his coffee.

Tuck had already eaten and was exploring Jaquar's study. From the hamster's comments, she understood that he found it a wonderfully fragrant and interesting place. She wanted to investigate, too, but from Jaquar's closed expression, figured that he'd hustle her out of his space and on to the less intimate environs of the island as soon as she took her last sip of the excellent coffee.

She'd already noticed that his octagonal room captured more sunlight than Bossgond's round Tower.

He had more bell jars than Bossgond—for experimenting with weather? And a lot of what most Earth people would call magical tools—staffs of different woods and metals, *wands,* ceremonial knives with no edge and wickedly sharp daggers. There was also a collection of small boxes, as varied as the staffs, and Marian longed to open them all and see what treasures they held.

The chamber had an underlying elegance that was so much a part of Jaquar. She took her gaze from the sweeping shelves of tidy books to the man as he lounged, and a stray thought came that he'd be devastating in a tuxedo. Not that she'd ever see him in one.

He wasn't what she'd expected. Of course she'd only met him briefly, but she'd sensed he was trying to sweep her away with his charm. Since they'd met again, he hadn't acted deliberately charming at all, and she liked that.

In fact, she liked him, and the Song that twined between them. They had much in common—love and concern for their family, a passion for study, and weather Power. Absently, she drained her cup and set it on the tray.

"Are you ready?"

"Yes."

He whistled a note and the dishes disappeared. Marian grinned. For all the times she'd seen the spell, it was still one of her favorites. She'd learned the task her second evening with Bossgond.

Jaquar tilted his head, his gaze fixed on Tuck, who was

sniffing the lowest shelf of boxes. "Tuck, Marian and I will be spending the morning outside. Will you be fine here?"

"Yes." Tuck didn't even look in their direction.

"Can you please stay in this room?"

Tuck hesitated, raised his head and looked at them. He bobbed. "Yes."

"Thank you," Jaquar said, still polite.

His manner toward Tuck warmed Marian. That was another thing she and Jaquar had in common—they liked and respected Tuck. Marian had always sensed that Bossgond wanted to dissect Tuck, searching to see if the atomball he ate was still lodged somewhere inside.

Still courteous, Jaquar led the way to the narrow curving stairs and started down them. Marian carefully shut the door behind her, testing it to make sure it was shut, then followed Jaquar.

He strode from the bottom of the stairway turret through the hallway on the bottom floor of his Tower and threw open the heavy front door. Bright sunshine painted the hallway floor yellow. Interesting that both Bossgond and Jaquar had main entrances that faced east—was that a male thing, an innate preference to look toward Lladrana and not out to the sea, or did all main doors face east?

He went out and stopped at the edge of a golden line—his protective spell, no doubt—and carved a door in it with his telescoping wand that currently was the size of Alexa's baton.

Marian stood at the threshold and inhaled the scent of Mue Island—it was as different from Alf as Jaquar was from Bossgond. There was more of the mainland scent, since the island was closer to Lladrana; there was also more ocean because the island was smaller. The fragrances of the island soil and flowers and trees varied subtly, and were more pleasing to her than the astringent air around Bossgond's tower. The atmosphere burgeoned with early summer.

Her spirits lifted and she caught herself humming counterpoint to the tune of the island, a tune that was one chord of the melody comprising Jaquar's personal Song. Then Marian sighed. Would she be here on Amee long enough to fully develop her own Song?

The wish to stay condensed into a hard kernel of yearning within her—something she couldn't fulfill if she wanted to be near Andrew.

Jaquar motioned for her to join him. When she did, he hesitated a moment, then took her hand, closing his fingers over hers. Warmth, and simple pleasure at the easy link flowed through Marian and she smiled up at him.

He returned her smile, and it reached his eyes, banishing the dark shadows of grief.

"As I said last night, we'll start with wind and clouds. The best place for that is on the western coast of the island where the wind blows in from the ocean." He shrugged. "There are only a couple of tiny islands that no one of the Tower Community has claimed between Mue and the Brisay Sea."

Excitement bubbled through her. She would have rubbed her hands, but wanted to keep her fingers in his. "Great!"

He chuckled. "I don't anticipate that you will have any problems with the clouds—that's Second Degree Scholar work and you are at the upper edge of Third Degree."

Her step hesitated.

"What?" he asked.

"Third Degree means something entirely different—a negative connotation in my own language."

Interest sharpened his gaze. "What?"

Oh boy. How to define the phrase? "It is a very harsh interrogation by the authorities." And then "the authorities" needed explaining.

They had walked across a meadow of tall grass to a grove of evergreen trees, and Marian looked back to see the Tower in its entirety.

As she'd suspected, the lower two floors were of greater diameter and the reddish stone looked small, more like cobblestones or bricks. The other three stories were definitely octagonal, with large pairs of pointed windows, airy and graceful from the outside as well as the inside.

She frowned. Every few feet around the lower two stories were jagged dark marks, like soot or gunpowder. She stopped and stared. "What happened?"

Jaquar tensed beside her, then replied neutrally. "Even as a Circlet, fire isn't my strong suit. As I raised the Tower and called Lightning, it came—and singed the stone, *and* pointed directly to my keystone. I couldn't clean it, so the only option was to call it down several times to keep the stone's location secret."

"There must be twenty marks around the base of your Tower."

Jaquar dropped her hand, turned and strode away. "I called a lightning storm. That was the result. I was still quite young at the time."

It was obviously a sore point, so she abandoned the subject and hurried to catch up with him. "Is the meadow close?" She hadn't walked so much since her trip to Paris as she had the past two and a half weeks.

"Close enough. Your practice with clouds—" he glanced up as if confirming there were plenty to work with "—should only take a quarter-hour. Then you can progress to other 'air' lessons such as Calling the Wind. The meadow is flat and also a perfect spot to practice Wind Dancing."

Calling the Wind. Wind Dancing. Anticipation zipped through her. "How lovely," she said, and swung into step with him.

He looked down at her and chuckled. "You're a Sorceress through and through."

"A scholar," she said, nodding. "I always have been." Wistfully, she thought back to her apartment, her old studies. They'd been ongoing, but not nearly as enticing as learning magic—Power.

The moment they reached the meadow, he put her to work. They lay side by side on the sunny grass and looked up at the clouds. After all the time she'd spent with the terrariums, it was easy for her to send her mind and will and Power into the sky to shape the clouds and move them around. She was concentrating so on proving her worth that the awareness of his big body beside hers, nearly touching, almost didn't register. Almost.

She couldn't afford the distraction of thinking about the strong aura of him, the well-formed muscles, the thickness and sheen of his hair....

It had definitely been too damn long since she'd had sex. And the moment *that* idea crossed her mind, the cloud she'd been herding disintegrated into a dozen little ones. Luckily, Jaquar had just said, "Done." Her timing had been perfect.

Still, she didn't roll over to look at him, but scrambled to her feet, took a handkerchief from her gown pocket and wiped her forehead. Then she grinned at him, pretending the heat in her had been generated by her Power instead of thoughts of rolling around with him. "What's next?" she asked.

His eyes narrowed, then took on a twinkle. The little Song between them spiked in intensity and beat, but he replied with a smile, "Now you Call the Wind."

16

Marian clasped her hands together to keep them from trembling with excitement. Her first real use of Weather Magic came now!

Again Jaquar's instructions were succinct and the Songspell easy to learn. The whistling words and rushing rhythm made innate sense to Marian, as if she'd always known this Song. She only needed to discover it within herself.

So she lifted her arms and spoke-sang the spell, and a gentle breeze wafted tendrils of her hair that had escaped her braid, then died when she laughed, forgetting to hold it. She looked to Jaquar, aching to share her delight in this first real proof of her magic. Bossgond was so old, she didn't think he remembered what it felt like when magic was new and exhilarating and shooting through your veins.

Jaquar was relaxed, leaning against a tree and smiling at her. Since he also had the old-memory look in his eyes, she guessed that he recalled very well how she felt. Their eyes met. Another moment shared.

A bubble of happiness broke from her mouth in a giggle. She lifted her hand to put it over her mouth at the silly sound, then let her fingers drop. She didn't need to be anyone except her essential self here and now, did not need to wear a mask, to project an image. So she laughed and stretched her arms high and shouted, "Yes!" Then, "What's next?" she asked eagerly.

He didn't move from the tree at the edge of the clearing, staying out of her magical space, giving her room to work. His brows rose. "Now you summon a stronger wind." His gaze turned considering. He rested his hands on his hips, nodded decisively. "I think you are ready to Call the Zephyr, the wind you will use most often over land to modify weather, and Dance with it." He swept a judging glance over her and she sensed he was examining the potency and energy of her Power. "Ready?"

Marian shifted, settled into a stance that connected her with the island. "Yes."

"This is the Zephyr Songspell." He sang it and the richness of his tenor thrilled her so, that she had to ask him for the first words again. She flushed when she didn't get it right the first time. Patiently he repeated the words.

She mouthed the whole Song to herself, then looked at him with drawn brows. "Can I alter a few words? They seem a little—" she opened and closed her hands as if trying to grasp something "—masculine. Or something."

He tilted his head. "Which words do you want to alter? Tell me your Song."

Running through it again with the minor modifications, she waited, not breathing, until he nodded. "That will do fine.

You *are* a quick study, and progressing, too, if you are shaping the Songs to fit you."

She nodded in return, licked her lips and loosened her shoulders. Then she raised her arms and sang.

The breeze spun around her, bringing all the scents of spring—the wildflowers as well as the awakening soil, the hints of dark pine and fading blossoms from the forested hills—and she laughed in delight.

"Keep control," Jaquar instructed, "but provide more energy, more Power, more stirring and *push*. See if you can have it lift you from your feet. The air is already in motion, it shouldn't be too difficult."

The thought of it, and her breeze, took her breath from her. She followed directions. In her mind's eye, she visualized her large yellow mixing bowl, the whisk she used to beat eggs, and applied the memory of physically whipping the eggs to the use of her Power. In an instant the wind increased, battered her, flipped her gown high around her waist, lifted her several feet in the air, spinning her. The little grooming spell on her long hair didn't survive. Strands lashed her face. Her laugh turned into a shriek, part excitement, mostly fear.

She didn't know what to do next. The wind was too strong for her.

Hold. Jaquar's calm voice came in her mind and she didn't know if he spoke to her or the wind. *And still.*

The rotation of the air—of her—slowed, and she lowered. She misjudged the height and the moment when the breeze stopped, and landed awkwardly off balance. She took a couple of stumbling steps, windmilled, but fell.

Then she stared at the blue sky and the clouds…clouds she could move and shape. She stretched out her arms—she felt as if she were breaking from a constricting cocoon. Yes. More, more, more!

Jaquar's shadow fell over her and the man himself looked down with an odd expression on his face, as if he'd been surprised by some new fact that killed a pet theory of his.

Marian laughed. Though handsome as the devil, he was like many other scholars she'd known. Like her.

So she smiled up at him.

His face scrunched further, emotions warring behind his gaze. Then a great breath escaped him. He smiled, sadly, shrugged and offered her his hand.

She took it and welcomed the Song that rang between them. It was all part of the beauty of the day.

With a tug, he drew her to her feet.

And into his arms.

She glanced up at him in surprise and he took advantage of her parted lips to press his mouth on hers…and everything else faded.

The kiss seared through her like a scorching wind, leaving her knees so weak that she leaned against him and learned him in a whole new way—his body in intimate comparison to hers. Taller, broader, stronger.

Harder.

Except his lips—they were soft and intoxicating, nibbling at her mouth just as the sensuality of their Song nibbled at her reason.

For a while she just gloried in the rush of passion, of all the sensations that told her she was strong and womanly and desired. His arm was a solid bar across her back, holding but not forcing. His other hand curved around her hip, then squeezed as he exhaled a small groan. The tip of his tongue penetrated her mouth and she tasted him, exotic and spicy and rich as the darkest bittersweet chocolate. She wanted more of this, too.

The music was nearly overwhelming. If she let it, the melody could sweep away reason and logic and sense. Something that had happened before only at the peak of orgasm. She should be frightened at the undercurrents and riptide of passion, but instead it was tempting, for once in her life, to forget reason and only *feel*.

His hand went to her bottom, brought her into his body and against his hard erection. A moan of hunger escaped her—she wasn't positioned quite…right. But his mouth had moved from hers to below her ear, trailing down her jaw to her neck, and her skin heated and her pulse pounded and she thought she was melting into him. The beat of their music wound tight.

A moment later he lowered her to the ground, followed her down to lay beside her, his hand going to her breasts.

The ground was sun-warmed beneath her, but it hummed an alien tune. No familiar Song of Mother Earth, but something odd and thready and broken that jolted her from the haze of passion.

She rolled away. His hand reached, but she kept moving until she was beyond his grasp, beyond his close scent that called to her to mate. Marian forced herself to one elbow, then the other. Panting, she dared not look at him in case she lost all rationality again. The man was definitely dangerous.

He stood and said nothing. She didn't think he'd offer his hand again, but in case he did, she scrambled to her feet.

She'd known the sexual awareness was there, had half-fantasized about the man, but didn't realize until now how utterly she could succumb to him. It wasn't just fighting her own attraction to him, but fighting his great magnetism. And the Song that spiraled between them burst into full orchestral

Power when they touched. Too many things were in the "minus" column, but the way her body felt, the way he made her feel beautiful were huge pluses.

Not looking at him, she shook out her dress—unnecessary since there weren't any wrinkles—to give herself something to do. Then her hands went to her hair and she tunelessly whispered the grooming spell that tucked strands smoothly into a braid. He gazed at her.

"I thought," he said in a husky voice, "you had a repetition of that vision you received the moment we met so soon after you were Summoned. But that isn't why you drew away, is it?"

Marian composed her expression and looked at him. His eyes were deep blue, and she thought she could see sparks in them. His lips were more red than she'd seen on any Lladranan. She ran a tongue around her own and found them plump, and the taste of him jolted her once more. She took a step back.

"No." She wasn't sure she could explain why the Song of the world of Amee had affected her so.

"Since we are on the topic of our first meeting, what revelation *did* you have about me?" His muscles tensed.

"I don't know," she said on a sigh, and met his now cool gaze. "Just that you were my doom." It sounded stupid.

He stood and looked down at her, expression serious. "My emotions were raw at that time."

She narrowed her eyes. He was still keeping something from her—but what right did she have to demand he tell his secrets? None. They had a lot in common, but they weren't close friends. Acquaintances, colleagues—with him being the senior—perhaps even bordering on lovers… That might be it! She worked it out in her mind, slowly speaking the logic aloud.

"Are you talking about a bond between us—like I have with Bossgond—that might have harmed me?"

"My emotions were raw," he said again, with just enough emphasis for her to know that he hated admitting it.

"I've learned that bonding with people here can keep me on Amee instead of returning me to Earth during the Snap." She turned her arm so he could see the two magical tattoos—Bossgond's yellow bird and Alexa's jade baton.

Jaquar's mouth twisted. "You already have two bonds, and you still want to go back to your brother." He started walking, but not toward his Tower. Another lesson? Perhaps. They were both dedicated scholars.

"Bossgond has been solitary for a long time. He knows how much my brother Andrew means to me and has said he'd help me return—perhaps even come back to Amee if I'm successful in helping my brother. So he won't hold on to me." Marian matched steps with Jaquar. "As for Alexa—she's from Earth so her bond isn't completely Lladranan. She, too, understands about my brother and wouldn't keep me here against my will."

"Sounds logical, but what is logical in theory is not often true in reality," Jaquar said softly.

Soon they reached a tiny cove surrounded by rock. Narrowing her eyes, Marian thought she could see the coastline of Lladrana—so this was the eastern side of Mue Island.

"You are excellent with Wind— Fourth Degree edging into fifth," Jaquar said. "Let's work with Water and Rain. There are several pools in the cove where you can practice tides and surf and wave. The cove itself is an excellent shape and size to develop rain. We won't work with thunderstorms today—that is best conducted on the far southwest of the island."

That was a blessing. Marian was beginning to feel tired.

Jaquar gestured to a nearby pool. "Why don't you start with something simple, like evaporating the water and holding it in the air."

Marian walked over to the pool, smiling, then stopped. "I can't." She shook her head. "There are creatures in this pool. I can't harm them." She glanced at Jaquar, to see an approving look in his eyes.

He nodded shortly. "Good. You have a strong ethical basis *and* a realization that the use of your Power to modify Weather could greatly affect them."

"Thank you," she murmured.

"However, the residents of this particular pool won't be affected by your evaporation unless you also draw all the moisture out of their bodies—"

Ick.

"—and I'll be here to ensure that doesn't happen."

That's when the work began.

The water was slippery—as slippery to hold with her mind as it was to cup in her hands. Time and again she slowly lifted the water, to find it escaping her mental grasp before she could fold it into the air. She started enthusiastically with about a pitcherful, but after a couple of hours she was down to a cupful, and of that, could only make a few drops evaporate.

Jaquar was so even-tempered that it grated on her nerves. She sweated in the warm sunlight and he lounged on a rock, writing on a scroll and watching her lack of accomplishment.

Exasperated, she rounded on him—and found his patience was nothing but a pose, his mouth curved in an amused smile.

"What are you laughing at?"

He just raised his brows. "I was wondering if you would prove to be the exception to the rule that Weather Sorcerers are better in one element than others. It would have been trying if you were perfect."

Marian stopped in midsnarl, relaxed. Then she rubbed her temples. "The water is so damn *slippery.*"

"It is at that," he said in suspicious agreement.

"I suppose you have no trouble with water."

"I had the same amount of trouble with it as you are having when I was a first-degree Scholar."

She sighed. "A long time ago. So it will take me years to become proficient with it."

"Probably, even though your Power is strong and you've advanced rapidly, this could be your weak point."

She had others—her need for perfection was one. She grimaced. "I suppose we should call it a day."

"Yes, I have my own studies this evening, but I will leave you with my entire medical library to peruse."

That drove every other thought out of her mind. "Great!" Her eyebrows dipped. "Something—I don't know—something today made me think that there *is* help for him here." She couldn't understand it, but once she spoke the words aloud, she knew it was true. She instinctively believed Lladrana had the answers her brother needed.

Jaquar stared at her thoughtfully. "Everyone has been speaking about you—that would include Alyeka, and she knows your world and ours. Today you called the Wind and the Zephyr. There might have been notes of a tune, perhaps even a melody within the winds that told you this."

She blinked at him, then wondered if she'd *ever* understand enough about Lladranan Power.

When they reached Jaquar's tower, his huge black flying horse was cropping grass near the building. The sight of packs loaded on the volaran made Marian blink. Nothing in the world—in *two* worlds—looked less like a beast of burden.

It raised its head, tossed its mane and whinnied. Marian heard a faint *Heyy* in her head, obviously a greeting. It watched her with huge dark eyes, seeming as interested in her as she was in it.

Jaquar strode over to it and stroked its neck, his face softening into a smile. Then he glanced up at Marian. "This is Nightsky. He is honoring me with his companionship." Jaquar whistled and the packs vanished in a riffling breeze. Marian made an involuntary sound—she'd noticed the hem of one of her gowns and it was hard to see it disappear again. She bit her lip and looked up at the Tower.

"I sent them to my study," Jaquar said.

She nodded.

"Come meet Nightsky."

There was nothing she wanted more. She walked slowly to the volaran, held out her hand, fingers down, for him to snuffle. *Heyy,* he said again, aloud and in her mind. Slowly lifting his muzzle, he sniffed at her hair. *Good.* It was more of a feeling and an image—of a lump of sugar—than a word.

Marian laughed and Jaquar smiled. "Not many volarans deign to speak to humans. We are honored." He bowed to the horse, who blew air from his nostrils.

Going to the steed's other side, Marian stroked him herself. His coat was finer, silkier than a horse's, feeling almost like tiny feathers, over a strong muscular body. She frowned. "How do they fly?"

She met Jaquar's eyes.

He raised his brows and smiled. He patted the volaran again. "We have studied that and have come to the conclusion that they are pure magic—Power."

The volaran felt awfully solid to her. She narrowed her eyes at Jaquar. He shrugged.

"Very well. It's a combination of aerodynamics—" the word barely translated in Marian's mind "—and Power."

"He's real, physical."

"Of course."

Marian shook her head, smiling. Pleasure emanated from the winged horse, wrapping around both her and Jaquar. The smile faded from Jaquar's gaze, turning into something more—affection, tenderness. They held the stare and the late-afternoon air warmed, almost sparkled, definitely hummed. Added was the resonant note of the nearby Tower and wildness mixed with Power that was Nightsky.

The soft mood spun between them—affection, respect, this shared moment that contented them both.

A sharp trill of metallic chimes echoed from the open window of Jaquar's Tower. His expression turned wry. "I'd say that Bossgond sent you a crystal ball and he wants to speak with you."

Bossgond. *Andrew!* The old man had promised to keep track of Andrew for her. She ran to the door of the Tower, flapped her hands at Jaquar to hurry him up. It didn't work. He sauntered to her.

She gritted her teeth, she wanted to hop up and down. "Bossgond may have news of my brother, Andrew!"

Jaquar's brows winged up. "What?"

"Bossgond has binoculars focused on Earth—Exotique Terre—and my brother."

"Those binocs of his are trans-dimensional?"

"Yes, yes!" She stepped aside and let him chant the opening spell under his breath. He strode through the corridor and over to the stairs. She hurried after him.

They ascended fast and flung open the door at the top. He stopped and she tried to jostle by him, but the man filled the small doorway. She poked him and he stepped aside, shaking his head and staring.

She followed his gaze. Tuck had unwrapped all the packages and had made a nice nest of her underwear. Marian trapped a groan in her throat, felt her face warm with embarrassment. It wouldn't be so bad except the garments were like her—Exotique.

The chime came again and she leaped for the small yellow glass ball sitting atop the folds of her maroon dress. The orb was small enough to fit in her hand. She curled her fingers over it and said, "Hello? Hello?" When nothing happened, she shook it, like it was a snow-globe, then stared at it futilely.

Jaquar plucked it from her hand, held it in his palm and tapped his thumbnail against the glass. "Bossgond," he said.

Bossgond's face stared out at them, scowling.

"Andrew?" asked Marian.

The old man's frown deepened. "He looks as usual. Salutations, Marian."

She let out a relieved breath. "Salutations, Bossgond." She dipped her head a little in courtesy.

He studied her, face smoothing into his usual grumpy wrinkles. "I need—wanted to ensure that you were well."

"Very well. Today I heard something in the wind that said I might find help for Andrew."

Bossgond snorted, looked at Jaquar. "Report on the Scholar Marian," Bossgond demanded.

Marian's face went perfectly blank. An oral evaluation with her present?

"She is progressing well," Jaquar said easily. "Level five with Wind, a solid level one in Water."

Grunting, Bossgond said, "Has a problem with Ocean, eh? Wasn't noticeable in the ecospheres."

"No," Jaquar agreed.

"Told you she was best with Lightning, so is naturally

weakest with Ocean. Have you given her any practicums in Lightning?"

Jaquar's cheeks tinted red. "No. That will come the easiest, and the best Lightning Study grounds are at the far end of the island."

"Very well. I heard from Chalmon that the maw of the nest is quite active."

Marian listened sharply. This wasn't a topic she knew of or understood.

Jaquar shrugged. "It has been so the past few days. Hard to extrapolate what is happening or may occur."

Bossgond grunted again, turned his stare back to Marian. He smiled, and Marian nearly jumped at the unexpected charm of it.

"The cook is good, Marian." Bossgond licked his lips. "Thank you."

She returned his smile. "You're welcome."

He seemed hesitant. "I miss you," he said gruffly.

Touched, Marian felt tears behind her eyes. "I miss you, too."

"I'm working on a Sending to return you to Exotique Terre. We can probably do it in the time period you require—three more weeks."

Squinting into the small orb, Marian could see his desk piled with papers and scrolls and books. She cleared her throat. "Thank you."

He nodded, glanced at her, then Jaquar. "Proceed with her training. When she is close to Circlet in all areas, bring her back to me."

Jaquar raised his eyebrows, but all he said was, "Yes."

"Good studies," Bossgond said, and the crystal ball went dark.

"Marian! Jaquar," Tuck said, sitting in his nest of Marian's underwear.

She hurried over and picked him up. Holding him up to eye level, she said, "Hello, Tuck."

"Hello, Marian. Hello, Jaquar," Tuck said. "Marian did well today?"

"Very well," Jaquar assured the hamster seriously. "She has great Power and will and is rapidly learning basic technique in Wind. She just needs the skill of control."

Marian flushed at the memory of tipping and falling in the wind. She hoped she did better with Lightning.

Tuck nodded. "I will tell Sinafin."

Jaquar continued. "She is not as skilled with Ocean."

Tuck waved a paw. "Water is not as important for Marian as fire."

They stared at him, then at each other. Though they both had a thirst for knowledge, Marian sensed Jaquar was as reluctant as she was to question Tuck about Sinafin. This whole conversation seemed to be straying into prophecy. From the tension in Jaquar's muscles, Marian thought he no more wished to learn of the future or Sinafin's agenda than she did.

"Nice garments," Jaquar said, and Marian realized he was staring at her underwear. He grinned wickedly. "They look better on Marian, though."

With a sniff, Marian set Tuck on her shoulder, scooped up her clothing and held out her hand for the crystal ball.

Suddenly she wanted to be alone and as far away as she could from all the strangeness—which meant holing up in her rooms. "With your permission, Circlet Jaquar, I would like to retire to my rooms and eat dinner there." Maybe she could conjure up food that was close to American cuisine. "I think you have an appointment this evening."

All expression vanished from his face, and Marian stilled in wariness. Cool, unreadable blue eyes met hers.

"That I do. I will transfer my lorebooks on medicine to your desk." He turned and walked away.

Tuck's claws dug into her shoulder. *Danger,* he said.

"How do you know?"

"Sinafin said—"

"Am I safe here in the Tower?"

He came up close and rubbed against her neck, his soft fur comforting as well as tickling. "Yes."

She nodded decisively. "I'll be careful." Walking to the stairs, she started down. There had been that warning premonition about Jaquar. Thinking about the man—his sad and steady blue eyes, the lovely dance they'd shared, the fun of playing with the Wind—created a warmth inside her. The sexual attraction between them was potent. She also liked him a great deal—and that was a priority. Never again would she let simple physical attraction lure her into intimacy with a man as she had with the late, unlamented associate professor Jack Wilse.

But Jaquar Dumont was not Jack Wilse. The Sorcerer had a *presence,* probably from his mastery of Power, that Marian believed Wilse would never have.

Jaquar definitely made her insides tingle and her toes curl. What harm could it do to have a good, hot fling here in Lladrana?

She didn't know.

She had no idea what sort of ramifications emotionally, but more importantly, socially, a sexual affair might entail. The worst was the idea of a bond. They already had a potent Song between them—stronger even than hers with Bossgond, and that had included blood.

She'd have to beware of becoming emotionally involved with Jaquar. She couldn't afford to have sex with him—not if it would bind her to Lladrana.

17

Though Marian had gone to her rooms to feel less alien, the rooms were, of course, as different from her own apartment in Boulder as everything else on Lladrana was different from her other life. She sat at the intricately carved desk, which repeated the pattern of Jaquar's golden circlet, and brooded. By the time she'd reached the apprentice suite a few minutes earlier, books and scrolls had already materialized on her desk.

Tuck had clamored to explore, so she'd put him down and heard scrambling and peeps in the background as he took stock of her quarters.

She'd spent most of her time in practical lessons and hadn't read much the past few days—a unique situation for her. Usually she consumed books, both fiction and nonfiction. After eyeing the books, she knew when she opened one that it would be in unfamiliar script. She *had* bonded with Bossgond, who certainly knew how to read, and Alexa who probably knew how to read in both English and Lladranan, so Marian *should* be able to read, too.

She propped her head on her elbows and rubbed her temples. A slight *whoosh* came to her ears, and the Tower's atmosphere changed subtly. Jaquar was gone.

Tension drained from her, and only then did she realize that she'd been waiting for him to leave. Now she was totally alone for the first time since she'd arrived on Lladrana, and it felt… good. Not at all scary.

As he flew on Nightsky to Chalmon's island, Jaquar considered Marian. Since the dance the night before, she had seldom left his thoughts.

Jaquar shouldn't want to bond with Marian. She wasn't staying in Lladrana, and the heartache wasn't worth the passion. He lied to himself. With Marian, he felt so alive, so complemented by another person, that he knew the sex would be better than he'd ever had.

But he wanted more. He wanted what his parents had had.

Bossgond had called to check up on him, and that fired Jaquar's blood. As if Bossgond thought he'd hurt her…continue with his original plan. It had been tempting, until he kissed her. Then Sending her to the Dark's maw had become impossible.

Even now, unemotional logic said that her connection with the weapon-knot made her perfect for the task of destroying the nest. All she had to do was pull a thread…and kill herself.

Perhaps that was not true. No one knew how Powerful the knot was, whether it would destroy the nest, whether it would kill if she used it. But he wouldn't mention this to Chalmon and Venetria.

No one knew whether the nest would be wounded, how

much, if Marian was Sent there. So logic bolstered his emotional decision. He wanted vengeance, but not at the expense of an injured Marian. His goals had changed. He would not use Marian as a weapon against the Dark. He'd convince Chalmon and Venetria not to act on their own. Now he must concentrate on teaching Marian, and *her* best weapon would be Lightning.

Marian still hadn't opened a book when Tuck cheeped excitedly, "What's this, what's this, what's *this?*" A scrabbling noise. *"Food!"*

Marian tilted her head. She didn't recall having any food in her rooms. There was a crash from the bedroom. It sounded... Earthlike. Dread speared her, she shoved back the chair and ran into the bedroom, yelling "Light!" Fire crackled to life in the fireplace. Crystal globes flared brightly.

Tuck put his paws over his eyes, squeaking indignantly. "Hurts!"

Humming, Marian lowered the light, then saw the destruction. Her stomach cramped.

Tuck sat in the midst of the remains of her PDA. She stared at it, horrified. Tiny electronic parts, as esoteric to her as any magic she'd learned, were scattered in bits around the hamster. Anger flashed through her. She'd considered the PDA her very own tangible link with her homeland. It had been the symbol of the control she had over her life, the knowledge she'd mastered—control that was currently missing in the chaos of adapting to a whole new world. She stared at the hamster, who sat back on his haunches and groomed his whiskers with tiny claws. Obviously he had the digits and Power to open the computer.

"What have you done?"

"It was dying."

She flinched. She hadn't wanted to admit that, even though she'd only been turning it on for a few seconds at a time to see familiar colors and menus and notes that represented her old life.

Tuck burped. "So I ate it."

"What?"

"I opened the nut up and ate the kernel. Now I know everything it knows."

Marian was speechless.

Tuck squeezed his eyes shut and emitted a huff. When he opened his eyes, they were all too sentient, all too understanding of her emotions. What had she kept in her Personal Notes section?

"Just like I ate the golden nut Sinafin gave me, I ate the nut inside that thing that beeped."

It had—every morning when it was time to leave for her bus to work, when she had important meetings, lunches, parties. Thanksgiving at her friends', for heaven's sake! Somehow she couldn't see Tuck beeping.

"You know everything?" she asked weakly.

"Pick up the laundry every Tuesday evening at 6:00 p.m.," he said, then continued, "Andrew's birthday March twenty-second."

"That's the appointment book," she confirmed. "May I pick you up?"

"Yes. It was a tiring dinner."

"Oh." She took Tuck, went to the armchair she'd created in which to talk to him and placed him in his tufted nest. He curled up and watched her with bright black eyes.

Marian settled into the deep chair. It conformed to her body and she sighed in pleasure. With a wave and just a little grief, she dissolved the remnants of her PDA into molecules and sent them into a storage lattice of Power that Bossgond had shown her how to use and had sent with her things that were now spread out on the bed. She wasn't sure how she'd use the complex molecules but was sure she'd figure out something.

Tuck blew out a breath.

She shook her head. "I really can't see how I can play Solitaire with you."

He hunched up and hummed quietly, just as her PDA had!

"Watch."

Midway between them, a small image of her last Solitaire game appeared.

"Wow. I'm impressed." She was beginning to enjoy herself. "Music?"

His eyes bulged even more than normal and he opened his mouth. Strains of "Over the Sea to Skye" played on guitar poured forth.

Marian listened, entranced, tears again coming to her eyes. This time they rolled down her cheeks. That had been her favorite track on the last album Andrew had given her. She summoned a tissue, wiped her eyes and blew her nose.

"You played that one the most," Tuck said, sitting again on his rump, paws in front of him.

"Yes."

"I didn't understand music before. Your music in the square nut is different from the Songs I learned when I crunched the golden walnut. I ate the shell of that nut, but not yours."

"I'm amazed that you could eat the meat of my 'nut' at all," she said.

He opened his mouth in what she'd come to know was his smile. "You liked the nut and didn't want it to die. I wanted more mind-food. I thought how I could do it, and I *did*."

Like person, like animal companion. "Yes, you did!" Songs. That meant prophecies in Lladrana. What sort of Songs had the golden walnut carried and Tuck absorbed? "So what did the Songs in your first nut say?"

His whiskers twitched, his paws clasped each other. "Sinafin said I was not to tell."

Marian could probably coax it from him, but respected him enough not to try. *She respected a hamster.* That sounded crazy. She bit down on her lip. He was an intelligent being, and he was her friend more than he was a pet or animal companion. And now he was the only thing she had from Earth. Her eyes widened in horror. And what would she do if she lost Tuck? The bits of plastic and glass and metal around him that had been her mainstay in Colorado were nothing compared to him.

She'd have to find some way to protect him.

He said, "You do not need to worry. I am very strong. I will live long, now, and I have much Power."

She wondered how much hamster and how much magical being Tuck was. It would be fascinating learning what he could do. Like Alexa, Tuck was now a mixture of Earth and Lladrana.

A twinge of anxiety nibbled at her. She didn't know how she'd be able to take him back to Earth. If he retained his Power on Earth, she shuddered at the idea of his falling into scientists' hands.

After chittering to get her attention, Tuck said, "I want to go back to my house now. I have good drink and salty nuts there. I want my better food."

Marian wanted to listen some more to Earth music. Instead she gestured to the speaking tube by the bed—this one with a trumpet painted like a blue morning glory and the tube a green stem with embossed varicolored green leaves. "Jaquar's study is locked to me. Can you climb up that?" Four floors.

He perked up. "Yes." Staring at her with his protuberant black eyes, Tuck said, "I'd like to go outside tomorrow with you and Jaquar. You can watch me."

"Are you sure?"

"Yes." He nodded emphatically.

"Very well. Ready to go upstairs?"

"Yes."

Marian set him in the bottom of the tube. He grinned at her, cheeped, and zoomed up the shaft. The opening strains of Mozart's "The Magic Flute" echoed down and kept her company as she headed back to her desk. Lladrana had changed Tuck, wondrously. Perhaps it could change Andrew, too.

Impatient that he had to explain himself to other Circlets, Jaquar strode into the parlor of Chalmon's Tower. Venetria and Chalmon stood by the large table, arguing. They stopped as soon as they saw him.

"Salutations," Jaquar said.

Chalmon placed a hand on Venetria's shoulder. "I think we all agree that we must cooperate and that the Dark can no longer be ignored. It was for that very reason that we had the Marshalls Summon our own Exotique."

Jaquar said, "Since she comes from outside our community, and is exceptionally Powerful, I think she will be an able leader, given time."

Frowning, Chalmon said, "We definitely need a report on the Exotique. That is why we asked you to come. We must learn when she will be ready to infiltrate the Dark's nest. All the signs point to the maw opening in the next couple of days. Will the Exotique be ready to enter then?"

"I have another idea," Jaquar said. "Perhaps we can form a team to seal the maw. Close their own shield. We may not be able to infiltrate it and learn of the Dark, but we could delay, perhaps even stop the master and the horrors he controls."

Chalmon tapped a crystal ball. "One of the younger Sorcerers tried to lob a fireball in—nothing. We've tried everything, and nothing works. All our Power slides away from the place. Nothing penetrates and nothing sticks." He grimaced. "Ten people have attempted spells."

Jaquar's gut tensed.

"Is it true the woman is already a Third Degree Scholar?" Venetria asked.

"True."

Both Chalmon and Venetria exclaimed in astonishment.

"When do you anticipate her becoming a Fifth Degree Scholar or a Circlet?" Chalmon asked.

Jaquar had already considered the question, estimated the time, lengthened it to protect Marian. "I believe no longer than a month."

"That's not soon enough." Chalmon's voice hardened. "I believe the maw will open within the week. We must send Marian in to learn of the Dark, to harm the nest and perhaps destroy this once-human master who taunts us and directs the horrors."

"I think your plan disastrous," Jaquar said. "What can you hope to learn through her?"

"I've made a little echoing spell—it will send back all she sees and hears when she is within the nest," Chalmon said.

"No," said Jaquar.

"It was your plan in the first place!" Chalmon snapped.

The words were like a blow to the chest. He nearly staggered. "Made in the heat of anger and vengeance."

Chalmon lifted and dropped a shoulder. "That may very well be true, but what choice do we have? You saw what *one* sangvile did. Its damage multiplies rapidly. Marian is very Powerful already. She might be able to return by herself. Who knows what she could do."

"I am her teacher and protector. I will not allow this," said Jaquar.

"The Exotique Marian would not have been sent to us *now* if we weren't to use her for this purpose," Chalmon said.

"That's convoluted thinking," Venetria argued. "That sounds as if you believe in fate and not free will. Why do you think that now when you never have before? Or is it only that you want to sacrifice someone else?"

Red flushed beneath Chalmon's skin. "Don't call me a coward."

"Why shouldn't I? You haven't plane-walked to that place. I have." Venetria gestured grandly. "Jaquar has."

"Plane-walking is not one of my talents," Chalmon muttered.

"You'll sacrifice her. Is it so easy for you? I always thought you were a man of character," Venetria said.

Chalmon's face contorted in anger. "I want to protect *us*. If that means sacrificing some stranger, so be it."

Venetria said, "I'm not sure we should—"

"You always vacillate!" Chalmon accused. "I tell you, the worst monsters are about to spew from that maw. Dreeths. Sangviles that could easily target the Tower Community and eat us all!" He grabbed Venetria's shoulders. "Woman, your island is the northernmost! Close to the damn border where those monsters congregate. Your defensive shields are pitiful. I won't lose you."

She stared at him, eyes wide. Her mouth trembled. "You would go to such lengths to…to keep me from harm?"

Chalmon shuddered. "Everyone of the Tower Community

has seen the memory-vision of how the sangvile attacked Aly-eka. I won't have that happen to you. And that was only one sangvile."

Face set in hard lines, he stared at Jaquar. "Dreeths fly, and have you forgotten that if the boundary is not fully Powered between magical fence posts—and there are plenty of gaps—a horror can manifest as far inside the country as one of its own reached?"

"That hasn't happened in known history," said Jaquar.

"No? But all our Lorebooks say that it's true. And the sangvile was in Castleton, in the Castle, in Coquille-on-the-Coast! Once the nest opens and another of its kind spews out, it could manifest in one of those places!" Chalmon said. "We have no choice: if Marian can harm the nest, we must Send her."

Jaquar fought for the woman he'd come to admire. "We could go to the Marshalls—specifically to the Exotique Alyeka, and ask her help in penetrating the force that shields the maw. She's a trained warrior—both physically and magically. She knows what we're facing. She's fought a sangvile twice. She is one of us, now, a Lladranan. We could use her as a spearhead into the maw, follow her in. That could work."

Silence filled the chamber as all three of them considered the plan.

"I always liked that idea." Venetria's face shone. "She can penetrate the nest's shield and the rest of the Marshalls will fol-low immediately. We could go, too."

Her Song was utterly sincere, and Jaquar relaxed.

Chalmon sat on a sofa and leaned back, pulling Venetria down and close to him. He smiled patronizingly, his usual ex-pression around Jaquar, and nodded. "A good idea."

"And the Marshalls can move fast! They're used to mobilizing quickly," Venetria said.

Eyebrows raised, Chalmon said dryly, "If Bastien and the other Marshalls don't kill you for mentioning the idea to Alexa."

Jaquar decided to speak to Bastien alone, first. Relief flooded him that he'd found a new plan. Chalmon and Venetria had been convinced. "I'll contact Bastien and Alyeka in the near future, *before* the maw opens again." His gaze swept the room. "Alyeka is a very Powerful, strong, experienced fighter and foresighted woman. I think she'll agree to spearhead our force." He smiled sharply, "And she is linked to the Marshalls. We will follow. And do you think any Marshall won't support her? They *always* work as a team."

"The last time the Tower and the Castle tried a joint effort—some two centuries ago—it didn't work," Chalmon said, considering.

"Who will hold the focus of this combined Power?" Venetria frowned.

Jaquar smiled. "Why, our Exotique, who is bound to Bossgond and Alyeka. I will provide support, since I had a tentative link with Alyeka, and thus the Marshalls, in that last battle." He met each Circlet's eyes, impressed upon them his determination and confidence that this was the right path to take.

When no one denied his logic, he bowed to them all, turned and left.

Just before he shut the outer door behind him, he heard Chalmon say thoughtfully, "Do you think Jaquar's bonded with our new Exotique, too?"

"There is definitely a chord sounding between them," Venetria said.

Jaquar closed the door, smiling a little. He had won the game, and Marian would never know the depths he had sunk to, when ravaged by grief.

For Marian, the books hadn't been too hard to read after all. At first, the sight of the words seemed to sear into her head as if they were written in neon. But when she put her finger on the words, trying to learn the alphabet and sound them out, she heard the sound-songs of them in her mind.

By the time she felt too exhausted to continue her search through the Medical texts, she knew how to read. Some of the more complex words still stymied her, and connotations and concepts might be difficult, but overall, she was pleased with her work. She didn't think she'd be able to read aloud anytime soon, though. And as she dressed in her nightgown and climbed into her bed, she wondered how soon the language of Lladranan—reading and speaking—would vanish from her mind when she returned to Earth. Would she go to France in the future and speak with a Lladranan accent? Or would she have to relearn French?

She smiled to herself as sleep crept close. Her concentration had been intense, and with the unaccustomed activities of the day, she hadn't been able to read more than a couple of hours—not even long enough to listen to the entire "Magic Flute." But she had found small traces of information regarding something the Lladranans called "cortifremi," which sounded like MS. As she slipped into sleep, hope filled her that she'd be able to find a magical—Powerful—cure she could apply to her brother.

She awoke to stifling dark and stark terror. The horrible sound of swooping wings accompanied the brush of dusty feathers on her face. She screamed and heard no sound.

This was not a nightmare. She was awake, cold sweat coating her body. She couldn't move.

The *thing* perched on the bottom frame of her sleigh bed, eyes gleaming.

18

Clutching the covers until her fingers hurt, Marian stared at the bird. A black vulture with a bare red head.

It stared back. There was something about the tilt of its head, the glow of its eyes, the…the…delicacy of its Song. It loomed about a foot high. Weren't vultures bigger?

Sinafin? Marian sent the being a mental call. Sweet relief poured through her.

The glittering black gaze pierced her. She could have sworn a splinter of pain entered her chest.

Are you sure? whispered like dry dust in her mind.

Marian wasn't at all sure.

The bird lifted wings and sidestepped down the footboard with the sound of sharp claws scritching against the wood, raising gooseflesh on Marian's arms. Her heart thundered in her ears. *What do you want?* Even if she could move, she didn't know if she'd be able to speak.

Are you trying to talk to me? asked the creature. *I can't hear you. Try harder.*

The tone slapped her mentally—an order, nearly a compulsion.

Sinafin? Marian mind-whispered.

A flash of blue lightning blinded Marian, and when the spots faded from her vision she saw the creature was now dead white, a skeletal thing. Only the eyes were alive, and they were cold and demanding.

But Marian knew what it was. It *was* the magical shape-shifter, the feycoocu. Sinafin. What did the being want of her? Marian could think only of Alexa's parting words. *Sinafin can be trusted to do what is best for Lladrana.*

I can't hear you. Lightning flashed again and, blinking, Marian saw the vulture was now covered in a long black robe, a cowl draped over its head, showing only beak and glowing red eyes that stared at her inimically.

It clicked its beak in threat. Marian moaned. No sound emerged. *She could make no sound!*

I can't hear you. You must call louder. The vulture hopped down from the rail, robe flapping, and lit on her feet. Claws curled over her toes. It felt heavy, pressing hard against her feet. Marian shrieked silently in her head.

Marian watched in horror as it extended one clawed foot and set it down on her ankle. It would walk up her body! She thought her heart would burst from the terror.

Her mind gibbered, then put syllables together in a mental cry. *Sinafin!*

I can barely hear you. Try harder. Another step and it settled on her ankles, not heavy now, but moving with a dry rustling that made Marian tremble.

Sinafin!

Better. Try again.

SINAFIN.

It stopped, foot raised, ready to step up on her shin. Its beak opened in what appeared to be a grotesque smile.

SINAFIN! Marian screamed with her mind. Pushed aside fear to grasp at the elusive wild Song of the small magical being. *SINAFIN!*

Marian envisioned it as a *she,* a pretty fairy. *SINAFIN, FEYCOOCU!* The bed seemed to vibrate with the force of her mind-call.

The vulture flew—backward—to the footboard. Tilted its head. *Louder—use all your senses, all your will.*

The feycoocu was a fairy, with black hair and blue wings, with a wild, delicate, fascinating Song. She had smelled of… of…a spicy floral scent. She was *not* heavy, she was light. An… aura…a rainbow of Power surrounded her. Marian clutched the knowledge to her, built the little being as a three-dimensional entity. Marian used all her senses. Holding the image of the feycoocu in her mind, Marian yelled, *SINAFIN!*

The Tower itself seemed to tremble with the reverberation of her cry.

Sinafin perched on the curving wood of the footboard. *That might do.* Her wings were hunched up around her head.

You have learned your lesson. The bird shot by Marian, curved beak skimming her face, leaving a tingle. *Tell no one of this.* It disappeared through the wall above Marian's head.

"L-light," Marian gasped, and all the wall sconces, every candle and both fireplaces flared to life.

It wasn't enough. She was chilled and could think of no spells that would warm her.

She was so cold she couldn't think—from the terror? Had Sinafin harmed her somehow?

As the trembling subsided, Marian began to scrape together some logic and reason. If Sinafin acted in the best interests of Lladrana, why had she terrorized Marian? How could that help the land?

And she wasn't going to let a—a *vulture* intimidate her, keep her quiet. No. Sinafin wouldn't hurt her. If Sinafin was once a creature like Tuck—or if Tuck could metamorphose into a being like Sinafin—a feycoocu was not an evil or cruel entity. The reasoning cut through the last dregs of terror, let other thoughts well up—how Marian had initially been amused and pleased with Sinafin, had sensed that the fairy had been concerned for her, later approved of her.

Sinafin had said she loved Alexa. A being like that wouldn't torture without reason. Would she?

"Let's send the hamster ball to the Dark nest," Chalmon said calmly as soon as they heard Jaquar's volaran take to the skies.

Venetria jerked. "What? We decided to follow a different plan."

"No," said Chalmon calmly. "Jaquar decided to remove himself from his original plan and try another. It has merits, but he'll fail. The Marshalls won't listen to him, and even if they do, they will take time to think and act. Didn't they wait nearly a year before informing the rest of Lladrana that the fence posts were falling? Summoning an Exotique was their last, most desperate solution to the problem."

"They are committed to fighting the Dark now," Venetria said. "There are many more of them. They'll listen to Jaquar and move quickly." She was speaking fast, but she liked the new plan, didn't want the worry and guilt that had enveloped her when she'd considered the old solution to the Dark.

Chalmon snorted. "Have you ever heard of a Marshall plane-walking? They won't cooperate with us, and they won't want to fight on an ephemeral plane."

"But we don't have the experience of the Marshalls in working together to do a Sending or a Summoning. We might not be able to send the Exotique into the nest."

He raised his eyebrows. "That's why we need to follow through with the experiment." He glanced at the water clock. "Other Scholars and Circlets who agree with me will be arriving momentarily to help."

"Tonight?" Venetria said blankly.

Chalmon brushed a soft kiss over her mouth, the pure tenderness in the stream of his Song softening her.

Then the doorharp trilled and Bossgond answered to the first of fifteen people. Venetria watched, torn, as he calmly prepared for plane-walking, a skill he wasn't proficient in. Finally, he was ready, and gestured the others to ascend to his Ritual room on the top floor.

That had been open and ready, too, and Chalmon hadn't told her.

"I know you are conflicted on this matter. I want to make it as easy as possible for you." He held out his hand. "I need our Song, too."

"What plane do you visit?" she asked dully.

"The fifteenth."

"One Jaquar does not frequent."

Chalmon shrugged and his lips thinned. "You insist on remaining at your vulnerable Tower. I will protect you with my last breath."

She tossed her head. "You want information about the Dark—"

"We all do."

"You want to destroy the Dark's nest."

"A worthy ambition."

"Not if it means sacrificing an innocent woman!"

"We've had this discussion." He dropped his hand and turned to the door. "Come or stay."

"What if I say I will live with you until the Dark is destroyed?"

He turned away, glittering gaze meeting hers. "Will you?"

"Yes."

"Promise on your keystone?"

"Yes."

He inhaled deeply, then let out the breath. "Then I'll say we should go forward with this experiment, just to see what happens."

"Will you consider Jaquar's new plan?"

"We will wait and watch."

How long? She didn't want to push him, because then he would turn intractable. A great weight bowed her down. She would be making hard choices. Walking up to him, she put her hand in his. "I'll come."

The Ritual passed quickly, as if each person had been practicing it. Only Venetria and Chalmon and a third Circlet with an explosive arrow would actually travel, the rest sang Songs that bonded them temporarily to Chalmon, sending him strength. He, in turn, would allow those left behind to experience what he did. He held the strange orb of the Exotique's companion in his hand. It still smelled.

Venetria struggled to stay on the fifteenth plane, and Chalmon helped her. Finally they reached the observation point overlooking the Dark's maw.

Watch for me, and tell me the next time the shield darkens.

Her form wavering, Venetria watched. *Now!* she cried.

With a mental grunt of effort, Chalmon threw the clear hollow ball at the nest. Another Circlet lobbed the small arrow of an explosive spell.

The ball penetrated the shield.

The seething maw stilled.

The arrow broke as it hit the shield.

It worked! the other Circlet screamed. *Exotique essence harms the nest.*

Venetria lost control, and Chalmon and the other had to hold her within this plane.

But the arrow failed. The Exotique Terre artifact was not strong enough. Chalmon's mental voice held the hollow echoes of doom. *Watch the nest,* ordered Chalmon. *Send me word when it is active once more.* He cut all the strands but Venetria's that sent him energy with a sweep of his arm. His form shuddered, wisped into nothing. She followed, fearing what would come back to his tower, where she would stay with him.

Finally Marian called Alexa. *Alexa!* she shouted.

Through her bond with the other woman, Marian felt a pulse of surprised fear. *Shit, Marian, could you scream a little lower? You woke me up.*

Marian closed her eyes. It had worked! She'd added a little wind-spell chant to her call and it had worked! She giggled. It sounded high and nervous to her ears. No more crystal balls for her.

Is Sinafin there? Marian asked, opening her eyes and scanning her place for the dozenth time.

Mind grumbling, Alexa seemed to check, then said, *I don't see her. She is her own person. I don't keep tabs on her.*

Marian puffed out a breath. *Alexa, she was just here, in my rooms at Jaquar's Tower. Terrorizing me.*

What?

I swear she did the best she could to scare me out of my skin. She was a vulture.

A vulture, huh. Another name for buzzard, right?

Yes.

Alexa's mind-tone almost sounded amused. Marian received the impression that Sinafin had been everything from a cockroach to a chinchilla. Then Alexa's mind turned to thinking. *I hate to say this—*

Marian could almost see Alexa making a face. *Yes?* She prompted.

But if Sinafin terrorized you, it was probably for your own good.

The chill of fear crept back into Marian's bones. She wrapped the comforter tighter around her, hummed the little fire-tune that had gone out of her head earlier. Warmth enveloped her, but her insides remained cold. *That doesn't sound good. The deductions one makes from that statement…*

Yeah, Alexa agreed. *If she's terrorizing you for your own good, she probably thinks you're gonna face something even scarier.*

She did say I'd learned my lesson.

Huh, Alexa said. *Then I'd be sure to practice what she taught you. What lesson?*

At that moment a siren shrieked—and it was Alexa hearing it. The sound punched through their connection accompanied by Alexa's sweeping emotions—feelings spurred by upcoming battle.

Gotta go. Invasion alarm. They aren't supposed to attack at night. Something's up.

Marian received an impression of Alexa jumping from bed, racing to her chain-mail, baton flashing into her hand and Bastien at her heels.

Take care.

Yeah, Alexa sent absently. *Like they say in e-mail, "virtual hugs."* But her mind had fallen into a strange rhythm.

She was preparing for battle. To fight and kill monsters, perhaps to die.

God bless! Marian sent strongly, then broke the connection.

She slid from bed to pace the room a few times, then, when she was warm, slipped off the comforter and spread it back over the bed until it was perfectly aligned. Then she crawled under the covers and hoped for sleep without dreams. And prayed for Alexa.

Jaquar's flight back to Mue was full of thoughts of Marian. The sight of her as she'd called the Wind haunted him. Her dress had lifted to show her body—the body he was trying hard to forget that he'd seen naked twice—and the odd undergarment she wore only accentuated her loveliness. Her hair had floated around her, deep red with fiery highlights.

Most tempting of all were her blue eyes, wide with discovery and excitement, and the joy on her face. How was he going to resist the temptation of all that?

He gritted his teeth. He would have to. Marian intended to return to her home and her sick brother. If *his* parents had needed *him,* nothing would have stopped him from helping.

Jaquar had rediscovered his honor and thanked the Song he hadn't committed an action that he would not have been able to live with. He wasn't about to stain his precious honor by having sex with Marian and binding her to Lladrana through him when she believed she was needed elsewhere.

So perhaps he should help her hunt for medical aid for her brother—the sooner she was gone, the sooner he could craft a new life without his parents and continue on.

He might even consider taking an Apprentice.

When Nightsky and he landed near the Tower, Jaquar saw no light from Marian's windows. She must be asleep.

He realized he'd wanted to see her, spend a little time in her company, just enjoy the humming notes between them. Best she had retired.

Jaquar sniffed the air. A storm was coming. It would bring rain for Marian to practice manipulating—and lightning. Though it was years now since he'd called the lightning storm and it had raged beyond his control, he shuddered. Still, Bossgond was right: Marian had an affinity for Fire.

Though Jaquar would never match her mastery in that element as a Weather mage, he knew how to call the lightning, ride it even. Better yet, he could teach her the basics, guide her practices and watch her learn and become proficient with her Power, and that was almost as good as using it himself. He didn't think she'd ever—quite—match him in controlling Wind and Air.

He would teach her. He would protect her, and instruct her how to protect herself.

So Jaquar tended to the volaran, then went to his rooms and, listening to the rising wind, fell asleep.

A sound woke him. An odd noise he'd never heard in his Tower. Foggy with sleep, he listened, heard clicks coming from the speaking tube near his bed.

Before he could determine the source of the noise, a tiny, cold, sharp-clawed paw patted his face. He jerked in reaction but stopped the whistle that would have flung the hamster against the wall.

"You are thinking of Marian," the little being squeaked.

He'd been dreaming of her—lush and wanton and laughing in his arms as they rolled on the bed and she opened her thighs and her mind and— He grunted noncommittally in response to Tuck.

"You should go to her." Two small paws tapped his cheek. "I don't think so."

"It would be best if you go to her and mate. I am Marian's companion, but I want to stay here in Lladrana. Her place is here, too. She is a Sorceress." Tuck hissed, "The feycoocu says she should stay."

Ah, the instigator and the reason the mousekin was bothering Jaquar. "You mean the feycoocu wants me to bond with Marian so that when her Snap comes, she will be more likely to remain here. Marian is concerned for her brother—that's who she wants to help. That's who she's bound to the most, emotionally."

"That should change. Andrew is good, but he is not as important as you."

The brother wasn't as important to the hamster or the feycoocu as Jaquar, is what Tuck meant. Jaquar didn't want to listen any more to the creature.

"I'm not going to have sex with Marian just to please you or the feycoocu."

The hamster withdrew his paws, but a moment later, Jaquar felt the tug on his hair and scalp as the rodent climbed onto his head.

It sat on his forehead, warm and furry…and tickling. Rolling his eyes back, Jaquar could see the gleam of Tuck's tiny black eyes, serious with a knowledge that Jaquar didn't want to face.

"Your Songs match," Tuck said.

Jaquar didn't want to hear that.

"She belongs here. With you. With me. With Bossgond."

"That may be what you want, may truly be best for her, but Marian must decide for herself."

Tuck grumbled, huffed, climbed down to walk back and forth across Jaquar's chest. "You won't go to her tonight?"

"No. If we…mate, our pleasure will be a mutual experience, one she wants as much as I. I will not seduce her. Furthermore, I will endeavor *not* to bind her to me with a strong sexual tie."

More mutterings from the hamster. Finally Tuck sniffed and said, "It would be better if you love tonight, in the Tower. Best if you twine your Songs into one. But we must trust the Song."

The philosophy was far beyond what Jaquar thought Tuck could achieve. The hamster had been talking better, too. Jaquar wondered how Tuck had made the intellectual leap. The feycoocu? Practice? Jaquar didn't know, but uncomfortable personal conversation or not, the whole episode was going word for word in his personal Lorebook.

"Good night," Tuck said. His claws skittered as he stepped into the speaking tube.

To Jaquar's amazement, the hamster flew up.

A moment later, Jaquar found himself smiling. There were now three beings in this Tower who were masters of Air.

When she met Jaquar at the door to his study the next morning, Marian noticed a constraint between them in their stilted conversation. Perhaps he thought that she was going to ask awkward questions about where he'd disappeared the night before. Marian didn't consider it any of her business, but didn't know what formalities or rules there might be between student and teacher. She was certain that she didn't want to talk to him about Sinafin's visit, and he'd no doubt ask if she commented on his night.

So breakfast talk was desultory. One glance at Tuck's house showed Marian that he was curled up in a ball in the plush room he'd taken as his sleeping space. The sitting room that adjoined Tuck's "bedroom" was piled high with his hoard.

Marian shook her head at the sight. "I think Tuck has finally adapted to Lladrana and gone back to his old nocturnal habits."

An odd expression crossed Jaquar's face, but all he said was "It seems so." He hesitated, gestured to the trees thrashing in the wind outside the Tower windows. "A storm's coming in. The height of the front will strike the northwest part of Mue Island midafternoon. This is excellent weather for you to practice Water Power. The hike across the island is an hour, so we should leave after lunch."

Forcing a smile at the thought of a long hike in bad weather just to fail at lessons, Marian agreed to the plan. He was the prof, after all.

He must have guessed her thoughts, or perhaps the notes stringing between them went a trifle flat, because he smiled genuinely. Pushing his clean plate aside, he leaned forward on the table and whispered, eyes glinting, "We can also see how you do with Lightning Magic."

Immediately Marian cheered up. She felt her eyes widen. "For real? I'm very good with Lightning in the ecospheres. It's my best subject. But you'll let me try it in a real-life situation?" She found herself whispering, too, in excitement.

Jaquar chuckled. "Yes. A practicum."

Marian nearly shuddered with delight. "This is going to be the *absolute best* class in my entire career."

He set his hand out on the table, palm up. His gaze was gentle.

She put her hand in his, squeezed his fingers, then noted the rolling melody streaming from him to her and back, redoubling in strength. Lifting her glance to his, they connected that way, too. His eyes had deepened to dark blue, blue she hadn't seen on Earth—Lladranan blue, or perhaps it was the silver glints in them—magic, Power. Power blue.

"Your eyes are so beautiful," she said.

His expression closed and he pulled his hand away, stood and banished the dishes. "Be prepared to leave for the shore after lunch. Practice Water and Lightning in the spheres this morning for at least three hours."

Well, that was certainly a dismissal. Consultation with the prof over.

Marian stood and curtsied formally, which made Jaquar narrow his eyes as if he wondered whether she was being sarcastic. She looked once more at the sleeping Tuck, then went down to pursue her studies.

When she started working with the ecospheres, she understood she'd always used the wind or the sun to work with the water, not handled that particular element itself. She flushed again at the thought of how easily she'd failed in the task the day before of holding water in the air, and how well she'd thought she'd been progressing before that. Sighing, she knew she'd had a touch of hubris and had been squelched.

She studied hard, experimenting with water for a solid hour, starting with the smallest terrarium through to the largest. Her efforts at mastering water in the terrariums were mediocre. To truly master Water magic, she'd need step-by-step instruction from Jaquar.

After struggling with Water, she spent some time with Lightning, then looked over the lesson plan and found she'd completed every task. She spent another half-hour being creative with Lightning, then went back to Water before she finished manipulating the elements.

Marian was deep in her medical reading when Jaquar announced lunch. She had it sent down in a dumbwaiter type device, and ate at her desk, reading. When her waterfall clock pinged that she had a few minutes before Jaquar came down, she freshened up and donned her sturdiest gown to hike across the island. Still, she waited for him for about five minutes, not daring to immerse herself again in the scrolls. She wished Tuck or her PDA had been around to set the alarm— the waterfall clock was too imprecise for her taste. She eyed the thing. Surely there were better timepieces. *Some* Circlet had to be studying time.

Jaquar arrived and knocked on her door. He was dressed in a cape the color and texture of duct tape and wore the stupidest hat Marian had ever seen, low crowned and broad brimmed but not nearly the elegant proportions of a gaucho's. Furthermore, it was made of some horrible gray material that reminded Marian suspiciously of the texture of "soul-sucker" that she'd seen in Alexa's and Bossgond's images.

She drew back a little.

"I was right. It's raining and there are lightning storms at the shore. This storm will provide you with good practice with water *and* fire," Jaquar said. "Rain or running water is easier to work with than pools or even the tide." His smile was warm. "Do you have a rain cape?"

"Actually, I do." It was still marked with yellow birds as befitted Bossgond's Apprentice, but she didn't care about that. She went into the bedroom and pulled it on. As she crossed back into the living room/study she noticed that Jaquar had not stepped over the threshold, and her heart began to pound. She hadn't invited him in, and he respected her enough that he hadn't entered without her asking. So different from some of the men she knew. Like Jack Wilse.

His head tilted to the side and she saw his nostrils flare. He smiled again. "The place holds your fragrance. From what I can see, you've made it your own. Good."

"Where's Tuck? I thought he wanted to go outside

today—and with at least one of us watching him, he will be protected."

Jaquar pulled a face. "In the rain? He was disgusted when he saw it on the windows. I think he's rearranging his hoard."

"Always a hamster's favorite thing—besides eating. They are originally desert animals."

"Ah." Jaquar touched her shoulder and the cape rippled. When the fabric finished moving, it was plain gray, no pattern of little yellow birds.

Marian chuckled. "Thanks." She pulled the hood of her cape over her head.

"You are welcome. You'll need a hat to keep the frink—" He stopped, a considering look coming to his eyes. "Perhaps not. Frinks don't seem to fall around Exotiques." He offered his hand, and she took it.

Once again, she sensed that he'd experienced an emotional sea change in the time they'd been apart.

He opened the door and they stepped out. The odd pinging on the small flagstone patio stopped. Blinking rain from her lashes, Marian noticed the rain looked less dense than before.

"Lovely, no more raining frinks," Jaquar said in satisfaction. His grin flashed. "There are definitely more benefits to having you around than just looking at your lovely person, Marian." He squeezed her hand.

On the way to the beach, Jaquar quizzed her about her studies in a casual manner that made her feel as if he wasn't judging her or holding to strict expectations—not nearly as harsh as she judged herself, and his standards for her seemed lower than her own. Was she being too hard on herself again? Too concerned with perfection? Probably. No one could say that Jaquar wasn't an excellent teacher or a very Powerful Circlet.

Now and then they paused while Jaquar patiently instructed her in Rain Power—once when it was pouring, once in a drizzle, once in a light shower. He was right—rain in motion was a lot easier to manipulate than still water.

Finally they reached the beach and it wasn't more than a minute before lightning struck a few yards away. Marian itched to get her hands on it, wrap her mind around Lightning Power.

Instead, Jaquar made her practice with storm-tossed waves and tide pools rippling with rain for what seemed like hours.

Then a roar came from overhead and lightning struck close, and Marian lost her concentration and the bit of rainstorm she'd been managing.

The lightning sang to her—to her mind, but even more, to her blood. She knew it, each crackle, each beyond-hearing hiss and zing. Even before Jaquar showed her, mind-to-mind and by demonstration, how to weave it into patterns, how to Send it, Marian knew the Song. Linking hands with Jaquar's, he called it and controlled it, forking it down beyond their feet, sending streaks across the sky.

She'd never felt anything like it—*nothing* so Powerful, so satisfying as playing with lightning, creating designs. It was as if she'd taken the electricity inside to sizzle in her blood. As if she *was* lightning.

He'd start a Song to teach her, and she'd pick up the tones, the rhythm, the melody and sing herself. Marian's Song of Lightning, the words more facile on her tongue than his.

So, eyes narrowed as if he gauged her every note, he set her tasks, and though she knew they were tests, she just laughed. Nothing came easier to her in her life than taming lightning.

She danced it across the sky, sent it from cloud to cloud, from cloud to ground, to rock, splitting a boulder. She made tiny sparks, long forks, curtains of the stuff.

Spectacular.

She played, she designed, she drew and dismissed. And finally as the rain pounded down and she'd done all he'd said, she whirled around in the wind and faced him, grinning.

He smiled back.

But as she took stock, she realized something in the Song of Lightning was missing. Something she hadn't grasped. It was not complete.

Marian lifted her face to him, questioning.

"You need practice *inside* a storm." He gestured to a cliff. "From there we could step into the wind and let it take us through the storm front." His eyes had deepened to dark blue and the expression was pure challenge.

But Marian had always loved storms. "Ayes," she agreed in Lladranan.

Jaquar grinned and held out his hand. She put her hand in his, liked the connection when his long, elegant fingers folded over hers.

"Let's go!"

They ran up the hill. She wasn't in the best of shape, but Jaquar matched his steps to hers, not dragging her, not pushing her. She liked that, too.

He led her to a huge rock jutting out in space. Though she wasn't usually bothered by heights, the wind was strong and another large curtain of rain was marching closer.

Jaquar stepped forward and closed her cape, smoothed it over her body, sealing it. The Lightning Song was inside her and transformed into sexual sparks. She trembled beneath his touch. A smile hovered on his lips. He kissed her nose but didn't speak above the rain, the thunder.

Instead he moved behind her and wrapped his arms around her middle.

What next? she asked, because there *had* to be a next.

Sing with me. He took up a spiraling chant.

She followed.

When the melodic line was established, he dropped his voice to harmonize. At the next break in the chant, he said, "Ready?" There was a tone in his voice that told her he'd step back if she wanted.

"Ayes," she said.

"We'll do this together." He started a low, intricate chant.

After a few measures, she felt the cadence of it, figured out the twisting chords.

"Now!" he cried. A gust of wind blew them into the air.

For an instant, she was only conscious of his arms around her—the strength of him, physically and in his psi Power. His body was pressed to hers and many Songs wrapped them both. His Song and hers and theirs, and the Song of Mue Island, the Song of the Air and the Storm and the Ocean. All rang in her mind like an orchestra.

Then the sheer magnificence of the storm, of their wild ride inside the clouds, whirling with the wind made her shriek with excited laughter. Oh, she could experience this *forever.* The glory of it was beyond human comprehension. She felt the vibration of Jaquar's chest behind her and didn't know whether he laughed with her or Sang, and it didn't matter.

They followed the storm winds for a while, then a black fist of a cloud loomed, could not be avoided. Something about it chilled her. It didn't *feel* right. When they were in it a fog dulled her senses. She clamped her hands on Jaquar's wrists and told herself she could feel his muscle, sinew, bone under her fingers when she doubted, when her fingers grew too cold to tell. The cloud battered her with a mean sleet she writhed to avoid, ducking her head. The Songs faded to a horrible hum like a high-pitched cry of a straining car engine, a series of *pings* that were nearly beyond her hearing.

She felt pummeled for an endless time, then they dropped— straight into a rain cloud where sweet water drenched her, slicked her hair, stuck her magical gown tight to her body. She could hear the Songs again, and Jaquar shouting in her ear.

"Look ahead," he cried. "Lightning. Do you want to try and ride it?"

All the joy in the storm, the reckless energy around her throbbed through her on a rising tide of music. "Yes," she screamed. "Yes, yes, yes!"

Now we call the lightning and ride it!

19

A flash of fire rolled over them, encased them. Took them.

Whisked them up with the speed of light.

Snatched her breath so she couldn't sing.

They dipped, fell, and Jaquar's voice came rich and deep.

They spun in a sea of electrical sparks. In heavy, dewy clouds.

Curving his hand around hers, he lifted them, spread their fingers, palm out. Marian followed his movement.

Call the lightning now!

She did, so again they were swept away, shot from cloud into night, plummeting downward.

Jaquar held a note, Marian joined him.

And time slowed.

They were on the bolt itself, shooting from the cloud, across the sea to other clouds.

The speed was awesome, something she shouldn't have been able to experience. Couldn't rationally explain.

Jaquar stopped singing. And Marian lifted her voice and *sang* and they rode the lightning.

Finally a huge arcing stream, thicker than both of their bodies, caught them, sent them rushing down to land, darkness punctuated by city lights.

As they zoomed down the lightning, Jaquar guided them so they lit in a field and avoided the town. The rich soil had been turned, ready for planting, and it, with the scent of ozone and the feel of the lightning still fizzing in her bloodstreams, made her crave sex. With Jaquar and only Jaquar. She didn't want to think, didn't want to weigh the pros and cons, didn't want to speculate what consequences might occur from their coupling. She wanted to tear his clothes off.

So she did. She shoved off his cloak, grabbed his tunic and ripped, and he stood staring at her. She yanked at his pants and then he was clothed only in a loincloth. Her breath caught in her chest at the sight of him. It was raining, slicking his muscles, droplets defining them. He was beautiful.

She'd never seen a better proportioned man—broad shoulders, lean hips, muscular thighs… The pounding of the rain around her thundered in her ears. He stood tall and sexy and, in this instant, hers. She knew it.

Her hands curved over his shoulders, then his nostrils flared, his expression went wild and he yanked her to him. His body was hot and hard…and ready. Then his mouth was on hers, wet and demanding. She opened to him.

They slipped and fell to the ground, landing softly. She didn't know if that had been his Power or hers, or Amee's, but she heard overwhelming orchestral chords that combined into a pulsing, rhythmic drumbeat. A sexual beat. She cried out as her own clothes disappeared and warm rain slipped down her body in a sensual caress.

His hands were on her body, sliding, stroking, probing, the sensations so intense she could only cling to him, yearn for him.

And his tongue was in her mouth and she was tasting him as he took her. Their bodies met and melded, arched and twisted. Their minds touched and linked and shattered with pleasure.

Marian lay under his weight, panting, enjoying the lovely Song, the sluicing rain, the heat of him. She'd never felt so abandoned, so free. Her mind had totally blanked, not a rational thought to be found.

She laughed.

A tremor went through him. His head was next to hers and he whispered, "Marian." The richness of his tone, the lilt of it made her quiver.

Long moments passed as they lay together. Finally he shifted beneath her and she let the reason she'd banished in experiencing the physicality of the now, rush back to fill her head.

The rain had stopped. She used a hook of Wind to lift and hold her, dry a bit of ground and set her on her feet. With a three-note spell, her dress—warm and dry—slid over her head and draped her. It was a little harder to find her new underwear, and when she did, she drew on the panties, but used a pocket in her gown to hold the bra. The dress bodice was doing just fine as a foundation garment for her breasts.

By the time she'd dressed, the sheathing clouds had dissipated to show a large, white moon. The night sky held swaths of stars. She tilted her head back to experience the night, found a bubble of happiness shimmering through her. She felt lighter, freer than she had for a long time. Too much work and not enough play. And what spectacular play sex with Jaquar had been!

She rolled her shoulders, aware of the new range of movement now that the tension built up over the past few weeks had eased. Smiling, she looked to Jaquar.

He stood gazing down at her. Inscrutable.

"Do you think we made a mistake?" she asked.

He pushed his stupid hat onto his head. "I don't think we need to talk about it."

Men were the same even across worlds.

"All right," she said coolly.

He took her hand. Music crashed through her—the intensity of emotion from him made her stumble and he slid an arm around her waist. His tender actions seemed at a variance from his cool manner, so she set his earlier words aside. She didn't want to analyze anything—his words in relation to his actions and emotions, or her own.

"I have you," he said, his voice softening.

"I have you," he repeated, lilting, and she didn't know if he meant that he wouldn't let her fall or that he was keeping her as a lover—reluctantly. She shivered from the strange fury of emotions she'd experienced in the past couple of hours and he stopped to drape his cape around them both, pulling her close to his side. Still befuddled, she nevertheless realized that they kept pace with each other—she lengthening her stride a little, he shortening his own. Their steps matched. Something else she didn't want to consider right now. She shook her head to clear it, looked once more at the brilliant sky glittering with at least two veils of stars—was there more than one arm of a galaxy visible? As she inhaled deeply, fresh air helped clear her mind, while the ruts of the soil centered her.

She cleared her throat before she spoke. "Where are we?"

With his free arm, he gestured to a smooth area in front of

them. "The road between the Marshalls' Castle and the town of Castleton."

Marian stopped, looked up at him. "That's on mainland Lladrana," she croaked.

He raised his eyebrows. "The wind took us to the mainland. The lightning storm was wide. I thought it best to ride the lightning down here, near one of the most populated places in Lladrana."

Again, Marian stared at the sky. No trace of clouds. She found herself shaking her head in disbelief. "One hell of a way to travel!" When she said it, another bit of knowledge jolted her—she'd picked the word for "hell"—anfer—from his mind! Her Lladranan accent was now near perfect, and her comprehension of the nuances of the language a great deal better than they had been.

His hand squeezed her hip, his eyes darkened. "I can't ride the lightning by myself. I don't have the skill or Power."

She swallowed hard. "You showed me how, you controlled our descent." If she'd been by herself more than likely she'd have plummeted to the ground and made a large dent. End of Marian.

Now his teeth gleamed in a smile. "I'd traveled that way with the last Weather Mage, Sorceress Entanra, when I was an Apprentice." He shrugged. "And I knew the theory, of course."

"Of course," Marian said faintly, trembling.

He wrapped his arms around her. "Shh," he said into her hair.

She felt his warm breath, but couldn't seem to stop shivering.

"You have the knowledge to Ride the Lightning, to Dance with the Wind. If you don't think about failure, it won't happen."

"Are you sure?"

Chuckling, he said, "No."

Oh yeah, that made her feel a whole lot better. Her nerves were shot. The intimacy between them was growing and that scared her, too. She *liked* him far too much, didn't dare become deeply attached to the man if she planned to return to Earth. No future in it, and she didn't know if she had the finesse to handle an affair. The emotional connection between them was already stronger than it would be for any casual fling.

She needed balance. So she stepped away from the comfort of his arms, but was still glad when he slipped his arm around her waist.

She looked at the road, glanced up the hill and saw the dark hulking shadow of the Marshalls' Castle. Alexa. She sighed in relief. Alexa would be the perfect person to help Marian sort out her feelings. So she gazed toward the Castle and sent out a mental call. *Alexa?*

A fleeting surprise throbbed to Marian from her link with Alexa.

Marian? You sound close.

I am close, on the road between the Castle and Castleton.

Confusion. *Why did you fly in?*

I didn't, Marian sent dryly. *I rode the lightning as part of my training and we ended up here. Jaquar is with me.*

Pure stupefaction throbbed from the other end of the bond with Alexa, then curiosity, excitement. *Rode the lightning! That is so cool!*

Jaquar's mouth tilted up, and Marian knew he was hearing a small echo between Alexa and her. He urged her onto the road and they turned to the Castle.

We'll be at the Castle shortly, Marian sent.

Wait! I'm at the Nom de Nom, a Castleton inn that the Chevaliers frequent. The noise around their mental bond increased. *Oh.*

I think Jaquar knows of it. See you in a bit, Alexa said.

Marian glanced up at Jaquar. "Did you hear? Do you mind going to the Nom de Nom?"

"I heard. Are you sure you want to visit the inn? The Chevaliers can be...rowdy." Again his arm tightened around her waist, and she thought she felt a tendril of jealousy. Chevaliers were the knights of Lladrana, those who fought the horrors. They probably were real testosterone guys, adrenaline junkies.

A chuckle rumbled in her throat before she could stop it. "You're an exceptionally sexy man, Jaquar."

He stiffened, then picked up the pace. "You think so?"

"Very, and so does Alexa."

"She does?" He sounded pleased. "By all means, let's go to the Nom de Nom. Is Bastien there?"

"For you to tease by flirting with Alexa?" She pinched his arm. "You're with me, and I don't approve of that sort of behavior."

Jaquar laughed.

They neared the town gate. The archway through the walls was well lit by huge white balls of magical illumination. Two guards garbed in green and blue stepped into the arch.

Jaquar didn't hesitate in his stride. "Sorcerer Circlet Jaquar Dumont and Exotique Scholar Marian."

The men's mouths dropped open and they separated to each side of the arch.

"The Tower's Exotique!" one whispered in excited tones. "No one's seen her except the Marshalls and the Tower. This will be something to tell!"

"She's a nice size," the other said. "Not like that strange little Marshall."

There was the sound of a blow, a grunt from the guard. "Marshall Alyeka has always been kind to me. Keep your mouth shut, dolt," one said to the other.

Marian could feel their gazes on her as she walked away. Irritation at the men surged. Obviously news of her visit would be spread far and wide, probably by morning.

Jaquar guided her along wide sidewalks through the equally wide streets and elegant squares of a town. The city looked more like late Renaissance or early Industrial Age than Medieval. Each building had a caged magical light.

Yes, Alexa was right. There were a lot of interesting aspects of Lladrana.

She heard the inn before she saw it—and felt it vibrate to her bones from the huge and Powerful Songs. She slowed a little, tilting her head, trying to sort through the Songs. "So many Songs, so rich," she murmured.

Jaquar looked startled. "The Nom de Nom is three blocks away."

Marian just shook her head, tried to piece together what she was experiencing. "Songs of one person, two…"

"Those would be paired fighters, a Shield and Sword for defensive and offensive work."

Frowning, she said, "Some crisscrossing and almost *woven* nets of Songs."

"Chevaliers working together as teams when necessary."

"Some Songs have one primary tone and branch off, adding other little tunes."

"Ah." Jaquar led her around a turn. "Probably a Noble with Chevaliers sworn to him or her." Jaquar waved to a three-story building that seemed so old it leaned a little. "The Nom de Nom."

Just before they reached the threshold, Jaquar stepped away

from her with a little sigh. He ran a hand through his hair, smoothed his clothes, then looked at her. He touched the shoulders of her gown and adjusted them a little. After one comprehensive, sweeping glance at her, he nodded, his mouth quirking in a grin. "Any dishevelment you have could be attributed to a wild lightning ride."

For an instant, his hand curved softly around her cheek. "You are quite, quite fabulously Exotiquely beautiful."

She stared at him, stunned.

Then the door opened before them and some Chevaliers emerged, bringing the scent of smoke and beer. Marian blinked when she saw four women and a man, all equally tall, all dressed in well-worn leather. They hesitated a moment at the sight of her and Jaquar. The men goggled at Marian. Then the women muttered greetings and went off, hauling the man with them. A spicy musk lingered from their passing.

"What's that scent?" asked Marian.

"Volaran."

Flying horse. She hadn't noticed that Nightsky's fragrance had been so strong.

"This will be your first exposure to many Lladranans," Jaquar said. "And a group not of the Tower Community. Ready?"

Marian nodded.

He grinned again. "It's been a long time since I've been in here." He tilted his hat. "Not since my early youth." Sweeping open the door, he held it for her to enter first.

Noise and color rushed over her. To her right was a long bar with many Chevaliers—men and women in equal number— lounging against it, talking. She had the feeling women had been part of the fighting force for as long as men had. She saw people ranging from an older man who looked as tough as beef jerky to a fresh-faced teenaged girl who walked toward them. Her eyes widened as she passed them, and she dipped her head in greeting.

Others stepped back, giving Jaquar and Marian a clear path. She blinked and finally saw Alexa at the last booth on the left. The Marshall stood and waved, grinning.

Each booth held four or more people, except the one just before Alexa's, which held an intense couple clutching hands and sharing a strained conversation and potent Song underlaid with deep sexual tones. Alexa's booth held only her.

When they reached the booth, Jaquar indicated Marian should slide along the leather seat closest to the wall and face Alexa. He followed, placing his body between Marian and the Chevaliers.

"Salutations, Marian," Alexa said, and Marian heard the more casual *Hey, Marian* in her mind.

"Salutations, Alexa," Marian said.

"Salutations, Alyeka," Jaquar said.

Alexa inclined her head to Jaquar. "Salutations, Jaquar."

"I don't see Bastien," Jaquar said as Alexa sat. He slid his hat to the far corner of the table near Marian.

"No, he's at the Castle volaran stables. A wild, pregnant volaran flew in and asked for his help. Apparently she thought the birth would be complicated. My personal assistant, Marwey, just updated me—you saw her on the way out."

"*You* have a personal assistant?" The words escaped Marian before she could stop them.

Alexa laughed and sat. "I have a personal assistant, and *ten* Chevaliers." She rolled her eyes. "Some of the Chevaliers should be in Bastien's employ, but he doesn't like being a boss. Do you want beer, Marian?"

A serving woman had sidled to the table. She stood near Alexa as if believing even a slightly known Exotique was better than a strange Exotique and a Sorcerer.

"Do they have wine?"

"I wouldn't recommend the wine here," Jaquar said. "The mead might be acceptable."

"I'm drinking tea." Alexa lifted her mug. "They keep it for me."

"Mead is honey wine, right?" Marian asked, searching her memory.

"Ayes," the waitress confirmed.

Marian smiled at her. She took a step back.

Marian said, "Mead is fine."

"I'll have lager," Jaquar said.

Though the barmaid looked like the type of woman who enjoyed flirtation and male attention, she smiled superficially at Jaquar and hurried away.

Jaquar lifted Marian's hand to his lips and kissed it, then linked fingers with her. Alexa tilted her head and her eyes unfocused. Marian sensed the Marshall was studying their auras and listening to the Song surrounding them—a Song that clearly rang of recent sex.

Her eyebrows dipping, Alexa sent Marian a questioning glance. *Do you realize you've formed a sex bond with Jaquar?* She said mentally to Marian.

Hard not *to realize that,* Marian said. *I know what I'm doing.*

Alexa appeared doubtful but didn't contradict Marian.

At that moment the server bustled up with a wineglass she deftly slid to Marian, and an ale mug for Jaquar. A silver coin appeared on the table near Jaquar's mug and the woman squealed and scooped it up.

Marian smiled as she hurried away, then took a gulp of

mead that tasted of spicy herbs, wine and honey. She tilted her head back and saw them.

Heads. Mounted on the wall.

Monsters.

Her hand holding the glass went limp and crashed to the table. She forced herself to swallow instead of spew the drink.

She couldn't tear her gaze away from the awful creatures. These were the real thing of the holographic images Alexa had shown her. Render—black, bristly fur, wide mouth opened in a snarl with awful, sharp teeth. Two paws were mounted, too, each with six curved razor-sharp claws. Slayer—yellow head covered with spines, wicked tiny eyes. Soul-sucker—reptilian gray skin, round sockets for eyes and nose, a torso sporting two arms with two tentacles framing each arm. Her gaze went to Jaquar's hat, which he'd put on the table. Definitely made of soul-sucker.

Gulping again and again to keep her mead down, Marian tried not to think of them attacking the humans here. Attacking and killing.

Her stomach rolled. She put a hand on her throat to force the sickness down, but still tasted the "tassy water"—as a young Andrew had named bile—preceding nausea.

Alexa gripped Marian's hands hard, and a soothing balm sifted through Marian from her.

Jaquar scowled and said, "What is it?" He set an arm around her shoulders.

"Just keep your eyes from the upper third of the room," Alexa said in English. Marian got the idea that she was upset on Marian's behalf, and slipped into the language for that reason. Lladranan would never be Alexa's first language—but if Marian had the chance to stay, her English would dim.

Marian took a couple of deep breaths, redolent of beer and

fire smoke—oddly, the latter comforted her, too. The smoke carried the tang of fire and Marian drew it within her. "It's the heads," Marian said.

"Whose heads?" asked Jaquar.

Another thing that Alexa from Earth understood and Jaquar didn't.

Alexa grimaced. "Sorry, I was appalled when I first saw them, too." She shrugged. "But now I face the real things often enough that they don't faze me."

The fire smoke that had warmed her blood turned cold. Alexa battled these things. Marian wanted to hug the woman, wrap her close, take her home. But Alexa had found a new home and a new destiny and it seemed to suit her—she was truly a warrior woman at heart.

Their eyes met and Marian saw wry wisdom in Alexa's. "I'm happy here," she said softly.

Marian forced a smile and a nod. "I can see that," she replied in Lladranan.

Alexa wrinkled her nose. "Okay," she said in English, then switched to Lladranan. "I could use a better skill for the language, and an easier time of riding lessons, both horse and volaran. Do you ride?"

"Ayes," Marian replied in Lladranan.

Looking at Marian with narrowed eyes over her mug of tea, Alexa sipped, then put her cup down. "You have it easy."

"I was an Apprentice and am now a Scholar, still studying to become a Circlet. *You* became a Marshall that first night."

Alexa cheered. "You're right. It was awful passing those Tests, but I did get them all over with." She sighed. "But it took me a while to Pair, and until then no one considered me a full Marshall." She shrugged again. "That's over with." Leaning forward with a renewed light in her eyes, Alexa asked, "Can you really ride lightning?"

"Ayes."

Wriggling in delight, Alexa said, "That's so cool. Could you teach me?"

20

Jaquar squeezed Marian's shoulder and his attention was pulled back to Alexa and Marian. From the corner of her eye, Marian had watched him play male eye-and-attitude games, warning other men away from the table.

He said, "No, Alexa, Marian can't teach you how to ride lightning. She hasn't mastered the technique herself, and you may not have Power that's linked to Fire to learn."

Alexa pouted, then cunning crossed her face. Without a word, her jade baton appeared in the center of the table standing on end and the bronze flames burst into fire, both real and magical.

An instant of silence, then came sounds of scraping chairs and rustling garments. Marian glanced around to see the Chevaliers—both male and female—who had been casually leaning at the bar now studiously faced it. The sharp whispers from the booth behind Marian stopped. No one looked at Alexa's table.

Only Marian felt Jaquar tense, otherwise he kept an impassive expression.

"Point taken," Jaquar said.

"Very impressive," Marian said.

With a wave of Alexa's hand, the baton disappeared, probably back under the table and into its sheath. Since Alexa didn't peep, Marian deduced no fire had burned her, nor was the baton hot. Definitely impressive.

Relief seemed to ripple through the room, voices wove back into normal conversation. Alexa gazed around thoughtfully. "They still think I'm an unknown quantity, ready to go off like a rocket."

"They aren't the only ones," Jaquar murmured. Marian agreed.

"Two Exotiques and a Circlet Sorcerer, all strange folks, and the place is still full of Chevaliers." Alexa nodded in satisfaction. "Goes to show how tough they are."

Marian thought anyone that could hang around in a rough place like this with a bunch of monster heads decorating the walls had to be tough.

Jaquar said, "I think about a quarter of the room emptied when we joined you."

Shrugging, Alexa scanned the men and women again. "The crème de la crème of the Chevaliers remained," she said.

Marian decided Alexa personally knew everyone who was left. "I know I can't have a baton like yours without becoming a Marshall," she said, "but do you think I can have a magic wand or something?"

Alexa's eyes opened wide. "You'll get a magic telescoping

staff. All the Circlets of the Fifth Degree have them. Didn't they tell you?"

"No."

"They never realize the holes in our knowledge." Alexa shook her head.

"I've figured that out," Marian said.

At that moment the outside door opened. Alexa heard it, looked up and narrowed her eyes. The door shut, and a new, strong Song approached them. It was the most intricate, Powerful and potent Song Marian had heard since coming to Lladrana. The sheer richness of the music overpowered her for a moment. She realized it was the Song of a married couple—soul mates.

A few seconds later the young woman Marian and Jaquar had passed on the way in stopped at their table. On her shoulder was a warhawk. The girl was followed by a young man who wore bright purple Chevalier leathers. These were the two with the wonderful Song.

Eyeing the hawk—Sinafin—warily, Marian addressed her. "Salutations, feycoocu," she said.

Sinafin preened, then nodded. *Salutations, Scholar.*

"Salutations, feycoocu," said Jaquar.

To Marian's surprise, the bird stepped from the girl's shoulder to Jaquar's. He blinked as if also amazed.

The girl gestured to Alexa to scoot over. With a frown, Alexa moved to the corner, muttering about people taking advantage of a small person. The girl sat next to Alexa and the young man seated himself next to the girl.

"This is my personal assistant, Marwey, and my Chevalier Pascal," Alexa said.

Marian noticed a bright purple badge on Marwey's cloak,

and once again looked at Pascal's tabard of purple. She couldn't help staring at Alexa. "You like purple."

Alexa growled. "It's the traditional color for Exotiques. Be glad you aren't dressed in it and that everything around you isn't purple."

"You're kidding, right?" Marian blurted in English.

Alexa buried her nose in her large mug. "Tho." The Lladranan "no" echoed hollowly.

Staring at the young couple sporting the hideous color, Marian shook her head.

Pascal's eyes fired. "It's a perfectly good color!"

Marwey pinkened and nodded.

"Maybe they don't see the exact shade we do," Marian said weakly.

Alexa's eyebrows rose. "They are an aural society."

Interrupting Jaquar's stare-down with the bartender, Marian addressed him. "What do you think of Alexa's…livery?" She thought "livery" was the word for what a noble person dressed the subordinates in their household in.

Jaquar glanced at Pascal's purple leathers. "Bright. Interesting."

Marian and Alexa shared a glance.

"I have purple clothes, purple bed hangings," Alexa said gloomily. She glared at Sinafin, the feycoocu. "A purple *muff!*"

"Really?" Marian couldn't believe the being who'd frightened her so badly the night before could be anything as innocent as a muff.

A crash of breaking glass diverted everyone's attention to the bar. Then a streak of purple caught Marian's eye as Sinafin—a muff—rolled off Jaquar's shoulder and across the table to land in front of Marian.

My visit last night was necessary, said Sinafin. Her mental voice was soft as a whisper, meant only for Marian's ears. *I am sorry, but it was necessary.*

Marian figured that was the best apology she'd get from the creature. The thickly furred muff rippled, exuding comfort. Hesitantly Marian petted the muff and it warmed under her fingers, sent her a few bars of "Over the Sea to Skye."

With a sigh, Marian gave up her anger and continued stroking Sinafin. Lovely animal, ugly muff.

Marwey glanced at Pascal. He studied Jaquar and Marian, shrugged.

"Alyeka?" Pascal said.

"Yes?" said Alexa.

"I have something of importance to ask and think it must be spoken of now," Pascal said. He squared his shoulders, discreetly nodding toward the booth behind Marian and Jaquar.

Jaquar straightened and gazed at the younger man. The muff rolled away from Marian and off the table to the bench beside her, then onto the floor.

"What is it?" Alexa had set her mug down and had tilted her head as if trying to hear any Songs coming from the booth.

Marian herself heard erratic, harsh rhythms. Two Songs inextricably melded together, both hopeless.

Alexa frowned. "I don't understand what you want."

Marwey's lips tightened. "Koz and Perlee Desolly. They're friends of ours. They're—"

"Desperate," Pascal finished. "They Paired against the wishes of the noble they flew under and both were dismissed from his service. They're independent now and penniless."

"Reynardus," Marwey said flatly.

Glancing at Marian, Alexa explained, "Bastien's father. The former Lord Knight of the Marshalls."

In urgent tones, Pascal said, "The Desollys need support. A

helping Song. Knowledge that they're good Chevaliers, good people."

Hands wrapped around her mug, Alexa nodded. "I understand. Most of Reynardus's fliers are now with Luthan or Bastien and me."

"The thing is—" Marwey wet her lips, swallowed "—we're not sure how Luthan and Bastien feel about Koz. He's antagonized them both in the past. And—uh—Bastien and Perlee—well, they played together for a while."

Alexa scowled.

Marwey continued. "But only for a month or two, and they both moved on. It was a long time ago."

Alexa was shaking her head.

"Please, Alyeka," said Marwey. "Take them on. We will—"

Holding up a hand, Alexa stopped the girl's tumble of words. "I can't believe you hesitated to ask. Of course they can fly under my banner," she said. Then her tone sharpened. "They're good, and will fit in with my team?"

"We'll make sure they do," Pascal assured her.

"All right, then." Alexa screwed up her face. "I think I still have plenty of zhiv to pay two more Chevaliers."

A yip came from under the table and a small dog scrambled up to Alexa's lap, then hopped onto the table, where it panted, swiped Alexa's cheek with a long, pink tongue and curled into a ball. It was the shapeshifter Sinafin, the fey-coocu frog-fairy-vulture-hawk-muff.

Marian stared at it. "A miniature greyhound?" she murmured.

"Yes," Alexa said, petting the dog. "They don't exist in Lladrana."

"Of course not," Marian said politely. "That would be too easy."

She shared a smile with Alexa. Then the other woman stood on tiptoe to peer over Marian's head into the booth behind her.

Alexa looked at Pascal. "What rank do you want to give the Desolly Pair?"

Pascal jutted his chin. "Koz deserves Fourth."

"Fourth rank. He must be good, then," Alexa said.

Pascal slipped from the bench and strode to the other booth. The voices behind Marian stilled, took on the lightness of casual conversation. Then Pascal began speaking in quiet, reassuring tones.

Moments later the emotion throbbing from the booth behind Marian was a relief so pure it held giddiness.

Jaquar tapped a finger on the table. The small gesture had the three women looking at him. "Alyeka, do you have any dreeth teeth left, or, better yet, a spur? There are several Circlets who want those and will pay dearly for them."

Alexa rubbed her hands, grinned. "Oh yes." She looked at Marian and wrinkled her nose. "Gruesome trophies."

The couple from the other booth approached Alexa's table with Pascal. Koz was a big, raw-boned man of bluntly handsome features. Under his arm he sheltered a startlingly beautiful woman with amber eyes and dark brown hair that grew from a widow's peak. Marian hypothesized that she, like Jaquar, had some old Exotique blood—interesting, since progeny from Earth-Lladranan unions were rare. She wondered if a Circlet had kept track of the bloodlines, the genetic code...

"Swordmarshall Alyeka Vauxveau, I present to you Koz and Perlee Desolly, who I think would make an excellent Chevalier Pair of the Fourth Rank for your household."

"Thank you," the woman whispered.

Koz's jaw worked. "I promise you, Swordmarshall Alyeka, you will never regret this."

"Welcome to my household, Chevaliers." Alexa held out her hand.

Desolly touched her fingers briefly with his own, then half bowed. "Thank you."

The woman and Alexa shook hands.

"I will pay for your lodgings in Horseshoe Hall or the Keep," Alexa said.

"Thank you, Lady," Perlee said. She smiled up at Koz. "We'll have our own rooms. How wonderful!" She bit her lip, glanced back at the booth they'd left. "We can move in immediately… we have our dufflecases."

Alexa smiled and waved a hand. "Fine. I'm sure Marwey and Pascal have it all planned out. Go ahead." Her eyes twinkled at Marwey, who slipped from the bench and started out of the inn.

The Desollys and Pascal followed.

Alexa tilted her cup. It was empty.

"Do you want more tea?" asked Jaquar.

"Not here. I have a better cache up at the Castle. Let's go there." Alexa looked at Marian and a small trill of notes ran in the Song between them. "You can stay in the suite under mine. In my Keep Tower," she said proudly. "It's really great except it's always been assigned to an Exotique, so there's the purple factor."

She turned to Jaquar. "You can stay in the…" She frowned. "Where *do* Sorcerers and Sorceresses stay when they're at the Castle?"

"We have never stayed in the past, but perhaps it is time to be more active," Jaquar said.

"Didn't stay in the past?" Alexa jumped on the admission. Her eyes narrowed. "Since this war with the Dark has escalated, all the Marshalls are living in the Castle rather than on our own estates. It's time the Tower Community establishes a presence in the Castle, too."

Jaquar's teeth gleamed in a smile that wasn't quite nice. "I agree, but you bait me. Well, let's see. We could raise a Tower in the middle of one of the Castle courtyards."

Staring at him, Alexa said with heavy irony, "Oh yeah, that will work."

His brow furrowed as if he pondered her phrasing. Marian chuckled.

"The Castle is called The Marshalls' Castle," Jaquar pointed out. "We of the Tower would be on your grounds—you would have the strategic advantage."

"Heaven forbid that any of the communities of Lladrana would work together to save us all from the Dark," Alexa snapped. "Turf wars. Shee-oot."

Jaw flexing, Jaquar said evenly, "I said I want to end that, but I will also remind you that the Marshalls kept the knowledge that the fence posts were falling and the horrors were invading from the rest of the country until far too late. No wonder the Marshalls have alienated other segments of our society."

"Did we hide that knowledge, indeed?" Alexa stood, planted her hands on the table and leaned forward, every small inch of her exuding menace.

"Not you—those before you." Jaquar raised a hand in peace.

"Can you tell me that none of the Tower Community knew what was going on?" she said in a dangerously low voice. "That no one tracked the Dark? Tell me that you all didn't remain quiet, too, watching the Marshalls struggling to staunch the flow of horrors. That you didn't hesitate to inform the other members of Lladranan society. That you stood back and let Chevaliers die fighting until I asked for your help. That you didn't really join this action until you all knew a sangvile was loose and it was feasting on your own."

The inn had fallen silent, everyone focused on their table. Anger and suspicion swirled in the atmosphere. Did Alexa know she was stirring up a mob? The wait staff had vanished.

Jaquar paled beneath his golden skin. He stood, looming over Alexa. It had no effect on her. "I will say that we made mistakes, individually and as a community." He swept a glance around the room. Many of the Chevaliers turned back to their own business. One tough, rangy man met Jaquar's eyes. "Mistakes we have paid for." Grief laced his voice.

Alexa sighed and raised her hands, palms out. "Peace between us. As we say in Exotique Terre, 'That was then, this is now.'" A considering look came to her eyes. Her smile matched the one Jaquar had given her earlier. "I suppose we Marshalls could claim one of those islands off the west coast that you Circlets like. Establish a presence among you, instead of making rooms available here in the Castle." She straightened.

Choking, Jaquar flung up a hand in what Marian recognized as the gesture of a fencer when hit. "That isn't necessary."

"Then the Tower needs a presence here in the Castle. Permanent rooms. To *work with* the Marshalls and the Castleton City Guildfolk." Alexa's glance speared Marian. "Try to integrate the Tower Community with the Marshalls."

Marian opened her mouth, closed it, then stood.

Jaquar reached out and took her hand, raised it to his lips. "For tonight I'll stay with Marian." He paused.

When she didn't contradict him, she felt some tension leave his stiff body.

"Tomorrow we can tour the Castle and choose rooms for the Tower Community, should any wish to come and stay."

"I'll expect you at the Marshalls' Council Meeting tomorrow morning," Alexa said.

"Of course. I'll be there."

The outside door opened, and as fresh, cool night air poured in, Marian felt some of the negative emotions in the room flow out—given a little push by Alexa and some of the Chevaliers. Marian was impressed at the teamwork, the willingness to help. Her vision shifted slightly and she heard Power—a ready tune of support from the flying knights encased Alexa, and washed to Marian, too, out of respect for Alexa and her obvious acceptance of Marian. No tune reached Jaquar.

Sinafin yipped. *That was very well done. It is a good start.* She approved.

Marian saw some Chevaliers nod and realized the feycoocu had broadcast the comment.

A middle-aged, sturdy woman of obvious authority strode to them.

Alexa inclined her head to the woman, gestured to Alexa. "Lady Hallard, Representative of the Chevaliers to the Communities of Lladrana, let me introduce you to Exotique Scholar Marian Harasta."

The woman's dark brown eyes studied Marian. She nodded once, briskly, and shot out her hand. Marian untwined her fingers from Jaquar's and took the woman's hand, found it hard with calluses. Obviously this woman didn't send her Chevaliers into battle without her—she led her Chevaliers in battle.

"Salutations, Marian, pleased to meet you." She dipped her head at Jaquar. "Sorcerer Circlet Dumont, good to see you. We need all the help we can get." She hesitated, then tramped away to the bar and the tough, rangy Chevalier that wore her colors—gray and yellow.

"Let's go now," Alexa muttered. "Before everyone in Castleton shows up to meet you and ask you questions. At least you speak the language well," she said enviously. "Better than I do."

She swept out in front of them. Jaquar plucked up his hat and set it on his head, left the booth and stepped aside for Marian, then brought up the rear. Marian was amused that she was sandwiched protectively between the two.

No one stopped them.

The night air was brisk, the sky magnificently star-studded. The air smelled pure and with her inhalations, Marian tasted Song—the tang of the City, the mainland of Lladrana.

Once they left the vicinity of the Nom de Nom, the streets and squares were quiet, though not dark. Plenty of windows were lit, showing that the culture wasn't simply dawn-to-dusk.

Marian and Alexa walked together and Jaquar trailed behind, talking with Sinafin who had changed into warhawk form when none of them were looking and rode on his shoulder.

Soon they reached the road to the Castle. It was uphill. Marian straightened her spine and tried not to think of her aching feet. At least the magical slippers had wonderful arch support.

Alexa took off at a rapid pace. Valiantly, Marian kept up. "Alexa," Marian said in English, trying to keep a whine from her voice. "Can you slow down a little? I walked two hours to a beach, practiced Power lessons for another three or four, then rode lightning here." She glanced back at Jaquar, who was talking to Sinafin. "Not to mention…other activities. My body feels like…" Her muscles felt whipped, but her inner core felt glowing at riding lightning and the sex afterward.

"Oh? Sorry. Those 'other activities' can really wear a person out." Alexa grinned up at Marian.

"Yes. How far is it?"

"To the Castle? About two miles."

Marian suppressed a groan, but Alexa sensed it anyway. "Not used to walking, eh?"

"No. Bus."

"Car." Alexa sighed. "I'm a bad horsewoman. Of course, since I used to be a *terrible* horsewoman, that means I'm improving. I haven't ridden alone on volaranback lately, not since I broke my arm again." She shook her head. "I fall off. Everyone, including the volarans, is appalled. Maybe I have an inner ear problem. No, can't be that because the jerir got in my ears all three times and that would have healed."

She continued talking, but Marian paid no mind as she struggled to grasp the wisps of memories that had come from Alexa during their blood-bond. "Wait!" Alexa stopped, Marian gestured to continue walking and they did, but she said, "The jerir pool—a healing pool. It healed awful wounds."

"Yes, it did," said Alexa. "And little cuts and scrapes, and bruises. Everything. We used all the benefits up and had to send the remaining sludge away. I think to some island where a Circlet could study it." She put her hand on Marian's arm. "But I don't know how jerir is for diseases. You might want to speak to the Castle Medica or Swordmarshall Thealia. I know they're working with a black-and-white baby who swallowed some jerir. Black-and-whites usually have bad Power flow, but whether that translates into bad brain synapses or what, I don't know."

"Maybe, just maybe…" Marian whispered.

"Marian, if jerir was a cure-all for black-and-white problems or anything else, I assure you, rare as it is, it would still be used *a lot.*"

Marian sniffed back hopeful tears that had lodged in her throat. "You're right, of course. But it's an avenue to explore."

"Of course." Alex stared at Marian. "You really do look exhausted."

"Thanks a lot." Marian shrugged. "I ache."

"The Castle baths are spring fed. Hot springs," Alexa said. She skipped a little up the road.

Marian nearly closed her eyes at the energy radiating from the woman.

"Hot springs," Marian repeated reverently.

"Yup. The best are the Chevaliers' baths in the bottom of Horseshoe Hall. Efficacious minerals, good Powerful soothing spells, a series of different temperature pools." Alexa waved. "Whatever you need."

"Sounds wonderful."

"They're also the busiest. Probably full right now. Co-ed bathing." Alexa slid a glance Marian's way.

Marian was shaking her head.

"Yeah, I know, I don't care for it, either. The Marshalls have a fancy public bath in the bottom of the Keep—pretty mosaic tiles, greenery." She cocked her head. "No one's there right now. It's co-ed, too, so Jaquar can keep you company. Between the two of you, you could ward the door and make it private." Alexa wiggled her brows, then sobered. "Marian, you *do* know that every bond you make—with Bossgond, the blood-bond I forced you into—"

"Don't you say that! I agreed."

"You didn't—don't—know all the ramifications—"

"Maybe not, but I'm an adult. Don't take my choices away from me. I don't want you feeling guilty over this."

"Oh, all right. But to continue my warning from my vast experience of three months—every bond you make with someone here, with Amee itself, will tie you here, and I know that's not what you want. You have one helluva a Song going with Jaquar already."

"I know."

"Just saying—"

"Thank you, but I'll be fine." *I have to be.*

21

Whether Jaquar had noticed that their pace had sped up, Marian's agitated voice or a ruffling of the Song he shared with her, he caught up and walked with them.

Actually, he strutted. "The feycoocu has graced me with the gift of her name."

Marian and Alexa shared a glance. "Sinafin?" they asked in unison, looking at the bird.

Jaquar's mouth twisted. "I should have known both of you knew it."

Of course, said Sinafin. *They are Exotiques. All the Exotiques will know my name.*

His eyes narrowed with calculation.

"That reminds me," Marian said, switching back to Lladranan. "The woman we met at the Nom de Nom, Perlee Desolly, looks as if she has some Exotique blood. I was under the impression that children from Exotique-Lladranan unions are rare."

"True," Alexa said. "But they do occur. My estate—the one gifted me as an Exotique—and you'll get one and a salary, too, Marian—was established by an Exotique who had children." Alexa stared straight ahead. "I doubt Bastien and I will have children. It's not good to bring children into the world when both parents are fighters." She shrugged. "And if Lladrana ever wins this war, I still don't think we'd be blessed. During the two visions I had of my life on Earth or my life here, children were not in my future. We practice birth control, anyway."

"How?" asked Marian.

Now Alexa turned her head and smiled. "Really a curious person, aren't you, Marian."

Marian was glad the dark would not show her flush. "Yes."

"Only to be expected, you being an academic and all. But I would have thought that Jaquar would say something about it—or Bossgond, even."

Marian stared at Jaquar's profile. "They didn't."

Jaquar shrugged. "It didn't come up. I know Marian can't stay. I did what was necessary." Sinafin asked him something and he turned his head to talk with her.

"Powerful people—such as Marshalls or Circlets—can control bodily functions. During sex we usually turn up the body heat and kill the little swimmers."

"Sperm?" Marian asked.

"That's it," Alexa replied cheerfully. "Fry 'em to hell." She waved her hand. "Poof. They're gone."

"Interesting," Marian said. She was almost distracted from the topic she wanted to pursue. "Has anyone ever kept track of all the mixed bloodlines through genealogy?"

"Like an Exotique descendants' Lorebook?" Alexa asked.

"Yes."

"I don't know."

Marian caught Jaquar's attention and repeated the question.

"I haven't heard of any," he said, and picked up the pace so that Alexa nearly had to run.

"Didn't your parents ever discuss your heritage with you?" asked Alexa. She wasn't even panting.

"No. I was abandoned as a child. In Krache." He gave a humorless smile. "A seaport with few decent people. My adoptive parents found me living in the streets there."

"Oh," Alexa said. "Sorry."

Sinafin rubbed her feathered head against his cheek, crooning.

Alexa stared at Jaquar, then shook her head. "Well, at least I don't have to look at that hat anymore. Bastien made it for himself, you know. Really ugly hat."

Marian followed the new conversational lead. "Very ugly hat. Uglier than your purple muff."

Sinafin clicked her beak in amusement.

They arrived at the main gate of the Castle. The Marshalls' Castle. Marian had visited a couple of castles in France, but this one looked more like Windsor than a French chateau.

There was a drawbridge, and the edge of the iron portcullis showed near the top of the entryway. The hallway beyond the gate must have been at least fifteen feet long, leading into a courtyard.

Since Jaquar and Alexa walked quickly and the buildings overshadowed the grassy courtyard, details were lost.

Alexa headed toward the far door of the yard. "This is the lower ward," she said. Pulling her jade baton from its sheath, she pointed it at a large, square wooden door with iron strapwork and hummed two notes. The door banged open. Marian caught horrified looks on the faces of two uniformed soldiers as they flattened themselves against the inner wall.

"Sorry," Alexa said. "I didn't know anyone was minding the door." She slipped her baton back in its sheath and stepped over the foot-high threshold of the door.

Jaquar chuckled and did the same.

As Marian followed she met the eyes of the soldiers—both middle-aged, one man and one woman—and found them staring at Jaquar, then her, mouths open.

More gossip would circulate, for certain.

Alexa waved to the massive Keep. "Thealia's Tower is the closest, mine is behind hers, overlooking the cliff." She angled toward it.

This yard wasn't grass like the previous one, but stone. A huge round building about three stories high dominated the far end.

Jaquar held out his hand and Marian took it. He gazed down at her, smiling. Did she look as lost as she felt at this turn of events?

Sinafin emitted a piercing cry and Marian wondered if Alexa had kept track of all of Sinafin's forms; it seemed the creature had an infinite variety. The hawk flew across the yard.

"She's going to Bastien and his laboring volaran," Alexa said.

"This is Temple Ward," Jaquar said. He gestured to the round building. "That's the Temple where the Marshalls Summoned you."

Memory images clicked into place of the gigantic round room, a pentacle, an altar. "If I want to return to Earth, should I leave from there?"

Alexa halted, glanced back at them. "Probably best. The Marshalls are the strongest team in the country. I don't think a band of Circlets would have the experience in blending their Power to accomplish such a difficult and delicate task. Or you can wait for the Snap."

"I'll figure out how to recompense you for sending me home before I leave. The timing of the Snap is too uncertain," Marian said.

They entered a cloister walk of open stonework arches that ran along most of the Keep, then went to the far Tower, where there was a door. Alexa ushered them through and into a large hallway. She indicated the left wall. "That's the Marshalls' Council Room." When they came to an intersecting corridor—another wide hall—Alexa turned left. "The hall at the end of the building opening to the right leads to my tower. I'll show you to your suite, then I think I'll check on Bastien in the volaran stables."

So they traversed the corridors and mounted the stairs in Alexa's tower. As in Jaquar's Tower, the steps were a tight spiral of stone.

Alexa crossed the circular inner entryway to a door and flung it open, then turned left down a dim, narrow passage and threw open another door. "Your rooms. Be glad the Marshalls only used an incredible amount of purple in my suite." She grinned at Jaquar. "You should know lighting and housekeeping spells—you might want to dust." Then she hurried away.

Whistling several notes, Jaquar entered as light flickered in crystal orbs on the walls.

"It's beautiful," Marian said. She stared into a richly colored bedroom—rugs of complementary patterns, a wide expanse of windows that followed the curve of the tower. To her right was a huge canopy bed, complete with curtains.

Marian stared at the bed. The heat of her blood seemed to rise until it pulsed just under her skin, sensitizing every nerve.

She was intensely aware of Jaquar standing beside her, though she didn't turn to look at him. She could hear his every breath, sense the waves of his aura, and the melody between them rolled like thunder in her ears, in her heart. She barely breathed herself, afraid that moving might shatter her mind, the sensory input was so great. She didn't know how she stood the feeling throbbing between them.

"I can't," she whispered in English.

But he must have known it was denial.

His footsteps were mere brushes of shoe upon thick rug, yet she heard them…retreating. At the door, he murmured, "I'll be in the Keep baths at the lowest level. Follow our Song if you wish to join me."

A slight disturbance of air indicated the opening and shutting of the door.

Marian trembled violently, took one step, two, toward the bed. Fell across it. She panted and tears leaked from under her eyelids. She lay there for a moment, doing nothing but existing, as if her mind spun in starry space, scattered into electrical impulses that were stars, no thought, only being.

She was afraid her heart had developed a small crack that could wrench it in two. One part of her longed to stay in Lladrana, become a Sorceress, fulfill her natural potential…learn more of Jaquar.

The other part would always need Andrew—for brotherly love, to protect and be protected. Her family.

How could she merge the two?

She could return to Earth and stay.

She could return to Earth, explain everything to Andrew and return to Lladrana.

She could stay in Lladrana—but, no, that was not truly an option.

The most exciting, the most frightening possibility of all was to convince Andrew to return to Lladrana with her. But could she? What if he would live longer and better on Earth? What if there really was no hope for him on Lladrana? What if she couldn't come back, let alone bring Andrew with her? What price would they pay to return?

And why was she thinking of all these abstruse matters when there was a sexy hunk of man waiting to pleasure her in the wet, steamy, exotic baths…? Because she was afraid her feelings for Jaquar played a big part in her decision.

But, of course, there was such a thing as thinking too much, overanalyzing. That was exactly what she was doing now.

Marian stretched, and grit pricked her skin—dust from the road? Caked mud from lovemaking in the field? Electricity of her body attracting particles during the lightning ride? Probably all three.

She hopped from the bed and did a quick exploration of the tower suite. She was becoming well informed about tower living arrangements. This one had a bathroom with a shower, but no bathtub, as usual.

Definitely time for a wash.

Humming—and realizing she was lilting a portion of the tune that linked her to Jaquar—Marian let the notes seep into her, lead her feet instinctively. An interesting alternative to thinking—simply following instinct. She seemed to be much more tied to the world and people and Songs here than on Earth.

She reached the lowest level of the Keep. Instead of dark and dank, twisty passages, she found well-lit corridors that were wide.

For a moment she hesitated outside the door. Their previous sex could be rationalized away as excitement from playing in the storm. If she went in now, they'd join together again—knowingly and deliberately on both their parts.

Letting her emotions, her sexuality, surface and overwhelm the sharp thoughts, Marian pushed the door open.

He stood waiting for her, shining droplets scattered over his body. The lush setting of colorful mosaic tiles complemented his golden skin, dark hair, blue eyes. A man in the prime of his life, he moved toward her with muscular power and grace. He could be a sultan, a water god. He was a Circlet, a great Sorcerer. A magnificent man.

An aroused man.

Her insides began to tremble as her body readied for him. No need to suppress logical thought patterns now—they were gone. Memories whirled through her of his hands, his lips, the sound of his low groan as he climaxed. She wanted it all again. More and longer.

She wanted to glide her hands over his firm muscles, feel the teasing prickle of his body hair. She wanted him over her and in her.

So she held out her hand, but he stepped past her. Half turning, she saw him place his palm against the door A maroon light flared around his fingers as he crooned, "Private and special, softly keep this place for us alone."

That Song was a tune that repeated again and again in her mind as he came to her, smiling.

Eyes locked on hers, he took her hands, lifted one to his lips, turned it over and pressed a tingling kiss into her palm, then did the same with the other. He loosed her hands and her fingers curled inward, to hold his tender kisses.

His palms curled around her shoulders as he leaned forward and kissed her forehead, then her eyes closed as he touched his lips to each eyelid. He was undoing her, utterly. Nothing in the universe mattered save him, his soft mouth, his gentle wooing of her. She didn't even care that he comprised her world. No warning alarms rang in her head. Only the deep languid feelings stirring inside her were important. Only the yearning that would coil tightly, demanding to be assuaged.

Her eyes opened again as he kissed the tip of her nose, brushed her lips with his. All so reverent, as if he was cherishing her. Her breath left on a moan.

She raised her own hands, placed them on his face, felt the elegant bones beneath his skin, saw the shadows under his eyes that grief had painted. Yet nothing in his touch, in his bearing, in his Song reverberated with grief and she was glad she gave him surcease from that emotion. She stroked his lean jaw, slid her thumbs over his full lips. Lips she had to taste. She tilted her head and drew his mouth to hers.

The meeting of their lips was the most exquisite thing she'd ever felt. Promising. Infinitely promising. She could believe anything with his mouth against hers. Feel everything. She opened her lips, feathered her tongue across his lips, savored his taste of wild forest herbs, of wind, of man, bringing it into her to keep.

His tongue followed suit, traced his taste over her lips, relished her, then plunged into her mouth, penetrating, exploring, as if all her essence could be learned from this kiss.

He broke the embrace and stepped back, his eyes dark, his face taut with passion, his chest rising and falling with ragged breaths. When he raised his hands they trembled, and he met her eyes and laughed. "What you do to me, Lady. Beauty—of heart, of mind, of body, of *Song*. I have never heard such a compelling Song." Fisting his hands as if checking they still obeyed him, he crushed the fabric of her dress at her shoulders, then lifted the gown from her, tossing it aside to lie like an emerald shadow.

A raspy noise caught in his throat as he studied her. He shook his head. "Exotique. Who knew such splendor existed—pale skin, red, red hair, nipples the color of—" Again the groan and head shake. "Beyond any Lladranan delights."

Frowning, he said, "What happened to that—that garment which molds your breasts?"

She felt herself blush, and since it started above her breasts he watched with interest. "My bra?" She nodded to the gown. "It's in a pocket of my gown."

"Yet you wear the lower piece that emphasizes your femininity."

It was nothing more than a pair of high-cut panties.

Jaquar shuddered. "You'd best hurry and bathe. I have already done so. I can't stand the wait for you much longer."

She shucked her panties, scanned the tile for puddles and avoided his tracks as she hurried to the pool. She decided it was long and deep enough for a flat dive. The Marshalls did themselves proud.

The water—warm and gliding silkily against her skin—full of herbs, she guessed. Her fingers touched the bench jutting from the pool wall and she surfaced. She shook her head to fling her hair from her eyes and glanced around.

Jaquar slowly walked to the pool. She thought she could see the heat of desire emanating from him in the steam.

Marian ducked under, then bobbed back up. She wanted to soak her bruised body—later. She spied a dish of soaps, grabbed the first one and began a scrub. She'd just done her hair when Jaquar put his hands under her arms and drew her from the water.

She gasped, but before she could protest, he was washing her thoroughly. She moaned and hung on to him as his slick hands caressed her, massaging her breasts until all she could hear was her own panting. He was relentless, sliding his hands over the curve of her hips and belly, up and down her legs. His fingers delved between her thighs, exquisitely, knowledgeably. Her balance wavered.

Her vision dimmed, but her sense of smell heightened. The fragrance of the soap rose to her nostrils—aloe and something sharper that reminded her of deserts more than green Lladrana. It mixed with a luxurious scent that she realized with a touch of self-consciousness was her own arousal. Then there was Jaquar's natural scent, and his own musky arousal. She whimpered as the combination blew through her like a scouring wind, hollowing so she could be filled with something else, something new.

And filled with man.

She swayed toward him.

His hands were strong around her waist. "Take a breath. I'll rinse you, then…then…"

She closed her eyes and inhaled deeply.

"By the Song, your *breasts*…" he murmured. She was raised, then lowered gently into the water that lapped against the soles of her feet, causing her toes to curl. The water flowed up her calves to her knees, to her thighs. Then it warmed her sex, and she shuddered, she was so aroused. He slipped her farther into the pool until her breasts floated, nipples tight, and she began to moan.

"Breathe!" he warned.

She shut her mouth. The water caressed her neck, rose over her face, tingled her scalp as her hair spread out.

He smoothed his hands up her body under the water and she could do nothing but twist under his touch. His fingers untangled her hair, then he caught her under her arms and pulled her out of the water.

Releasing her breath in a puff, she finally opened her eyes to see his face taut, and a flush on his skin that affected her even more. She *needed* him.

The cool air evaporating the water on her contrasted with her heated blood, coiling her arousal tighter. She'd never been so aware of her entire body, and the throbbing of her sex.

Then he settled her on a soft, fluffy bathsheet, big enough to hold them both. One of his hands curved around the back of her neck, bringing her lips close for his kiss. He plunged his cool tongue into her mouth as he angled his body over hers, slipping his knees between her thighs. The roughened brush of his body hair against her sensitized skin had her arching to meet him, welcome him.

He thrust into her, long, deep, powerfully.

She sucked on his tongue, stared into his eyes. He withdrew slightly, lunged again, and she shattered into bliss.

He groaned and followed.

Their Songs merged, took from each other, gave to each other.

Changed them both.

Marian felt enveloped by him. His warmth surrounded her, and the exotic fragrance of bath and sex whirled around her. Time slowed.

Finally, he lifted his head and his gaze was as piercing as ever.

She outlined his cheekbone with the pad of her thumb, chuckled. "You are back to thinking, Jaquar?"

He opened his mouth, hesitated, cleared his throat. "*You* can talk." He set his brow against hers. "I'm going to roll us over into the pool for a quick cleansing."

"I don't think—"

The water slid over them. They didn't hit the bench as she'd feared. Nor did they separate. Jaquar kicked, found his feet, and his hands slid to cup her bottom, entering her.

He flexed his muscles, *all* of his muscles, and Marian began the spiraling climb to the center of the storm once more.

"What's going on in there? Open up now!" a woman shouted from outside the door, banging on it.

Jaquar jerked, withdrew. He grasped her hand and pulled her to the corner stairs leading out of the pool.

"Don't make us use our batons to get in," threatened the woman. She sounded like an angry parent scolding unruly children.

Marian couldn't help herself, she laughed.

There was silence, then a more subdued shout. "I don't recognize you."

"It's Exotique Marian and Circlet Jaquar," Jaquar said coolly, taking a large terry-clothlike robe in midnight blue from a hook on one of the pillars. He wrapped himself in it, then brought another to Marian. It was purple.

Surely this was Alexa's robe.

It was too long for Alexa. It was *Marian's* robe. She was so bemused by the startling color and its very presence that she allowed Jaquar to help her on with it. He stood behind her, overlapped the front and tied the belt in a loose knot, then brought her back against him.

He felt hard and solid and wonderful. His breath was sweet and warm next to her ear. Tenderness flowed from him.

"Ahem," rumbled a male outside the door. "These *are* the Marshalls' baths. And *we* are the Marshalls, yet the door is warded for privacy against us. Do you think you could finish up quickly in there? Training took place in mud fields today."

"Quickly?" whispered Jaquar. "I think not—not this next time."

Heat washed over Marian. "We're coming out. Jaquar, can you dismiss the ward?"

He heaved a sigh. "If I must." With a wicked grin, he continued, "Our loving will be better in bed, anyway."

Heavens. An-*ti*-ci-pa-tion. Marian swallowed, fiddled with adjusting her robe. She hoped they didn't look as if they had had hot and sweaty sex, since they hadn't. It had been more like hot, *wet*, slippery sex. On the other hand, it was probably too late to impress the Marshalls. The damage of this little scene was already done.

On his way to the door, Jaquar picked up her panties and put them in his pocket.

"I want those!" Marian demanded.

He shrugged, rolled their clothes together and tucked them under his arm. He touched the door with one finger. "Open."

"Thank you," the man outside muttered.

Jaquar stood aside and people swept in. The first was a huge man, already shirtless and showing a massive chest covered with scars. Another was a stately woman with narrowed eyes.

Marian dipped in a little curtsy. "Salutations."

"Salutations," the woman said. "And to you, Jaquar."

He inclined his head to the group, "Swordmarshall Thealia."

Some moved to opposite sides of the room and behind openings Marian hadn't noticed. Dressing rooms?

Jaquar caught Marian's hand in his own. He smiled charmingly at Thealia. "Sorry to delay you. We rode the lightning tonight and got quite dirty."

Those who were still in the main bathroom froze.

Thealia opened her mouth, hesitated, then shook her head and waved toward the door. "We have business to discuss. Depart."

"Of course," Jaquar said. Tugging slightly on Marian, he led her away.

After he shut the door, he waited for a moment, and Marian heard the rise of excited voices.

Jaquar smiled in satisfaction. "That will give them something to talk about."

Tucking her hand in the crook of his arm, he led her to their suite under Alexa's rooms. This door, too, he warded for privacy, and Marian watched him and knew she'd learned enough to do the little whistle spell herself.

He came back to her and put his hands on her shoulders, rested his brow on hers. "In the baths, I was too aroused to think. But I want our coming together to be sharing and mutual pleasure, Marian. An act of conscious decision. Sleep with me," he said unsteadily. "More, take me into you and merge with me and hold me and rock me to infinite Song." He removed her robe in a quick sweeping movement. "As I will do for you in return."

She'd never believed a person could talk too much, but Jaquar certainly was doing so. What was that old movie line? "Shut up, you fool, and take me to bed." Worked for her.

He grinned, and laughter rolled from him. He swung her up into his arms.

22

Jaquar didn't sleep well. All he wanted to do was forget himself in Marian's tight body. But he had to speak to Bastien. Once the Marshalls agreed to the new plan to assault the Dark, Marian would be completely safe. As it was, he was certain he had a couple of days before Chalmon and Venetria would act. Chalmon might have derided the Marshalls when it came to making speedy decisions, but most Circlets were even slower. And Chalmon and Venetria alone could not Send Marian; they would have to convince others to help. That, too, took time, and Jaquar had heard no rumblings.

So he dozed and finally heard Alexa return—alone. He dressed quickly in just a robe and walked to the volaran stables. The night was quiet, the sky blazing with stars. Except for a patrolling guard, he was the only one abroad. Even when he passed from Temple Ward to Lower Ward, he saw few people. If Chevaliers were partying, it was in the Nom de Nom or the tiny inn in the outer Castle wall.

He met Bastien as the man exited from the stable passage into the ward. Bastien stood and stretched, breathing deeply. He smelled of sweat—volaran and his own—and other odors that Jaquar didn't want to identify.

Bastien grinned and joined him. "Beautiful night!"

"The volaran mare?"

"Very fine! With a fine filly."

"Excellent."

"That it is." Bastien made to throw an arm around Jaquar's shoulders and chuckled as he stepped aside. "So, Circlet, what do you want of me? Permission to raise a Tower in the middle of Horseshoe Close, here?"

"As if you could grant such."

Bastien laughed, touched the baton at his hip. "I have more influence now."

"I've come to speak of the Dark." Feeling a little wary of the shadows, Jaquar walked to the middle of the ward and slowly began to return to Alexa's tower. Bastien accompanied him. "Is this about plane-walking and finding a maw of evil?"

"You've heard?"

Bastien shrugged. "Rumors."

Jaquar told him of his first trip to the nest and the master's words, then laid out his new plan.

"No," Bastien said flatly, muscles tense. He was all warrior now. He swept his fingers through his black-and-silver hair. "I can't plane-walk. I don't have the control due to the remnants of my wild Power. I am Alexa's Shield, her protector, her Pairling. I will not allow her to fly into this battle without me."

They'd neared the gate to Temple Ward, and didn't speak

until they'd passed through and were beyond the guards' hearing.

Bastien frowned. "Besides, Alexa is an Exotique. She is tied to Amee by me, and the rest of the Marshalls, but her bond with the world is not as strong as that of someone who was born here. She could get lost among the planes." He glanced at Jaquar. "If it were on *this* physical plane, we'd fight, but not otherwise."

"It is Marian's task, then, to fight the Dark in its nest." Bile rose in Jaquar's throat. He'd make sure she didn't go in alone, and that she was Circlet of the Fifth Degree before they attempted it.

"No," Bastien said, and it took a moment for Jaquar to realize what he'd heard.

He stopped outside the Assayer's Office and stared at Bastien. "No?"

Bastien shook his head. "I can't think her task is to destroy the nest all by herself. Powerful as she is, I don't think she could do it. She might harm it, but if she didn't destroy the Dark, too, the nest would regenerate."

"True."

Walking to the entryway of the Keep, Bastien said, "All indications show that every community of Lladrana must be integrated and cooperating to destroy the Dark."

"Also true." They'd reached the landing below Marian's suite.

"Don't say anything about this to the Marshalls' Council tomorrow morning. I want to tell Alexa myself, and I need awhile to figure out how to do that."

"Very well," Jaquar said, and watched Bastien take the stairs up.

His plan was ruined, but only he and Bastien knew. Jaquar

had a couple of days to come up with a new one, but he wouldn't do it alone; he must consult with Bossgond.

He entered the suite and watched Marian sleep. Her skin was so pale in the moonlight, her body so beautiful, her expression so pleased, it made him ache.

Jaquar went and showered, then returned to her. As he slowly woke her, caressed her into moaning passion and took her on another wild ride, he wondered how long he would have her.

He loved seeing the passion and affection in her eyes, the hint of hero-worship. That would die when he warned her, told her what he himself had set in motion.

He'd dealt with too many deaths lately.

It was dawn when Chalmon dismissed the Circlets and Scholars who had been practicing the Sending ritual and looked at Venetria. "Your contribution to the Sending Song was weak. I can't do it without you."

"Even though I don't agree with you?"

His lips quirked. "If you were violently against this, you'd be throwing things at my head. Preferably my glassware." His face hardened. "But it *must* be done. The nest will open again soon, I know it!" He shrugged and moved around the room restlessly in an atypical manner.

Venetria narrowed her eyes. He was sensing something she wasn't—she could tell through the fluctuations in their Song. His Power picked up minute variations in the Amee's Song. Venetria shivered.

"It will be bad, very bad if the maw spews out horrors at this time."

She hesitated. "Perhaps we should consult the Singer."

He barked laughter. "You think I didn't consider that? I

visited her the night before last and was granted an audience. Not a Song, for she knew our affairs as usual, but a meeting. Apparently she's received many Songs recently. No wonder." He strode to the model of the nest he'd made. She didn't follow. The thing disturbed her with its slow, inimical pulsing.

Venetria asked, "What did the Singer say?"

Another short laugh that was no laugh at all. "One sentence. 'Do what you must do.'"

She just stared at him. "That's all?"

Pacing, he nodded sharply. "I had the feeling that the Singer had received many conflicting Songs of future events." He stopped and pivoted to face her, his Song all determination. "We must continue with our plan."

The cry escaped her. "Send an untrained woman into the maw!"

"Partially trained and very, very Powerful. If anyone has the chance to destroy the nest and live, it is Exotique Marian. We'll watch. There is a good chance that once she opens the nest it will be vulnerable to us!" He frowned. "As for being untrained—who knows but that raw Power might be more effective against the nest than trained? The more she is instructed, becomes a Circlet, the more she is learning Amee's ways and dimming her Exotique Terre essence."

"That's merely rationalization."

He swung on her in fury. "You think so? I don't. If you cannot help me in this…" He didn't end the sentence.

She knew what he meant and her heart seemed to shatter into a thousand fragments, only held together by sheer will. Or perhaps her terror of losing him. She couldn't breathe. Her studies had lost much of their allure and now he was the most important thing in her life. She didn't think he felt the same, and didn't dare tell him. She said, "I will Sing with you."

He straightened, his expression calmer—had he, too, feared their Song would break?

Marian awoke to the doorharp, followed by a knock: *"Shave and a haircut. Two bits."* She smiled sleepily. Despite the fact that Alexa would stay in Lladrana, some of her thought processes would be pure Earthling for as long as she lived.

But Marian didn't want to think of Alexa's life span. Like Andrew's, it could be far too short.

Untangling herself from Jaquar, who grunted and reached out an arm to keep her close, Marian rose from the bed, grabbed the purple robe and opened the door.

Alexa grinned up at her, noted the purple robe and rolled her eyes. "I see the Marshalls were ready for you. There's probably a robe like that in every building's baths."

"Huh," Marian said brilliantly.

"Do you want to joint the Marshalls' Council Meeting this morning?"

Marian just stared at her in horror.

Alexa laughed. "Guess not. Well, there's plenty to explore around the Castle." She waved. "Feel free."

"I thought I might visit the baths again."

Chuckling, Alexa said, "A woman after my own heart. The most private is the Ritual Bathing Pool in the Temple, but it's also the coolest."

Marian would like to get a good look at the Temple and discover if there was any possibility that she could Send herself back to Boulder on her own.

Alexa whistled sharply. Marian jumped, then goggled as Jaquar appeared beside her, fully clothed in his maroon Sorcerer's robe and wearing his Circlet of figured gold. Dressed for success. Wow. She'd have to learn that trick.

Looking approving, Alexa smiled. "Come along, Jaquar. I'll excuse Marian from the meeting, but not you. I'm sure the Marshalls have lots of questions about what's been going on in the Tower Community."

Jaquar darted a glance at Alexa. Then he brushed back Marian's hair and kissed her lips softly. "Good morning."

She couldn't help smiling up at him with all the far-too-gooey feelings she felt for him. "Good morning, Jaquar."

"Well, it looks like another example of a Lladranan man being a fabulous lover," Alexa said with a chuckle.

Jaquar just raised an eyebrow. He turned to Marian, caught her around the waist with a hard arm and ravished her mouth. He left her mind reeling, heat welling inside her. She stepped away from him, gave him a little push to send him on his way to a dreary meeting.

"Go away, you two."

"See you later," Alexa said. "You might want to visit the brithenwood garden. I'd like to know what you think of it."

Marian found her gown and underwear in the bathroom. They hung suspended in air in the shower stall, and she just stared for a moment, mouth open. Nibbling her lip, she deduced that Jaquar had "washed" them with some sort of spell, particularly since his shirt, trousers and loincloth also floated midair. That thought, of course, made her wonder if he was wearing anything under his elegant robe. She banished the distracting idea and dressed.

The Keep was cool, as was the cloister walk outside it, but the day was sunny and bright. Only a few soldiers and a couple of Chevaliers were around as she strode up the walk and stopped under the Temple portico. The door to the Temple was huge and wooden, but all she did was lift the iron ring of the latch and it swung inward, opening, the scent of incense wafting out.

She let the ring slip from her grasp and took a step into the dim building, closing the door behind her. For a moment she just stood as her eyes adjusted to the light. The room was fully as big as she remembered, sectioned off here and there by intricately carved screens that didn't reach the high ceiling.

Following the curve of the wall, she explored. Most of the wall on each side of the door held a built-in stone bench with velvet cushions, and piles of lush pillows here and there. She ducked around all the screens and found a dining room, a toilet closet with sink and octagonal, tiled tub, even a place to sleep that held several mattresses covered in silk. There were fireplaces, and light came from the high windows.

The ceiling showed huge beams studded with Power-storage crystals and wheel-chandeliers. Very interesting.

Finally she moved to the area of the room that held the altar and a large pool. When Summoned, she'd thought the pentacle that the Marshalls had used was incised in the stone. Since Bossgond and Jaquar both had permanent pentagrams, she'd continued to think so, but her memory had played her false. Hands on hips, eyes narrowed, she scanned the room, tested her Power against it and received incredible echoes of great spells, bell-tones from the crystals above and the chakra lamp-chimes.

There was no permanent star and circle. Which meant that the Marshalls created the symbols when necessary, probably drawing and angling them in the direction that would vibrate the best with their goals.

Scrutinizing the stones, she found a bit of a vermilion outline of the pentacle that she'd fallen into. She also discovered an almost flaming blue-green line that might have been the color of the pentacle used to Summon Alexa, if her memory of the images Bossgond showed her were true.

Hands clasped behind her to prevent her curious fingers from betraying her by touching the altar, she noted the tools, gleaming with a polish from use and care. The lamp-chimes drew her. Different-colored candleholders looked cut from gemstones. A small mallet lay near them, and Marian could recall the Power of the sounds wrung from them. Her fingers itched to take the mallet and run it across the seven chimes. Would they sound different unlit? What of the size of the candle, or the candle's wick—would that affect the sound? Marian didn't know.

She studied the gong. It looked to be about nine feet in diameter and of hammered, polished silver, with not a smidgeon of tarnish. Again she wanted to unclasp her hands and test—flick a finger and thumbnail against the gong, see what happened.

Better not. Stepping back, she didn't release her entwined fingers until she was far beyond temptation. She looked at the pool. She knew it had once contained the famed healing-liquid, jerir, but now it definitely held herbal water. She glanced at the door to the Temple. No way was she going to bathe in full view of anyone who walked in.

So she returned to the little octagonal pool to wash and shampoo. The moment she stepped from the bath, the bottom opened and the water disappeared. Wow. New water, with flecks of plant matter she hadn't noticed, flooded into the pool from eight sides and it was full again in minutes.

Marian rolled her shoulders, shook out her arms and legs, testing her limbs. No doubt about it, she felt *good* from the bath. Efficacious herbs and minerals, as Alexa had said.

As she walked back to the door, she paused by the large pool and considered it. She hadn't done any lessons today and maybe working with water inside, *here,* might be easier.

Go ahead, Sinafin said. She was a frog again, sitting by the pool. *The Temple is for all human endeavors. Bathing, eating.* The frog grinned. *Practicing Water lessons.*

"Will the Temple and the pool *help* me? I don't want to succeed in lessons here if I can't duplicate them elsewhere."

The frog let out a reverberating *crooaaakkk* that raised the hair on the back of her neck. *Now any advantage is neutralized. I will watch but will neither guide nor add my Power.*

"Thanks." She guessed. She stepped into a wide shaft of sunlight, settled into her stance, called her Power. It was easier now, as if she could sweep all the latent sparks of static electricity from the atmosphere, as if she could process sunlight flowing through the windows into sheer fiery energy. With complete concentration, she followed Jaquar's instructions step by step, not daring to modify any of his Songs of Water Power.

She stared at the pool, tried to evaporate some water. As with her first lesson, she used too much. Sighing, she let the cupful fall back into the pool and began with a droplet.

It worked. She held it, dispersed it into the air, could find it and reform it if she wanted! Yay!

The sun glinted in her eyes, so she closed them. She felt the rays enveloping her, the warmth of the light, the very yellowness. There were other colors in the spectrum, other stars adding their signatures to the light, and she gathered them all, used them on the pool.

She opened her eyes. She'd done it!

Congratulations! croaked Sinafin, glowing green.

With a whoop she danced over to the feycoocu and patted her cool frog head. "I did it!"

You will not forget this lesson, either.

Marian didn't want to think of her previous one with Sinafin. She much preferred Jaquar as a professor.

"One more time," she said, rolled her shoulders and stepped into the shade, keeping her eyes open. This time she tweaked the Songs Jaquar had given her. She held her breath as she collected the slippery water, kept it suspended in the air with her mind, evaporated it—dispersed it into the air—then lifted it to the ceiling, forming a rain cloud. With exquisite precision, she let the misty rain pour down, missing both Sinafin and herself.

The feycoocu hopped over to the rain and wallowed. The little shower ended quickly and Marian punched her arms in the air and shrieked, "Yes!" Then she whirled around, stopped. If she *had* let the rain fall on her, she could have dried herself easily with a warm breeze, intensified sunlight on her clothes and not her skin. Oh yeah!

Now dry the stones, Sinafin said.

Grinning, Marian did.

I will see you later. With complete dignity the frog leaped to the door and through it.

Exclamations came from outside the Temple. Marian chuckled. She skirted the altar and gong. Despite her recent success with water, she didn't trust herself to keep her hands from poking into Powerful instruments that were best left undisturbed by a foolish student—strains of "The Sorcerer's Apprentice" ran through her mind. She surely didn't want to explain any dancing brooms or gong rolling off its stand or gemstone lamp-chimes cracking, or a strange Song emanating from the Temple.

Her imagination ran riot at all the havoc she could cause. She supposed it was an honor—the amount of trust everyone placed in her that she wasn't being watched.

She left the Temple humming, and walked through the courtyard and gate and down to the Lower Ward. There she lingered a moment, observing people train in a circular area with swords and shields and staffs. They were good, and as exciting as any historical movie. Better choreographed, too.

A scent came to her nose that she recognized as volaran and she found her way to the Landing Field. There she observed a couple of Chevaliers depart, one Sword and Shield Pair of male lovers land.

She gave them privacy and turned away to the maze that linked the Landing Field and the Keep and Alexa's brithenwood garden.

Wandering through the maze, Marian knew that she liked this place. Oh, the Castle could never be home to her as it might be to Alexa—though Alexa had her own estate, too. But Lladrana, the world of Amee, resonated inside her. Just walking on the soil was an experience; she seemed to draw a bit of energy into herself at each step. Even water now answered to her Power, left her a bit of fluid strength. Dancing with the wind energized her, too, not to mention riding lightning!

She couldn't imagine herself doing any of those things at home. Not in Boulder. Maybe, if she was very, very careful, she could find some deserted mountain meadow in which to practice. If she even had enough Power on Earth to summon a wind. Her stomach tightened. Somehow she didn't think everything she learned here would work there. How much more effort would she have to use to do magic on Earth?

One more thing she didn't know.

But she did know that she was greedy. She wanted to be the Powerful woman she was becoming, the woman who could play in storms, dance with the wind, ride lightning. The woman who could cook and clean and *create* with magic. Yet

Earth held Andrew, and her mother. Perhaps, with the perspective she'd learned here, the new experiences, somehow she might be able to bond with her mother, love and be loved as family should. She could hope.

Marian laughed when she reached the door to the brithenwood garden. It was small. She'd have to duck, but Alexa could open it and walk straight through. No wonder Alexa liked it. Marian opened the door and hunched her back as she entered the garden. It was one of the most beautiful places she'd ever seen.

The tree that gave the garden its name, the brithenwood, stood tall and willowy with white bark and deep green, narrow spearlike leaves. The scent was floral, but unique as if the perfume comprised several "notes" instead of just one—perhaps the leaves and the bark exuded fragrance as well as the blossoms. Looking up, Marian could see that the top of the tree still held a few white blossoms.

Around the brithenwood was a bench, and two tracks of stepping stones wove through the tangle of garden that was lush with textures and colorful flowers.

Something—the tree, the walled garden itself—dispersed serenity like a scent. The Temple had been serene, too, with an underlying muscle of Power—a place that had seen sanctified Rituals for ages. This garden brought the peace of nature. The tall gray stone walls emphasized the blue of the sky, the low wooden door seemed to hold the world at bay.

As she crossed to the bench, Marian spied a twig about five inches long and half the width of her finger that had fallen from the brithenwood. It was a pretty thing, so she picked it up and slid it into her pocket. Then she sat beneath the tree.

Since the morning was so peaceful, Marian decided to meditate. She drew her legs up and crossed them, rested her hands on her knees and emptied her mind. When a thought or observation occurred, she let it drift by, fade.

The Songs around her helped. Not only the individual Song of the tree, but the sprightly notes of the flowers, the buzzing of bees, the rustling of grasses and leaves in a small breeze, all combined into a lulling melody.

Until a horrible screech jolted her. Her eyelids flew open and she saw a peacock strutting around the garden, tail fully unfolded. Marian choked.

"Sinafin," she said. "Peacocks are male. Peahens are not nearly so colorful."

A beady eye turned in Marian's direction. Sinafin sniffed and continued her progress around the garden.

Marian closed her eyes again, but this time couldn't settle. Which was just as well, since a minute later the door banged open and Alexa tromped in.

Meeting Marian's eyes, Alexa winced and flushed. "Meditating, huh? Sorry." She slammed the door shut.

"I take it the meeting did not go well?" Marian said.

"A couple of the Marshalls put Jaquar's back up and he danced around what the Tower Community was doing about the Dark. I brought up establishing a Tower presence here and you'd've thought I proposed razing the Castle!"

Marian frowned. "Well, I was Summoned for some task, I know that. It's probably rallying the Tower Community, *making* them a community instead of individuals. Then having them integrate with the Marshalls. But that doesn't mean the effort will be welcomed by the Marshalls."

"I'll work on them," Alexa said grimly, fingering her baton in its sheath as she sat next to Marian. Then she saw Sinafin parading around, opening and closing her feathers. "A peacock again." Alexa snorted.

"I told her that peacocks have the pretty plumage and pea-hens are subdued, but she ignored me," Marian said.

Alexa said, "By the way, word has spread that you're here, and a Scholar of the Fourth Degree—"

"Fourth!"

Alexa raised her brows, and her smile widened. "That's what Jaquar told us."

"Wow. Just one more degree—"

"And *Finals,* probably worse than your doctoral exams. Mine sure were worse than the Bar exam."

Marian subsided. "You're probably right."

"Anyway, people will be coming to meet you." No sooner had Alexa said that than a loud knocking sounded at the garden door.

"Who's there?" shouted Alexa.

"Luthan and Faucon," called a man's voice.

"Bringing gifts for the new Exotique," said another voice, rich and cultured.

"A moment," Alexa called, but she turned to Marian with a smile. "One really amazing thing about being an Exotique is people give you stuff to make you remember them, like them. And—" she raised a forefinger "—since Exotiques are inscrutable in their thoughts and actions, those gift-bearers don't necessarily expect a return on their investment. The trick is not to be greedy." She pulled a dark red stone out of her pocket and showed it to Marian.

Marian stared, open-mouthed. "That looks like the ruby in one of England's royal crowns."

"The Black Prince's ruby. It's really a spine." Alexa flushed a little. "I like jewels."

"Who doesn't?" They shared a smile.

"I *earned* this. I'm sure you will soon have skills to trade."

"We are still out here," the first voice called.

"Just a minute," Alexa shouted. "I need to tell Marian about you two."

"That's a few words for Luthan, but I would take much longer," said the second voice, which Marian decided was Faucon.

Alexa bit her lip, shot a glance at Marian. "I don't know if you've run across this before—"

"Across what?"

Shrugging, Alexa said, "Some of the Lladranans instinctively like or dislike us. I think it's a visceral thing."

Marian blinked. "No, I haven't experienced that."

Alexa nodded. "You're about to meet two handsome, sexy and honorable Chevaliers. Luthan is Bastien's brother and the Representative of the Singer to the Marshalls. Faucon is a high-ranking noble."

"I take it one of them has this instinctive like-dislike reflex?"

"They both do. Try not to think badly of the one who has the revulsion. He's embarrassed by it."

"Revulsion? It's that bad?"

Alexa wiggled her eyebrows. "And the opposite is the *attraction*."

"Oh boy," Marian said under her breath.

"Come on in!" Alexa called, before Marian had time to really think on all the ramifications of Alexa's words.

The small door opened and two men ducked under the lintel and entered. They carried scrolls.

"Now there's a pair," Alexa whispered. She leaned closer to Marian.

The first man was dressed in immaculate white Chevalier fighting leathers that bore no stain or scar. Remembering the garb she'd seen in the inn the night before, Marian could only think that the clothes must have a spell on them, or he'd dressed up—to meet her? His hair was black with a wide streak of silver at his left temple and a smaller brush of silver at his right. His eyes were brown like most of the Lladranan men, but he was taller than average, and they were a tall race. His build was lean and muscular, his face was narrow, and something about him reminded Marian of Bastien—so this must be Luthan. His expression was somber.

The second man was only an inch shorter and his body type less lean and more athletically muscular—mesomorphic. He had medium-sized streaks of silver, denoting Power, at each temple framing a face as elegant as his voice had been, and strikingly handsome. He winked at them. Marian sat up straighter.

Luthan halted a few feet from them, took a breath. He looked braced for something, then a shudder moved through his entire body, but he remained expressionless. Alexa caught Marian's hand and squeezed in silent support. *Try not to hold it against him,* she said with quiet sadness. Alexa had dealt with a brother-in-law who'd found her revolting.

Marian nodded.

The man came up and bowed formally, looked to Alexa.

Alexa sighed. "Luthan, Lord Vauxveau, Chevalier Fifth Rank, Representative of the Singer to the other Communities of Lladrana, please meet Marian Harasta, M.A., Exotique Scholar of the Fourth Degree."

"I was instructed to introduce myself to you and assure you of the Singer's support in all things." He held out his hand.

Just then, Marian recalled that this was the man who had prophetic visions, like her friend Golden Raven back home. Marian wondered if his was strongest when touch-activated, like Golden Raven's. Now it was her turn to brace herself. She put her fingers in his and he bowed gracefully over them.

The peacock screeched.

Luthan dropped Marian's hand.

Both men turned.

Faucon bowed. "Salutations, feycoocu."

Luthan inclined his head. "Salutations, feycoocu."

Marian wondered if one or both of them knew Sinafin's name.

A smile lifted one side of Luthan's mouth as he set two books and three scrolls next to Marian. "Here are some Lorebooks from the Singer's Abbey that she sent you. She also told me to inform you that Alexa, here, was the one who mended Bastien's bad Power flow."

Marian stared at Alexa, who pinkened and shifted.

"It was an accident. I did it—um—instinctively."

Faucon jostled Luthan aside, bowed deeply and sent Marian a charming smile. "I see that Exotique Terre has supplied us with another gorgeous woman." He took Marian's hand and lifted it to his lips. "Your wish is my command."

Had he really said that? Marian went over the line in her head, translated it into English, French, back into Lladranan. It scanned the same in all languages.

His fingers stroked her palm and a flicker of heat entered his gaze. Obviously this was the man who was immediately and innately attracted to Exotiques. Marian told herself not to be so pleased, it was nothing personal—but it felt *very* personal. "One of my ancestresses was an extraordinary Medica and Sorceress. I bring you copies of her studies."

Withdrawing her hand, Marian smiled. "Thank you."

His fingers dipped into a pocket of his breeches. When he withdrew it, he held a small, square bottle of dark-green stoppered with a tiny cork. "I have a small pool of jerir on one of my estates, and had this liquid harvested for you. My ancestress said this was the greatest amount of jerir a person should imbibe."

"Huh." Alexa eyed it. "Guess I didn't swallow any more than that in my three dips or I wouldn't be here."

"A devastating thought," Faucon assured her. He handed the bottle to Marian. "With my compliments. Would you like to join me for—"

Luthan dropped a hand on Faucon's shoulder. "No, Faucon."

Faucon stepped away from Luthan, scowling. "I will not listen to any specious lies from you this time, Luthan."

Shrugging, Luthan said, "It was only a word of warning. I've been told there's a very strong Song linking Scholar Marian and Circlet Jaquar Dumont. Of course, if you *want* to irritate the Circlet—"

Faucon's jaw set. He glared at Luthan, turned his glance to Marian, shook his head and sighed. "My timing is off once more." He bowed to Marian again. "Truly, Scholar Marian, should you need anything I can provide, send word."

"Thank you," Marian said, slipping the bottle into her pocket.

Sinafin shrieked and made to herd the men from the garden.

For the first time, Luthan smiled fully. "And farewell to you, also, feycoocu." He bowed to Alexa and Marian and left. Faucon gave a small salute to Alexa, another melting smile to Marian, and followed Luthan from the garden.

There was a short silence after the door closed behind the men, then Marian said, "Lladrana certainly grows handsome men."

Alexa chuckled. "Yes, indeed, and my Bastien is the best of the lot."

Marian shrugged. "Tell me about curing Bastien."

Shifting again, Alexa said, "Well, uh, it happened during sex."

"Oh." Marian was eager to know, but couldn't find the right words to pursue the topic gracefully.

"To be precise," Alexa said, looking away, "I noticed that Bastien's crystal star had a flaw during sex, and afterward, I removed it."

"What crystal star?"

Alexa looked surprised. "When we make love, we both project multi-pointed stars that touch and meld together."

"Oh."

"That doesn't happen with you and Jaquar?"

"No, I, uh, don't get visuals. Mostly I just get swept away by this spectacular wave of music."

They met each other's gazes, began to laugh.

"Oh," Alexa said.

They laughed some more.

Alexa tapped her fingers on her baton sheath. "That's interesting. You might be better suited to Lladrana and Amee than I, since you seem to have a more aural than visual sense. I'm gonna have an accent for the rest of my life."

Marian touched her fingers to the books beside her, sending her mind and intuition questing, hoping to receive an indication that help for Andrew lay within one of the tomes. Nothing.

"Perhaps when you get back to Earth, you'll still have Power, at least enough to cure your brother," Alexa said reassuringly.

"I hope so," Marian murmured.

"It will be interesting to know whether and how much Power works on Earth."

They shared another smile. "Yes," Marian said.

A cautious tapping came on the door. It creaked open and a young man poked his head inside.

"Oh, you're here," he said.

Alexa shrugged. "Come on in, Urvey."

Steps dragging, the youngster did. Marian thought he was about the same age as Marwey—late teens. He was dressed in fighting leathers and a midnight-blue tunic that after a few instants, Marian placed as Bastien's livery. Bastien's servant, then. He darted a glance around the garden as if it were a strange and threatening landscape.

"This place sounds funny," he said.

"It's mostly our Exotique Songs," Alexa said. She tilted her head as if listening, touched Marian on the forearm. "Though since Marian is still connected with Earth—Exotique Terre—I can hear echoes of my mother planet, too."

Alexa looked a little wistful, but nothing in Alexa resonated with a wish to return to Colorado. She was certain of her course. Marian envied that.

Urvey appeared unconvinced. He fingered the piece of paper he held.

"You have a message?" asked Alexa, putting out her hand.

Shifting his feet, he stared at Marian. "It's for her. And the Circlet," he whispered.

"Oh," Alexa said. "Marian, this is my husband Bastien's squire, Urvey Novins. Urvey, this is Exotique Scholar Marian Harasta."

He was not like any squire Marian had envisioned.

Urvey bowed. "My pleasure," he said.

"Salutations." Marian nodded, then held out her hand.

Urvey dropped the note in it. The paper was slightly damp. Marian unrolled the paper and read the letters easily—a benefit of her bond with Jaquar.

Guildsman and Townmaster Sevair Masif requests the presence of Exotique Scholar Marian and Circlet Jaquar

Dumont to discuss the matter of Weather Magic and frinks. Please come as soon as possible.

Though the note was courteous enough, Marian felt searing anger.

23

Blinking several times Marian handed the message to Alexa. "Frinks are worms that fall with the rain? I've never seen them," Marian said to Alexa.

"I have, but only once." Alexa looked up with a frown. "I think I'll go with you. I don't know what Jaquar's relations are with Sevair, but the underlying tone of this note concerns me, and I won't let him push you around. He's a nice guy, really, so I don't know what's wrong."

She was throbbing with curiosity.

"The Guildmaster's journeyman is waiting in the cloister walk outside the Keep," said Urvey.

"Can you call Jaquar mentally, please?" Alexa asked Marian.

"You don't think we should refuse?"

Drumming her fingers along her baton sheath, Alexa shook her head. "I don't think it's a good idea. The various communities of this society are distant enough. I'm sure one of our jobs is bringing them together to fight the Dark. Let's not alienate a good man."

"All right," Marian said, and stood.

Alexa rose, too. With obvious relief, Urvey ran to the door and held it open for them.

Jaquar! Marian called, holding an image of him in her mind.

Alexa took Marian's forearm, smiling. "Just tell him that you got an invitation to visit Sevair Masif. From what I know of men, he'll insist on accompanying you. Then we can hand him the note on the way down."

"All right," Marian said. *I am going to Castleton to meet with—* She had used visual symbols for herself and the city, but had no symbol for Sevair. Taking the note back from Alexa, she scanned it for any sort of icon, noticed a stone block and a hammer.

Marian? Jaquar asked. His voice was filled with affection, making her smile. He sounded as if he were in the Keep somewhere.

I am going to Castleton to meet with Sevair Masif. She sent the mental image of the stone block and hammer.

What?

For a third time, Marian began forming the pictures she needed to communicate mentally with him. *I am going to—*

You're going to the cloister walk outside the Keep, he said, obviously more accustomed than she was to sorting images from their mingled Songs and occasionally touching minds.

I'll meet you there, he finished.

"It worked." Alexa grinned.

"I guess so," Marian said.

Since they had to go through the maze, Jaquar was already in the walkway, leaning against a post with his arms crossed, when they met him. Another youngster about Urvey's age, dressed in dark gray livery, stood in simmering silence.

Addressing the young man, Alexa said, "Marian, may I introduce you to Jumme, Townmaster Masif's journeyman."

Marian hesitated, then dipped a curtsey.

The youth responded by whipping off his hat and making a flourishing bow such as Marian had never seen outside of the movies.

"My pleasure." His voice vibrated with sincerity, and a little more.

"Do you know—" Alexa started, gesturing to Jaquar.

"He introduced himself," Jaquar said coolly, pushing away from the pillar to take Marian's hand and tuck it under his arm. He scanned her face. "You look a little different."

She smiled. She wasn't ready to tell him she'd mastered Water. She wanted to be able to practice outside in the ocean and be perfect when he next tested her.

"Do you want to ride?" Jaquar asked. "It's only a couple of miles, but riding—"

"No, thank you. Let's walk. It's a beautiful day."

So they walked, two and two—Alexa and Jumme, and Marian and Jaquar—back down to Castleton.

Sevair Masif's gray stone house sat across from a pretty green square. Both the outside and the warmly paneled interior were distinctive and obviously quality work. The earthtone furnishings of the den Marian, Jaquar and Alexa were issued into were of excellent material and well-tended.

Jaquar led Marian to a small beige couch that would hold two, and Alexa took a chair of deep gray.

Sevair stood stiffly behind the desk. In a work shirt, his arms and shoulders appeared well-honed by his occupation. He was as tall as Faucon had been, and like Luthan, he had a streak of silver hair on the left side of his forehead.

His jaw was clenched, his eyes narrowed. He leaned forward on long, scarred hands, piercing Jaquar with his stare.

"Weather Sorcerer Circlet Dumont, were you ever going to answer our requests for help?" he asked icily.

Jaquar stood and straightened to his full height—a couple of inches taller than Masif, but not as heavily muscled. He still managed to look down his nose. "I received no request for help."

Masif's gaze snapped with angry fire. His jaw flexed, then he said, even more coldly, "Every few months for the past two years, we sent a message to you asking for help."

Jaquar's manner changed subtly, from challenging to listening. He shook his head. "Townmaster Masif, I received no message. How did you send it?"

"Through the Marshalls, to be forwarded to you—" He stopped, glanced at Alexa who was no longer lounging in her chair but sitting up straight.

Making a disgusted sound, Masif moved to a chair—not the one behind his desk, which would give him a better placement for authority, but one near the fireplace. "The Marshalls. They didn't forward our messages. They never responded to our questions themselves, and now I learn that they actively worked against my Townspeople." His fingers fisted, released. "The Marshalls let my people worry, turn into mockers, and betrayed us."

"One moment!" Alexa raised a hand, her brow knit, and Marian could hear the faint echoes of Alexa's conversation with the other Marshalls. After a minute, Alexa said to Masif, "The Marshalls made the decision not to tell you that they didn't know how to combat the frinks. However, neither Thealia nor any of the older Marshalls received any messages from any Townmaster to pass along to the Tower Community or Circlet Jaquar, the Weather Sorcerer."

"Reynardus." Masif's mouth thinned.

"Not necessarily," Alexa said. "When was your last message?"

"A few weeks ago…"

"After I'd joined the Marshalls?"

"Yes."

There was silence. Finally, Masif stood and bowed to Jaquar. "My apologies. It looks as if the problem regarding a traitor is mine. And forgive me my inhospitality. Would you like tea?" he asked Marian.

"No, thank you."

Jaquar offered his hand to Masif. "I am sorry."

Masif clasped Jaquar's hand and the men's energy merged, flared, their Songs ringing in the harmony of like minds. Both looked a bit stunned. Masif dropped his hand and took a step back. Jaquar came and sat beside Marian, setting his arm along the back of the sofa behind her.

"I am also sorry to tell you that I can do nothing about the frinks," Jaquar said. He huffed out a frustrated breath. "I've tried, the Song knows how often I've tried, but I can't *sense* the frinks in the clouds. Not all rain clouds carry them, and there is no pattern as to which do and which don't."

"Before Alyeka came, every rain brought frinks."

Jaquar rubbed his left temple. "Then perhaps they develop at a lower altitude than I can operate inside a cloud—they might even form as they leave a cloud. I can only tell you that I don't know much about the matter, despite intensive study." He shrugged. "They are elusive to me."

It was obvious he didn't like admitting that. Marian shifted closer to him in comfort and Masif's gaze went to her.

"Last night there were heavy rains on farmer Ciboul's fields. Since Alyeka came, the outer fields that border the road to

Castleton have received fewer and fewer frinks in the rain. But the inner fields, frinks were still a problem—until this morning. Ciboul reported to the Citymasters' Council that there was no sign of frinks in several fields."

Marian felt herself blushing. Suddenly she recalled the deep ties everyone seemed to have with the land. Would the farmer have realized she and Jaquar had had sex in his fields? How mortifying.

Jaquar said, "I was instructing Scholar Marian in weather yesterday, particularly storms and lightning. We rode the lightning onto a field near the road between the Castle and Castleton, then walked out to the road."

"Excuse me," Marian said. "But what do frinks look like?"

Masif smiled. "I anticipated that question. It appears as if I am the tutor for the Exotiques in frinks. You learned of frinks with me, didn't you, Alyeka?"

Alexa shuddered. "Yes."

The Townmaster walked back to his desk and took out a round pottery bowl. He shook it a little and the sound made Marian's skin crawl. It was reminiscent of rattlesnake tails, with an added tinny note.

"Ewww," said Alexa.

Masif stopped beside her and showed her what was in the bowl. "Ewww," she said again, took the bowl and wrinkled her nose, then handed it to Marian.

Marian decided to be more classic in her exclamation. "Ick." The bowl was full of little metallic shells that looked like articulated, armored cocoons. Each was about three inches long and as wide as her thumb. She grimaced. "Double ick."

Jaquar took the bowl and poked his finger into it, stirring the contents. The repulsive, tinny scritching sound came again. Marian and Alexa shuddered.

"Most frinks that fall, die. Only some survive and burrow into the soil," Jaquar said absently. He picked one up. Holding it by one end, he wiggled it.

Marian leaned away from him. "It sounds like a rattlesnake tail, only worse," she said.

Jaquar and Masif looked at her quizzically.

"Yes!" Alexa said. "That's what they remind me of. One of my foster parents had a rattlesnake tail. Ick."

"Ewww," said Marian at the same time.

Turning it over in his fingers, Jaquar frowned. "Even this shell has weight. If I felt these in the clouds, I'd know it."

"Oh!" Marian stared at Jaquar, wide-eyed, understanding now what they'd flown through in that black cloud the afternoon before.

They all looked at her.

Jaquar's scowl vanished and he sent a little tune to her, which echoed back with her puzzlement.

"What?" he prompted.

With an inward shrug, Marian tried an explanation. "That black cloud, with the—the sleet." It hadn't been sleet. It had been frinks. The thought of those obscene things pummeling her creeped her out. "The noise instead of the Songs."

"Marian," Jaquar said quietly. "I saw no black cloud. I would not have taken you into a cloud with sleet. I'm a Weather Sorcerer. I know which clouds hold ice pellets. We went into rain, yes, but not sleet. I heard no strange noise." He kept his cool, blue gaze on hers.

Marian lifted and spread her hands in a helpless gesture. "I don't understand."

"She's an Exotique. Perhaps she can perceive the frinks that escape your notice, Circlet," Masif said, equally coolly.

Never looking away from her, Jaquar nodded. "Perhaps so. Tell us."

Grimacing, Marian looked at Masif. "Could I have that tea now, please?"

"Certainly." He picked up a horn that wasn't connected to anything and ordered tea.

Momentarily distracted, Marian asked, "How do you do that? Is the horn magic, or—"

Masif smiled. "The horn has a small spell on it, but, I, too, have Power."

"Oh." She narrowed her eyes and stared at him, trying to see his aura. Nothing.

Jaquar put the frink back in the bowl and set it aside. Then he wiped his hands on a handkerchief and grasped her hands. Until his fingers touched hers, Marian hadn't realized how cold hers were. He rubbed them between his own.

"Tell us about the cloud."

With a frown, Marian searched her mind for details. "I don't know when or where we blew into it." She lifted and dropped a shoulder. "Playing in the storm was so exciting, I couldn't measure time—you know how it is."

"I can guess that you got caught up in your work." Masif smiled at her.

At a tap on the door, he opened it and took a small tray, which he placed on the low table in front of her.

Marian made herself strong, sweet tea, and curved her hands around the china cup for the comfort of a known thing—a china cup of tea. The men were unknown, the furniture slightly different. Songs of the people in the house flowed around her in music unknown on Earth. A hot cup of tea was familiar.

When Alexa followed her lead and smiled at her, Marian was even more comforted.

"Marian?" Jaquar prompted, more teacher to student than lover to lover.

She sipped the tea. It was good as tea went. She drank a bit more. "As I said before, I can't judge when or where the cloud was, but it was huge—a big, black cloud shaped like a fist." Jaquar tensed beside her, but she continued. Frowning, she looked into his eyes. "I nearly lost contact with you. I couldn't *feel* you. So I grabbed onto you, hard."

Nodding shortly, Jaquar said, "I remember you doing that, but not when or where, either." He glanced at Masif. "But it was her first Storm Ride. It's not unusual to have a student panic."

Masif poured himself a cup of tea. "Rather like taking an Apprentice up the scaffolding of a spire, I'd imagine. You're not sure what they'll do when the excitement wears off."

"Sounds right," Jaquar said.

Marian continued with her story. "Anyway, my head went foggy. The Songs disappeared. There was this awful noise like pinging, then an—" She looked at Alexa and said in English, "It sounded like an engine revving too high, ready to blow."

Alexa nodded.

Marian turned back to the men. She didn't know the Lladranan word for *engine,* hadn't seen any such thing. "A very high-pitched noise, long and rising. Then I felt things hitting me. I thought it was sleet." She glanced at the pile of frink husks and quickly away, then gulped her tea.

Reaching out, Alexa patted her arm. "Hideous."

Marian tried a weak smile. "Yes."

The men stared at her for a long moment.

"I would say that the Townmaster is right. You felt the frinks, even their evil cloud, while I didn't. Something the Dark can mask from us but not you, perhaps. Extrapolating from the experiences of both you and Alyeka, the frinks cannot make contact with you, or if they do, they die."

"This is a great discovery," Masif said. "With your aid, Scholar, we might forestall any more frinks from falling live and burrowing into the ground." He looked at Jaquar again. "Does the Tower Community know what evil the frinks will do to the land?"

Jaquar shook his head. "No. We are watching them, just as you Cityfolk and farmers are. We do not know what disaster they might be germinating. We have no records of frinks, no Lorebook in which they are mentioned."

"Nor do the Marshalls," said Alexa.

"Not good," said Masif.

Marian took one last cup of tea and prepared to disappoint the man. "I'm sorry, but I will not be able to help much." She met Masif's intent gaze. "I have a sick younger brother at home. I am studying as much as I am able, with the hope that something here might help him, perhaps even cure him and others who have his disease. But I can't stay here in Lladrana." She braced for anger.

Instead Masif's face went impassive. He turned his head and the light touched the wide band of silver at his left temple. "I lost a young sister," he said, almost too low for her to hear. He jerked a head at Jaquar. "The Circlet lost his parents. I do not doubt that if we had had the chance to save them by visiting Exotique Terre and returning, we would have done so."

"Thank you," Marian said.

"We Guildspeople of the cities and towns and fields thank *you*," Masif said gravely.

They took their leave, and a few minutes later, Jaquar and Marian strolled through the streets of Castleton. A Chevalier joined them and he and Alexa dropped back to speak of Castle politics.

"It's a pretty city," Marian said. "Very clean."

"Very. Not like the one I grew up it, but Krache is a seaport in the south, a lawless city in both Lladrana and the country to the south, Shud."

Marian squeezed his hand. During their lovemaking, when they were connected mind to mind, emotions to emotions, she'd received flashes of memories from him. She supposed he had experienced the same. At least it wasn't as detailed as the memories that had flooded her during the blood-bond with Bossgond.

"I'm sorry," she said.

His smile was crooked. "I know that your childhood wasn't pleasant, either."

Marian shrugged. "How many people do you know who had a great childhood? Alexa didn't."

"Of the Circlets? Most, I would say. Extraordinary Power tends to show itself early. If their own parents weren't of the Tower Community, they'd be fostered, then apprenticed to a Circlet while still young. For instance, both Chalmon and Venetria had an easy childhood and student life."

As he said it, Jaquar felt another tingle at the back of his neck, as if they were being watched. He'd experienced it a couple of times since they'd entered Castleton—once when they'd entered the city gates on the way to speak with Masif and again when they'd left the stonemason's home.

They were in a busier portion of the town, with small shops and narrower streets. Mentally, he stretched his Power, and caught a flicker of pulsing Circlet Power and a glimpse of a tall, lanky youth and the bright green cape he wore. Chalmon's recent student who'd raised his Tower and advanced to Circlet had chosen that color green as his own.

Jaquar set his arm around Marian's waist. They were lovers now. He knew a little more of her mind, and how completely unaware she was of some aspects of Lladranan culture, like the competition between the Towers. He'd protect her.

The Marshalls' Council Meeting this morning had not gone well. He'd told them of the plane-walking and the dark maw and the master—but not all of the master's words—and they'd demanded information about where this evil place was, despite the fact that he'd told them the Tower wasn't sure of the location.

He'd spoken of the Circlet observers and the Marshalls had insisted that they receive all previous and future reports of the watchers. The Marshalls wanted the *Tower Lorebook*. As usual, the Marshalls did not listen but commanded. Jaquar had hoped this would be different now that Alexa was part of the Marshalls, but tradition and ingrained distrust of the Tower were too strong to overcome, at least in one meeting.

Marian sighed and leaned into him, and Jaquar realized that they'd just passed through the city gate and onto the road up to the Castle. He'd been lost in thought.

She hadn't demanded to know what he was thinking, hadn't chattered or tried to converse while he was in deep thought. A jewel of a woman. Truly a Scholar and a lady.

As she kept step with him, the Song they'd made between them resonated low and potent. Her body brushed against his, hip and thigh. Under his arm her waist was soft and supple. Her fiery hair, different in texture than any he'd known, caressed his cheek. The fragrance of her rose to his nostrils and he inhaled, believing that he could never get enough of that scent.

But she was bent on returning to Exotique Terre. Now that he'd bonded sexually with her, he knew firsthand of her love for her brother, how much Andrew meant to her. Jaquar could not keep her from the young man. If Jaquar's parents had been alive, or if he had stronger bonds with other Circlets and they had the time and incentive, he'd have proposed that they Summon Andrew. But even then, the young man's health was too fragile for that. Not that the Circlets of the Tower worked together well. They simply didn't join together often enough to practice merging their energies. They hadn't had a strong enough outside reason to cooperate.

Until now.

The sangvile and the threat of many sangviles all feasting on the rich Power of Circlets in a few days scared Jaquar down to the bone. And he was sure he wasn't the only one. Even Bossgond had expressed a fear of the monsters. Time to consult the old mage. He'd help with a plan.

Marian hummed a little tune and Jaquar's focus returned to her. The tune, like so much else about her, was unfamiliar. He liked it.

He liked *her.* More—she fulfilled him. Sex with her wiped his mind clean of concerns. Her conversation stimulated him. Her joy in learning her Power reminded him of his own past, helped him recall lovely moments between himself and his parents, instead of remembering them as gray husks echoing of emotional torture.

She stumbled and he steadied her, held her close, noting with wry amusement that his heart rate sped up at the contact.

Marian smiled up at him and his thoughts scattered.

He wished she could stay. He'd court her if she stayed.

The idea terrified as well as delighted him. He'd been spoiled by his parents' Pairing. They were a rare Circlet Pair—equal, trusting partners. Much more likely was a string of lovers, or a live-in lover who wasn't a Circlet, or the bickering and mistrust shown by Chalmon and Venetria. Before Marian, he'd never thought he'd be so lucky as to find a Circlet who'd complement him. His rough early childhood had made him cynical enough that he hadn't aspired to a Pair-bond with a woman.

Now there was Marian.

Her hand slid into his and the touch of her fingers along his palm fired every nerve in his body. He was completely, achingly aware of her and aroused.

He glanced to the side of the road. No wonder, this was the place they'd appeared last night.

Blood had rushed under Marian's skin, too, and since her coloring was so much paler than a Lladranan's it was easier to see. Enticing.

How fast could they get back to their bedroom?

24

As they walked up to the gate, a deafening alarm shrieked.

Alexa passed them, screaming, "Let me by!" People got out of her way, fast. The Chevalier she'd been talking to ran with her. The Castle guards stiffened, became more alert.

Bastien appeared at the far end of the thickly-walled entrance tunnel, grabbed Alexa and dropped a chain-mail tunic over her. Two other people came to dress her in armor. An instant later the sound of volaran wings beating the air reached Marian. People tilted back their heads and looked up. At least twenty volarans took to the sky in the first wave. Marian recognized several Marshall Pairs, as well as noble and independent Chevaliers, flying singly and in twos.

"Let's go!" Bastien said, and whistled. A huge dappled volaran strode into view.

Marian's heart clutched. Her friend was going into battle. She didn't know what to say, what to do, could only stand and stare. Though Bastien's face was creased in a wide, fighting grin, Alexa looked pale under her helmet as she squared her shoulders.

"Good luck!" Marian shouted.

"Merci!" Alexa called back, in Lladranan.

Bastien dipped his head to Marian, picked his Pairling up by her waist and tossed her onto the volaran. He leaped to the flying horse's back behind Alexa. "Fly!" he cried.

The volaran's muscles bunched, wings extended. He took to the air, disappeared behind the Castle walls, then soared above them. Other volarans flew in formation behind Bastien and Alexa. Marian saw Pascal and Alexa's new Chevaliers, Koz and Perlee, all riding beautiful volarans. Under her helmet, Perlee's hair showed red in the sun and she stroked her volaran's neck and laughed with excitement. Koz glanced over at her and smiled. They looked years younger than the desperate couple Marian had first noticed at the Nom de Nom the night before.

Alexa and Bastien were the only ones who rode double—because she didn't ride well, didn't fly well, Marian remembered.

The klaxon stopped and the great silence pressed on Marian's ears, not mitigating the dread in her stomach. People moved around them, going in or out of the gate, on their daily business. Marian clutched one of Jaquar's hands in both of hers.

More shouting came from beyond the gate, and another wave of volarans rose. This time their leader was Luthan Vauxveau in his pristine white fighting gear. His hair was wet as if he'd been bathing when the alarm sounded. No woman rode with him and his expression was severe.

Marian gulped. "Alexa's gone," she said, her voice raspy.

Jaquar slipped his arm around her waist. "Yes."

"I thought since she found the answer to the fence posts, there would be fewer battles!" The connection between Alexa and her grew every day, as did their affection.

Marian and Jaquar were now alone on the road.

He urged her forward. "The Marshalls can now raise more fence posts and energize the magical boundary that keeps the horrors out, but there are still old gaps, and the ancient posts continue to wear out and fail."

They came to the gate and the Castle soldiers looked at Marian, intrigued. Then one stared at Jaquar and her eyes hardened.

"The Marshalls fly to defend Lladrana from the Dark. What does the Tower Community do to defeat the evil?" The soldier sneered.

"I reported to the Marshalls of the Tower's efforts this morning," Jaquar said. "The Marshalls are responsible for sharing the information."

Marian raised her chin. "We destroyed a mass of frinks in the clouds yesterday," she said.

The soldier's expression softened. She gave a little bow to Marian. "Our thanks. Exotiques are such a boon in these dangerous times. Thank you for coming to help us."

Marian nodded, flushing. She was a fraud. She'd been learning her Power and playing, and the only help she'd given was inadvertently. She hurried with Jaquar through the Castle gate and into the Lower Ward.

There she saw great activity. More Chevaliers, even a Sword and Shield Marshall Pair, ran to the stables and Landing Field, continuing to respond to the silenced alarm.

"What am I going to do?" Marian murmured under her breath. Lladrana needed her. Alexa needed her. Surely Marian should fill the position of Tower Exotique as Alexa had that of Castle Exotique.

The longer Marian stayed, the more she was torn.

Andrew needed her. How could she abandon her old life? Andrew? Her mother?

How could she turn her back on this new opportunity that fulfilled her more than her life on Earth had done?

"Come," Jaquar said, as if he felt her agitation through their sex bond. He led her through Horseshoe Close, to the stables and inside to a small training ring.

There stood a lovely roan volaran watching a tiny cream-colored foal. The beauty of the sight caused new tears to sting behind her eyes. The little flying horse was practicing running, stretching its wings, and now and then hopping into the air and gliding a few feet. The mare looked on indulgently.

Jaquar leaned against the rail. "Bastien asked the mare if the foal, which is a filly, can stay with him and Alexa and train to be Alexa's mount." Jaquar chuckled. "By the time the foal is adult, Alexa should be ready to fly on her own."

Marian watched the small horse, exploring as all babies explore, learning new things every minute. She knew Jaquar had brought her here to give her pleasure, and the visit had, for a moment, but now all the uncertainties of Lladrana's future seemed emphasized.

"She's going to be a battle mare, then." Marian choked, her gaze following mother and child as they circled the ring.

Jaquar drew her into his arms. "Yes. We live in a difficult time. An era that wouldn't have been so hard if our ancestors had concentrated on discovering the nature of the Dark and defeating it." He snorted. "They studied its creatures, deduced how to contain the invasion of the horrors and, when that worked in general, went on with their lives. A terrible mistake." A hint of bitterness emanated from him.

Marian circled him with her arms, leaned against him and closed her eyes. The solidity of his tall, strong body comforted her—the woodsy scent of him, but most of all she was reassured by his determination to find out the nature of the evil that threatened Lladrana and work with others to destroy it.

"I can't stay." Marian opened her eyes and stepped back, repeating the words that had become her mantra. "I must return to Andrew."

Jaquar smiled sadly, brushed a thumb over her cheekbone. "I know. So we have a short time together. But I will help you, Marian. Bossgond and I will make sure that you return home." His voice lowered. "Perhaps you could consider coming back…and bringing Andrew if possible. As you saw, Exotiques are prized."

He leaned forward, brushed his lips against hers, back and forth, sensitizing them. "Before you leave, we will generate a plan for you to come back. Please consider, Marian."

She swallowed. "You think we could do it?"

His eyes fired. "We can try."

Slowly, she shook her head. "I don't know if Andrew is strong enough."

Jaquar dropped his arms. "Bossgond watches other dimensions. He knows a great deal about the Dimensional Corridor and will try to make all the Exotiques' trips safe and easy in the future. He is studying Summoning Power and Ritual to the exclusion of all else. I am a master of plane-walking. Between us, and with Alexa, we should be able to bring you back, and Andrew, too. The gate soldier was right, Marian—Lladrana needs you." Jaquar grasped her hands, lifted one and kissed its back, then did the same with the other. "And I think you need Lladrana, as well." He shook his head. "I don't know much of your life on Exotique Terre, but the Song wouldn't have chosen you for the Tower Exotique if you couldn't enjoy a life on Lladrana."

Marian withdrew her hands. "I'll think about returning. But only if I can bring Andrew and if this place would be good for him, too." She met his eyes. "I'll want to see all your plans and Rituals for Summoning us before I decide."

He chuckled and swept her a bow. "I'll ensure that you do, Scholar Marian."

That reminded her. "You told the Marshalls I was a Fourth Degree Scholar."

"I lied."

"What!"

Setting his brow against her forehead, he snagged her gaze with his. Such beautiful blue eyes he had, and now they were open and earnest. "When we left Mue Island you were a Fourth Degree Scholar. You have Circlet status now, I think perhaps as much as second degree already. You learned to control the lightning ride—that should have made you Circlet status… There was something more, too—when you found and faced and defeated the frinks in the clouds."

Her breath came heavy, but she couldn't look away from him. "Second Degree Circlet?" What would her mastery of Water lift her to?

He straightened, nodded. "Yes. But it is Bossgond's place to Test you, and you won't come into your full Circlet Power until you raise your Tower."

Marian shivered. "So quickly."

Jaquar took her right hand again. "Lladrana needs you, so the Song found the most Powerful Exotique in your land." He chuckled. "And you have good study habits."

She nodded. "A thirst for knowledge. I always have."

"Circlets of the Tower are like that." He turned to go, tugged on her hand.

Glancing back, Marian saw the little filly nursing. So young, so tender, such a huge fate in store for her. The mare's gaze, wise beyond that of a mere horse, met Marian's. "She might die in battle with Alexa," Marian said of the foal to Jaquar, envisioning a hideously bloody volaran and rider, dead and pale.

Tho. The negative grated in Marian's mind. With a jolt, she realized it was from the mare.

Jaquar halted. His head lifted and turned, looking at the mare as if he, too, had heard.

He and Marian stared at the mare.

The volaran observed them with steady eyes. *Alexa and Fleche will not die in battle together.*

Releasing her held breath, Marian said, "Is that her name, Fleche?" It meant *Arrow.*

The mare snorted. *Alexa named my filly Cloud, but her True Name is Fleche Obscur, "Arrow for the Dark."* The volaran's words Sang of Power, of fate. *I was sent to foal here by the head wild stallion. Fleche is his filly, too.*

Jaquar bowed to the mare. "Thank you for sharing your knowledge. We take our leave, now."

The mare dipped her head to nuzzle her filly, but kept one shining eye on them. *I would not tell you more. It is not for you to know. You are not Our Exotique.*

Marian's stomach turned over.

Jaquar nodded. "The Chevalier's Exotique, the Exotique of the Field."

The mare lifted her head and neighed a laugh. *The Volaran Exotique.* Then she turned away from them and focused on her baby.

Marian was glad to hurry away from the stables, matching

Jaquar's long strides. "Chevalier Exotique," she found herself muttering.

"Swordmarshall Alexa is the Marshalls' Exotique, the Exotique of the Castle Community. You—" Jaquar squeezed her fingers "—are Circlet Marian, the Sorcerers' and Sorceresses' Exotique, the Exotique of the Tower Community."

"And one will come who is the Chevalier Exotique."

"Or the Volaran Exotique—depends on your point of view, I suppose. Do you have people well versed in volarans in Exotique Terre?"

Marian thought of all the ranches in Colorado, of the rodeos and horse shows, the breeders and associations, even of the polo club. Her mother stabled two horses. "We don't have volarans. But my land, Colorado, has many horses." She drew in a deep breath. The scent of volaran clung to her gown, the Song of the mare and her filly still played in her mind. "Alexa comes from the largest city in our area. I come from a smaller city close to Alexa's that is a seat of learning. But we have horse breeders and horse farms. We are well known for our ranches." What sort of person would be Summoned as the Exotique for the volarans? Would it be another woman or a man this time?

If it was a woman, would she accept her destiny on Lladrana or seek to return like Marian? Since she'd be a Chevalier, too, would she form a stronger bond with Alexa? Alexa would have another close friend, then, a woman who had belonged to both worlds, too. Envy swirled through Marian. She had no close friend like Alexa at home.

Marian wished Andrew were a horseman.

"How many?" she asked blankly. She should know, but was a little too shaken by the pressure of fate, of options spinning in her head to recall right now. Maybe if she waited, Andrew would be Summoned.

Jaquar ushered her from the Lower Ward into Temple Ward and they made for the Keep. "How many Exotiques can be Summoned in the next two years? Why, the same amount as there are communities of Lladrana. Six. Obviously the Song has a master plan, but what it is, the Singer hasn't told us."

She glanced at him and saw that though his voice was light and ironic, his eyes were narrowed and his lips had an irritated curl to them. "Six." Marian sighed.

He pressed her fingers in reassurance. "And obviously you two ladies are here to provide a link between the communities, so we will be able to combine and function as one. Perhaps we can destroy the Dark."

"Two years," Marian breathed. Everything might be resolved in two years. An incredibly short time.

Jaquar walked fast, whether out of suppressed anger or some other passion, Marian didn't know. "Probably more. Each Exotique must learn of Lladrana, complete her own task, whatever that is." He definitely sounded angry.

But Marian didn't know why he was furious, and since it didn't seem aimed at her, she ignored it, still caught in the idea of other Exotiques, the grand plan that might be unfolding. What would she be doing on Earth in a little over two years? Even working to fund her last years, she should be finished with her doctorate and cozily settled into an academic career path.

How flat that sounded.

Andrew might be fairly healthy and active. Or he might be dead.

She shuddered. She'd been thinking that leaving through Ritual and being Summoned back might be a possibility. Jaquar had spoken as if such magic could be done. But she was deluding herself into thinking it could be quick and easy. Or cheap.

The Tower had paid the Marshalls to Summon her. Those very Marshalls were out fighting today and would continue to battle. Some could die, and the strength of the Marshalls' Power diminished.

They reached the cloister walk outside the Keep and Jaquar said, "Sit with me, Marian," in a tone that made her blood turn cold.

Marian looked at him, eyes wide, and stilled. Her Song fluttering, she sat.

Jaquar joined her and took her hands. "I wanted you to concentrate on your studies, but there are things you must know. Just before you came, I followed the sangvile who killed my parents back to its nest—the home of the Dark." He told her everything, and as he watched, her skin went pale, even her lips took on a tinge of white. It was fascinating—and wrenching—to watch.

Her breasts rose and fell with quick breaths, her hands went cold in his. He folded his fingers around hers, sent warmth to them.

She finally said, "My task is to plane-walk to the maw and destroy the nest?"

"No!" He believed that with every note in his body.

She tilted her head, frowned. "It must be."

He thought back to what Bossgond and Bastien had said, both men less emotionally involved with the nest and Marian than he. "It can't be now. Your bond with Amee is not strong enough to plane-walk."

"But the horrors—"

"The horrors have invaded Lladrana for centuries. We are watching and waiting, and planning. Every Apprentice, Scholar and Circlet in the Tower Community knows how to kill sangviles with fire. Some wear amulets. You—" he leaned forward and kissed her brow "—my lovely Circlet, Summon fire with a thought."

"It must be my task," she repeated.

"But not now," he said firmly. "No one could expect you to rise to Circlet so soon." He rubbed her hands. "I'm working with Bastien and Bossgond." He wanted to hear, soon, if Bastien had any ideas. They must speak as soon as possible.

"Bastien?" Marian looked startled. "This is a Tower problem."

"No, dear one. This is a *Lladranan* problem—you taught me that. I think your task must be to organize us to be a viable force against the Dark."

"I see," she said. She leaned against him for a moment, then stood.

He was grateful when she dropped only one of his hands and they linked fingers with the other.

"I want to go up to the suite, now." Her smile was lopsided. "I'd like thick walls around me."

He kissed the top of her head. "You are so brave."

She wasn't brave at all, but once again buried under a huge amount of information—and expectations.

Jaquar wrapped an arm around her waist, but she still felt cold. She wanted to be in a quiet place where she could shove aside her emotions and begin to think logically.

As soon as they reached their suite in Alexa's tower, Jaquar flung open the door.

Loud chimes rang a few notes of Bossgond's public Song, then his peevish voice boomed. "Where are you two? Do you know how difficult it was to find you? It took me time away from my studies. I need to consult with Jaquar. Contact me at once."

Bossgond would not speak with her. When she'd called him via the crystal ball in their suite as Jaquar was changing into

more everyday clothes than his formal Circlet robe, Bossgond
had painted a strained smile on his face and his eyes had
shifted away from her. He'd wanted an in-person meeting with
Jaquar as soon as possible but had not invited her.

Marian continued to mull over different scenarios as she
rode double with Jaquar back to Mue Island on a huge volaran
that Bastien's squire had loaned them. Apparently the Pegasus
had never flown over the Brisay Sea and wanted the adventure.

Bossgond must have known all along about the Dark and
the maw and the imminence of it opening and spewing out
monsters and how she might be able to harm the nest. But
he hadn't said anything. That comforted her. Wait! He *had*
said something. He'd told Jaquar that Marian couldn't plane-
walk. Furthermore, she *knew* Bossgond had treated her like
a regular Apprentice. Every time she had asked any Circlet
what they wanted of her before, they'd said "learn." She had,
but she wouldn't be around to pay them off, not quickly.
When she came back… She lifted her chin. When she came
back, she'd fight—in her own way.

The trip didn't take long enough to sort everything out. Jaquar explained that Powerful volarans, and Bastien's were all
very Powerful, had "distance magic" that shortened the flight,
as if each beat of wings carried them many miles instead of
yards. Soon they were circling down near Jaquar's Tower.

Wait, wait, I am here, cried Tuck's voice in her mind.

Jaquar cocked his head and the volaran's ears flicked as if
they'd heard her hamster, too.

Oh, how she wanted her hamster! She pinpointed Tuck: to
her horror, he was *outside.* Not only that, but he was beyond
Jaquar's security forcefield. She wanted to scream and carry on,
but since he was obviously safe, she suppressed the urge,

though both Jaquar and Tuck must feel her distress through their bond with her.

Sure enough, Jaquar tightened his arms around her and soothed. "He's fine." Jaquar chuckled. "He isn't stupid. He has Nightsky with him."

"Oh." Marian let out a relieved breath.

See, strange beastie? The volaran they rode turned his head back, blinking with curiosity.

"Yes," said Jaquar. "Look for your fellow volaran, Nightsky."

Their volaran angled toward the far side of the island. It was easier to see Nightsky, of course, than Tuck. Nightsky galloped down the beach, stopped and lifted his wings in greeting to the one they rode.

As they descended, Marian finally saw Tuck jumping up and down on a rock jutting into the ocean, waving his paws and squeaking madly. *I am here!*

Since he appeared so delighted with himself, she could only smile. Their volaran gently spiraled down. He nodded at Nightsky, then delicately stepped over to Tuck. Lowering his head slowly, he eyed the hamster, then snuffled at him.

Tuck squeaked with laughter, patted the volaran's big nose with a tiny paw. *Pretty vo.*

"Vo?" asked Marian.

"Volaran," Jaquar said, dismounting and helping Marian down. She stood a moment, leaning on him until she got her legs back from the ride.

"Of course," Marian said.

Their communion done, the volaran lifted his head from Tuck, then turned and greeted Nightsky, nickering. Marian sensed the other, telepathic communication between the two volarans, but could not understand it.

Jaquar hunkered down so he was close to eye level with

Tuck. "Well, Master Tuck, did you have a good time outside? You certainly scared Marian and me with your adventuring."

Tuck looked away. "Not speaking to you."

Raising his eyebrows, Jaquar stood. "Is that so?" Without waiting for a response, he went to the volaran they had ridden in on and stroked him from nose to tail, singing. Marian observed how the coat seemed to gleam, how the volaran moved more easily. Jaquar had groomed him and given the flying horse more Power, to make the return flight.

When Tuck screeched for attention, Marian walked over to him. He sniffed. She bent down and stroked him with her forefinger. He huffed.

"I thought we'd agreed that you wouldn't go outside," she said. She couldn't lose him.

"For one day and night only." Since his black eyes bulged, they couldn't slide slyly in her direction, but he tried.

"I see." She bit her lip. "I was very, very scared when I knew you were outside."

"Nightsky was with me."

"Yes, thank you for bringing him with you."

"We talk. He's a good vo." Tuck sat back on his haunches. "I wanted to see the ocean. I heard the ocean." He opened his mouth and sound of surf—Earth's waves—rolled out in counterpoint to the island's. "I never saw the ocean."

"Oceans are hard to come by in Colorado."

"I only saw the front yard. It was little."

"Yes, it was—is." It was about a three-by-six-foot piece of grass at garden level. Suddenly, with all her heart, she wanted to be back there, back before everything started.

But Tuck twitched his whiskers and rubbed his paws as if dismissing the subject.

Bide well, Exotique, Bastien's volaran dipped his head at her. *Bastien returns.*

Trepidation for herself was swallowed by fear for Alexa. "The battle's over? Is Alexa all right?"

Most live.

Marian winced.

All you know well, live, said the pegasus.

Well, that was good news, though she felt sad for the strangers. She curtsied to the flying horse. "Thank you for that information, and for the excellent ri—flight here." She thought she was doing well, acting naturally when her head buzzed with options—go and never return, go and heal Andrew and come back, go and bring Andrew back, stay and fight the nest. Surely the cowled figure in her dreams was this evil "master."

The pegasus looked out to the ocean, then studied his surroundings in all direction. He bowed to her, whinnied and sent mental messages to Nightsky and Jaquar, then took off again, flying inland.

Jaquar glanced at Marian, his hand on Nightsky's neck. "Nightsky is ready to go. We should leave shortly so I can consult with Bossgond and return before the evening meal." He scowled. "You're fretting. Do you want me to stay?"

"No. I want you to talk to Bossgond. But even more than that, I want you to bring him back here so *I* can talk to him." By the time they returned, she'd have her thoughts in order.

He looked at her soberly. "I'll do that. Return to the Tower. Go to my study and Sing *'Open, water, access.'* The floor in one corner of the room will open to a large square pool. Practice Water." Prof to student. The words reassured her enough to make a small joke.

"Still not willing to eat with Bossgond, even with the new cook?"

"I would rather eat with you," Jaquar said simply.

Tuck grumbled.

"Oh, and Tuck," Jaquar added.

"Bossgond called," Tuck muttered. "Other Circlets called. Much noise. Worse than telephone and answering machine." He made a high beeping noise like one of the sounds Marian's PDA had programmed into it, and opened his mouth. "Call me *at once* on my new cell number 720-MRS-RICH," issued from Tuck in Marian's mother's perfectly elocuted tones. Marian recalled she'd recorded the message with her PDA just in case she couldn't remember the new phone number. As if she could forget MRS RICH.

Jaquar laid a hand on her shoulder, his face shadowed. "Your mother?" He shook his head. "I couldn't understand the words, of course, but our link told me it was she. She doesn't treat you as you should be treated, with respect." And Marian felt *his* response to her mother's message through the bond. He was grateful he'd had loving parents. Marian had reminded him of that.

"I must go," he said. Gently, he pulled her into his arms. He tipped her chin up with one hand. "You are so lovely, inside and out." Brushing a thumb over her lips, he said, "So very worthy of respect and love."

25

Marian's heart thudded hard as she stared into the deep blue of Jaquar's eyes. The waves along the shore crashed, the odor of the briny ocean nearly overpowering the scent of man, of Jaquar, that she craved. All her senses were extraordinarily keen. She thought she could feel the weight of his gaze as it traveled over her face. Knew she could feel their auras, their Power, mingling. Their bond opened, emotions flowing between them. Tenderness. Respect. The faint edge of love.

He bent his head and his lips touched hers softly, yet a yearning stormed through her. His lips pressed hers, withdrew.

He stepped back. "I must go. If I stay an instant longer, we will mate on the sea."

She nodded.

Jaquar took another step back. "Go to the Tower. Beware of other Circlets." He ran for Nightsky and jumped onto the volaran's back. The flying horse leaped into the sky, lifting with wings and Power. They flew in the direction of Alf Island and Bossgond. Jaquar lifted a hand to wave.

I'll be back before dinner! he sent, mind to mind.

Fear spiking again, Marian didn't wave back.

Tuck gave a tiny growl to attract her attention. He looked up at her, his face furrowed in a hamster scowl. "You left me alone a *long* time," Tuck accused shrilly. Marian picked him up, but he wouldn't settle in her hands and he nipped the fleshy part of her thumb in irritation.

"Ouch!"

"Serves you right," Tuck said. "I was lonely. I was afraid for you. Many speak through the glass ball but not you and not Jaquar."

"I'm sorry."

He sat back on her hand, his little chest puffed out. "I am your companion now. Sinafin says so."

"And of course Sinafin is always right," Marian murmured.

Tuck nodded. "Yes."

Marian sniffed.

Tuck had a hard time narrowing his bulbous eyes, but he tried.

Marian chuckled.

"You remember that she is teaching me, and when you raise your Tower I can become a feycoocu."

All humor faded before renewed anxiety. What did Sinafin know? What would the feycoocu tell Marian if she asked? She stared at Tuck. What did he know and what would he tell her?

"Let's go back to the Tower and have a little talk."

"And food," Tuck said.

She'd bribe him with anything. "And coffee."

Tuck scrabbled up to her shoulder, set his pointy claws through the material of her gown, tugged at her hair.

"Ouch!" Marian said. "Let me make a pocket for you." So she did, right above her breasts.

Tuck settled himself inside. "Nice. Warm. Heart sounds good. I'll take a nap." He wriggled a couple of minutes more.

Marian eyed the cove, almost wanting to see if her mastery of Water worked here, too.

Almost. She decided that Jaquar's pool would be another good test.

She found the path from the beach to the interior of the island. Nibbling her lip, she visualized a map and thought this beach must be on the southwest portion of the island.

The sun's warmth soaked into her, reaching every cell. She was a Circlet and specialized in Fire! Lightning, as a matter of fact. Now she only had to prove she had mastered Water.

How much would she be able to do in Jaquar's study? She thought one of the reasons that she hadn't been able to manage Water was the pressure of having Jaquar watch her—and judge her work. Always disliking error, she became paranoid about making mistakes while in his company. She'd never had an intimate relationship with a prof before—not that he was much like any teacher she'd known.

The attraction between them was so strong—not only physically, but of like minds and values. She had the idea that if she was given a choice between furthering her studies in Power or having Jaquar as a lover, she'd choose the man. That notion scraped her nerves—it sounded too much like her mother, who needed an admiring man around at all times.

So Marian stretched her legs on the walk back to the Tower. Her body was toning up, as much due to daily exercise as the calories she and Jaquar burned off in bed. He was such a fabulous lover.

But no doubt he'd want to see how she progressed with her

lessons in Water. She grinned. She was hoping to show him she'd mastered it!

To bolster her confidence she crafted and refined a tune, and hummed what she whimsically called "Marian's Rain." It was both a mnemonic song to prod her memory for the right steps, the right *feelings,* she should have when practicing the cycle of seawater to rain, and a Powerful Songspell.

She was nearing the protective circle around the Tower when she stopped and stared at a carriage, without horses or volarans or even *wheels,* sitting in the meadow. It was an elegant equipage of bright green and gold with small pink-and-white striped flags on each corner.

Before she could figure out what it was, the Circlets Chalmon and Venetria walked from the direction of the Tower, calling, "Marian!"

Beware of other Circlets. Fear gripped her. They were between her and the Tower! But she could run, find a place to stop and open the protective circle. Escape.

She turned and raced. A hot splinter of pain speared into the back of her right shoulder.

Dizziness. The ground rose up. She managed to land on her side, sparing Tuck. *Tuck…stay…still.*

She fought unconsciousness, but wished she hadn't when she heard Chalmon say, "This was all Jaquar's plan. I wish he'd stayed to carry it through."

His voice rang with sincerity, and Marian knew he'd spoken the truth.

Marian woke suddenly and completely. She stood in the center of the smallest of several pentacles increasing in size that were incised into the flagstones of a huge courtyard between stone theater seats open to the evening sky.

To her right, beyond the courtyard, was an opening to the theater where the carriage sat. To her left was a dilapidated Tower. She recognized this place. Parteger Island, the Tower Community gathering place.

It would soon be full dark, yet it was still light enough for Marian to see about thirty people watching her.

Trapped.

26

Tuck stared up at her with wide eyes from her bodice pocket.

About twenty people stepped up to an outer circle about six feet from her. They placed their palms out, spread-fingered as if holding her in place.

Marian's breath stopped. She threw herself bodily against the barrier.

It didn't give. They had her caught inside the pentacle.

"Line up around the pentacle, immediately," Chalmon commanded those who hung back. He stood on the inner circle closest to her, along with Venetria and three other Circlets—just beyond arm's length, though she reached and reached with fingers curved like claws.

Fear dried her mouth, buzzed in her head as she strove to reason at what was happening. She'd wanted to be Sent home to Boulder. It looked like she was going somewhere else, and she trembled to imagine where.

A young man looked uneasy. "I don't know about this—"

"If you won't stand with us, stay out of the way or leave." Chalmon's voice was hard. "The best estimate is that the Dark maw will open and release monsters, including sangviles targeted at us, before morning. We must prevent this!"

"I don't like this," a woman said. "I'm only a Scholar, and wasn't told of this. I won't do it. An Exotique is a precious resource, and this is gross betrayal."

Damn right. Marian struggled to break free of the bonds again, this time buffeting the forcefield with her mind. Her Power fluttered like a butterfly inside a killing jar, though she saw sweat running from the Circlet's headbands down their faces.

One against far too many. She could hardly breathe. She didn't know what was going on, but sensed it was very, very bad.

"Where are her teachers—Bossgond, Jaquar?"

Good questions. Venetria raised her voice and began an intricately toned spellchant that drowned out others, and the Power wove thick around her. Marian's palms dampened. Where was Jaquar?

"This was Jaquar's plan in the first place," Chalmon said. "He's been informed of the danger of the nest opening shortly, and is on his way."

Oh God. Doomed.

Just like that first premonition she had when she arrived in Lladrana. She wanted to shriek. She fisted her hands and flung mental bolts of Power toward the shield, fueled by sheer hurt and anger and fear. The invisible trap held.

"We must link and conduct the Ritual *now*. Join us or not." Chalmon stepped into place, slapping his right hand into Venetria's left. All around the circle people linked hands.

The Song swelled, added harmonies. Marian was caged with pulsing beams of red light sounding like the rush of a mighty river. She swayed, glassy-eyed, as if not only her body was captured and controlled, but her mind, too.

When she saw Jaquar running toward her, she sent him loathing, her mouth open with a silent shriek of horror and betrayal.

He stumbled. His gaze bored into hers. His face was all angles, tight expression. She couldn't read him.

She couldn't face him, either. Underlying her fear, her rage, her desperation was the burning acid of his lying and treachery.

She'd turned her back on him! Jaquar's fury at the others dimmed beside his anger at himself. He should have told her what he'd originally planned, but he hadn't wanted to see her respect for him destroyed.

Fool.

He had to reach her, prevent the others from Sending her, or go with her into the maw.

No price was too much to pay.

Her head tilted away from him. The Song between them ceased with a sudden, sharp shock. She'd cut the link.

Agony whipped through him—pain at the severing of the sex bond and all the emotions that had attached to it and spun delicately between them.

She shuddered time and again, hunched her shoulders, but did not face him.

He reached the outer circle of Circlets and Scholars and they blocked him—moving, dancing, arms linked. With gritted teeth he grabbed the clasped hands of a man and a woman passing by, inserted himself into the energy stream and winced when a crash of cymbals ripped through him.

But they hauled him up, kept him on his feet, moving forward in the circle. His mind wheeling to find balance, to *think*.

The loud chant diminished as it transformed to a voiceless Songspell that traveled mind to mind and was below hearing. He reached for the meaning of the words, struggled to comprehend, to counter.

But he could not stop it. The melody being forged was too great, created by Powerful, determined people, for once in concert. They were Sending Marian to explore and harm the nest—atop the shoulder of her gown was a tiny crystal ball that would relay the sights and sounds of the Dark's headquarters to waiting observers.

He broke from the outer circle, ignoring the cries of the participants as he wrecked their energy flow, and staggered toward the inner circle. One glance at the five people and he had another thing to be thankful for.

Bossgond wasn't there. They had spent some time discussing the rumors he'd heard of Jaquar's original plan, then how to watch the nest. They'd come to no conclusions about how to attack or destroy it quickly. Then the old mage had drawn Jaquar into a long discussion about the Dimensional Corridor and Sending Marian back to Exotique Terre. Jaquar had returned to his Tower later than he'd planned, to hear Chalmon's curt call. Doubt had crept into Jaquar's mind as to whether Bossgond had delayed him on purpose. But no, *he* hadn't betrayed Marian. Her mentor hadn't betrayed her.

No, Jaquar, her lover, had.

Narrowing his eyes, Jaquar gauged his timing to push into the inner circle, past the swirling figures to the pentacle and Marian. The Sorcerers and Sorceresses of this round danced with hands clasped but arms outstretched between them. And with each step, the music rose, nearing a crescendo.

There! Jaquar flung himself between two tall men, under their arms, into a stinging, ear-pounding thump of a drum. *Bang!* He pushed, penetrated the field, fell to his hands and knees, felt warm blood run from his nose.

He lurched to his feet, hurtled forward to the red-sphere cage surrounding Marian. He reached it, tried to penetrate the forcefield. Cacophony pounded through him—hissing, screaming, noise. He pressed onward. He had just touched Marian's fingers when Venetria ordered, "Go!"

Chalmon's deep voice followed. "Go!"

Jaquar grabbed for Marian's hand. Missed.

"Go!" chanted a third Sorcerer.

The spell cloth encasing the weapon-knot Jaquar had snatched from his Tower fell from his fingers into Marian's palm. It was the strongest weapon he could give her.

Her hand jerked closed over the thread.

Once again she turned terror-filled eyes upon him, and he knew in that instant that she thought his actions, too, had been part of the spell, of the plan.

"No!" he screamed, but he didn't know whether she heard him before she vanished.

Utter silence descended—except for the echoing of his last *no,* around the stone theater of Parteger Island.

At the last minute, when terror overcame the haze in her mind, Marian understood that the Power flow was uneven, flawed. Unlike the Marshalls, this group wasn't accustomed to working together. Further, none of them entirely trusted one another or the process of connection.

Deep inside, Marian screamed. It was bad enough that she was the puppet and the tool of this group. To know that they might be incompetent in their spell was terrifying.

What would happen to her?

Off balance, the Circlets' minds and will yet managed to merge for one clear moment, and they flung Marian to the Dark maw. She shivered and shuddered and spun through planes of existence she hadn't known about but recognized through the touches of minds against hers.

Wind didn't take her—she could have mastered it. Lightning didn't sweep her through the night—she could have bent that to her will. She traveled on the *push* of minds, on the waves of sound of a mighty Songspell.

Mordantly, Marian realized their aim was off. They had not shared a common vision of their target.

She rubbed the cloth Jaquar had given her and the outer covering fell away. The weapon-knot twined around her right middle finger.

Betrayed. Emotional pain stabbed her, tears backed behind her eyes. They were sending her to the heart of evil, and Jaquar had given her the weapon to destroy it—though she didn't know how to use it. It probably would kill everything, including her.

She flew through gray landscapes, through black space studded with a glistening swath of stars. Then she plummeted down, down, down to a seething black place with an open maw that looked like unhealthy red flames, like a scabby, open mouth with razor-sharp teeth.

She hit a Powerful shield that slimed her as she plunged through, screaming until fear took her very voice.

Tuck squirmed in her chest pocket. Just the feel of him calmed her. She wasn't alone. She had someone to protect. As she fell through rocky darkness and saw a stone floor rising, she twisted and landed hard on her side. Again.

"Oomph!" Her breath thumped from her body and she lay stunned, gasping.

The *smell*—of putrefaction, burning, dead things rotting. She didn't want to inhale, but her lungs struggled to suck air. All this time on Lladrana she'd become more and more aware of sounds, but now odor overwhelmed her. She flopped an arm over her nose to try to limit the stench. Already she felt it seeping into her clothes, her hair.

Her mind cleared enough to take stock of her surroundings. Dark brown cavern walls, oozing damp. A pitted, rocky path upward, blackness shrouding the cavern and any passageways beyond her feet. The air was hot, sulfuric, laden with the horrible odor.

All too familiar from her nightmares.

Chittering frantically, Tuck popped from her pocket and scrabbled to her neck, where he patted her face. "You are okay. Okay. Okay!"

Just the sound of the English term steadied her. Her next breath succeeded; she drew air into her lungs.

It tasted vile.

She choked and coughed and doubled over. Tuck clung to her hair, patting, whispering, "We are fine."

She didn't think so, but couldn't spare the breath to tell him.

A horrible *thud* came from the dark corridor beyond her feet, followed by scratchy, ragged breathing.

Not her own.

Her heart beat hard enough for her to feel it. Just like in the dream, something huge lumbered at her. Ready to eat her. Or worse.

She'd been in Lladrana long enough to know there was worse.

Marian scrambled to her knees and found that her magical dress had ripped and showed no signs of mending itself. She couldn't spare the Power to fix it. She'd need all her wits, all her energy, all her Power to escape this.

The maw of the Dark. The center of the evil that was invading Lladrana. They'd sent Tuck, innocent Tuck, with her. Bile coated her tongue and the back of her throat.

She would survive, and they would *pay*.

Jaquar would pay the most.

An awful croaking echoed in the cavern. Slow, slithery movements sounded, closing in. Marian hopped to her feet, swept up Tuck, thrust him in her pocket. But he wriggled and escaped.

"No, I want to be out. I want to *see*."

Marian didn't.

She had to move!

Grabbing her gown, she straightened it with a flip of the fabric, saw that the tear was mending threads one at a time as if the spell labored against the noxious atmosphere.

A small crash of rock behind her made her jump.

Which nightmare would this be—the vicious, huge monster she couldn't see, or the evil once-human Sorcerer? The master that Jaquar had told her of.

Not one of them—not Bossgond, not Jaquar, not any of the others—had given her any real information about this place. She had no knowledge of her enemy, of his weaknesses, nothing she could use to craft even a half-assed spell, let alone a perfect spell, or at least a competent spell.

Tuck set his claws in the shoulder of her gown. *Run!* he cried mentally.

Marian ran. She had no breath to spare for prayers. Her feet thudded up the cavern. There was enough reddish glow-light for her to see as she ran.

Which nightmare? Would she break out onto a cliff edge and see Andrew lying dead? How could she? What were those fearsome dreams—predestined truth, or fiction?

They seemed all too real right now.

She bumped off the wall, and an odoriferous slime-smear decorated her sleeve, her arm hurting where she'd hit the rock. Like in her dream. Pumping lungs, pumping legs. Her shoes seemed loose, not tight around her ankles or cushioning her soles. *Flop. Flop.* The more she thought about her shoes, the more she felt them slip.

Chhrrrhh. The hot breath of the creature touched her back. Adrenaline flooded her and she ran faster than she'd ever thought she could.

The passage twisted, and she careened from one wall to the other, no pain now. Too frightened. Ran into something that gave before her—cloth over a doorway? And she was through. Was this the cliff edge? She pivoted, slammed against the wall.

Beside her, the tapestry went up in flames.

She stood on a huge ledge, but it wasn't outside. She was near the top of a cavernous room on a great balcony. To her right was a wooden rail that looked all too flimsy. Roars and rumbles came from below.

"Well, well, well," creaked a sly voice. "What do we have here? A little intruder."

It was the man in the cowled robe, but he wasn't a man, he was a giant—nearly a third taller than she, with misshapen hands furred with hair on the backs, the only flesh she could see. He might once have had the coloring of a Lladranan, but his skin now showed a distinct shade of green.

He rose from a thronelike chair and walked slowly to her. She couldn't see into the hood that covered his face but got the unsettling impression of movement, like a mass of wriggling worms, or tentacles. Marian set her back against the wall.

At that instant, the monster chasing her lumbered through the doorway.

Lurching from side to side, it reached the balcony, stretched its wings and tottered to the rail.

A dreeth. A small dreeth, but still terrifying.

The flying dinosaur's leathery wing-tip brushed against an invisible forcefield over the railing and sparked. The beast hissed. Flames shot from its mouth.

Marian gulped. "I didn't know dreeths were fire-breathing." The comment came from her, all right, though she didn't know what possessed her to speak.

The once-man chuckled wetly. "I am working on it. But if they have fire, they must be small. I picked the image from the Exotique Alexa's brain." Another snicker that made Marian's skin crawl. "You Exotiques *do* have a rich imagination for monsters."

Marian tried to keep images of movies, of graphic novels, of fantasy gaming cards showing evil beasts, from flooding her mind, ready to be culled and used by this creature.

The dreeth turned toward them.

"Go!" The cowled figure waved a three-fingered hand studded with pus-filled lumps at the dreeth and the rail. A shimmer and hum and the forcefield vanished. The dreeth screamed as it flew away.

Marian was sure that whatever awaited in the room below was worse than what she faced here. At least it sounded as if there were massed monsters down there, but still... She crept toward the rail, looked over it.

Sure enough, there were at least a hundred. She recognized slayers, renders, sangviles—three more dreeths, these gigantic. There were other horrors, lesser and greater, that she had no names for. Most of them were eating live, writhing animals. Would she be dinner, too?

The inhuman creature rasped laughter. "There is no escape

for you that way. There is no escape for you at all." He advanced on her. "An Exotique Scholar, what a prize. What shall I do with you? What pretty hair."

His hand reached for her, stopped. His head tilted. "What do we have here?"

She froze in terror. Tuck hid in her hair. *Please, no, not Tuck.*

The man-beast roared with laughter, his fetid breath washing over her, a drop of spittle hitting where her neck curved into her shoulder. It burned. Marian set her teeth against a scream.

She shrank against the wall. She had to *do* something. She'd survived in her dreams! Blue fire had sizzled from her fingertips. She had no clue what blue fire was, how to find it within her Power, how to use it.

Think!

"You have a little spy. Something the Circlets set upon you. How cute."

He couldn't have said "cute." No, he hadn't—she'd just heard it, filled in the blank. She wondered how much she was feeling, sensing from him, and what she actually heard. What was real.

"But I am the Master and though I enjoy toying with you, it is time to send your poisonous presence where you cannot affect the nest. Yes, I am the Master." White, curved fangs gleamed in the darkness of his hood. His fingers, elongated and multi-jointed, plucked a little glass orb the size of a marble from her shoulder. She hadn't even known it was there.

With thumb and forefinger, he flicked it over the rail. There was a tiny flash, a roar from the monsters.

"Oooh, and you have a mousekin, too. An Exotique animal with Power, also a threat to our home," the un-man said. "I think I have sensed his essence before." He reached again.

"No!" Her fingers closed on something in her skirt pocket—the brithenwood stick.

"Yesss." Now his voice was sibilant, snakelike. His fingers curled and claws sprang from the tips, swiped at her neck, severed a swath of her hair. Missed Tuck.

"No!" She flung the brithenwood, wrapped in anger and Power. It struck his eye and pierced it!

He shrieked in agony, plucked the stick from his eye and dropped it, snatching his fingers back. A droplet of blood fell on her hand, burned as much as his spit, trickled to her wrist tattoos and flashed white, searing her.

The Power of his pain and rage lifted her from her feet, flung her over the rail to fall to the horrors below.

Death. And her last sight would be the deformed mage, eye exploded, black blood coating the empty socket, trickling down his cheek. Long tentacles around his mouth wriggling in pain.

But he slowly closed his fingers into a fist and her fall halted. She hung suspended in air.

Not such an easy end for you! His malevolent voice hit her like cudgels, bruising. *You are Powerful. I will suck that Power from you, drain it drop by drop, and your agony at its slow loss will make it all the tastier, all the stronger for my own use. And when my little horrors need some special energy, I'll carve off a piece of you for them. I wonder what will go first? A finger? Perhaps a whole hand or foot…*

The monsters screeched and the noise drowned out even the master's mental words in her head.

After a long moment when he communed with his underlings, he turned back to her, flicked his fingers. The blow was a strong backhanded slap that snapped her head back. With a screeching yell he sent her into the dark place. *Go, now, to the larder where your obscene alien vibrations do not disrupt us. Go!*

Larder. Larder. Larder. The word reverberated in Marian's mind, increasing in loudness with every repetition until it struck her unconscious.

27

Marian awoke to nothingness. To silence and darkness and no physical sensation. She could hear, see, *sense* nothing. Knew nothing.

Was nothing.

She had not a bit of control in her life, in her fate. Panic shredded her.

She couldn't hear her breath or her heartbeat.

She couldn't smell any fragrance from her dress or even her own perspiration.

Nothingness.

She screamed.

There was no sound.

No intake of air, no taste on her tongue.

She couldn't feel the gown against her body.

Worse, she couldn't feel *herself*. She tried to close her hands into fists, felt no flex of muscle, no pull of tendon, no touch of finger on finger, fingers curled into palms.

Biting terror filled her, shrouded her mind.

What was left of her?

No body.

Only mind.

For untold aeons she screamed inside until her fear subsided from sheer weariness.

Slowly, slowly one thought connected to another. She became aware again.

Was she dead?

Was this limbo? Absence of sensation. Best definition of limbo she'd ever come across and she was living it. Maybe she was living it.

If she was dead, why was her brain still working? Why did she still have an idea of self?

Marian.

She was Marian Dale Harasta.

Relief fluttered through her. If she could think, perhaps she could somehow get out of this mess.

With her mind.

She'd had Power once.

Before she'd failed.

She'd made mistakes. She'd not listened to her instincts, she'd trusted the wrong man, she'd failed.

Humiliation flooded her, self-accusation. She'd *failed*. And now she was here, in limbo, unable to control anything.

Maybe.

Inside her head she sang a spell to move the air.

Nothing.

She tried licking her lips.

No tongue, no wetness, no plump lips.

Thought vanished under quivering fear.

But this time the descent into panic was shorter. She believed.

She reasoned. She knew her identity, she felt hot and cold—or perhaps it was just the recalled wash of hot and cold through her body as it reacted to emotion—icy fear, flushing embarrassment, guilt.

Marian Dale Harasta.

Yes, the edge of panic receded. She still hung in the limbo of the lost. It wasn't as dark as she had thought. Perhaps that had been black terror pressing upon her brain, binding her spirit. She thought her eyes were open but saw nothing but grayness, like fog. It tricked her mind into making shapes where she knew there were none.

Was Tuck still with her? Hanging on to her shoulder? She hoped so but he could be biting her ear and she wouldn't feel it. Perhaps he hadn't lost reason like her. Maybe she hadn't thrashed around in panic and bucked him off. She could only hope he was with her and coping better than she.

Was the knot still twined around her finger like a ring? She didn't know. She couldn't feel it, so she certainly couldn't fumble to untie it.

Once more she moved her feet, but could not feel the stretch of tendon. Dark humor welling up, she sent instructions to her feet to close together, to tap heels together three times, her mouth formed the words *There's no place like home.*

It didn't work. She hadn't expected that it would. She couldn't feel her feet or any vibration in her throat.

She was truly helpless. Her worst fear come true. And nothing she'd done all her life to be perfect had saved her from this. None of the knowledge she'd slaved to learn, to remember, could help her. None of the innate Power she'd felt and honed in Lladrana could save her. All those lessons—useless.

Lessons. The word sat in her mind like a silver splinter. Pointed, hurting a little, prodding her, like there was something she should remember. What?

At least she had her brain. She could think. She didn't know if time passed in this limbo, or how it passed. Whether nanoseconds or years passed in the worlds outside. Whether she herself aged.

Another tiny bit of calm trickled through her—at least her mind still worked. Perhaps her studies provided her with help after all. She might be able to amuse herself for quite a while, and that could keep her from going mad…again.

She wasn't pleased that she'd lost control so totally, given herself to fear and panic and self-condemnation at a stupid mistake.

Well, she should cut herself a break—no one she knew had ever experienced what she had, found themselves suspended in nothingness. So who knew what *they* would have done? How could she measure herself against the unknown courage of someone else? Except she did it all the time.

She'd gauged her prettiness, her sexual attractiveness, her social skills against that of her mother, or other girls and women in Denver society. Had always found herself lacking there.

She thought of Andrew. She wondered if tears welled up in her eyes, if her throat closed, because the tightness she felt in her spiritual heart should have brought such physical reactions. Her love for Andrew was, and had always been, powerful and unconditional.

Thinking of Andrew steadied her. She wondered how he was doing in his new retreat, whether she'd found any way to help him, or could have found some in the future.

Marian considered whether—when—Alexa and Bossgond

would miss her. Fury overwhelmed her at Jaquar's betrayal, at his last gesture of shoving the weapon-knot in her hand so she could destroy the nest, while destroying herself, as well. He *had* been her doom and she hadn't listened. Instead, she'd listened to the stupid, false Song between them and his words. She'd been so pleased that he'd found her beautiful, so blinded by their lovemaking.

Another lesson wasted.

Lesson.

Maybe the thrill of riding the lightning, of feeling immense Power crackle through her, of the acceptance by Alexa and Bastien and the Marshalls in the Castle had made it easy for him to deceive her. Especially after that ghastly experience with Sinafin.

Knowledge blinded her: she could have sworn it flashed white-hot and atomic in her mind.

You have learned your lesson, Sinafin had said. And before that—in the endless moments of *that* traumatic experience, the feycoocu had repeated again and again, *I can't hear you.*

As if Sinafin knew that Marian would have to call for help one day....

Hope nearly sent her spiraling into mindlessness again. To hope and attempt and fail was worse than not hoping at all.

Easy, easy. She tried to take deep, even breaths. Inhale, hold for a count of eight, exhale. She didn't know if her body did as her mind directed, but either way, it couldn't hurt to pretend. Harking back to Earth lessons, Marian visualized a stream of white light entering her body, through her head, flowing down her as she imagined relaxing tight muscles one by one. She'd been meditating for a couple of years and easily sank into a different state—a state of clarity and altered brain waves.

Reaching deep, gathering the greatest amount of self, and Power, and sheer will, she yelled at the top of her lungs, *SINAFIN! FEYCOOCU!*

Very, very faintly she heard a whisper. Too quiet to understand. Perhaps even imaginary. Marian collected herself again. Screamed again, putting an extra punch of Power—she hoped—behind her call.

SINAFIN!

Another tiny…echo?

Marian built an image of Sinafin in her head as the feycoocu had taught her—but unlike that time at Jaquar's Tower, she didn't see Sinafin as a fairy. No, this time, the shapeshifter was the warhawk, sitting on Jaquar's shoulder in the Nom de Nom.

Marian "closed" her eyes and brought back every sensation, physical and emotional, of that scene. The smokiness of the bar, the red leather of the booths beneath her, Jaquar's warm and tender arm across her shoulders— The image faded. Damn it!

Again she built—this time from the emotions out. Now she realized Jaquar had an aura of a man well satisfied with sex and the anticipation of more. Alexa sat across from Marian—quivering with curiosity and yearning to ride the lightning, deep green eyes alight with interest. The Song between them flowed with Alexa's pleasure that Marian was there as well as friendliness, affection. Alexa was solid in the vision. For a moment their Song filled Marian's mind, and she held it close, worked to remember it.

Jaquar—*do the breathing exercise even if you can't feel it*—Jaquar had been a man throbbing with sexuality, a Circlet radiating Power. A lover, a man who'd weathered and come to terms with his grief. An underlying, innate note in his being had matched hers—an Earth tune, from the last essence of Earth blood he carried. The Song they had made together—passionate, wary, inescapable, tempting. Marian remembered that tune too well. Before it could hurt her, she gently, gently drew away, but kept it in her mind.

She recalled other portions of the scene—the twisting and twining notes of the individual Chevaliers standing at the bar. The lower, duller strains of the bartender and barmaids.

The intense emotions of the couple in the booth behind her that Marian hadn't noticed at the time, came back—love, desperation, shock at Alexa's offer, thrilling hope and acceptance. Incredible relief. The Song between the two Chevaliers.

The Song of Marwey and her lover Pascal. Deep, abiding love with knowledge of their past, commitment to each other and a shared future.

The Song of Marian herself. Bright with Power, intricate and weaving chords from Earth into a Song of Lladrana—or vice versa. She knew that Song now—Song of her bones and blood—though she couldn't feel them. Song of her heart and mind. Song of her soul.

All these twisted like strands of harmony into a thick rope that Marian used to gather her Power and send it forth in a great shout that rolled from her, taking everything she had. *SINAFIN. SINAFIN. SINAFIN.*

Marian? The voice was muted but clear. Relief rushed between them.

Help! Marian thought she should be weeping buckets with the word.

Hold on. I have your Song-rope, Alexa said grimly.

An instant later Marian felt a surge of Power come to her. She imagined a warm embrace from the smaller woman—ephemeral, but true.

And her wrist burned. She could *feel* it, feel the pattern of the heat—Alexa's jade baton.

Where are you?

In the nest. In limbo. In the larder. Marian suppressed a wild surge of black laughter. *The evil Sorcerer called the Master who serves the Dark cast me here.* Whatever happened, Alexa needed to know what was going on.

Wait to tell me. Call again. You are not alone. Send ropes to your friends.

Help! The word shot from her. Was caught.

I have you, said Jaquar.

Again she felt desperation—this time from him. Rage. Her whole body heated with warmth. She felt the curling of her toes, the very lifting of hair on her scalp. She didn't want the warmth. But she wanted to go back.

I have you, he repeated.

She didn't reply, but used her turmoil of emotions to send another call. *BOSSGOND!*

Here! His voice was deep and old and solid.

Alexa said, *I am joined with Jaquar and Bossgond, hand-to-hand. Bastien is arriving momentarily. The Marshalls are here in the Castle Temple. We will bring you back.*

Marian shuddered, felt the tremor through her body.

Marian! It was Tuck, warm fur rubbing against her neck. *I have been talking and talking and you didn't say anything.* He sounded fearful.

"Sorry, Tuck," she said, and her tongue felt thick, her throat clogged with tears—of panic and hope and relief. She cleared her throat and said, weakly, "Could I hear a little Beethoven? The Ninth, please?"

Tuck vibrated against her and the orchestral piece rumbled

from him. She breathed deeply, enjoying the sensation of her lungs filling, expanding, emptying, shrinking. Blessed sensation.

She still saw nothing but fog.

Time to Call for Sinafin again, Tuck said. He chuckled in her mind. *You Call and I will broadcast Sinafin. Soon we will be Summoned to the Castle Temple. Then we can go home.*

Home. She didn't know where that was—her first thought was of Bossgond's Tower, then her apartment. She didn't ask Tuck where he meant.

Power roared to her from Alexa, strong and wild.

Alexa? Marian asked.

Bastien is here. So is Sinafin. Call her again.

Sinafin! Marian shouted.

I am here. You did very, very well, Marian.

Marian gulped at the praise, lifted her arm and saw the deep emerald velvet. She wiped her eyes on the sleeve.

Alexa broke into laughter. *Beethoven's Ninth! We can all hear it! You should see the Marshalls' faces. Stopped them in their tracks.*

I have Called Circlets I trust as well as those who hurt you, Bossgond added. *My friends will link with me. And Jaquar. With the Marshalls' help it will be but a puff of breath to bring you back. You are bringing us together, the Castle and the Tower, this day. Well done, Marian. It will be only a few moments....*

I'll hang in here, Marian sent to Alexa, and her friend laughed again.

One by one new Songs were sung to Marian, drowning out Beethoven, so Tuck stopped the Earth music.

Songs of people were so much more fascinating. As each Pair of Marshalls was added—Swordmarshall and Shieldmarshall—three Songs enriched the links between them, each individual and the Pair Song.

In her mind, Marian saw the Circle gather and expand as others joined. After Alexa, Jaquar's Song was the strongest—cruelly familiar, though she'd cut the bond between them.

She knew she had, she'd felt the whiplash of it, then the empty place inside her where it had sung.

Jaquar hadn't spoken to her after those first words, and she hadn't talked to him. It was hurtful enough to realize that he was the second person who'd heard her. If they'd had more time together, he probably would have been the first one her Song would have flown to.

Would he have ignored it? Would he, could he have brought in the strong force that Alexa had to save her? Marian didn't know, but she dreaded facing him and the other Circlets, trying to be civil.

When all the Marshalls had joined the Circle, the rainbow brightness, the incredible Power Marian sensed amazed her. It was far greater than the Power the Circlets and Scholars had used to Send Marian to the Dark nest. Even Bossgond's and Jaquar's Powers looked puny.

The Marshalls' individual Power might not have the depth and breadth of a Circlet's, but they were used to working as a team. No wonder the Tower Community had given the task of Summoning Marian from Earth to the Marshalls.

Marian's shoulders sagged in relief. She knew she'd be saved. The change in her body caused her to spin slightly in the nothingness. She lifted her hands as if she could paddle as she might in water, and caught sight of the weapon-knot wrapped around her finger like a fancy ring. Bloodred and pulsing, as if it, too, soaked in Power from the Song-web that wove around her. Though, that image wasn't quite right for sound instead of sight. She was more like a solo performer surrounded by a huge and mighty orchestra. She smiled at the notion.

Now her immediate fears were banished, Marian had time to truly think. She laughed shortly. Atavistic fear had banished thought, the physical triumphing over the mental as usual in a human being.

She was deep in the Dark's nest. Dare she try to destroy it with the knot? She sensed the knot had several spells woven into it and each, when loosed, could do damage.

No, said Bossgond. *I will demand all Lorebooks of weapons or knots to be sent to me. We will study them together.*

Another wisp of relief. Marian swallowed hard. She'd be going home with Bossgond, not staying at Jaquar's.

Tuck sniffed in her ear. *I love my house.*

Two jolts swept her as familiar energy, tainted with guilt and shame, came into the Circle. Venetria and Chalmon.

They begged to add their Power to Summon you back, Alexa said acidly. *And Sinafin agreed. Hardly anyone goes against Sinafin. Know this, Tower Community.* Alexa's voice reverberated and Marian knew that she spoke in a loud voice to the whole Tower, as well as sending her speech mentally. *When a community Summons an Exotique, they must provide her or him with an estate and life-stipend. That is true of this Tower and Exotique Marian. You will gift her with an island and zhiv—or you will pay zhiv to the Marshalls in return for an estate on mainland Lladrana, should she choose to stay with us. As for those who sent Marian to the Dark nest, you all owe her a life.*

That stunned Marian. She was owed a life—by about twenty-five people.

Emotions roiled through her.

Anger. They had sent her to her death.

Vengeance. She would make them pay, each and every one.

Then glee! Did she have a bank of favors to be sent home and bring herself and Andrew—God willing—back, or what?

She'd let Bossgond and Alexa and Sinafin collect for her. Marian giggled. She figured no one was going to set themselves against Alexa or Bossgond, either. Good.

And she had repaid the Tower for all the teaching Bossgond and Jaquar had given her. She could go back to Boulder with a clear conscience in that area, free of any emotional debt.

Ready, Marian? asked Jaquar.

Ready, Marian? said Alexa an instant later.

Yes!

You know where the nest is. Situate yourself in the coordinates. Then visualize the Castle Temple and come to us! Jaquar said.

Marian shut her eyes, glad she'd spent some time exploring the Castle Temple—that morning? She pictured the huge open space, the wooden screens, the rafters with Power crystals glowing. The altar with the chakra lamp-chimes of precious stones filled her mind, as did the great silver gong. She'd never forget the details of the pool where she'd mastered Water.

Her memory harkened back to her previous Summoning there, the Marshalls in colored robes wearing batons at their sides. Bossgond and Jaquar, Venetria and Chalmon in their formal robes, with circlets gleaming on their brows. She brought Tuck from her left shoulder and cradled the hamster in her hands, curving her fingers around him. She held him tight to her breasts. He huddled down inside the protection of her fingers.

The music rumbled, surrounding them, encasing them in a sparking sphere of lightning! Marian lifted her foot to touch the arcing energy, and she and Tuck rode the lightning that rippled with chimes.

Crack! Bong!

Her feet thudded against soft carpet and her knees bent, absorbing the shock.

28

Choking, Marian opened her eyes to see a circle of sixty people still enveloped in an aurora borealis undulating with Power. All had hands linked and raised over their heads.

Gaze locked on hers, Bossgond lowered his arms, softened his voice, drew the chant to the end. The circle broke hands.

Tuck wriggled and Marian opened her fingers. The hamster flew to Alexa's shoulder, where Sinafin sat. He started chittering as if telling all their adventures.

Propelled by the need to feel another person, Marian flung herself into Bastien's arms, and he and Alexa cradled her close.

Marian felt enveloped in life, in…in…*honor.* All the slimy horror of the Dark nest and the master faded. The underlying evil intelligence that lurked there had seeped through her pores and down to her core like malevolent oil. This, too, diminished when surrounded by Alexa and Bastien. Good people, dedicated people.

"Marian," Jaquar whispered.

She didn't take her face from Bastien's shoulder.

"Don't touch her!" snapped Bastien in a cool and deadly tone that Marian hadn't heard from him before. "You may return to your island." He spoke over Marian's head. "Venetria and Chalmon, you leave a list of those who perpetrated this wickedness upon Marian, then return to your islands, also. You are not welcome here. Consider how much your life is worth. That is how much each of you must pay to Marian for this grievous wrong. Every Circlet and Scholar who took part in the Sending will forward to the Marshalls a statement of what they owe Marian—the value of their own life. They will pay—forever, if necessary. We Marshalls will keep the accounts."

"My life is worth anything I have, everything I have," Venetria whispered.

"I, too, will pay anything she requests from me," Chalmon said. "But I will point out that the plan succeeded. The maw did not disgorge monsters. It was harmed by her presence. It does not appear as if the nest will send out horrors for an unknown amount of time in the future. All is quiet—"

"Watch!" Tuck shrieked. He opened his mouth and held up his little pink paws tipped with white claws.

Marian stared as a hologram appeared, recalling that her PDA had video- and sound-recording capabilities. Tuck could report everything to the Marshalls. What an incredible show-and-tell!

"*No!*" *Marian whispered. Her face was pale and set, hair wild and looking as if it glowed red. Her eyes were wide. She trembled.*

"*Yesss.*" *The mutant Sorcerer's voice was sibilant, snakelike. His fingers curled, claws sprang from the tips, swiped at Marian's neck, severed a swath of her hair, missed Tuck.* The image bobbled.

"No!" Marian cried. A green-brown stick sparking with Power shot from her fingers. It struck the master's eye and pierced it!

A shudder rippled through everyone in the room.

Alexa cleared her throat. "Nice shot. Excellent weapon. What did you use?"

With one last squeeze for Bastien, Marian stepped away from him and Alexa.

Marian flicked her robe, trying to remove dirt. "A brithenwood twig I found in the garden here."

"Interesting," one of the female Marshalls said. "I would say it had special qualities. We must investigate this."

"Yes," Chalmon said, a little too loudly. "The information Marian sent back about the Dark's nest will be invaluable in our fight against it."

Jaquar's right fist slammed into Chalmon's jaw, knocked him to the ground. Venetria hurried to his side.

Jaquar looked straight into Marian's eyes. "I swear, Marian, by my most solemn word of honor, by my parents' lost lives, by the keystone of my Tower, I *did not* participate in this action."

Anger fired inside her. "You set me up." Her voice was shrill—and accented with French.

Apparently he understood, because he lifted both hands, palms out. "I *swear,* Marian, I did not betray you."

Sinafin clicked her beak.

She steadied her nerves and spoke slowly and clearly. Marian met Jaquar's dark sapphire eyes and said, "You *knew.* They said it was your plan." She shot a glance at Chalmon and Venetria, who had withdrawn to one of the screens that partitioned the Temple.

Marshalls flowed between her and the Circlets, as if protecting her.

He reached for her, stopped. "Long ago."

"You gave me this." She held up her hand, fingers spread to show the dark bloodred weapon-knot encircling her finger, wide enough to reach her first knuckle.

"For defense. I arrived too late." His mouth twisted.

Too many feelings whirled inside her, like storm clouds shaking with thunder and lightning.

Bossgond stepped forward, gently embraced her, kissed her on the forehead—and all that gesture did was remind her of Jaquar's tender habit of talking to her with his brow against hers.

When Marian didn't hug Bossgond back, he dropped his arms and took a step back. She glanced at him. He looked older than when she'd last seen him.

"I knew, too," Bossgond said. "I heard rumors but did not act. Did not tell you about them."

She had sensed he was avoiding her, hiding secrets from her. His dark brown eyes filled with grief; his shoulders slumped.

Marian drew in a deep breath. "Maybe tomorrow I can forgive you." She didn't look at Jaquar when she spoke to *him*. "I don't know if I can ever forgive *you*."

From the corner of her eye, she saw him flinch, incline his head in acceptance. He walked into the shadows near the circular walls of the Temple, out of her range of vision. Since she didn't hear him open the large door, she knew he stayed.

Bastien draped an arm around her shoulders. "Come have a late dinner."

Another surging fear swamped her, made her lean against Bastien. "How…how much time passed?"

Alexa took one of Marian's limp hands, squeezed it. "You were gone for about six hours."

Marian nodded, moved away from Bastien and withdrew her

hand from Alexa's. Much as she'd like others to fight her battles, they were *her* problems and she had to deal with them.

She scanned everyone in the room. Many she didn't know—Chevaliers and the Circlets whom Bossgond had called. But she recognized all of Alexa's and Bastien's household that she'd been introduced to. She saw the Chevalier's Representative, Lady Hallard, and her staff; the Singer's Representative, Luthan Vauxveau. The sexy noble Chevalier Faucon.

So many people had helped her!

They'd come when she Called, given her support when she needed it, even if they didn't know her.

They were fighting a war against monsters and were finally coming to work together.

She stared at every Circlet who'd come to retrieve her from the Dark. A greater number than those who had Sent her, and of all ages, from a teenager who fiddled with his circlet as she nodded to him, to a woman who had to be as old as Bossgond but wore her white hair high and held her matronly body proudly.

She was blessed.

Then she swept her glance to Chalmon and Venetria. Venetria didn't meet her gaze. Chalmon watched her from under hooded eyes.

Marian curled her lip. "You attached that—marble—to me and saw and heard everything before the master found it and destroyed it." She lowered her voice. "But you don't know what happened after that." She gestured to Tuck. "Tuck can show others, the Marshalls, the *good* Circlets, what happened. I can tell them what happened." She paused significantly. "I can tell them of what I know and my deductions from my experiences."

Venetria bit her lip. Chalmon reddened. They hummed with

suppressed desire to hear. Served them right—perfectly right—
that she would tell the Marshalls and not them.

"I know something of the master and what he serves." She
waited a beat. "And the reason the Dark invades."

Jaquar soaked in the solitary splendor of the baths beneath
the Noble Apartments, a building across the courtyard from
the Keep. No one joined him. He wasn't sure whether or not
the other Circlets considered him an outcast, but the Chevaliers and Marshalls viewed him with distaste.

Alexa and Bastien had whisked Marian off somewhere. Re-
flexively he mentally reached for her through their sex-and-
affection bond. Nothing.

He groaned and rubbed his chest over his heart. It hurt,
the cutting of the bond, the instinctive searching for her
and finding nothing, the knowledge that he'd ravaged her
emotionally and lost whatever affection and respect she'd
had for him. The bond had been more than sex. How much
more, he didn't know, but dangerously close to love on his
part, a more-than-sex-and-affection bond.

Marian had no affection for him now, and there sure
wouldn't be any sex with her in his future.

He wanted to close his eyes and let the bath water lap away
his tension. But he dared not.

He'd tried sinking into himself, listening to the sound of the
gently moving water and letting it soothe his mind as the hot
water eased his body, but when he shut his eyes he saw Marian.

Marian dazed and terrified within a red cage of Power...
Marian white and trembling, with a wide streak of newly silver hair at her left temple, clinging to Bastien, hiding her face
from Jaquar... Marian too hurt to look at him directly...

None of those images were ones he wanted to see again, or remember.

He didn't want to recall Bossgond's flinty and accusing gaze, either. The older mage had not spoken, not looked at him except for one scorching stare that made Jaquar feel four years old with a mess in his pants.

Bossgond and the other Circlets had socialized briefly with the Marshalls, and accepted lodgings in the Keep. No doubt they were surveying the suite Jaquar himself had chosen that morning for a representative of the Tower to occupy.

Enough! Time to regroup and plan. He must offer Marian all his support, mend the rift with her. Then he would work with Bossgond and Bastien and the Marshalls to neutralize the nest. He was the best plane-walker.

Soft footsteps whispered over the stones. Jaquar sat up; the movement caused water to slosh up to his chin. Luthan Vauxveau disrobed and slid into the six-person tub with him.

"Salutations, Circlet Dumont," Luthan said quietly.

"And to you, Chevalier Vauxveau," Jaquar said.

Luthan slid down the bench so that his shoulders were underwater. He rested his head on the padded neck roll surrounding the tub and closed his eyes.

Jaquar was at a loss. He didn't know Luthan well, and everyone else in the Castle was avoiding him—why wasn't Luthan? Deciding he didn't want to know, Jaquar settled back into the welcoming hot water. But a hum of tension lived in his muscles.

After a moment, Luthan said, "The next couple of days are going to be very important. I wanted you to know."

As if the past few had been commonplace! Jaquar recalled that Luthan Vauxveau had a small gift of foresight. He was also the Representative of the Singer, the prophetic oracle of Lladrana. Which had brought him to Jaquar?

"You wanted me to know so I could do what?" asked Jaquar. Luthan didn't open his eyes. "Be alert."

When the silence became too heavy for Jaquar to endure, he left.

Marian choked down some herbal tea that was supposed to be calming, and managed to eat half of her small dinner in the Marshalls' dining room. Tuck was sleeping in her breast pocket, limp with exhaustion.

She felt discombobulated—sometimes mind and body working together, sometimes distanced from her body, uninvolved with her emotions. Time moved in jerky increments. Slow moments of tolerating dinner conversation. Fast flashbacks to the Dark evil's nest, when her mind worked to remember every tiny nuance of the experience, consider it, correlate it with every other small fact. She needed to be sure of her conclusions.

"Marian?" Alexa said.

Looking up at her concerned friend, Marian understood that Alexa had spoken her name more than once. "Do you want to bathe or go to bed?" Alexa asked.

A bubble of hysterical laughter caught in Marian's throat. Use the elegant, colorful baths of the Keep where she and Jaquar had made love? Slip into the sheets of the same bed they'd slept in, then later torn up during sex?

She didn't think so. "No. And I don't want to sleep in that suite under yours, either."

"I understand," Alexa said. She looked to Bastien.

He smiled at Marian. "We've put you in the suite under Swordmarshall Thealia and her husband."

"Oh. I'm sure that's fine. It has a shower stall?"

"Yes," said Alexa.

Bastien leaned forward, covered one of Marian's hands with his. "So you're buzzed on the battle aftermath, mind humming, muscles twitching, too restless to sleep—"

Marian's eyes widened. "I didn't go into battle."

"You certainly did," Alexa said. "Against the master, and won."

Shaking her head, Marian said, "I didn't win, either."

"You're alive and safe. He's crippled and his plans are shot to hell. That means you won," Bastien informed her cheerfully. "So what do you want to do to wind down? Walk to Castleton and back? It's a nice night—um, early morning."

A little shudder passed through Marian. She didn't think she could face the expanse of dark sky, even sparkling with the stars of two sweeping galaxies. The panic that had coated her had been too black. "I want to visit the brithenwood garden." She only knew that when she said the words.

"Sounds great." Alexa smiled at her and stood.

Marian coughed at the pun. "The garden *does* have a great Song."

"Fine with me," Bastien said, rising.

"You're going, too?" Marian got up from her chair.

He smiled genially, tucking her right hand in his left arm, angling his right elbow out for Alexa to take. "From now on, *Circlet* Marian, you will be escorted at all times. You are too valuable a gift to be unprotected."

Marian didn't know whether she liked the idea or not.

Alexa winked at her. "I've lined up Faucon Creusse to be your companion."

Then Marian realized what Bastien had called her. She looked up at him as he led her from the Keep to outside the Castle and to the shortcut through the maze. "You know I'm a Circlet?"

Bastien shrugged. "The strength of your Power was evident as soon as you landed inside the pentagram. Fifth Degree Circlet."

Marian gasped.

Alexa hurried forward to open the garden door and went through. Marian and Bastien ducked under the lintel, then Bastien closed the door behind them.

The scent was marvelous, comprising of early summer flowers, the brithenwood tree itself, sweet grasses and the faint tang of the deep forest to the west. That reminded her of Jaquar's scent. She automatically tested their bond. It was gone. She'd cut it deliberately. Marian swallowed.

Alexa was helping her to the seat around the tree. Then the small woman shifted from foot to foot before Marian.

Alexa cleared her throat. "Um, Marian. Uh, I don't want this to be a shock to you like it was to me." Alexa touched Marian's hair.

Marian jolted. "I've gone white?" No! She was far too young.

"No," Alexa said.

Marian relaxed.

"Not totally," Alexa said. She took a wide lock of Marian's hair at her right temple and tugged gently. "Just this much."

"Feels big," Marian muttered.

"It's very attractive," Alexa soothed.

Bastien kissed Marian's fingertips. "Very attractive. The color of your hair is exquisite. The streak only emphasizes it."

"Oh," Marian said hollowly. She was torn between wanting a mirror immediately, and hiding forever from the fact that she wore a silver Lladranan Power streak.

Alexa plopped down beside Marian. The Swordmarshall fluffed her hair. "The question is, will my silver stuff grow golden with age? That's what happens here—the older the mages get, the more golden it becomes."

Marian chuckled. "You aren't a native. I don't think so."

"I don't, either." Alexa sighed.

The short exchange had lightened Marian's mood.

There was a rustle in the branches above her. She looked up and saw a blue squirrel. She blinked, but it remained blue.

The Song chose wisely when it Summoned you, Circlet Marian, Sinafin said. *You are close to fulfilling your specific task.*

"Not yet," Marian said quietly. "Not until I tell everyone tomorrow at the Marshalls' Council Meeting my deductions." She frowned, fretting. "And there's one bit I don't quite remember...."

Alexa hugged her. "You will."

Bastien smiled with wicked charm. "You're an Exotique Circlet—nothing will escape you."

Sinafin dropped a brithenwood branchlet in Marian's lap.

29

Tuck woke Marian up by tugging at her hair. "Pretty, pretty," he said. "Now you look like a Circlet."

Marian grunted and rolled over, feeling as stiff and sore as if she'd been beaten. Groaning, she stretched cautiously, inch by inch. The bruises from when she'd pinballed through the caverns painted her skin in blues and purples. Ick.

But she could feel her muscles, and that was way over on the plus side.

She hadn't had any nightmares. That was good, too. She buried her head in the pillow, wanting more sleep.

Tuck nattered on. "We are going to report to the Marshalls. I will use my amazing abilities and astound them all."

Marian cracked an eye open, saw the suite that had been furnished for a teenage girl. Full of ruffles. It really didn't matter. The shower had hot water and the bed was soft.

"I am going to be a star," Tuck said.

"Is that so?"

"But to be at my best, I need *food*." He smiled, showing his little teeth.

She subsided back into the pillow. "Ask Jaquar—" Just that easily, she reached for their bond, and all the hurt of a love-affair gone bad crashed over her. She put her hands over her heart to keep it from cracking with the grief.

Their bond was no more. She'd cut it in anger and fear and the horror of betrayal. Nothing had changed that. She should want a connection with him again.

Jaquar had said he hadn't betrayed her, had tried to save her, then given her the weapon-knot. Her eyes went to where it rested on the bedside table.

She noticed tear tracks on the pillow, and her chin wobbled. She'd cried in her sleep for him.

But her judgment for men had been wrong again. She'd trusted a man who could send a person to a hideous death. The original plan had been his. *He'd* put the idea of sending her off into the maw of the Dark into Chalmon's and Venetria's heads.

Tuck said, "Yes, Jaquar would feed me well, but I don't know where he is. He must be in the Castle, but his heart does not beat in the Keep. I need food *now*. Much food. Excellent quality food. *Now!*"

Marian was distracted by Tuck's observation, and it was so much easier to consider an intellectual problem than to wrestle with the emotions ripping her apart. At this moment thinking was good, feeling just plain hurt. Switch to reasoning mode.

"You can tell who is in the building by their heartbeats? You can recognize that?"

Tuck pulled her hair.

"Ouch!"

He grinned at the two strands he held in his paws. "You must listen to me, and get me food."

They weren't in Jaquar's or Bossgond's Towers, where Tuck had stashes. Marian certainly was his caretaker again, and she didn't want him running around the big Keep by himself. "All right, all right." As she sat up, another groan tore from her. Despite the couple of weeks she'd spent here, being physically active, yesterday had tested her body to its limits.

Grumbling, she moved to the wardrobe. It held two gowns. One she'd worn for the past two days. She checked it, but there was no sign of the tear she'd seen in the Dark's cavern. It looked and smelled fresh, but she didn't know if she could wear it again. Too many memories—donning it in the morning after great sex with Jaquar... No. She should *not* think about that.

She should focus on Tuck and her presentation—report, debriefing?—with the Marshalls and Circlets. Probably some high-ranking Chevaliers and other community representatives to the Castle. There'd be a full house. It would be as bad as her doctorate oral exams.

Somehow it didn't scare her. She wondered if that was just the nonchalance that came after a truly terrifying, life-threatening-and-worse experience, or if she'd grown beyond her compulsion to be perfect. She hoped she'd grown.

"Come on!" Tuck hopped up and down on her bare foot, his claws scratching.

Marian took the other dress out. It was purple.

Still, she put it on and scooped up Tuck. He'd like the elegant Marshalls' dining room. She wondered what the reaction would be to a hamster sitting on a linen tablecloth, eating fruits and nuts from a bowl. The thought amused her.

When she opened the door of the suite, a rangy man in well-worn Chevalier flying leathers pushed away from the wall of the entryway.

His bow to her was minimal and had little grace. "Marrec Guardpont. Chevalier attached to Lady Hallard's household. She's—"

"The Representative of the Chevaliers to the Marshalls. I take it you are my escort?"

"That's right."

She studied him. Tall and strong like most Chevaliers. He looked tough, with lines beside his steady brown eyes. He had small streaks of silver at each temple, denoting modest Power. Marrec radiated solid responsibility.

"I saw you in the Nom de Nom a couple of nights ago, and you were with Lady Hallard last night when everyone Summoned me from the Dark's nest."

"I added my bit," he said, then gestured for her to go before him down the stairs.

He was a man of few words, but the knife on his right thigh and the sword on his left made her think he was most definitely a man of action.

Running bootfalls of more than one person sounded. Marrec slipped in front of Marian, drew his sword, tensed.

Surely there wasn't any threat in the Castle? In the very Keep?

"Let's be cautious," Marrec said, and Marian stiffened. Was he telepathic? Empathic?

At the next crossing corridor, guards ran past. They didn't even look at Marian and Marrec. The rest of the walk to the dining room was without incident.

Bossgond found them as Marian was finishing the last bite of the croissant that came with her eggs Benedict. Tuck was still munching. Marian had had to remind him time and again that a hamster with cheek pouches stuffed to twice his size was not elegant or star material.

As soon as Marrec saw Bossgond, he pushed his chair back, stood, bowed to her and inclined his head to the older mage, then left the dining room.

"The Marshalls and other Circlets await," Bossgond said as he stopped by their table. He eyed Tuck. "The hamster will show us what occurred during your tribulation in the Dark's nest?"

Tuck withdrew his nose from his bowl and sat up straight, paws curled inward. "Yes," he said, then opened and curved his mouth roundly in the way Marian knew meant he was about to broadcast.

She picked him up and stroked him, head to tail. He wiggled in pleasure. "Not yet, Tuck. Let's save it for the Marshalls." She set him on her shoulder and he began grooming, paying particular attention to his whiskers.

"I'm ready," she said, but now her stomach jittered.

Bossgond took her elbow. "Jaquar will be present, and afterwards…"

Marian frowned down at him. "Yes?"

Sighing, Bossgond led her from the room and down the wide corridor. Finally, as they made the last turn, he said, "Jaquar and I collaborated on a Ritual to Send you back to Exotique Terre and return you—and perhaps your brother—from there. The timing is difficult, but we think it might be done within a week."

At that moment, Luthan Vauxveau, Bastien's brother, opened a door, saw them and gestured them to him. On the door was a fancy harp. Underneath was written in elegant gold lettering "Marshalls' Council Chamber."

The Marshalls and Bossgond's Circlets sat in a long rectangular room with a scarred and dented wooden table and elaborately carved chairs.

Alexa took a chair with a stack of pillows atop it. The chair back showed a sword. Bastien sat to her left, in a chair carved with a shield. Other Marshalls followed, in color-coded pairs, sitting in appropriately carved chairs.

Luthan Vauxveau took the chair that showed a woman lifting her arms, head thrown back to the stars, her mouth open. He was the Representative of the Singer, the Lladranan oracle, Marian remembered.

With a big smile, Bossgond slipped into the chair with a carved back of a tower. He tugged Marian's hand and she sat next to him in a chair with a shield. The other Circlets followed. Jaquar was at the far end of the table. After one glance at his strained expression caused her stomach to pitch, Marian looked away, observing others.

Lady Hallard greeted Marian with a short nod, then took the chair showing an almost three-dimensional volaran on its back.

Everything neat and tidy. Everyone in their place. Marian approved.

As soon as they all settled, Lady Knight Swordmarshall Thealia Germaine called the Council to order, then introduced Marian—as a Circlet of the Fifth Degree.

Marian stood, not knowing exactly where to start. Then Tuck ran down her arm from her shoulder to her hand, which lay on the table. He strutted to the middle of the table, sat back on his haunches, wiggled his butt as if to get comfortable and opened a rounded mouth.

A projection like a hologram appeared in front of him, in a three-foot sphere.

Marian stood dazed and vacant-eyed in the middle of a series of pentacles. She woke suddenly and completely, then threw herself against a barrier.

It didn't give.

"Line up against the second pentacle immediately," Chalmon commanded.

Tuck showed everything in gruesome, colorful, amplified detail—from his own perspective. Marian couldn't watch, wanted to put her hands over her eyes, to slink from the room. Instead she sank back into her chair, closed her eyes and suffered through the betrayal again.

She heard a chair slide against the wooden floor, and someone came to stand behind her. Jaquar didn't touch her, didn't try to renew the bond between them, but his aura wrapped around her in warm support. She didn't know how he did that, but she was grudgingly grateful for his presence. Everyone else around her was completely enthralled by the show.

Now and then people gasped with horror, swore or muttered phrases she didn't understand. The comments around her were often drowned out by her whimpering, moaning, occasional screams in the movie.

Her hands fisted in her lap. Bad enough to relive this, without understanding that she hadn't shown much courage.

When she heard Tuck squeaking wildly, "Marian, Marian, Marian!" she opened her eyes to see herself, face expressionless and body completely motionless, surrounded by a backdrop of black, seething smoke.

Marian froze in her seat. The larder. Obviously Tuck hadn't been affected.

In the hologram her eyes darted from side to side, but appeared unseeing. She opened her mouth and screamed so loudly that the small diamond-shaped windowpanes rattled and jolted several of the people at the table. Jaquar tensed behind her. She realized he was swearing under his breath, words she couldn't guess at.

Now Marian couldn't look away from herself hanging there. In the hologram, her hands fisted and lifted before her face. "Maybe we should fast-forward, Tuck?"

Alexa choked. She looked pale and turned tear-filled eyes to Marian. "What was happening to you?" Her whisper was hoarse.

Shrugging, Marian said, "Nothing. I felt nothing. No physical sensations at all." She grimaced. "That's why you see all the contortions—"

"Quiet!" snapped Thealia, cocking her head to listen.

On screen, Marian was tapping her heels together and chanting, *"There's no place like home."*

She squirmed in her chair.

Alexa choked on a sob, sniffled. Her lips curved upward. "Might've worked, who knows?"

"It didn't." Then she realized that in Tuck's movie, a low chant hummed around her. She strained to catch the words. Everyone at the table did.

Thealia hissed and leaned back in her chair. "I can't quite understand the words. They're mangled."

A murmur of agreement ran around the room.

Marian looked at Alexa. "Alexa?"

Alexa shrugged. "No, of course not."

"They're French," Marian said.

Everyone stared at her.

Flushing, Alexa said, "I'm bad with languages."

Marian tilted her head. "And maybe some bastardized Latin. Anyway it started out with the witches' scene from *Macbeth*."

Alexa's mouth dropped open. "You read Shakespeare in *French?*" Then her brows drew together. "Like 'eye of newt, toe of frog'?" she asked in English.

"Yes." Marian translated for the Lladranans. "We're listening to archaic French and Latin demonic spells. Maybe that's why I came to the conclusion I did."

At that moment, Marian-in-the-movie twitched and began screaming, "Sinafin!"

"I think we should definitely stop this production," Marian said.

"No, let's watch it to the end," Thealia said.

Sitting back, Marian noticed that Jaquar had taken his seat at the end of the table. His hands were tight fists atop the table and he appeared to be staring into space.

Beethoven's Ninth Symphony filled the room, and both Marian and Alexa broke into relieved laughter.

Luthan leaned forward and asked Marian, "What is the name of this Song again, Circlet Marian?"

"It's the Ninth Symphony by Ludwig van Beethoven."

His lips moved as if memorizing the information. Then he nodded and resumed his impassive expression.

Tuck soon finished with the show and Beethoven's music cut off abruptly. Tuck exhaled a huge sigh and rocked onto his back, paws curled. If Marian hadn't felt the strong thrum of his Song through their bond, she'd have thought him dead. Not even a digit twitched.

"Tuck!" Alexa cried.

"He's weary, but not debilitated," Marian said. She scooped him up and cradled him in her hands. "You were a star," Marian whispered to him. He opened one gleaming eye, closed it. Then she set him on her lap.

"Get some food and water for the hamster," Thealia ordered.

A woman Marian hadn't noticed before stared at Tuck, then hurried to the door. "What kind of food?"

"Nuts, Umilla, bits of fresh fruit," Alexa said patiently, and Marian realized the serving woman was a black-and-white, like Bastien.

Marian felt erratic bursts of Power pulsing from her.

The woman bobbed her acknowledgment and scurried from the room.

"So." Thealia tapped her finger on the table, gazing at Marian. "What are your conclusions?"

Inhaling deeply, Marian prepared herself. "The master is a Circlet gone bad."

"Over to the Dark Side." Alexa's mouth twitched.

Marian blinked. "Yes. When I was with him, I sensed he'd apprenticed with a Circlet on one of the islands, but the man failed when he tried to raise his Tower."

One of the female Circlets shivered. "When that happens, a mind can be fractured, the energy can warp one physically, too."

"A Circlet of the First or Second Degree," Bossgond said, shrugging with dismissal.

Irritation spurted through Marian. The people in this room were the most Powerful in the land, perhaps in the world of Amee, but most displayed the arrogance that came with such power.

She met Alexa's steady green gaze. The woman dipped her head and Marian felt another tie of kinship. Marian had all too often been sneered at when she appeared in the "society" circles her mother preferred. And Marian knew there were several "misfits" at the table. Bastien, the black-and-white; herself; Alexa, the Exotique and former foster child; even Jaquar. He was a man who'd been abandoned as a boy because of his Exotique coloring. Yet all of them had found their way into the circles of Power.

The door opened and the serving woman brought in a large bowl of nuts, a grainy composite that looked like granola, and bits of apple and pear. Tuck perked up in Marian's lap.

He reached the bowl as it was placed on the table and dove in, chirping with delight.

"This 'Master.'" Bossgond fingered his lower lip. "He was very large. I can think of only four male Circlets who failed to raise their Tower." He named them. "And none of them was above average height or weight. Raising a Tower can warp you, but not add mass."

"Perhaps the one he serves gave him…more, or his diet." Marian shut her mouth. She didn't want to think about the tentacles on his face and what his diet might be.

Bossgond scanned the room. "All the Circlets here have raised their Towers. We cover several generations. Can you think of anyone I didn't?"

Silence held the room for several heartbeats.

"Bonhlyar," Jaquar said. "He was normal, too." An undertone in his voice made Marian think that Bonhlyar hadn't considered *Jaquar* normal.

"Bonhlyar," Marian muttered. It rang a bell. "Not—oh! He calls himself Mahlyar, now." She'd received a lot of information from his blood and spittle that had seared her.

"Ah," said Bossgond. "I was never convinced that his Circlet Testing was properly witnessed."

"What else did you learn of the master?" Thealia asked.

"He serves the Dark. He is the one who breeds and organizes the horrors, both in the maw and in a breeding ground to the north of Lladrana," Marian said.

"We knew that," said a Circlet.

"*I* didn't. No one told me," Marian shot back.

There was an embarrassed silence.

"We were informed rather late ourselves," Thealia said steadily. "Obviously the Singer has been right all along that the efforts of the various communities need to be integrated."

"The master forms them into battle groups, and orders them where the Dark wants them sent. The Dark has Power to transport them from the maw to other places, but not in large groups."

Marian licked her lips. "There's more." She felt the weight of their stares. "I think the Dark is not native to Lladrana."

"That has been extrapolated before," Thealia agreed.

"I think it came through the Dimensional Corridor." Marian frowned. "Though when I was in the nest, I got this feeling of...immensity...immense age and immense size."

"And immense evil," Alexa said. "Fire-breathing dreeths." She covered her eyes. "The master got that idea from me. I'm *so* sorry." She shook her head. "You were wise to shield your mind."

Marian blinked. "How did you know?"

Alexa dropped her hands. "Weren't you watching—no, of course you shouldn't have. But the Power aura around your head was quite clear."

They saw much more than she would have believed they could. It had been a mistake not to watch, not to see what everyone else had. She stiffened her spine. She'd have to live the events a third time, have Tuck repeat it for her again, so she could observe every nuance. She *hated* making mistakes. More often than not, they hurt.

Thealia leaned forward and pierced Marian with her gaze. "You were Sent there and Summoned back. When you were there, you formed an image of the location of the nest in your mind. Tell me you know where the nest is physically."

Her voice held the command of a spell, but only her emotional need affected Marian.

30

Marian looked around, managed a reassuring smile. "Do you have a globe?"

Someone whistled and a big globe appeared before her. Marian located Lladrana, followed the curve of the continent northwest beyond the two seas—one landlocked, one not—and pointed to an island of one high volcanic mountain. "Here," she said.

"Of course," whispered Bossgond.

"Damn!" Thealia slapped the table. She shook her head. "Too far to launch an immediate attack. We might ask for volunteers to survey the place."

"Not yet," Jaquar said. "Let the Tower observers gain as much information about it from all the planes, first."

Thealia pursed her lips, nodded. "Fine." She looked at Marian again. "Other conclusions? You said you knew why it was invading."

"I think the Dark originally came through the Dimensional Corridor here." She struggled to put into words the deductions she'd formed from clues she'd picked up unconsciously. She'd been too terrified at the time to put the puzzle together, but had since examined every detail. Shrugging, she pulled Tuck from where he was wallowing in his food bowl and put him back on the table. "Replay that time—" She gulped. "After the master struck me."

Tuck started the replay with Marian throwing the brithen-wood stick into the master's eye. Oddly enough, the bloody scene comforted her. She'd defended herself, and hadn't done too badly.

Then there was a roaring, a chanting not quite in sync. "This is what I heard. At the time, I was understandably not listening." She managed a strangled laugh at the memory of being suspended over the room full of monsters. "But I re-membered later."

Again the others frowned in concentration. Shook their heads.

"Tuck, can you choose the loudest group of chanters and refine the sound to project only their voices?" She had no idea of his capabilities.

Tuck stopped, waddled over to his water dish and lapped. Then he centered himself in the table, sat with paws curled in-ward and opened his mouth.

"Get it. Get it. Get it. We will get it, Master. Master. Mas-ter." The last word emphasized the sibilant.

"Sangviles." Jaquar choked.

A chill pall enveloped the room. Sangviles feasted on Power. Every person here would be a tasty treat. Marian shivered.

"I think the Dark entered Amee by the Dimensional Corri-dor and arrived in Lladrana first. When it moved on, it left something behind, and wants it back," Marian whispered, but the chamber was so quiet it was as if she shouted.

There was a full minute's silence.

"That's all?" someone sputtered. "Just give it back."

"You're not thinking," Alexa snapped. "Whatever it needs would only make it stronger, I'm sure. What we *don't* want is an even more formidable enemy. It is an immense Dark evil as it is, affecting the entire world of Amee. Amee cries," she ended softly.

Marian lifted her chin and swept the table with her gaze, meeting each person's eyes except Jaquar's. "Both Alexa and I know that Exotique Terre's Song is much stronger than Amee's, yet Exotique Terre probably doesn't have the same abundance and potency of Power. So how much greater was the Power on Amee before the Dark drained Amee's and broke its Song? Every minute the Dark feasts on Amee."

Bossgond grunted. "A very good question." A smile flickered on his lips. "Both the Exotiques are excellent students, good thinkers and natural Power Users. The Song would not send us anything less in this time of need." He stood and bowed to Alexa, then turned and bowed to Marian. "Good work. We now know more about the master and the Dark and the reason the Dark is invading Lladrana. There is much we still need to learn, and ultimately we must destroy the Dark before it demolishes Lladrana, but you have increased our knowledge base significantly. I salute you." He bowed again.

Marian sat up straighter. "Thank you."

"I think the Marshalls will want to discuss all the information they learned privately," Bossgond said to the Circlets. "You all, go disperse everything you heard to the rest of the Towers. Jaquar, come with me, we must speak of the Dimensional Corridor," he ended coolly.

"One moment," Swordmarshall Thealia said. "The Marshalls understood last night that Exotique Marian did us a great service, so we wish to thank her with a presentation of our own."

Bossgond settled down into his chair, eyes bright with interest.

Thealia lifted the speaker-horn. "Come in, now, please, Medica."

The door opened and a woman wearing a dark red tabard with a big white cross entered, holding on her hip a baby girl about a year old. The woman was a Medica—a doctor-healer. The child was a black-and-white, a person of potentially great Power that was fragmented and erratic.

Marian tensed. This was the child that had nearly drowned in jerir. She'd swallowed the magical brew—inhaled it, too.

The Medica sat in a chair with a shield carved on it. She put the little girl, clad in a diaper, on the table. The baby grinned and started crawling as fast as she could down the table.

Marian looked around. The Circlets observed the baby detachedly, the Marshalls wore goofy smiles and tried to attract her attention. She scuttled directly to Thealia's husband, patted his round face.

"Her name is Nyja," the Medica said. "Like many black-and-whites, before her dip in the jerir, her Power flow and mental processes were splintered." She inhaled. "I have copies of my notes of her condition before and after her plunge."

Marian felt Alexa simmer with anger through their bond, and sent comfort to her.

Like most black-and-whites, the child was subject to *frissons*, convulsions," the Medica continued.

Bastien, now master of his wild black-and-white Power, stiffened. Alexa twined her fingers with his.

The Medica pushed a book that looked like a journal onto the table. "I understand that your brother has that symptom?"

"He has muscle spasms," Marian said. The little girl was basking in the attention, going from person to person to play with each. Her Song was clear and steady and strong.

"Ahem." The healer cleared her throat and shifted a little farther from Alexa. "The night the babe was immersed in the jerir, she inhaled the liquid into her lungs, swallowed some, and—" the Medica sucked in a breath "—had a tiny hole in her skull. The jerir reached her brain."

"What!" Alexa jumped to her feet, furious.

The baby began to whimper. Alexa tromped to where the child sat and scooped her up, cuddling her. The little one settled against Alexa's breasts, obviously comfortable with her.

The healer had paled and did not meet Alexa's eyes. "We Medicas are very well versed in head trauma, treatment and surgery. The hole was drilled a few moments before the jerir experi—uh, therapy, and closed as soon as I revived her."

Alexa rocked and patted the baby, narrowing her eyes at the Medica. "I don't remember that."

"I beg your pardon, Swordmarshall, but you were not in a very observant state at the time." The healer still didn't meet Alexa's eyes.

"Feycoocu, is this true?" asked Alexa.

Yes, projected Sinafin mentally, strolling out from under Alexa's chair as a long-haired white Persian cat.

Alexa snorted. "I can see I won't get any answers from you— you're a cat." Her mouth snapped shut, then she sent a fulminating glance around the room. "I won't stand for such *experiments,* do you hear?"

Thealia rose and took the little girl from Alexa, looking

down at the Exotique Marshall. "We wanted to save our granddaughter."

Bastien curved an arm around Alexa and brought her against his body. "They tried something different to cure Nyja and it worked, evened out her Power flow."

Alexa fingered her baton.

"You think her brain was affected beneficially by the jerir?" asked Marian.

"Yes."

Marian trembled with excitement, with hope. "My brother's disease is one of the nerves, particularly in the brain and the spinal cord." But did a black-and-white's fragmented Power flow have any resemblance to multiple sclerosis? Could the jerir liquid help Andrew? And would he have to have brain surgery in Lladrana to cure him?

The Medica rose, then placed her hand on the journal. "These are copies of our notes regarding Nyja. She is an exceptional child, now." She gave a half bow to the room and left, back straight.

Marian stood and took the book, held it close. "Thank you," she said to Thealia.

Bossgond rose and snapped his fingers. All attention focused on him. He stood like a king, like the most Powerful magician in the world. "Exotique Marian was my Apprentice. I believe she has proven her worth to all of you. She would be an invaluable addition to the Tower and to all Lladrana in our fight against the Dark.

"I think you all know of her circumstances. She has an ill brother on Exotique Terre—Jaquar Dumont and other Circlets are prepared to return her to her home with the hope that we may Summon her back once again, and perhaps her brother, too. Who will stand with us in this endeavor?"

Thealia laid her hand on her husband's shoulder. "I speak for myself and my Pairling in offering our aid." She glanced around the room. "I would prefer if all the Marshalls agreed to be part of this Summoning, as we are the most trained in the technique."

"There are others to be Summoned in the future, too?" a Circlet said.

Luthan rose. "The Song predicts that the battle against the Dark will be most effectively pursued *and won* if four other Exotiques are Summoned. The other segments of our society are interested in people who will work with them. The best times for the Summonings over the next two years are known."

Bossgond said, "The calculations regarding Exotique Circlet Marian's travels through the Dimensional Corridor are specific to her and will not interfere with any other Summonings."

A burly-looking Swordmarshall rolled his shoulders. "More Summoning spells lie ahead of us. My Shield and I will participate in Summoning Circlet Marian. Good practice."

All of the other Marshalls murmured agreement. A huge burden of stress dropped from Marian's shoulders. She exhaled a prayer of relief.

Nodding at the Circlets, Bossgond said, "If you wish to take part in this exercise, both Sending and Summoning, please let me know." He turned to Jaquar. "Come with me and we will refine our plans. Marian, we will be ready to speak with you in about an hour."

Everything was moving so quickly. And so well! Marian just stood and watched the others file out until only Alexa and Bastien were left.

"We'll be behind you all the way," Alexa said. "If it can be done, it *will* be done."

"Thank you," Marian said.

* * *

Marian sat at the desk in her Castle apartment and studied the vial of jerir Chevalier Faucon had given her. It was a viscous dark liquid the consistency of thick maple syrup. When she held it up to the window, it was opaque to the light, but deep within the glass she thought she saw a sparkle or two. She didn't know what that was, and nothing in the research notes mentioned sparkles.

She'd already read the notes on baby Nyja, how much better the child had progressed after the submersion in the jerir than before. Drawings showed where the hole had been made in her skull. Marian had leafed through a fat volume on head injuries and surgery. Apparently the Castle Medicas had made that a specialty for generations.

Her thoughts kept straying from her studies, particularly since she thought she'd absorbed everything she could about the jerir and healing. She continued to consider the people of Lladrana.

The Marshalls and Circlets had ill-hidden their excitement at the information she'd given them. She suspected that they didn't think the price she paid was too high and that the ends justified the means.

Only Alexa, Bastien and Bossgond, the three closest to her, knew her trials and what it had cost her in terror and pain.

As for Jaquar, he'd looked as if he had suffered every step of the way with her. She still could not banish him from her thoughts. She shifted in her seat as she thought of their lost bond.

She tried to think about him in a logical fashion. Since she'd sensed facts about the Dark's maw, had reviewed them, and then had come to conclusions about the inhabitants in a way that had helped all of Lladrana, hadn't she also come to conclusions with Jaquar and Bossgond?

Yes. She leaned back against the soft pillow back of the chair and closed her eyes, remembering the atmosphere of Jaquar's Tower—the grief and rage and despair. She could believe him when he said his original plan was made in the craze of vengeance.

Objectively, she could envision how the whole scheme unfolded…and how Jaquar might have backed off when his sorrow lessened and when he came to know her, as he'd said.

After all, she'd only had that brief, deadly premonition about him once, the first time they'd met.

But reason did nothing to ease the very real hurt.

The little waterfall clock tinkled that it was time to join Bossgond and Jaquar in the chambers now allocated to the Tower, a suite of several rooms on the top floor of the west wall of the Keep. Prime space, she knew. She wished Tuck had been her PDA alarm clock and accompanied her, but after the meeting, Sinafin had carried him to the brithenwood garden.

Marian hesitated to see Jaquar again, didn't know what emotions would batter her. She set her shoulders, donning her most professional manner.

Picking up the vial of jerir, she stared at it again, seeking the glimmers. They seemed to symbolize hope, and she took comfort from the small bottle. She put it in her pocket as an odd talisman and touched it as she walked to the Tower's suite. She recalled how Alexa fingered her baton, and thought that if all went well, Marian herself would have a telescoping wand to hold and keep her fingers busy in the future.

Though she ran her thumb only softly over the doorharp, they heard her, and Bossgond impatiently shouted, "Enter." After a seconds' hesitation, Marian set her fingers in the door latch and pulled it. The door opened outward and she slipped into the room, then closed the door behind her.

Bossgond and Jaquar stood by a large library table under a bank of windows. The desk was covered with papers held down by various objects.

The men were a study in contrasts—Jaquar big and handsome and young, Bossgond small and bony and wrinkled.

But the sharpness in their eyes showed their minds, and Bossgond's Song had an echoing depth and brilliance that Jaquar had not yet achieved.

They were master Sorcerers.

Now she was, too.

Jaquar met her gaze with dark blue eyes shadowed with pain he made no effort to mask. She had to look away, especially since her loss of their bond throbbed with the same hurt.

"Come here, come here," said Bossgond. "Look at this sketch of the Dimensional Corridor that Jaquar and I have done."

She walked over to the table. The white papers only emphasized the green of the fields and forests seen from the windows.

The paper on top looked old. It showed an octagonal tube with round doors or portals on each side. She touched her forefinger to the drawing and inhaled sharply as the residual Song of the person who'd drawn this conjured up the brief vision she'd had of the corridor between worlds.

"Yes," she said. "It was like this, except I didn't notice all the doors, or that there were other angles with portals."

Bossgond said, "We believe this corridor links eight worlds, all generally alike, and the easiest passage is between opposite doors. The drawing shows the axis of Exotique Terre and Amee as the angles that are ninety degrees to us, or straight up. We think the angles slowly rotate so that eventually Amee is closer to some other world than Exotique Terre, but it is only from Exotique Terre that we have Summoned others."

"So I should ignore the other angular walls with doors if I am able to control my trip through the corridor." She sure didn't want to get stuck somewhere else, where dimensional travelers weren't understood or welcomed. Dreadful scenarios flashed through her mind. She banished them, concentrated on the drawing.

"That would be safest," Jaquar said in a raspier tone than usual.

"Indeed," Bossgond said absently, riffling through a stack of papers.

"The Dark knows of the corridor and can open it," she whispered.

Jaquar nodded abruptly. "Yes. Because it sent a render after Alexa. But we will protect you." His words hummed with a solemn vow.

Bossgond crowed when he found the page he wanted. "With the help of some of the other Circlets, we've calculated the days when you should be Sent and when we will Summon you back."

He shoved a paper at her. "This copy is for you, to take when we return you. These are the recent and upcoming dates that the Dimensional Corridor resonates best between Exotique Terre and Amee. As you can see, the best time to Send you would be the day after tomorrow, but that is far too soon to prepare us all for a Sending Ritual. If it were a Summoning, it would be different—we know how to connect and perform that spell, since we did so last night, but a Sending...no."

Marian took the paper and glanced down at it. She saw a bold red line-graph that peaked a couple of days from now, smaller apexes along the line. Lladranan dates were written horizontally beneath peaks and valleys. The largest peak, at the far left side of the paper, was the day the Marshalls had Summoned her. Another high mark was last night, when many of the Marshalls, Circlets and Chevaliers had pulled her from the nest.

Bossgond tapped the page Marian held. "Also included is the specific hour that is best for our Summoning Rituals." He looked at her from under lowered brows. "Since you were first Summoned when you were performing your own Ritual, I think it makes the connection between us and the chance for success all that stronger if you do so again. I have written the chant that we will be using to Summon you back, and the chant you should do at the same time."

Marian licked her lips. "I see." She smiled weakly. "You've been busy."

"I've had help," he said gruffly, nodding toward Jaquar but looking past him. "Circlet Dumont drafted the chant." Bossgond's voice turned stiff. "He knows you better in some ways than I do. Exotique Alyeka reviewed the words this morning."

"Quite an effort. My thanks," Marian said. She, too, dipped her head to Jaquar but didn't meet his eyes.

Bossgond said, "Your task now is to place the dates of Exotique Terre beneath the Lladranan dates, so the time corresponds to the moons and days that are the most familiar to you." He gestured to another small desk. "Do that now, and when you are finished, you can go." He looked pointedly at Jaquar. "The tension in this room is too high."

"Yes, Bossgond," Marian said. "When do you think you will Send me?"

He pointed to a yellow star on a date six days ahead. "Here, within the week, and the Summoning a few days after that."

Marian stared at the paper in dismay. Those times were a lot less favorable than all the previous times, and she wanted it better—perfect—for Andrew. "It's diminishing. Couldn't we wait until it builds again? Surely it does."

"Yes," Jaquar said flatly. "But the Chevaliers have already approached the Marshalls to do a joint Summoning for an Exotique of their own. I, and some other Circlets—but not Bossgond—have agreed to participate."

Marian forced herself not to tremble. "I see." She attempted another smile. "My wanting to return to Exotique Terre and then come back here has placed a lot of stress on you all."

Jaquar strode forward, held out his hand as if to touch her, then dropped it. "We need you." He cleared his throat. "Right, Bossgond?"

"Yes. Go do your work, Marian." Bossgond bent back over the table.

She took the paper to the small desk, picked up a feather pen and tapped her cheek with it. The first, highest peak showed the date of her Summoning underneath. It had been the night of the full moon on Earth. She'd never forget the May night—the full moon, the day before Andrew left for his retreat, the date of the big charity ball that her mother had expected Marian to attend. She knew the date well, and though she had come to think in terms of the days of the Lladranan moons—moon months—she'd kept track of the time that had passed. It only took her a moment to finish.

But before she could show it to Bossgond for his approval, the Castle's klaxon sounded.

31

Bossgond and Jaquar looked toward the south and the volaran Landing Field. Marian jumped from her seat, stuffed the piece of paper in her pocket, the note wrapping around the vial of jerir.

Hurrying to the windows, she reached them just in time to see the first flight of volarans take off—all the Marshalls. She caught her breath at the awe-inspiring flight. Sword and Shield Pairs in colorful battle armor flew, helms glistening.

The Circlets watched in silence as Chevaliers followed the Marshalls, lifting into the sky.

Marian bit her lip. "They fly to battle often, don't they?" Her hand went to the paper in her pocket. "What if they are gone—or an alarm sounds during my Ritual?" She hated being so self-ish, but didn't want to contemplate failure.

Again Jaquar lifted a hand as if to cup her shoulder. Again he didn't touch her. Bossgond threw an arm around her and squeezed.

"You are a Circlet, an Exotique. Lladrana needs you. The Tower needs you. I am sure the Marshalls will do as they did before—"

"Summon us at night? Both Alexa and I were Summoned at night, and it is rare for the horrors to invade at night." She was crushing the paper. "But all the rest of the good times to Summon are during the day." She'd noticed that.

"The Marshalls will commit to Summoning you and perhaps some of the more Powerful Chevaliers, too. If the alarm rings, others will go—lesser ranked Chevaliers."

Blood drained from her head. She leaned on Bossgond. "In that case, in sending Chevaliers without the most Powerful, I may be the cause of deaths."

"There are always priorities, some people who are more expendable than others. I assure you that the Marshalls protect Exotique Alexa more than any other person in their group, and they would do the same for you," Bossgond said.

Marian didn't like that thought, wanted for an instant to be held by Jaquar instead of Bossgond, since his face had gone expressionless. She sensed he didn't like that option, either.

Straightening her spine, she stepped back. "I'm finished with my exercise." She showed the crumpled paper to Bossgond. He glanced at it and grunted approval.

"I saw the feycoocu flying with Alexa and Bastien, so Tuck should be back in my rooms," Marian said. The strain of being with Jaquar, wanting him and their link, and disliking herself for that wanting, was becoming too much.

"Tuck will probably not wish to be Sent back to Exotique Terre with you," Jaquar said quietly. "May I have your permission to ask him to stay in his house in my Tower?"

Once more Marian had visions of Tuck being dissected by Earth scientists. "I don't think he should return with me. You may ask him, and if I am not able to return to Lladrana after I am sent, I would like you to offer to be his companion." She didn't trust Bossgond entirely with Tuck, either.

Jaquar bowed deeply. "I thank you for your faith in me in this matter."

Marian had no answer for that. She stared at Jaquar, wishing he'd been the incredible man she'd considered him, a man in her eyes that had fantasy aspects. Too good to be true. But he was all too human, and her disillusionment would take a while to fade. *He had plotted her death.*

Her judgment of men sucked.

Emotions churned inside her.

She turned to Bossgond with one last question. "What's next?"

He scanned the room around him with approval. "It has been a long time since I stayed at the Castle, and I've never been given the freedom of their library." He shrugged. "I don't think they know what treasures they have. The closer I bond with them, the easier it will be for us to link during Rituals. Also—" he grinned "—they are an excellent source of monster parts for spell ingredients."

That was another thing she didn't want to think of that might roil her feelings—Alexa and Bastien at war, fighting monsters, and claiming trophies of those that tried to kill them and were destroyed instead.

"So you want to stay here?" Marian asked.

"Yes. Some Circlets will visit me each day and we will tune to each other, facilitating a link when it becomes necessary."

"You want me to remain here for the six days until I'll be Sent back to Exotique Terre?" Marian sank into a nearby chair, trying to ignore the hum of Jaquar's Song that insisted on feathering along her nerves.

"Yes. The Marshalls should become better acquainted with you, your Power, your skills."

Marian sighed and rubbed her arms. "Where are my things?"

"At my Tower," Jaquar said.

"I have them," said Bossgond at the same time.

"Spread all over the countryside as usual," Marian muttered.

Bossgond glared at Jaquar. "You rent a volaran and gather *all* Marian's possessions in your Tower. *I*," he continued grandly, "will tell my cook to pack your things. Jaquar can fly to Alf Island, pick up the rest and deliver them here."

Jaquar narrowed his eyes but said nothing.

"Don't you want to check on your dimensional telescope?" Marian asked.

Bossgond's face went blank. The hair on the back of Marian's neck rose. He was definitely keeping something from her. She popped from her chair and gripped the front of his tunic. "Andrew is all right, isn't he?"

The old mage patted her hands. "He is alive and as well as can be expected." He craned to scowl at Jaquar. "What are you waiting for?"

Lifting an eyebrow, Jaquar said, "I have another task I must complete before I leave. I will, of course, follow your orders."

Marian got the distinct feeling that both Bossgond and Jaquar himself were punishing him for his actions. It made her uncomfortable.

Jaquar glanced at her, and she saw that despite his casual manner and cool words, his eyes were stormy. Was he watching her to see if she approved of him flagellating himself?

"You are welcome to stay in my Tower, ever and always, Marian."

"Circlet of the Fifth Degree Marian," Bossgond said pointedly. "When she returns she will be raising her own Tower, and I know she's chosen a place on Alf Island, with me!"

"The stress in this room is certainly beyond what my frail nerves can stand," Marian said. She spared a sober look for each of them. "I do want to return, but it will depend upon my brother Andrew's needs. It isn't certain that I—or Andrew and I—will come back to Lladrana, or that a second Summoning will be a success."

Marian couldn't settle down. She paced the tower suite. It had been decorated for Marwey, who now lived with her Pairling, Pascal, and reflected the innocence of a gently bred young girl. Marian didn't think she'd ever been that young or naïve, so the room evoked a vague discomfort in her.

Tuck had found a fluffy white pillow rimmed with lace on the bed and claimed it as his own. He snored peacefully in the center of the pillow, as if he were a living jewel or a gift ready to be presented to a dignitary. She smiled briefly, then drummed her fingers on the windowsill and stared into the maze below, tracing the path from the Keep entrance to the Landing Field, then the brithenwood garden. Her mind felt trapped.

No. Not just her mind. *She* felt constrained. People here had moved her around at their will. Events had been happening *to* her and she'd reacted. She wasn't in control of her life, wasn't even in control of her pet hamster, who had turned into an amazing entity.

Was she such a passive person?

She'd been learning.

She'd been developing her Power.

She'd been changing—she hoped.

Her will had been strong—at all times she'd acted with the foremost thought of helping Andrew.

There *were* times when she'd taken an active role. She had chosen Bossgond over the other Circlets when she first came. She had taken a lover. She had fought the master.

At no time had she acted impulsively. Was that a virtue or a failing? Perhaps she *should* have acted impulsively.

It was her wish to be Sent back to Boulder. It was her wish to return to Lladrana if at all possible, and with Andrew, too. Surely that wasn't passive?

Perhaps she couldn't sit still because she'd studied so hard that now she felt she needed to *act*. She prowled each room of the suite, looking out the windows at the day, scanning the clouds to check the weather. Maybe she could find a good frink storm to annihilate. She puffed out a breath and shivered when she recalled the feel of the creatures against her skin—but it would be something to *do*.

Again her gaze fell on the maze and the Landing Field beyond. It might be interesting to have a flying lesson.

At that moment she heard the strum of her doorharp and everything in her stilled. It was Jaquar. She knew without stretching her senses to hear and feel his Song.

She'd instinctively been waiting for him. Somehow she'd unconsciously understood, through their shared glances and body language, that he would come to her.

That she was his last task before he set out on the errands Bossgond had given him.

She cleared her throat. "Come in."

Jaquar entered, closed the door behind him and just stood and stared at her, yearning and torment in his eyes. "I need to talk to you." His jaw set and he held his body tight as if awaiting dismissal or rejection.

Marian shrugged with more casualness than she felt. Her heartbeat had picked up when he was outside her door. Her nerves now quivered at the sight of him.

He took a pace or two into the room. "I know it is too soon for you to forgive me." He shuddered. "I can't imagine what being in the maw was like. I deserve your disdain.

"I will say," he added in a low tone, "that when the sangvile led me to the nest, I was mad to get in there, to destroy it." His mouth curved down. "I tried. I'd have given my life to do what you did." He inhaled. "I was ashamed that I'd started the whole matter, and once I knew you, I didn't want you to find out and lose respect for me. So I planned on stopping it and you'd never know of my dishonor."

"You've explained yourself. Are you done?" she asked quietly.

Flinching, he said, "No. I wish to apologize deeply for my part in the ordeal you faced, to ask your forgiveness."

Marian nodded slowly. "I accept your apology."

He dipped a hand in his pocket. "This is not a bribe for your forgiveness. It is a gift. And since I know you are more concerned for your brother than yourself, it is for him." He withdrew a small golden stone like a tiger's eye that shone with Power. He cupped it in his palm.

"What is it?"

"Energy, to help your brother cross with you." He shrugged a shoulder. "I drew it down from the Castle Temple's storage crystals. Just imagine, energy from the strongest Rituals of the most Powerful team on Lladrana is captured here." He offered it to her. "They won't miss it."

She took it without touching his fingers. His face tightened.

The stone was warm from his hand and the bit of his aura clinging to the tiger's eye sank tingling into her skin. He said,

"The Medica told me they gave one to the baby after her dunk in the pool, and it might help with jerir."

"Thank you." She rolled it in her hand. The crystalline structure was full of Power in every lattice. "Though, I don't think I can convince a healer on Exotique Terre to drill a hole into my brother's skull and pour jerir onto his brain."

"Whatever you want of me, I'll provide. Before you go to Exotique Terre and after you return." He hesitated. "You do plan to return?"

She met his gaze. "Yes, if my brother agrees. I believe I have friends enough here who have the Power to Summon us back."

"You have more than a friend in me." His voice remained quiet and husky. He took another step forward, closer to her, just beyond arm's reach.

Marian stepped back.

Jaquar stilled. "What do you think the odds are that you will be able to convince your brother to come with you?" he asked carefully.

Slipping the stone in her other pocket, Marian stared out the window. "It depends upon his disease. If he is doing well, and there is a better prognosis for him, then we may stay."

"I cannot wish him ill, but my life will have lost something precious when you leave, Marian."

She really didn't want to hear that. Was he trying to win her over because of his shame, because he didn't like people thinking poorly of his character? That would be the basest motive.

"Thank you for the stone," she repeated.

"There was another reason I wanted to speak with you," Jaquar said.

"Yes?"

Jaquar shifted. "I haven't had many women in my life. But you are the most amazing, and I deeply regret what has happened between us. The Song between us was extraordinary. It developed so quickly, was so strong and complex." He braced himself. "I want…I want a bond between us again. Even if it is only acquaintances, only friends, I need that link." Once again his cheeks took on a darker color. "Please?" Then he stepped forward, stretched out his hand, palm up.

Marian swallowed. No one had ever said such things to her. She wanted to believe him.

"Please?" he whispered.

She lifted her hand.

He reached out and touched her fingers—and the Song between them mended instantaneously. Not a tiny link of affection, but a full-blown symphonic poem of respect, deep friendship, like minds, hearts that beat in tune. It echoed like fate along her nerves.

Then it happened.

Fog enshrouded her.

He started fading.

She saw him start to grab for her, then curl his fingers into fists and step back.

The Snap.

She let it take her.

Suddenly she was in the Dimensional Corridor with fierce winds whistling around her. She had no idea of the reason for the winds or what would happen if she calmed them, so she formed a forcefield around herself, using the Power that swept her around.

For a moment she let herself spin. Her life had just altered again. Her mind scrambled to keep up. She needed time to think!

On one of her spins, she saw a flash of bare flesh. She stopped her turn just in time to peer down the corridor and see her past self pulled by a red ribbon through the door the Marshalls had opened with their Summoning.

Shock hit her.

She was seeing the past! Those doors behind her opened on the past!

Marian wondered if she could go farther back than her own original experience in the corridor. Could she travel to where Alexa was being Summoned? Would there be some way for Marian to help Alexa defeat the monster who had attacked her? And if she did, would she change history for Alexa and even herself? Scary idea.

She moved away from the shining portal to current-day Earth, opposite the one she'd exited. She turned into the dimness of the past.

Marian hurried to the old door that had opened for her previous self, but it had closed. Marian-of-before was gone—now landing on the stone floor and meeting Jaquar and the Marshalls.

Her heart remembered the fear and pain and confusion. The door to her right—to Earth—closed into a small black crack, then vanished. A few feet into the future there was still a door.

A tiny rattle attracted her. Tuck in his hamster ball! She had to concentrate, focus if she was going to achieve her goals.

She scooped up Tuck, looked at him through the clear ball.

Bright unintelligent animal eyes gazed back at her. If she kept him now, would he develop as she had? She didn't dare change the past.

The wind whisked her gown around her ankles.

She had no time!

Always, always she was distracted and missed the optimal moment to act. She turned to the "Lladranan" side of the corridor and stared at the next door.

A passage she hadn't understood in the notes of the interdimensional traveler finally made sense, echoing in her mind. "One can never go through a previous door. An opening is available for only a single use."

Beat. Beat. Beat. She heard the rushing in her head and didn't know if it was her blood, the winds of the corridor or the pulsing of many world-Songs.

Perhaps it was time itself.

She pressed against the door and it opened on a bright rainbow. Why the rainbow? Because it was the past? Was it an omen for her? Would the rainbow appear just to her, or for certain Powered people? Or for everyone?

Focus!

She stood on the threshold, drew in a deep breath and felt as if fizzing champagne entered her body—what would it do to her? *Focus!*

Her hands gripped the plastic ball, relaxed.

Blowing on it as if it were a bubble, she set it gently wafting on a small breeze, watched as the ball—and Tuck—settled into the flowered meadow where she'd found him. A kaleidoscopic twist of her sight and she saw her former self speaking with Sinafin.

The door snapped closed.

Marian pivoted, fought against a huge wall of pressure that constricted her lungs, forcing air from them. Five steps into the past. Her eyes stung. Squinting, she saw that the door to her apartment had closed. The next dark door began to shrink.

She jumped at it, was struck with hard blows. She kept the image of her Earthly home strong in her mind. She slipped. Fell.

Into her apartment.

32

Gasping for air, Marian lay still, pulse thundering in her ears. Her senses dimmed and panic overwhelmed her for an instant as she viscerally recalled the grayness of the Dark's lair where she'd also lost all sensation.

"Uh, uh, uh," she moaned. Her limbs convulsed and she curled into a fetal ball.

Smell returned first—the scent of lily-of-the-valley incense. Distantly she heard her clock chime, her phone ring.

She blinked. Haze parted before her eyes. All the colors were brighter, more vivid, yet sounds, *Songs,* came faintly, were muffled. All except dear Mother Earth's Song.

Marian rocked to her hands and knees. Shook her head to clear it. The phone rang on and on. She stood and staggered until she reached it. The receiver felt odd in her hand—plastic, alien.

Bracing herself, she answered it. "'Lo."

"Marian, what are you doing still home!" her mother, Candace, shrilled. "You should be on your way. *Must* you irritate me at every turn!"

The sweep of innate love she'd had at the sound of her mother's voice vanished as Candace's words sank in. Marian leaned against the kitchen wall and stared at the calendar, the clock, the moon chart. It was only a couple of hours—no later—from the time she'd left.

"Marian, do you hear me?" Candace persisted.

"Ayes," Marian said. *"Mais oui."*

"That's not funny," Candace said. "I don't appreciate you being snide."

Marian rubbed at her temple. She was undergoing serious culture shock—something she hadn't anticipated.

"Get yourself down here at once, or I won't deposit the second half of your college fund. I did teach you to honor your word."

By the Song! "Sorry, Mother, I've been, uh, in an intense French seminar the past, uh, couple of days—"

"Just get down here as quickly as you can." Candace sounded furious. She hung up.

Setting the phone carefully back in its cradle, Marian pressed both hands to her head. Her mouth was dry—her whole body seemed thirsty. With measured steps she opened the refrigerator. The cold air blasted her and she flinched, she was so unused to it. Her hand curled around the filtered water pitcher, her fingers chilling at the touch. She kept her hand steady as she poured a tumbler full of water. Then she drank it down. And another.

She needed more—a full immersion, a bath. She might have time for a shower. Automatically, she undressed.

Candace was right. It was rare for Marian to break her word. She didn't recall ever doing so with her mother. Yet she'd done it when she'd left. Because of Andrew.

So much had changed, but her priorities remained the same. She wanted Andrew cured and only hoped that he could be convinced to come to Lladrana with her.

She also wanted a loving mother.

That wouldn't happen.

She'd once had hopes that she and her mother could build a mutually satisfying relationship. Now Marian had limited time to find words to reconcile with Candace. Marian's gut told her it couldn't be done. She'd have to leave one of the major threads of her life dangling, untidy, unfinished, never to be perfect.

It hurt.

Candace was already furious with her. It would be difficult for Marian to work her out of her stubborn anger.

The shower water cooled as it cascaded over her and Marian reluctantly turned the faucets off. She used minimal makeup and shimmied into her black evening dress. It fit better than ever. She'd toned up a bit in her weeks away—all that stair climbing.

She wound her hair into an elegant twist, grimacing at the new wide streak of silver over her left temple. Then she checked the small black beaded evening bag that she kept prepared for her mother's events.

And hesitated.

Her mind boggled at the thought of driving a stick-shift in the dark from Boulder to Denver. The traffic! She didn't know if she could do it.

But when she entered her living room again, the pentacle glowed. She saw it with new eyes. It held Power.

Marian closed her eyes. *She* held Power, too. She could feel it surge through her. It wasn't as strong as when she was on Amee, but she'd be able to do wondrous, magical deeds.

Slowly she moved into the middle of the pentacle. She knew the building where the fund-raiser was taking place very well. It was Candace's preferred place for charities, an old, elegant hall. That had once been a Scottish Rite Masonic Temple. Marian's lips curved. Plenty of star symbols there.

Even as she thought of that, a neon-blue star appeared in her mind—it was in a mosaic on the wall of a large balcony.

Perfect.

With a small chant, Marian raised her arms, Called the Wind and chanted that she wanted to be in the hall. The zephyr picked her up and whirled her. There was an emptiness, then her feet hit solid ground and her left hand touched small tiles. When she opened her eyes, it was to see her fingers in the center of the star.

Her breath rushed from her and she leaned against the wall. It hummed with the aftermath of Power. The remaining energy soaked into her and she accepted it gratefully. It was one thing to be a Circlet of Lladrana and practice magic there. It was completely different to do something magical on Earth, where she'd always considered herself a rational person and where magic didn't seem to exist.

The babble of cultured voices rose with the scent of costly perfume from the floor below. Marian let dislike of the event tremble through her, then set her shoulders and pushed away from the wall to walk with staggering steps. She barely made it a few paces down the hall to the ladies' room. It was blessedly empty.

She checked herself in the mirror. Her mouth fell open and she snapped it shut.

She looked better than *all right*. In the dim light she seemed to glow. Her hair was sexily tousled; her makeup appeared to have interacted with her skin to emphasize her eyes, cheeks, mouth. She stared, and felt a slight tingle as if she wore a shimmering coat of conditioner. An old word occurred to her, magic. *Glamour.*

Realizing she was wasting time—time her mother was counting in seconds—she left.

With the knowledge that she'd never looked better, and slightly hysterical, bubbling amusement at the effect of Power on her skin, Marian hurried down the old wooden staircase at the back of the building and into the ballroom.

She stopped at the bottom of the staircase to look around. The people and the party furnishings looked so strange after her sojourn in Lladrana. Nerving herself, she spotted her mother and crossed to her. She hadn't seen Candace in nine months, and she looked thin, pale and expensively elegant. She was speaking to two men with false affection. Her husband, John, smiled vacuously as he sipped champagne.

Candace's eyes widened, and for one instant Marian heard the faulty tune between her and her mother.

"Marian, how good of you to finally come," Candace said coolly. Her expression had hardened.

Marian felt as awkward and gawky as when she was twelve and had a growth spurt that sent her towering inches over Candace.

"Good evening, Candace," she said.

The men were introduced and bowed over her hand. Their auras had altered slightly—they were attracted to her, Marian realized. John stared at her.

Candace watched with sharpened gaze. The mother-daughter Song brayed with brass. With it came a word from Candace's mind. *Competition.*

Marian nearly gaped at her mother, but murmured something appropriate to the men and offered them a weak smile.

"Please excuse me, gentlemen, I must speak with my daughter alone." Candace smiled, too, then gripped Marian's arm in a clawed-handed squeeze and moved her away from the men.

Still stunned by the rapid shifts in her life, Marian didn't hear Candace's first few words.

"—at my wit's end to keep Trenton's new wife amused. Her name is Juliet. Go over there and keep her happy so I can work on Trenton for a plump donation." With a tilt of her head, Candace indicated a woman dressed in black knit tunic and trousers with a long, silver, fringed and beaded evening shawl draped around her. She moved a little and Marian saw the Chinese pattern for longevity woven in metallic thread on the back of the robe.

And she heard the woman's tune. Earthy, amused, strong. Clashing with Candace's own life Song. She listened to her mother's Song, which fluctuated between strident and whispered sharp notes…fading.

Shock rippled through Marian as she realized her mother was seriously ill, perhaps dying. She opened her mouth.

Candace discreetly poked Marian in her back. "Go do your duty."

Only a rusty, "Yes, Mother" escaped Marian. Operating solely on instinct, she walked up to Trenton's bride.

The woman took a glass of wine from a server who arrived at the same time as Marian. Needing something to settle her, Marian took a glass, too. It tipped, liquid sloshing dangerously close to the rim.

Juliet reached out to steady Marian's wrist. "Easy," she said, then, "Thank you," to the server who moved off with his tray.

A tinkle of connection sounded between them. Juliet gasped, dropped her hand. Her eyes widened, and Marian gained the impression that she hadn't heard the sparkling notes but had *seen* a shift in their mingled auras.

Then she smiled, quite genuinely. "How kind of Candace to provide someone interesting for me to speak with."

Marian choked on her drink. She spilled a few droplets on her bosom, watched them soak into her dress and disappear. It didn't look as if the material would stain. Good.

She racked her brain to recall the meager information her mother had given her about this woman weeks ago. "You, um, own The Queen of Cups store?"

"Yes."

"It's the best New Age establishment in Denver," Marian said, glad it was the truth. She wasn't acclimatizing as quickly as she had thought she would to being back home on Earth.

"Thank you." Juliet smiled. "What do you like the best?"

"Your books. Excellent selection."

Juliet looked askance. Did Marian have an accent? Did Juliet think Marian was as superficial as Candace? "And, um, your herbs. I bought a nice marble mortar and pestle the last time I was in."

Juliet relaxed. "We have a good stock of tools. We recently received a new shipment of pendulums."

Frowning, Marian said, "Pendulums can be quite attractive, but I've never used one." She didn't think she'd seen any in Lladrana, either. Did they use them?

With a tilt of her head, Juliet said, "Is something disturbing you? You seem…distracted."

Disconnected was a better word. Linked to Mother Earth, but that Song was subdued here in the city. It had faded to a hum that spoke more to her blood than her mind. Otherwise Marian was disconnected to everything around her, everything she'd been linked to a few hours ago.

Except Candace, and the Song between them was so pitiful it was depressing. Marian shook her head, hoping to jar a little sense back into it.

"Sorry, I'm just back from an…intense retreat. French." She smiled. "I'm a little tired and coping with language echoes."

Juliet narrowed her eyes. "Maybe you should have some food." Then, with a sweep of her arm, she called to a waiter who was circulating with small steak kebabs.

"Thank you," Marian said as she took three. She munched one quickly and then she and Juliet drifted over to a waste basket and dropped two of the bamboo skewers into it.

Juliet slipped the wineglass from Marian's hand and set it on a nearby table. "And I think you should have less to drink."

"Very wise," Marian said, then finished off the second kabob. She was ravenous, could eat ten of the appetizers. Was this a reaction to her using magic here, or to the Dimensional Corridor, or to landing on Earth again, or what?

"Marian," Juliet said softly, as Marian discarded the third empty stick.

Heat flooded her. "I'm sorry, as you said, I'm distracted, and here I came just to meet you. Please, forgive."

Juliet looked intrigued. "Just to meet *me*?"

Marian nodded. "Yes, my best teacher, Golden Raven, just left for the coast. I thought I'd talk to you about the Denver community and see if you could recommend someone comparable."

"Ah. Yes, I'd heard Wood Elk and Golden Raven were heading west." Juliet's brow furrowed. "You want another teacher?"

Actually, that was the last thing she wanted. Thinking on it, she had a surfeit of teachers lately, but Marian nodded anyway.

"Hmm." Juliet tapped her finger against her lips. "Do you get our newsletter?"

"The print one, but I think I'd pay attention to an online one more." That made Marian think about her PDA. She'd been careful not to touch it when she returned to her apartment. The intricacies of time-travel paradox had stumped smarter people than she. Marian caught herself rubbing her temples. "Sorry."

"Let's sit down." Juliet led her to a small sitting area against the wall. She took Marian's hands.

Their Songs flowed together in counterpoint. Juliet's eyes widened again.

"Your energy is fluctuating too extremely," she said.

Marian tried to withdraw her hands, but Juliet held tight.

"Breathe with me."

Of course! Why hadn't Marian thought of that? Too fuzzy brained. She let her eyelids drift closed. For several moments the women breathed together. At first Marian was aware of all the people and muted Songs around her, then she focused in on Candace's Song and felt her mother's disgust at her and Juliet. Marian sent love down the bond to Candace, but it seemed to dissipate against the shield of Candace's heart. In turn, Marian searched for emotions from Candace—pride in her daughter, respect, affection, love, *anything*—and only sensed a distant acknowledgment of blood, nothing more.

Finally she blocked her aching heart and emptied her mind, and found serenity, solidity. She withdrew her hands and opened her eyes to Juliet's considering gaze.

"I've been doing too much," Marian said.

"Of course." Juliet pursed her lips, tapped them with a finger again. "They are getting ready for the silent auction. I'd like to slip out a moment. I have something for you."

Probably a grounding crystal or an herbal drink. Marian raised her eyebrows. She should be wary. "Yes?"

Juliet nodded decisively. "Can you come with me out to my car a moment? I have it there. I knew it belonged to someone, but not who or when I'd meet the person—so I've been carrying it around."

A low hum seemed to rattle her bones—another feeling of premonition. Marian took another few discreet, deep breaths. "Yes."

"Great. Follow me." Whirling so her silver fringe caught the light and gleamed, Juliet headed quickly through the room to the exit.

They were intercepted by her husband, Trenton Philbert III, who was Marian's height and towered over Juliet. He set himself firmly in their path and raised a brow. "Going somewhere, Juliet? I believe we discussed this earlier."

Juliet rolled her eyes. "I've found the person the book is for."

Trenton shifted his gaze to Marian. His eyes cooled. "Ms. Harasta."

Juliet tsked and patted Trenton's arm, bringing his attention back to her. He smiled, harsh features softening. "Trey, you are making judgments again."

"An occupational hazard," the man said.

A lightning bolt of recollection hit Marian. "You're a judge, aren't you?"

"Yes." His tone was clipped.

Marian frowned. "Do you know Alexa Fitzwalter?"

His stare pinned her. "She disappeared about three months ago. What do you know of that?" His voice was harsh.

Too many conflicting emotions and ideas clashed in Marian's head. This return to Earth was as bad as her first hours in Lladrana. She put fingertips to her temples, trying to find words.

"Let me remember. Friends told me that Alexa was unexpectedly called away to handle a…delicate situation." That was true enough. Marian shrugged casually. "I didn't speak to her before she left and haven't since." *Not on Earth*. She kept that thought foremost in her mind when she met Trenton's eyes. "I was wondering if you've heard whether she's returned?" Maybe she could find a way to tidy up Alexa's affairs—take care of back rent, close her law practice.

"Her car was found abandoned near Berthoud Pass."

Shit.

Frowning, Marian said, "I don't know how to reach her. I never had her cell number." Again truth.

The man continued to weigh Marian's words. A portion of his Song pulsed from him—powerful, honorable, concerned and with a touch of personal Power—truth-sensing.

"Her office and apartment have been closed," he said abruptly.

Marian shook her head. "Then I guess I can't help."

"Where did you meet Alexa?" asked Trenton.

"We're gathering attention, and the silent auction is about to begin," Juliet interjected. She pushed at her husband's shoulder. "Go buy something outrageously expensive for me to support the charities and show everyone how much you love me."

He threw back his head and laughed. Even more gazes swung in their direction.

Juliet lifted her snub nose. "I have business with Marian. She needs the book."

Book? Trembling started within Marian. A book held infinite possibilities.

In an unexpectedly elegant gesture, Trenton took his wife's hands, kissed each of them. Then he looked at Marian again. "I'll get back to you later—"

"No, you won't," Juliet said firmly. "You will leave her alone.

I know you don't like unanswered questions, but I believe that's the best in this case."

Trenton looked pained, shot them a glance from under lowered brows, then strode back to the plush seats that had been arranged in rows.

As the auctioneer called the group to attention, Marian and Juliet slipped from the hall into the cool spring night. Tears stung the back of Marian's throat. She was home on Earth, in Denver, where she'd been raised.

Even the city air tasted good on her tongue. The lights were too bright to see many stars, but she stopped to look up and find Orion. The scent of blossoming trees wafted to her, even more familiar and comforting than the brithenwood. How could she give all this up? Her old, steady life. Her simple dreams. Her home.

A car door clunked closed and Marian realized that Juliet had left her to collect the book.

Marian looked around—the bright lights from Colfax Avenue, a couple of streets down, the huge trees leafing out, the interesting architecture of the hall…. She'd find none of this on Lladrana.

Could she return?

33

Juliet's silver shawl flapped in the breeze as she hurried to Marian and thrust a blue book into her hands. It was small but heavy, and bound in leather.

"Thank you," Marian said. "What do I owe you for it?"

"Free, on the house." Juliet started back toward the hall and Marian kept pace. "Will you be disappearing, too?" Juliet turned her head and smiled.

"Maybe." All this indecision wasn't like her. But the choice was huge and final. "I will definitely be leaving Boulder for California for a little while. Then I may disappear, and my brother, too."

"Then why did you ask me about a teacher?"

"In case I stay. I'm not sure what I'm doing and doubts creep in. And there's my mother—"

Juliet patted her shoulder. "You'll make the right decision."

They stepped into the hall and, instead of going to the ballroom where bidding was active, Marian crossed the lobby to a red leather couch and sat back against the squabs. Juliet sat beside her.

Looking down at the book, Marian received another shock. It was written in archaic Lladranan. She shivered and her fingers clutched the little blue leather book. She knew enough of the old language to read "Use...Knot...Unbinding."

Fate.

The intricate red-silk weapon-knot rested on her bedside table. In Swordmarshall Thealia Germaine's Tower in the Keep of the Marshalls' Castle. In Lladrana. On the world of Amee.

Her hands shook and dropped the book onto her lap.

"I *knew* you were the right person for the book," Juliet said. "You can read the language, can't you?"

"Yes," Marian whispered.

The door to the lobby swung open and Trenton stalked through. "I've done my part for the charities, now let's go home." He scowled at Juliet. "You're my bride. You were supposed to stay with me. You weren't supposed to abandon me, especially not for obviously better company than the folks in that room and more interesting conversation."

Juliet rose and crossed to him, smiling serenely. She patted his cheek, stood on tiptoe and brushed a kiss on his lips. "I'll do better next time you drag me to one of these, darling. Did you buy me something wonderful?"

"Yes. It will be delivered tomorrow." His gaze fastened on Marian. "I think I want to speak with Marian Harasta. I've been trying to figure out where her path might have crossed with Alexa Fitzwalter's."

Juliet linked her fingers with Trenton's, tugged. He didn't move.

Marian smiled slightly. "Colorado Shakespeare Festival in

Boulder?" After all, Alexa had quoted *Macbeth* correctly, she must like the Bard.

Trenton's eyes narrowed.

Pulling at his hand, Juliet said, "I think you want to go home for some fun."

He jerked his stare from Marian to settle it on Juliet, and grinned. "You believe you can distract me with fabulous and inventive sex?"

"Oh yes." She raised their joined hands and kissed his knuckles and walked away.

He followed, chuckling. "You are so right."

Marian was left aching for Jaquar and the tender affection they'd known far too briefly. And wondering what she could, what she would do...

She waited until everyone had left the fund-raiser, until her mother had overseen the departure of the catering staff and the efforts of the cleaning crew. Nothing but perfection for Candace.

When Candace sent her husband for the car, Marian joined her in the middle of the elegant, empty ballroom.

Candace sent her a brilliant smile, all teeth. "It was good of you to finally show up, Marian."

Ignoring the emotional slap, Marian pressed on. "Mother, have you seen a doctor?"

"Why do you say that?" Her eyes sharpened.

"You look a little...tired."

Candace waved the comment away. "The ball was quite challenging this year, but I outdid myself." Her expression turned smug. "I doubled donations this year."

Marian cleared her throat, tried again. "Now that the event is a success, you might want to slow down a little."

Straightening her bony shoulders, Candace said, "Nonsense, you know nothing about my life."

"I suppose not, but I think you should see a doctor."

Candace's lip curled. "Quacks, the lot of them. They haven't got a clue."

Marian's heart thudded. "You've been to see some! What did they say?"

"A lot of balderdash." She took off on a final inspection of the room. "I'm not listening to them."

She hardly ever listened to anyone. Marian caught up with her and grabbed her arm. It was nothing but skin and bone under her fingers. Her fear spiraled higher. "Mother!"

"How many times must I tell you to call me *Candace!* You don't listen. You don't remember."

"Mo— Candace, do you realize you're ill?" Marian couldn't give up.

"Oh, is that some of your New Age wisdom? I suppose you'll prescribe some nice herbal tea for me."

Marian didn't want her mother sick. Didn't want Andrew sick. Didn't want anyone she loved to die. "Let me review the doctor's reports and we can…"

Candace made a disgusted noise. "No. I'll live my life as I see fit."

"You're ill."

"I'm not."

"Let me help!" Marian cried, twisted inside.

Whirling, Candace glared at her. "You've never been a help to me. You barely arrived tonight on time, and did so only because of the money."

"No. Not entirely—" Marian's breath hitched.

With a nod of satisfaction at the room, Candace went to the light bank and flipped all but one switch off, then strode to the double doors to the lobby. She and Marian went through at the same time.

"Candace, I need to talk to you."

"I don't want to talk with you. Not now, and not later."

"A luncheon appointment." Marian caught her hand, fragile as a bird's.

Candace wrenched her fingers away. "No." She didn't meet Marian's gaze.

Candace's jaw firmed and Marian could barely see the scars of her last face-lift. Blue eyes the same color as her own scanned the lobby, then finally locked with Marian's.

"We simply don't have anything to say to each other, Marian. We are too different." Candace unlocked a closet, slipped on her fur coat and stroked it. Her hand trembled. Then she straightened her spine and headed to the front door. "Go away, Marian. I'll let you know when you might be of use to me. Go back to your pitiful, lonely little life. You may know book learning, but you don't understand anything about the real world or men."

"I— What about John? What does he think of the doctors' reports?"

Candace lifted her chin. "John supports me in all I do. As for you, I'll transfer the last of your college fund Monday. Then we'll be done with each other."

The words were like a blow. Harder than she'd ever heard from her mother. Impossible to bear without a cry of pain. "Why are you being so hateful?"

Candace swept out of the lobby into the night; Marian keeping pace. "I'm not being hateful, I'm being honest. You want to drag me around to doctors, as if you know best and they can fix my life. My life is *excellent*. Your life is the one that needs fixing. By the way, that streak in your hair ages you." She turned and locked the doors behind them.

"Mother, I'm moving away."

Candace waved for her car parked a block down the street to pick her up. "Is that so? Out to California with Andrew, I suppose. Well, from what I understand the Californians are even more fitness conscious than Coloradans. You'll have a hard time finding a man there."

More words she had to ignore. One last try. "I don't know when I'll be back. If ever."

"Don't be so dramatic," she said. As if already forgetting her cruel words, she air-kissed Marian's cheek as the chauffeur came around to open your door. "Bye-bye, Marian." She slid into the back seat of the car.

Just before the door closed, Marian saw the mask drop from Candace's face. It sagged with fatigue and sickness. Candace didn't know this might be the last time she'd see Marian. Candace really didn't care.

Hurt washed over Marian as the taillights of the car blurred in her vision. She stumbled to a bench flanking the doors to the hall. For a moment she just sat, absorbing the verbal slaps her mother had dealt her. Her shoulders slumped. There would be no rationalizing the words away, pretending they didn't happen, pretending Candace didn't mean them. With the closing of her car door, Candace had snapped the mother-daughter bond.

It was so fragile it had disintegrated into dust, and any remnants would be blown away by the time Marian reached Boulder.

The next day Marian awoke with a screaming headache and burning muscles. Daylight stabbed pain into her eyes. She stumbled from bed a couple of times to take aspirin, splash her face with cooling water, then return to sleep. Once, as she passed Tuck's cage, she tested the theory that everything had been a fever dream and opened the plastic lid to find him.

He was gone.

A glance at the taped pentacle in the living room showed that her PDA was gone, too.

She retreated to bed and slept the day and the night away.

Sunday morning she awoke ravenous. Once again she checked what she could to see again if her time in Lladrana had been a dream.

No Tuck.

No PDA.

And a beautiful purple velvet gown hung in her closet, with a container of jerir, a yellow stone and a crumpled piece of paper in the pocket.

As she ate breakfast, she studied the parchment. It *was* parchment, made from some finely scraped animal skin. The ink had dried bright and vivid, unlike most standard Earth inks, more like the ink of illuminated manuscripts that were specially made—of ground semiprecious stones, weren't they?

The second thing she did was log onto the Internet and searched for "Lladrana," "jerir," "Circlet," and any other unique words that might indicate other travelers.

Nothing.

No scientific data on Dimensional Corridors.

She walked to campus and around it, enjoying the late-spring day, the comfortably familiar sounds and sights of other students. She stopped and stared at her department building and thought of her future there.

After she made sure she was unobserved, she Sang a tiny wind into being. It swirled over a few grass blades, then died. The effort to call the wind was about triple what she would need to do the same on Amee. It left her hungry and with tendrils of a headache throbbing in the back of her skull.

She'd been avoiding weighty concepts, disturbed emotions, trying to be steady and stable all day long. But she'd have to decide what to do soon. Tomorrow was Monday. She couldn't see herself going in to work at the Engineering Department.

She had time, a little voice inside her whispered as she walked back to her apartment. She had nearly three weeks.

During lunch, she studied the timeline again and saw a day circled in brilliant blue, with a notation in Bossgond's hand. "Summon Marian and Andrew back to Lladrana."

Invisible ink, of course. She didn't know why she was surprised. Everything fell into place. Bossgond had seen her through his dimensional binoculars on Earth when she'd been in Lladrana. Naturally he'd correctly deduced what had happened, but had said nothing to her in case he might change what was or what might be.

Still, it made her shudder.

That afternoon, she went over her finances. They were in good shape and if she received the last of her college fund tomorrow she'd have plenty to live on before she was Summoned to Lladrana.

If she went. The day had been delightful. She'd steeped herself in the rich and sustaining essence of Earth, of her life as it had been.

The choice before her was just too gigantic for her to act hastily. She decided to quit her work-study job. Spring semester had just ended, and though she'd planned on registering for summer classes if she received her college fund, she could delay a while.

So she tidied her apartment and late in the evening began a tentative list of what she'd like to take to Lladrana, if she decided to return. When it was finished, she figured it would take a moving van to transport. Probably the most she could carry was a backpack, and Andrew, too.

Her sleep that night was peaceful and she awoke refreshed. Her first order of business was quitting her work-study job. She'd finished a big project and summer school would be light. Though the Dean was naturally grumpy about replacing her, he didn't seem too concerned.

Again she walked around the campus, strolled along downtown Boulder, enjoyed herself and considered her two lives. Everything seemed so clear in Lladrana.

She could have magic here. But could she integrate it into the life she'd planned? Not easily. Marian suspected that her trials in the Dark's maw was only the overture for a long opera. If she was to play her proper role in Lladrana, she'd be integrally involved in defeating the Dark. She already felt like she might have a bull's-eye painted on her.

And there was Jaquar. She didn't want to much think about him, either, but great quests would entail many other "greats"—sacrifices, betrayals, triumphs. She'd never had a man like him before and didn't think there was one walking the streets of Boulder who could compare.

She sat at her kitchen table and made a list—pros and cons for returning to Lladrana or staying on Earth.

Lladrana won.

With trembling fingers, she opened the *Lorebook of Knot-Weapons*. The volume was well organized, with simple knots first. It showed a picture of the knot, the description of its use including effects and damage, then gave visual instructions on how to tie the knot step by step. When Marian touched those pictures, a faint haze appeared as if a holographic picture should be projected. Not enough Power on Earth—though if

Marian sent her own Power through her fingertips, she could see the "movie"—hands slowly tying the knots.

Dread tightening her muscles, Marian continued to turn the pages. Her knot was the third from the end, "City Destroyer." Her mouth dried and she edged away from the book, setting her fisted hands on her lap. There was a long "Warning" section, describing how to encase the user of the weapon in a Powerful shield before its use. The shield chant looked complex and demanded perfect pitch. Which Marian didn't have.

Mouth dry, Marian scraped her chair back and went to the kitchen for a glass of filtered water, trying not to imagine what would have happened if she'd untied the knot.

It would have destroyed the maw—at the cost of her life.

The whole matter smacked of fate.

She'd have to use the book in the future, hopefully when she was very, very Powerful and had found someone to shield her. With friends, maybe—though she didn't think Alexa had perfect pitch, either.

Of course Andrew was her priority. She was sure she could convince him to return with her, but she'd have to ensure he believed her first. Could she connect with him in the Lladranan way? Let him *feel* her experiences?

She was happy and excited, until she called and spoke with Andrew's doctor.

"I'm glad you phoned," Dr. Chan said. "Since Andrew authorized me to tell you everything, I'll be blunt. His health is poor. He's underweight and vulnerable to infection. He has fallen several times the past few months and has been lucky not to break a bone. The intervals of time between attacks are shortening and the flare-ups are more intense and longer."

Marian clutched the phone. She hadn't known. It didn't sound good. If Andrew believed his mind was failing… She shuddered.

34

Marian forced herself to wait before going to California. Time had to elapse so she wouldn't see herself in Bossgond's binoculars. She kept herself busy changing her life.

She readied herself, poring over the Ritual chant Bossgond had written, retrieved the hard-copy notes of the Ritual she'd written for herself and refined it to dovetail with the Lladranans', and prepared the pentagram.

And she practiced. By the time the Marshalls and Sorcerers and others would Summon her and Andrew, she would be letter-perfect in her own Ritual.

Echoes of Lladrana reverberated in her days. One morning she found herself tense and nervous, then felt giddy with relief. When she looked at the timeline, she saw she'd Tested for Scholar that morning on Lladrana. So she bought a huge calendar and filled in the blocks with what she recalled of each day there, so she could "listen" for the echoes, feel the resonance of the emotions affecting her in Lladrana.

Finally, she took a flight to Andrew's ranch home in San Mateo, California.

As she went into his office, she noted the additional equipment for his deteriorating health. Canes and walkers stood in every room, his computer had a voice-recognition system for when his fingers lost mobility and an ergonomic keyboard for when his voice slurred. The sight of these made her eyes sting. No one should have to live this way, fall before an encroaching disease.

Marian called the retreat. When a counselor answered, Marian left a message that *she* had an emergency and needed Andrew, then gave his phone number as a contact.

He called a couple of hours later, sounding worried. "What's up, sis?"

"I need you, Andrew."

He swore. "I knew there was something going on that you weren't telling me about."

"I'm not the only one who's been hiding things," she said. "I spoke with Dr. Chan."

There was silence.

"I love you, Andrew, and I need to talk to you—about some life changes *I* am considering."

"You!"

"Yes. I've quit my work-study job and dropped out of school. I've been out of the country and have another…vocational offer, but whether I pursue that or just transfer to a California university is up to you. I want to get your opinion."

"Huh," Andrew said. "This can't wait until after my retreat?"

"I'm afraid not. The timing is difficult." She took a breath.

"And I spoke to people where I was about you and received a herbal medicine that might help."

"You're kidding, right?"

"No."

Again there was a long silence. It scraped Marian's nerves until she burst out, "Andrew, so much has happened. Such incredible events. I can't…I can't discuss this on the phone." To her horror tears clogged her throat.

"Shh, sis. I'll come home. You're at—my house, right?"

"Yes." She sniffled.

"You want to make the arrangements for a plane and car, or do you want me to?"

"I've got all the details ready."

"Of course, give 'em to me. I have a pencil and paper."

So she did.

"Looks good," Andrew said, then paused. "Thanks, Marian."

"What do you mean?"

"Thanks for saying you need me, for calling me with your news and making me feel…strong."

"You *are* strong, Andrew."

He snorted. "Not many people treat me like that, though. I love you—see you later."

"I love you, too."

As soon as she hung up, a tide of exhaustion overwhelmed her and she slipped into the guest bed and slept. And dreamed of Jaquar playing with her in a storm…

Marian woke to a commotion at the front door as Andrew paid off his driver and disengaged the alarm system. She dressed in her purple robe and hurried into the living room.

Andrew closed the door behind him and locked it, then took the walker standing by the door and leaned heavily on it as he stared at Marian. "My God, you look different."

She ran to him, trying not to show her shock at his thinness and infirmity. "I'm so glad to see you!" She hugged him gingerly, then returned to his comment. "Different how?"

Slowly he shook his head. "There's the hair, of course. That silver streak is very striking. Natural?"

"Yes."

"Too bad. Guess you really did have weird stuff going on."

Marian raised her eyebrows. "You thought I lied about it?"

"Fibbed." He smiled slightly. "Thought you were worried about me and spinning a tale to come live with me or something." He shook his head again. "You look…trimmer. In shape." He flushed.

"That's okay. Any more comments about my appearance?"

He narrowed his eyes. "You look more *yourself*. But more… You *glow*. You aren't pregnant or anything, are you? If you are and the guy dumped you, I'll kill him!" His expression grew fierce.

Marian took a step back in surprise. "No. Not pregnant."

"But there was a guy, I can tell."

Andrew took a couple of clumping steps toward her, and she realized he was very tired.

She wanted to rush to him and help, but instead indicated his recliner and took the one on the other side of the table.

He stumped to the recliner and lowered himself into it, still keeping his eyes on her face. "Did the jerk dump you?"

Clearing her throat, she shook her head. *She* had cut the bond between herself and Jaquar. "No, I dumped him."

"Wanna talk about it?" Andrew relaxed back into the recliner and shut his eyes.

"Not particularly."

"All right."

"Do you want me to—" But he was asleep.

For a time she watched him sleep. So beloved, this brother of hers. He'd been the only loving and stable person in her life. But she was deeply afraid for his health.

He was so much worse than she'd known. Or perhaps she was just looking at him with new eyes. Her mouth firmed. There wasn't much here that could help him, but maybe on Lladrana… She'd try *anything* to cure him. Dipping in, or perhaps even drinking the magical jerir. Paying the Marshalls any price to do a group Healing. The same with the Circlets. And the Friends of the Singer. Perhaps the Singer herself had Powers, could channel the Power of the Song to help Andrew.

Her options and methods might have changed, but her priority remained the same.

Since he was sleeping and she needed to do something, she went into the kitchen and took out a frozen casserole. It could warm until he awoke.

She picked up his duffel and unpacked it, set his medications on the table by his elbow with a glass of water and put the dirty laundry in the washer. She was transferring his clothes to the dryer when he called her name. She finished her task and walked to the living room.

"So, I didn't dream you," he said.

Leaning against the arch that separated the living room from the kitchen, Marian smiled at him. "No."

He rubbed his face, moved the recliner upright and drank some of the water. Serious gaze fixed on her, he said, "Sit down. Tell me what changed you and what you want to do about it. What you want *me* to do about it." A corner of his mouth lifted as if in pride that she'd asked for his help.

She didn't want to hurt him with the bond, would try to keep it light and easy at first and watch Andrew for any discomfort.

Walking over to him, she stretched and then curled her fingers, limbering them.

"What are you doing?"

Warmth crept up her cheeks. "I, uh—when I was away, I learned this technique for…connecting with people on an…emotional level."

He just stared at her, then he laughed, and it was so good to hear and see him this way that she drank in the sight and smiled herself.

After his last chuckle, he said, "All those New Age classes of yours—and where did you go, Tibet?"

"Not exactly."

He stretched out his hands. "Okay, lay it on me."

Instead of clasping hands, she bent and hugged him. A Song rose between them. Since Andrew stiffened, she sensed he heard it, too—the Song of the children of Candace. Closing her eyes, she felt tears well behind her lids. She was so *glad* to hold him. Without thought or will, her experiences on Lladrana flickered through their bond—fast and sketchy, but undeniably real.

His arms tightened around her. Then he shivered and withdrew. His face had paled, but his eyes blazed with wonder and excitement. "I can't believe it." Then he lifted a hand. "No, I *do* believe it, but it's fantastic all the same. Magic works and you have an affinity for fire."

He glanced over to the fireplace. "Care to light it?"

She sent him a withering glance. "It's gas."

"So?"

"So you have to turn the gas *on*. That's moving a lever, not lighting logs."

"Huh. Could you use some air to press down the switch?"

"Maybe I should draw down lightning on your thick skull."

He snorted. "Don't think you could do it." A wistful expression crossed his face. "I thought I got something about a hole in the skull and that special liquid—jerir?"

Marian licked her lips. "Yes."

"Didja bring the stuff with you and can I see it?"

"Yes." Marian went to the guest bedroom and returned with the bottle of jerir, which she handed to Andrew.

He took the solid proof of her trip to Lladrana in his hands, tilted the container back and forth, studied it under the light. The sparkles were harder to see under a lightbulb, but Marian spotted a couple.

"Real magic." He set the bottle on the table with his medicines. "You want to return, don't you?"

She met his eyes, let her fear show in her own. "I'm torn. It's a dangerous situation and it doesn't look like it's going to get any better soon." Taking a deep breath, she let it out slowly. "I'd have great Power and with great Power comes great responsibility."

"I'm glad that you feel that way."

A smile played on her lips, then faded. "I have to feel that way—otherwise I might succumb to pure greed or hubris or something."

But Andrew was shaking his head. "I don't think so. You've seen too much of what can happen with great riches and status in Denver society."

"Many of those people are caring, service-oriented individuals."

"But not Candace. What of Candace? You came back for me, and I thank you for that and am considering my new options. But I can't see you telling Candace about Lladrana, or convincing her to go there. Not her kind of place at all. You've always wanted a good relationship with Mother."

Marian braced herself. "I saw Candace Friday night. She's…dying." She swallowed hard. "I think she knows it. Cancer, probably. She won't do anything about it. Doesn't accept the prognosis. I got this through our bond—before she cut it."

Andrew swore, looked away. A moment later, he said, "It's hard, isn't it, knowing there's not a thing we can say that will make her take care of herself? I tried, now and then." His eyes turned sad. "I would have said that I didn't care. I do, of course. She is our mother."

"I don't think she has long—less than a year, perhaps."

Closing his eyes, Andrew sighed. "This is difficult for you." He shifted in his seat. "Maybe it's best that we do leave now. She wouldn't want us to be there at the end."

"You're sure of that? We couldn't give her comfort?"

"When did we ever give her comfort?"

"What if she changes her mind, her ways, wants us at the end?"

He opened his eyes, stared back at Marian. "Do you really believe you should forgo life on Lladrana because of a remote possibility that our mother will change her ways on her deathbed? If so, then I think you really don't want to return to Lladrana and the challenges there, but just prefer your steady, tidy life here."

Shock rippled through her at his harsh words. She staggered back to sit in the opposite recliner and frown at him.

His smile was humorless. "You wanted me here, *needed* me here to help you think about this radical change in lifestyle. Well, that's what I'm doing."

Marian rubbed her temples. "Not pulling any punches, are you."

"Since you'll be walking into circumstances that might get you killed, you'd better really be committed to that course."

She nodded, looked away, put his words in the back of her

mind to simmer. She'd consider them later. Taking an unsteady breath, she put a hand on her churning stomach. "You're talking like you'll come with me."

Nodding, Andrew said, "I'll give it good consideration. I know there's some time constraints. When would we leave?"

Marian dipped her hand in her pocket and withdrew the paper Bossgond had given her. Andrew examined it, turning it over and looking at both sides. He rubbed his thumb over it, scratched with his nail, even lifted it up and sniffed. Again he half smiled.

"Doesn't smell like Earth, but it does smell a little like you."

She hadn't quite accepted that she had a scent others noticed. "Huh."

Andrew chuckled, then glanced at the paper and read the English words at the bottom of the timeline. "I guess this big blue circle is when the return Summoning will be done?"

"Yes."

He nodded. "All right, about ten days." Carefully setting the paper aside on the table, he said, "That's enough heavy talk for now. Let's eat, watch some tube and get to sleep."

That evening, Marian lay in bed and waited—tonight had been the night in Lladrana when she and Jaquar had danced, when the first level of their connection had developed. She let the soft reflection of what was now occurring on Lladrana filter through her. Afterward, she felt a small but definite bond between her and Jaquar again—Jaquar-of-the-past and herself. She sat straight up in bed. Did Past-Jaquar now feel the bond with Earth-Marian as well as Lladrana-Marian? She thought he must, so the "Marian effect" upon *him* would be more than his effect on Lladrana-Marian or Earth-Marian. Not quite a double whammy, but still, it was something to consider when she thought of him—which was often.

Being on Earth gave her time and distance to reflect on her affair with Jaquar. She missed him, missed the companionship above all, and, of course, the sex. And she welcomed the renewed connection; this seemed to reverberate from the future, too, for just prior to the Snap, she'd linked with him again. A link through time. The thought made her shiver.

What would happen to that bond if Andrew decided against Lladrana?

She woke late, and by the time she dressed, Andrew was moving around the kitchen with only one cane and looking rested.

"Want me to make omelettes?" she asked.

He grinned and settled into a chair at the table. "Sure."

She got the ingredients together and began preparing.

A few minutes passed in silence. "I've decided," he said quietly.

Marian tensed as she folded the egg mixture over in the frying pan, then glanced at him.

"Yes?" Her voice was equally soft.

"I want to go with you."

She slid his omelette onto a plate and placed it before him, then went to work on hers, she was focused more on Andrew. "Why?"

He shrugged. "I think it's evident that my time and future here is limited." Then he gave a lopsided smile that tore her heart. "I'll take my chances on Lladrana."

She could barely breathe. "Really?" It came out in a high-pitched squeak that would have done Tuck proud.

Andrew picked up his fork and took a tiny bite. "I don't have much appetite." He continued to eat mechanically.

But when she finished making her own omelette and sat across from him, his gaze was as intense as a laser.

"Some people are born to do certain things. *You are born to be the Exotique Circlet Sorceress of Lladrana.*" His face hardened. "I don't *ever* want you walking away from that destiny. Promise me."

It wasn't often he demanded things of her.

She put down her fork, couldn't eat.

"Promise me, now. Nothing will stop you from returning."

She choked. He meant his sickness, his death.

"I—"

"I want this for you, Marian. All your life you've been look-ing for something, searching for that one skill that was com-pletely natural for the genius inside you. You had it and knew it subconsciously." He waved a hand. "Most sensitive people could tell that. Now you've found it. I *will not* let you squan-der your talent. Promise me *now.*"

"I promise." The words were barely a breath, but he heard them and nodded.

"Good." He closed his eyes again, a smile hovered on his mouth. "Always searching, all those classes…" He sighed.

Marian stared down at her omelette, too excited to eat. What had she done? She'd promised to go back to Lladrana and battle the Dark.

She might have been born to this work, but unlike her first week on Lladrana, the months to come wouldn't be fun and games and learning. Her future—their future, hopefully—could be brutal and short.

"Eat," Andrew said, "and I'll tell you how this will work."

Marian smiled, was able to pick up her fork again and eat. The omelette should have been tasty, but it was much like the ones she'd eaten with Bossgond. Still, like Andrew, she ate au-tomatically, for fuel.

Andrew said, "I'll get ready to travel. I think we should

leave from your apartment again." He looked around. "This house should sell pretty quickly, especially if I keep the price reasonable. I'll pull out money from my account and convert it to—what do the Lladranans use as currency?" He grinned. "No use going there a pauper if I can help it."

"You're sure you want to do this?"

"Of course." He chuckled. "I'm the risk-taker, remember? You're the cautious one, trying to get things perfect before you make a move."

"I'm doing better at that," she mumbled.

He tilted his head. "I think you are. Those Lladranans taught you more than magic, didn't they?"

She managed a smile. "I had a lot of challenging experiences."

"You'll have to tell me the whole story, from beginning to end—or at least the middle. We haven't reached the end yet."

"You'll really return with me." She searched his face and found his eyes steady.

"You're the one with the destiny. I'm the one with no future…here. We're family. Where you go, I go."

Tears rolled down her face. She reached for the paper towel she had used for a napkin and wiped her eyes, blew her nose.

He began eating again. "And you'll have to tell me about the man, too."

Her chest tightened. "The man."

"I felt him. But that can wait, it's all about me first. I'm not going over poor, and there is definitely other stuff I want to take with me. What do they use as currency, gold?" He winked.

"Uh, I don't know. I dealt mostly in trade." She frowned, trying to remember Alexa's experiences. "Jewels, Alexa had a ruby—no, a red spine."

"Even better." Andrew rose and took his plate to the sink,

washed it and his fork, frowning. "I didn't get that stuff about Alexa. Who is she?"

Marian finished the last bit of omelette, then walked up and gently jostled Andrew away from the sink so she could wash and put away her own dishes. She looked up at him with a twinkle in her eye. "Alexa was the first Exotique."

His goggle-eyed look was satisfying.

35

The following days Marian spent with Andrew were some of the most satisfying in her life. His symptoms eased and he became the vital, intelligent man he was when in remission. He delighted in Marian's small displays of magic, forged ahead in settling his affairs, closing his business and selling the house. In that, they worked well together. Andrew liquidated his holdings and bought gold and gems while Marian dealt with the paperwork of their disappearance.

They flew back to Denver by private jet a couple of days before they were to be Summoned.

On the night Marian's other self was thrown into the Dark's nest, Andrew took her to an expensive restaurant and kept her mind occupied by making her tell him stories of Lladrana. But her underlying fears remained and her body betrayed her by twitching until Andrew grabbed her and held her close.

The morning of the Summoning, Marian moved the two

cots she and Andrew had slept on to the building's storage unit and left them. She returned to a clean apartment, bare except for the items they would need for the Summoning. Andrew had placed his night gear in his pack, put on the music. He stood outside the scarlet-taped star and circle looking thoughtful. Their packs lay in the middle of the star.

"You know, this is going to look awfully strange to the property manager when he walks in."

"This is Boulder," Marian said tensely, reviewing her notes. Anxiety that her mind would go blank bit deep. "Besides, I'm going to leave the door unlocked. Maybe they'll think someone else laid the tape. I'm sure the brass incense burner and the mini music system will be stolen by the time someone in authority gets here."

Andrew patted her shoulder and shook his head. "I think they'll know you did it. Everyone knows you've always been weird, Marian," he teased.

Marian chuckled weakly, scanned his face, rubbed her throat. "Ready? You're sure you want to go?" They'd taped the pentacle together. Andrew had practiced the chant, too.

"Like the other ten billion times you've asked me—yes, I want to go. This is a real adventure." He adjusted his hat to a rakish angle. He wore a full leather suit of pants, vest, heavy jacket and an Indiana Jones-style hat. The hat reminded Marian of the hideous hat that Jaquar wore and she felt her heart pump faster at the knowledge she'd soon see him. For him, it would be a mere two days since she left, but for her it had been weeks.

He'd know that and factor it in when he pressed for a renewal of their relationship.

Marian wore her underwear and her purple robe. She'd packed a silk pantsuit and several pairs of jeans. She had some in Alexa's size, too, and was bringing a package of Tuck's favorite hamster treats. She had new electronic "nuts" for him—encyclopedias, books and music.

She set her shoulders. "Let's do it." She glanced down at her notes, shoved them into the center to consult.

"Easy," Andrew said as he caught her left hand in his right one.

His fingers didn't have tension running through them, his body was relaxed, Marian noted with envy. His right hand held the tiger's eye full of energy that Jaquar had given her.

She looked at her watch. "We're running a little ahead of schedule."

"All to the good. Let's start."

"I don't know…"

"You must believe we can do it," Andrew said.

"What if it's not right?"

He just chuckled. "I can't think that magic spells are so precise that there is no room for mistakes, can you?"

She didn't know, but it couldn't hurt to be as perfect as possible.

So they began the Ritual tailored to Earth Song and magic that Marian had crafted. They lit the incense together, closed the Circle, began the chant. Andrew's voice was low, deeper than Marian had ever heard, fervent-sounding.

He wanted to do this. The knowledge should have relaxed her, but it didn't. She was strung tight as a piano wire.

Mother Earth's Song rose from the ground through her feet, surged through Marian like a benediction. Andrew's fingers clamped over hers.

They chanted the final note.

A sizzling firebolt hit between their feet.

Andrew jerked. Marian gasped.

They shot into the Dimensional Corridor even as Marian

was thinking that the property manager wasn't going to like the singed carpet and it was good she'd reconciled herself to not getting her deposit back.

"Marian?" Andrew shouted over the winds roaring around him.

His eyes stared as if he didn't see what she did—a shining, nearly translucent portal across the hall from them. Through it she could see a huge Circle of Marshalls, Circlets, Scholars, Chevaliers…. But it wasn't the Temple at the Marshalls' Castle!

The incised pentacle was the one at Parteger Island—a place she never cared to see again.

"Marian!" Andrew shivered as if the winds buffeted him.

No breeze stirred the bottom of Marian's robe. *She* was in control here.

With a slight tug on Andrew's hand, she led him to the portal, and through it.

They dropped about four feet to the gray stone. Marian steadied Andrew as the breath jarred from him on landing.

Amee's Song flooded her, held her transfixed. Earth's Song diminished, left with a farewell of distant thunder, the image of a gray sky over the Boulder Flatirons, and the scent of ozone after a storm. Marian blinked back tears to see Andrew gawking around them, swaying.

Power sizzled through her—from the midmorning sunlight, the hot stone beneath her feet, the triumphant cry of Amee at the arrival of another warrior. Wind whirled around her like a thousand blessings, stroking her with love, from Amee—and from Jaquar?

His dark sapphire gaze fixed on hers, he stood linked between Alexa and another Marshall. Determination and promises flowed to her from him, through the emotional link that widened as their gazes locked. He nodded, then turned his head to look at Andrew. His eyes softened, a smile close to pity curved his lips.

Marian scowled. How dare he pity her brother!

"First question," Alexa called in English as soon as the last word of the Summoning chant ended. "Did you bring potatoes? You know they don't have fries here."

Marian laughed and Andrew grinned.

Lady Knight Swordmarshall Thealia Germaine cut the Ritual Circle by withdrawing her hands from those on each side of her and humming an atonal note.

Alexa strolled toward them, smiling at Andrew. "Hi, you must be Andrew. I'm Alexa."

Andrew took a step, wavered. Marian reached to brace him, but he shrugged her hand away and paced forward steadily, holding out his hand. "Andrew Reston."

Marian and Andrew had just stepped from the center pentagram to between the star-points when a screaming *whoosh* sounded behind them.

The shriek came from a thin, weedy young Circlet who yelled, "The maw opened. Danger. Danger! I saw it. An immense pulse of Darkness straight here—carrying horrors." He crumpled.

Wing beats and cries came from above. Volarans had risen to scream challenge to a dreeth, diving at it, clamping teeth on the fragile wings.

Marian whirled to see monsters pouring into the confined circle of the stands, trapping the Lladranans and her and Andrew—hulking renders, slayers ruffling their spines, the soul-suckers with twisting tentacles. Five black splotches of manlike sangviles glided toward them. She stood petrified.

But Lladranans fought in three dimensions.

Alexa whirled and ran to Bastien. He shrilled a whistle and a mighty volaran dipped near to the ground. Bastien threw Alexa onto the steed, then jumped on behind her. An egg-shaped force field snapped around them. They whipped out their batons and Bastien yelled a war cry as they flew straight for the dreeth's distended belly.

Their Chevaliers, Pascal and Urvey, Koz and Perlee and others called their volarans and followed.

The Marshalls coalesced into Pairs, then into a team, stripped their robes from their armor and waded into the fight, faces grim. A Powerful Song of destruction vibrated from them in low tones.

Most of the Circlets and Scholars stood as frozen as Marian. Bossgond wielded a staff that sent invisible energy, frying a slayer.

Sinafin in hawk-form flew over Marian and dropped a brith-enwood branchlet on her head, screaming, *Fight!* That jolted Marian from immobility. She caught the branch before it fell to the ground, held on hard. To her surprise, the twigs melded into the main stem, the forks came together, and she had a strong, beautiful wand that Sang of life.

Others were dying. Marian saw a male Chevalier Pair fall beneath five renders, ripping them apart.

Fight. It was a whisper inside her that had to grow fast, that had to stir her body into action. It didn't matter that she didn't know how. She had to try.

Jaquar ran to them, his telescoping staff the size of a wand. His lips were pulled back in a grin. He'd torched a sangvile and yelled in triumph.

Behind him followed a soul-sucker, and another speeding sangvile. "Watch out—" She'd meant to warn him, but he caught Andrew in a football tackle and draped him over his shoulder, running for the dubious safety of the deserted Tower.

Cold fingers encircled her ankle. Power stilled in her, began to drain. She looked down in horror to see a sangvile move its head to her calf, lips protruding.

Fight! Fire! Fire killed these things. She was the Mistress of Lightning. Fight before she died!

The Massster sssends his greetingsss, the evil thing hissed in her mind—violation enough to enrage Marian.

She pointed her new wand at it and shouted, "Fire!" Summoning Power from the anger of Amee in the ground beneath her. She allowed it to sear through her to free her wits, roll down her arm and charged from the wand to strike the sangvile and shrivel it to ash.

Her first kill.

She felt no remorse, only dedication to the cause of freeing this planet from the Dark that sought to claim it. She wouldn't stand aside. She'd learn to fight. This was her home now, these people her family as much as Andrew. She would defend them to her death.

Shuddering, she took a few seconds to scan the battle-ground. Most of the Scholars had fled after Jaquar, who was organizing them. Several Circlets stood ready before him.

To her surprise, Chalmon and Venetria had joined Boss-gond. A ragged Song rose from the three as they struggled to work as a unit, fighting a dreeth. Venetria used her staff to coat the creature's wings with ice, and it crashed. Boss-gond and Chalmon shot a thick sizzling stream into it, firing it.

Chevaliers fought on foot or volaran-back. Some had fallen, but their bravery and skill in facing the monsters and dispatching them impressed Marian.

The Marshalls were awesome to see—targeting a dreeth or a specific group of horrors, swooping down, and dispatching them. Not one Marshall—Sword or Shield—appeared to have a scratch.

Marian limped to the Tower where Jaquar was forming the Scholars and Circlets into a defensive semicircle. She couldn't see Andrew but sensed he was behind the line.

As she walked, she swung her wand like a weapon, shooting fire at the horrors—cutting two soul-suckers in half, setting a render afire. She learned not to shut her eyes as the fire hit, not to flinch as death claimed a beast. Her left foot that the sangvile had leeched onto was numb and dragging behind her, slowing her.

A scream of pain split the air above her. Marian looked up to see a small dreeth flame a rider and volaran. The rider fell and hit the ground two feet from Marian with a sickening *thud*. Marian pivoted, struggled to keep her balance.

It was Perlee.

"Nooo!" an anguished man shouted in her ear. Koz jumped from his own volaran, flung himself at Perlee, lifted her.

She was dead.

"No," he whispered, rocking her. "It can't be. This can't be right. This isn't fair."

Even Marian knew that life was rarely fair, and war never was, and this was her first battle. She swallowed hard, averted her gaze from the burned and broken Perlee. Setting a hand on Koz's large, trembling shoulder, she cried, "Come."

So many monsters. How could they all have appeared? A black death ray straight from the maw to here.

She shivered, pulled on Koz's arm. "Come! We aren't safe here."

He lifted a pale face, blind eyes staring. "She's my Pairling, we're bonded. She can't die. Not without me. She can't go away without me. She can't abandon me." It was a chant of his own. A chant rejecting death. A futile Song.

Thudding footfalls approached. Pascal, the head of Alexa's Chevaliers, stopped near them. "Perlee's gone, Koz. We have a fight to finish." His words were harsher than his tone. "Come along."

Koz did nothing.

Pascal stooped and pulled Perlee's sword from her loose fingers. To Marian's horror, he yanked Perlee from Koz's grasp, lifted her sword and plunged it into her body, through it, into the ground. Marian choked.

Perlee's body sank into the ground until all that showed was a depression of darker green grass, and her sword stood upright like a gravestone.

Koz roared in despair and swung at Pascal, who ducked, grabbed the man's arm and snapped, "Let's go. Horrors are advancing. Protect the Exotique!"

Looking down at her with dull eyes, Koz moved between her and a group of monsters rampaging toward them.

Adrenaline shooting through her, Marian ran haltingly toward the Tower, the men at her back. She plunged through the defensive line a moment before the horrors caught up with them.

The men joined the ranks and turned and fought. Jaquar stepped up with them as the beasts hit the line.

The battle had come to the Tower.

Jaquar, Pascal and Koz cut down the first wave of six—three renders, a soul-sucker and two slayers.

As a slayer died, it flung its spines into the defenders. A female scholar fell.

So did Andrew.

Marian screamed, her cry resounding off the black stones of the Tower. She rushed to his side, found the yellow spine sticking out of his shoulder. Without thought she grabbed it—acid seared her palm. Pain scoured her. She kept her gaze locked on Andrew.

His face was pale, beaded with sweat. He tried to smile. "Guess…I've…had…it. Not much of an…adventure."

"Nooo!" she moaned.

Jaquar was there. "The jerir, do you have it?"

Marian stared at him.

"The jerir!" he repeated.

She fumbled in her pocket where she'd put the bottle, dug it out. He ripped it from her hand, unstoppered it and poured it into Andrew's wound, then found the energy stone in Andrew's pocket and set it atop the injury.

Andrew jerked in her arms. She thought she saw his soul rise from his body. "No!" she cried. "Stay, stay with me."

With her own strong Song, Powered by physical and emotional pain, she encased him, drew him close. Held him. His soul hovered, then slipped halfway back into him.

Jaquar grabbed her hurt hand, took a vial from his pocket and upended fiery liquid over her palm and fingers. Her vision darkened. She fought it back.

Battle cries and roars came from the line. She turned her head to the protective rank of Circlets fighting. She saw Marshalls—Alexa and Bastien—zooming down on the monsters from behind.

Two Circlets fell. Then a render's powerful swipe hit Koz, swept him off balance, and his head hit the stone wall.

As Marian watched, the battle moved to the Tower, with all the monsters attacking, then the Marshalls and Chevaliers cut the horrors to shreds.

A shout of triumph rose. Soon all the survivors entered the Tower, which had become a hospital zone.

Marian stayed with Andrew, who struggled for life, laboring to breathe. She didn't let go of his Song, kept re-weaving the bond between them.

The two Castle Medicas who had helped Summon Andrew and Marian arranged the wounded around them, used their Power to heal. The Marshalls had consulted with the Medicas regarding Andrew, and Marian hated that he'd heard their whispered conclusion. He was an Exotique, too unknown and frail to be healed by a Marshalls' Circle. They could not help.

Would not help.

The Marshalls Healing Circle dealt only with the worst Chevalier casualties, slowly and steadily. They fought death and won.

Nor would the Marshalls help Koz. The Medicas frowned over the Chevalier. "He has a concussion. We have healed it, yet he does not respond." They shook their heads over him, then went on to other wounded.

The Scholars and Circlets had set up a Healing Circle, too, under Chalmon's direction, with Bossgond a part of it. Marian could sense from where she sat that the Circle wasn't as strong or as steady as the Marshalls'. Not as well practiced.

Something she'd definitely remedy in the future…

She didn't want to think of a future without Andrew. Had never wanted to imagine a life without her brother. She wasn't ready for his death so soon after the triumph of arriving in Lladrana.

Jaquar stayed with her, sitting beside her but not touching, keeping a low Song of comfort running between them. Now and then he would leave to join the Healing Circle. She missed him, then. He was only across the floor from her, but she missed him.

She prayed. The day crept by with agonizing slowness.

Finally Andrew's breath rattled in his chest. His eyes opened and his gaze fixed on hers.

Marian, he whispered in her mind.

She jerked, her fingers tightening on his hand.

Andrew. She infused her mental voice with all the love she felt for him. *I'm sorry—*

No! I'm not. He managed a smile. *An adventure. Live, Marian. Live large.*

Andrew—

No, listen to me. A hoarse sound that might have been the beginning of a chuckle escaped his lips. *Look, I have learned something new today. To mind-speak. Listen to me.*

He rolled his eyes toward Koz, who moaned. Medicas gathered around him. *I want his body.*

36

She flinched in shock. *No!*

Andrew projected mentally, *I learned something else today, too. I can see souls. His is leaving. He doesn't want his body. He is abandoning it, following his lady into death.*

No!

Yes. He is not fighting to survive, to live like we have. Like I am.

Andrew was right. She and Andrew had always struggled—against their mother—to live as individuals. Andrew had fought to live with his condition, sometimes from moment to moment, as he fought to live now.

Koz surrendered to death. His mind did not want to overcome the shock of his head injury because he was devastated by the loss of his Pairling. Even now, as life drained from his eyes, his etheric self, his soul, began to rise and separate from his body.

It is a big, strong, virile body, and I want it.

"No." But she whispered.

Yes. Come on, sis. You and I have read enough science fiction and fantasy, enough philosophy, watched enough flicks to know it can be done!

A bubble of sheer incredulity caught in her throat. *I can't—*

You can! You have great Power here. You have friends and allies and people bonded and indebted to you who will help. This is no time to lack faith in yourself!

But deep inside something gibbered insidiously, *I can't.*

You must! Look, his spirit is leaving, and you have me. You'll get all of me. Put me inside his body!

She had no time to prepare, no knowledge of how to do this thing. If it *could* be done. She wanted to deny that she could help. But Koz and Andrew were both in the arms of death. With luck she could save one. *Andrew.*

Linking Andrew's limp hand with Koz's, she put her hands around the men's joined fingers, felt the last pulsing energy of them both. She sensed how Koz was bound to the tiny echo of Perlee's Song and yearned to follow. Sensed how Andrew craved to live. As she balanced the rhythmic Songs of them, sweat slid down her face, her back, and her own true melody wavered.

Someone's hands curved over her shoulders. Jaquar. She should not be able to bear it, but he sent her strength and she used it. A gray form lifted from Koz, sped to where another shade—Perlee?—hovered. They merged and vanished. Pain speared Marian's head, her vision narrowed to Andrew's face. She gulped breaths but found no air.

Jaquar's grip dug into her shoulders. He was a rock she leaned on.

The Medicas drew back from Koz's body.

"No! Stay!" Marian commanded. She forced her hand to drop Andrew's limp fingers. "I have my brother and he wants to live. He will take this body. Keep it alive!"

They stared at her. One rubbed his forehead. "I have never seen a soul transfer. I don't know how it's done."

Marian didn't, either. She lifted her chin, kept Andrew close, wrapped tight in her love. With a thick tongue, she said, "I am a Sorceress, a Circlet of the Fifth Degree, I *will* do this."

Enthralled, the three Medicas stared at her. The leader nodded decisively. "We will keep the body alive."

She glanced at Andrew. The minute thread of life connecting his soul broke. There was a *snap*, an inner snap of Andrew separating from his body. The full weight of him, his will, his soul, his character, his personality fell on her and they spun into blackness, unconsciousness threatened. She gritted her teeth, but barely felt the action. Shoulders hunched, she fell forward.

Send me in, Marian, please, please, please, begged Andrew, like the child he'd been once.

She couldn't deny him then, and couldn't deny him now.

Wearily, lifting Andrew's being like a weight too heavy to be borne, she fumbled for Koz's hand, sensed the emptiness of his shell, knew the shape of all the crannies and caverns of him.

Someone moaned—was it her? Straining, she poured Andrew's essence into the body, tucked him in as if into a bed. The body jerked, ripping Andrew and Koz's hand from her slippery grasp. She grabbed, but missed him.

Bossgond was there, his hand linked to her right. Jaquar was on her other side, his fingers encompassing her left hand. And they were connected to all the Circlets on the field. Chalmon and Venetria poured energy into her. *Everyone* gave her support. Power trickled into her from unrecognized sources.

She reached with all her heart and mind and soul and recaptured Andrew, his whole being, and held him close, matched his whimpers with her own, turned them into hums of comfort.

Here is the body before you, Bossgond said. *The heart, the mind, the soul cavity. Do! We will help.*

Marian was afraid. *What if*—

You cannot doubt yourself! Bossgond snapped. *You must have faith that you can do this.*

Marian strengthened her will, let Andrew flow from her keeping, guided him into the body, holding him safe—for another stretch of seconds before her doubts ambushed her again. She fought them with the love she felt for Andrew, with the affection she felt from Bossgond, with the Powerful support she felt from Jaquar, but the transfer slowed.

Inside her head, Bossgond insinuated thoughts opposing the voice of her self-doubt. *Why do you think that you must achieve perfection or you will fail?*

Because I have always failed and it must be because I am not perfect. But with the admission, her heart felt lighter and more of Andrew sparkled into the body. Bossgond was distracting that part of her mind that doubted and letting her magic and Power do what needed to be done!

What have you failed at? Bossgond asked mildly.

Having my mother love me. Keeping Andrew safe. The failures rose huge in her mind.

Bossgond seemed consider that. *Perfection cannot be achieved. You can only do your best with the resources that you have. You did not fail with your mother. Your mother was the one who could not give you what you needed. It was a lack in her.*

I wanted too much.

Take the love I feel for you as a father, Bossgond said, and it poured into her. Love from the man, his pride in her, in her accomplishments filled her. She saw with awe that he thought she was beautiful, mind *and* body.

You did not fail Andrew. Jaquar's deep voice echoed in her mind. *He is here. He was not originally Summoned, but he came. You gave him new life. How can you think you failed him?*

Put that way, she couldn't. She let droplets of Andrew slide from her holding, sparkle into the mind-space, throb into the heart-space—that great heart of his—swirl into the soul-space. She released him with joy.

An arm clasped her around the waist and Power inundated her from Alexa. All the Marshalls linked with her. Marian went blind at the shock, the realization that through her the Power of all the Marshalls, all the Circlets, merged and cycled. Powerful people all, they provided Marian with all the magic she could need. Through her, they learned of one another, *accepted* each other. Distrust diminished with the intimate connection; trust and faith grew.

Take my love as a sister-friend, Alexa said, and that love filled Marian, banishing darkness and uncertainty. Alexa saw her as beautiful, too—as a strong woman of fascinating Power, full of love for Andrew, full of curiosity about life. In Alexa's image, Marian was laughing.

Marian smiled, relaxed.

Take my love as a mate, Jaquar said. The breath-stealing hugeness of his love roared through her like a river. She was a gorgeous woman. A woman who matched him in mind and heart. A woman who gave him joy as she learned, explored things. A woman who made him think and laugh and yearn.

How could she doubt herself? She couldn't. Her uncertainties vanished, defeated for now, as she gave her beloved brother new life.

She shrugged, settling the last of him into her Power stream, ready to transfer him with care. From Bossgond and the Medicas, she saw how to weave his mind into the brain, how to help him connect and spark the electrical impulses that were thought and memory and knowledge. From Jaquar and Alexa she expanded the heart-space where Andrew's emotions would live, sent them flowing there. And through Luthan the Chevalier Representative of the Singer, she received delicate touches from that elder woman, which mended Andrew's spirit, settled his soul.

Finally it was done.

Every little iridescent iota of Andrew gone from her keeping and into his new physical shell. What lingered and connected them both was the love they had for each other.

She slumped, black exhaustion descending, then fell into Jaquar's strong arms.

You are a Great Sorceress of Faith, he said, and his words comforted as darkness overwhelmed her.

Marian didn't think she'd been unconscious for more than a moment or two, because when she awoke, she was kneeling on the Tower floor next to Koz—Andrew. Afternoon light filtered through the windows, and circles of people surrounded her in a spiral, their hands beginning to unlink.

"Surely this was the greatest Power Circle ever created," a melodious male voice said near her.

She glanced that way and found a Shieldmarshall smiling at her, pleasure and Power in his gaze.

A Medica stroked Andrew-Koz's hair back from his head. "We will wake him in about two hours," the Medica said, smiling grimly. She swept a hand, indicating the room. "Combined wisdom says that the new mind must have time to settle in, but cannot be unconscious for too long or the inherent brain patterns of the past occupant will begin to overcome the new entity."

"The new *person,* my brother Andrew."

Dipping her head, the Medica agreed. "Andrew."

The shell of the Andrew whom Marian had loved all her life lay pitiful and deserted, green eyes wide and staring, face lax. Marian trembled and looked away. She couldn't stay here.

"I need air," she said.

Jaquar helped her to her feet. The rest of the Marshalls and Circlets were now participating in a single Healing Circle.

Marian gestured to the others. "Go help."

"I'd rather stay with you."

"I won't be a good companion." She needed to ponder events.

"You only have to be yourself. I'll just accompany you."

She linked her hands together, afraid the trembling in them would move to her whole body. "So much has happened," she whispered.

When she looked at Koz she saw only a large, virile Lladranan man. She flinched.

Jaquar hugged her. "He's there."

Pulling away, Marian turned her back on the scene. "I can't see him. I can only have faith that we accomplished the soul transfer."

Jaquar drew beside her, lifted her fingertips and kissed them. "You are the most amazing woman I know, and the most daring in your faith."

She stared at him. "I'm not—"

"You trusted people in a different land. You learned from them. Then you even returned to a world in great danger, a world that will demand much from you. You trusted us with your Summoning and with your brother. If Alexa can be called the Guardian of Honor, you can be known as the Sorceress of Faith."

Marian didn't know what to say. It felt as if a ton of responsibility was about to land on her shoulders. She didn't have the energy for that.

Andrew's former shell was gone. She gulped. She'd known that body as Andrew all her life. Would it sink into the ground like Perlee's? Would she miss it, mourn it, when she might have the real Andrew with her?

She shook the weird notions off.

Chants rose around them. Healing Power generated its own sweet smell that mixed with the sweat of those working, and the lingering stench of the monsters' bodily fluids.

"I want fresh air," she said.

He glanced at the open door of the Tower and the area beyond. "It should be safe. The Song knows, the Marshalls don't leave a scrap of the horrors around."

"I'm too tired to go far," she said.

"I'll be with you." He took her arm.

This time she didn't argue. She walked as steadily as she could outside, and her left foot still dragged a bit—in all the commotion she had forgotten to tell anyone about it.

"Why are you limping?" asked Jaquar.

"A sangvile—um—bite."

Jaquar swore and scooped her up. He whisked her back inside and to the Marshalls' Healing Circle. Marian didn't like being the center of attention again, but was pleased when she felt the sparkling connection with the Marshalls. She'd have to ensure the Tower Community bonded together better. Her wound was quickly healed, though a Medica scolded her and told her that her ankle would be weak for several days.

The atmosphere in the Tower was even more oppressive. Too many Lladranans. There were only two Earth people, herself and Alexa—even Andrew had a Lladranan body, and how much would that change him? She had faith that he'd only become a better person.

"My ankle is better enough to walk," she muttered to Jaquar, and linked fingers with him.

He looked at her, smiling. "Thank you."

"For forgiving you?" she asked.

"You have?"

She kept silent until they left the Tower and emerged into the strong late-afternoon sunlight. There she stopped to close her eyes and soak it up. The light refreshed her, reminded her she was alive. And so was Andrew.

When she opened her eyes, the first thing she saw was Perlee's sword in the ground. Next to it was Koz's. As her gaze swept the area, she saw about twenty other upright swords, some on the flagstones between the stands. None in the series of pentacles.

"All my fault," she whispered.

"I don't think so," said a voice behind her.

It was Chalmon. He and Venetria stood, looking bedraggled and exhausted, just outside the Tower door.

Jaquar stepped in front of her. "What do you want?"

"To apologize to Exotique Circlet of the Fifth Degree Marian Harasta," said Chalmon.

"You can't apologize for something that you don't regret," Marian said, stepping up to join Jaquar. When she thought of what this man and his cohorts had done, her anger spiked.

Chalmon eyed her warily. "That's true." He swallowed visibly. "And I still think that the knowledge we received was incalculable and the injury you did the nest saved many lives." He inhaled deeply. "But we were wrong to use you so, without your knowledge, and I apologize for that. I will always carry the burden of guilt that I was a moral coward and took the easy way out to forestall the consequences I feared."

From what she'd garnered through the link she had with Chalmon and Venetria, Marian didn't think anything about Sending her to the maw was easy for anyone. And Chalmon had been afraid the master and the monsters would invade Venetria's island and destroy his lover. Fear for a loved one made a person do strange things. Like die as Koz did. Like transfer a beloved brother's soul and spirit and heart into a different body.

Marian might understand why Chalmon had acted as he did, but she wouldn't forgive him anytime soon. She'd never trust him.

Turning to Jaquar, Chalmon bowed deeply. "And I apologize to you, Jaquar. I used your name to deceive Marian. I caused her to believe you betrayed her. I damaged your relationship with her."

Jaquar grunted. "Tell us why you don't think the attack was specifically because of Marian."

"I'm sure the Dark wants the Exotiques...neutralized. But the next was releasing sangviles," Chalmon said simply. "Those are particularly dangerous to the Tower Community. It's reasonable that the master had targeted this island as a stronghold for the horrors all along. In the past it has been rarely used, but is central to the current Towers." He shrugged. "I'd hate to think that the Dark is resourceful enough to target this island in two days. The timing may be due to Marian, but I believe everything had been planned."

He glanced around, his gaze lingering on the upright swords. "Parteger Island will never be the same. Nor should it be. I believe Circlet Marian will lead us now."

"Lead!" Marian exclaimed.

Chalmon's lips curved in a smile-grimace. "Organize us, then. We have been lax in cooperating, like spoiled children."

Marian was shaking her head, but Jaquar squeezed her fingers. She was torn by the idea—pleased and proud. But the weight of that responsibility pinned her heart.

"Excellent reasoning regarding today's attack, Chalmon," Jaquar said. His smile was forced, all teeth. "Now go."

"I don't know if his logic is sound," Marian said. Her damn self-doubt about her abilities was back.

"Then, know this," Chalmon said quietly. "Since you arrived, and your brother, too, Amee's Song is stronger. For that I will always thank you. And know also that I do not forget my debt to you. What I cannot pay in zhiv, I will promise in favors. My life is yours should you ever need it." He bowed and turned back to the Tower door, hesitating as if bracing for more work with others who disliked him. Then he squared his shoulders and went inside.

After Venetria watched him go, she gave Marian a strained smile. "I apologize, too. I knew what we did was wrong. I have no excuses. I don't think I'll ever forgive myself for my own actions." She squeezed her eyes shut, then opened them. "My life is yours, too, Marian. Just direct me in any way." She curtsied deeply and followed Chalmon.

Jaquar heaved a sigh. "Well, that interrupted my romantic walk with you."

Marian smiled, pressed his hand. "We were supposed to be on a *romantic* walk?"

Bringing her closer, Jaquar pulled her hand through his arm and began strolling again. "Yes, calming, uplifting, romantic."

"All that?"

His eyes were serious. "Everything I can give you, Marian."

He smiled. "Parteger Island is really very pretty. Quite pastoral beyond the theater and Tower." He waved a hand. "Meadows of flowers, orchards of fruit, groves of trees…"

"Your eloquence amazes me."

He chuckled with her. "So I'm trite." His tone turned serious. "You often leave me without words, Marian."

They had reached the outermost large pentacle. Jaquar grasped her other hand so that they stood facing each other. The heat from the sun wrapped around them, warmed the air.

His face was more lined than when she first met him. His eyes seemed bluer, his gaze definitely wiser. He'd suffered and survived.

As she had.

As Andrew had.

They all lived.

Even the streaks in his hair looked slightly wider than they had when he first stared down at her in the Marshalls' Temple.

"Our Song has revived, Marian," he whispered. "Listen to it."

She dropped her gaze and let the music surge around her, through her, cycle between them. It grew with every heartbeat, with every breath, with every moment her hands touched his. A Song more beautiful than she'd ever heard.

"Dance with me, beautiful Marian," he said, and led her into a waltz.

She closed her eyes and listened to their Song, and as she did, all the things he'd said and felt about her swirled through her bringing balm. He'd sent all his love, all his strength to her in her moment of need. He'd named her as mate—and Sorceress of Faith.

The tenderness now, of his arms, his steps, his body leaning into hers seemed like an unending caress.

The waltz ended too soon.

Marian met his eyes, saw his yearning.

"I love you," he said.

She closed her eyes. "I know. I care for you." She swallowed. "Deeply."

He brushed a kiss across her mouth, and Marian's lips tingled, heat bloomed within her.

Jaquar smiled. "We match, Fifth Degree Circlet Marian." *We should Pair-bond.*

A corner of her mouth lifted. "After seeing what happened to Koz and Perlee, I am doubtful."

He shook his head. "They were truly unlucky." He waved a hand at a Chevalier pacing the opening of the theater, on guard. "But look at Pascal. He is Paired with Marwey and neither would give that up. And all the Marshalls—"

Marian put her fingers over his lips to stop his words. "I must grow accustomed to my new life here first—"

"An excellent idea," Bossgond said. He tapped Jaquar on the shoulder. "Our wounded and Medicas must stay for a while, and the Marshalls would like you to restore the water lines."

They all walked back to the Tower, but when she reached the looming building, Marian tugged at her hands and Jaquar stopped.

She said, "The day is lovely. Peaceful. Let me consider my new life. Please give me a few moments alone."

He frowned and reluctantly let her go.

Thinking to see some of the aspects of the island that Jaquar had described, Marian circled the Tower. She breathed in the fragrant air of Amee but soon wanted to be near Jaquar again.

She'd just decided to go back when she stumbled straight into the arms of the cowled master.

37

She screamed, but it was too late.

The master raised a hand. The blow would kill her.

"I cry a sorcerous duel, now!" Bossgond shouted as he and Jaquar ran around the Tower corner.

Jaquar ran toward her. Bossgond tackled and sat on him.

The master, Mahlyar, stilled. His fetid breath whistled in her face. The tentacles on his face squirmed.

People sprinted out of the Tower, stopped.

"Dark Power or no, you are bound to a duel, Mahlyar, especially here on Parteger Island, the common gathering place of all the Tower Community, which you once were part of. I cry duel!" Bossgond yelled between panting breaths as he restrained Jaquar.

Not death at the master's hands, Marian thought. Or at least, not right now. Apparently she had a chance, pitiful though it might be.

Check your pockets, Jaquar advised. He'd stopped struggling. *You are the Sorceress of Faith. You can destroy it.*

Fight. Kill. Destroy. All the things she'd never wanted to do, never practiced, shrank from. She had to do it now.

"Your *pocket!*" Jaquar reminded.

She remembered. She had the brithenwood wand. The wand! She released a sigh of relief as she whipped it out.

The master laughed, clapped his hands. "Duel force field, nothing in and nothing out."

Jaquar said, *Remember your Power, your mastery over Weather elements. Storm and—*

A clear dome of rippling energy snapped over them and cut Jaquar's instructions off. Her world narrowed to herself and Mahlyar and the fight that would take place in a circle of fifteen feet.

She stood panting, eyeing him like a rabbit eyes a mountain lion, nearly petrified with fear. Fatalistically, she decided to do her best, at least cripple him enough that when the forcefield was raised, Alexa and the others could get him.

Even as she thought this, he waved a crooked, pus-laden finger in the air and made a door. It cracked open and dark slanted into the circle in beams. The dark death ray again…

She met its mad gaze. It was not human nor animal. It was not a "he."

"I can escape home," it said, so softly she thought only she could hear. "Or even better, I can bring others through after I've sucked your Power and eaten your brain."

A shudder seized her. She had to stand. She had to fight.

She had to win.

"You are such a failure, Marian," Mahlyar said, and his voice was all Candace—and others.

The words were thrown at her again and again, and with them images of people throughout her life who'd found her wanting by standards other than Marian's own. A teacher, a society debutante, another grad student, Jack Wilse…

"Enough!" she screamed. Screaming felt good.

She advanced with her wand.

The whispers of failure circled her again, and this time the visuals had solidified into three-dimensional people, all tall enough to make her feel childlike, and flinging failure after failure at her.

But this tactic wouldn't work. She had fought this battle earlier. Hadn't Bossgond bolstered her confidence? Hadn't Jaquar just named her the Sorceress of Faith? And besides that outside validation, she had her own true self-esteem.

She *was* a success! She had succeeded in goals that she'd set for herself. She had mastered her Power and become a Circlet. She had found a man to love and share her life with. Most of all, she had saved her brother.

And why was Mahlyar using these hateful puppets? To distract. He didn't seem to be doing anything else, like firing up a thunderbolt, he was just watching her. To test her? Perhaps. To psych her out. Yes!

And because he was afraid of her.

The knowledge dazzled her.

She aimed her wand at him, sent fire spearing toward him. Palm out, he deflected it.

"*You* are the failure!" She could play his game. "*You* failed to raise your Tower." It didn't sound too awful to her, but his features contorted. He shot a stream of darkness.

She jerked her wand, countered the stream, sent it into the ground at his feet. He snarled.

They circled. Anxious faces outside the dome—Pascal, Swordmarshall Thealia, Alexa—watched. She couldn't let their fear become her own.

He flung back his hood and howled, shocking her.

She jumped back. His face was patchy with color, bloodred, Lladranan gold, dead gray. A large brow ridge overhung his deep-set sockets. One eye showed small and red, the other hollow bone. Four-inch tentacles sprouted from around his mouth, three at each temple, thicker ones at the angle of his jaw.

Marian thought she'd go mad if one of those tentacles touched her.

His bolt of dark light caught her in the chest with hideous cold. Her heart slowed, her torso numbed. Her brain went foggy.

Then her left ankle gave. *No!* She hopped. Stomped her left foot, both feet. Her soles tingled as energy from the ground whispered through her. A tremor shivered through her. Not enough energy, not enough Power. Still, she flicked her wand and fire spurted. He waved it away, advanced with lips curled back showing sharp pointy teeth.

Marian set her feet, settled into her balance, raised her wand and summoned all the Power she had to shoot a flame.

With a finger-snap, Mahlyar built a shield to deflect her fire.

She stared as he kept coming.

He yanked the wand from her hands, shrieked with pain and let it fly. It hit the forcefield, then the ground.

So much for a wand as a weapon. Fear pooling inside her, she stooped and picked up a rock, threw it at him.

It hit his shoulder and he grunted.

This wasn't good.

Sneering, he flexed his fingers. Claws flicked from the tips, gleaming and murderous.

She ran for the wand. It was better than the rock, maybe still had some Power. She'd thrown a brithenwood stick once to good effect.

Scooping it up, she blessed adrenaline for her new strength. This time she whistled a short spell—"Kill, kill, kill"—and dredged up the last shred of anger and hate and destructive emotion from her body. She whirled and flung the wand, mind directed.

It skewered his left hand, torched it.

He screamed, blew on his hand and encased it in ice.

With evil determination, he flicked a writhing thread of dark energy at her. It caught her left ankle, twisted, twined. Trapped.

With one jerk he had her feet out from under her, was dragging her to him. He grinned, his black tongue licking over thick lips, his facial tentacles pulsing bloodred in triumph.

Terror immobilized her. She flopped around. Caught.

Think!

A pointed rock bit into her bottom.

Use the pain!

Use your Power!

From the sun. She reached and it flowed into her, energizing.

From the ground. Her nails clawed the ground and rich energy poured into her.

Energy. Power. Use it!

How?

She was a Weather mage. Lightning!

Yes.

She couldn't Call it from outside the forcefield.

But she could call it from inside herself. She formed the bolt, her whole body arcing as she sought to contain the energy. It ran through her head to toes to head, a closed circuit, escalating in Power, infusing every cell, sparking down every nerve. Suddenly her Power was *there*.

She stared up at Mahlyar, and he bent slowly down, grinning, tentacles curling, reaching, grasping.

She jammed her arms out, fingers stiff and spread. *Lightning!*

Blue fire zapped him, flung him back to hit the forcefield. He fell to the ground.

She stumbled to her feet and limped toward him. Her left ankle hurt—she sent a streak of lightning energy to encircle it, halted at the pain as her own Power burned away all traces of the Dark.

Mahlyar staggered to his feet and swept his right arm out, claws extended, gleaming and sharp. Sent a dark ray shooting.

With a thought, electrical Power rippled around her, shielding her. Nothing could get through from outside.

The next blue bolt of fire from her fingertips tore open his chest. She reached in and ripped out his blackened heart. It shriveled as she closed her fist around it, nails digging in. He screamed and the world shook.

The forcefield around them popped like a bubble and all the energy that they had confined and not used swept into her. Powerful energy, clean, sparkling, snapping energy, like a thunderstorm rolling through her and leaving lightning. She staggered and fell to her knees, dropped her head.

I will take that, Sinafin said in a tuneful voice. A beak pressed at her right fist, thrust through her fingers, snapped up the small stone heart in her hand.

"My God," someone said in English. Female. Alexa. "Shit, Marian, when you learn to fight you don't mess around." Her voice wobbled. "Ripped out the heart. Shit. I think I need to sit down."

A presence joined Marian on the ground. She felt it to her left.

She was full to bursting with Power, her skin stretched tight, the inner flesh of her lips turned out. All her senses were…off. She hoped they weren't fried, but suspected they were, along with her brain synapses. All fried. Poor Marian. Too bad. Such potential.

But she'd always known she'd come to this.

She heard whispering, then Bossgond said loudly, "She will never have such Power again. It is the best time for her to raise her Tower, I say!" He walked up to Marian and she saw him as a wavy ripple of shades of yellow in the air. The gold tone was particularly striking and she stared at it.

"Ahem." Bossgond cleared his throat. "Marian, it is time to raise your Tower."

Raise her Tower! The stunning idea nearly jolted her from the Power daze. She'd heard, read, thought a lot about that, but she wasn't ready. Oh no. Hadn't she overcome enough challenges today?

Someone took her elbows and lifted her to her feet. She didn't want to be upright or to think. She'd just look at the pretty gold—

"Marian," said Alexa. "You're staring at Bossgond's crotch."

Oops.

"Marian." Another male voice, reverberating across all the chords of her being. Soft, tender, caressing her name. Jaquar, who drew close.

She'd have thought Jaquar would be shades of red, like his maroon robe, but he was blue. From the palest gray-blue, icy-white blue to deep indigo. And the most beautiful blue was his eyes.

"Beautiful blue eyes," she said.

"Yes, yes," Bossgond snapped. "Let's get you to Alf Island. I know the place there that called to you."

"Heart to heart, soul to soul. Cleave. Transfer. Go. Come…" She wanted Jaquar's heart and soul to cleave to her own. *Cleave* was a word used in the Christian marriage ceremony, wasn't it?

"Take her other arm, Jaquar, and let's *move* before her brain explodes with an overload of Power!"

Just escaped brain being eaten to face brain exploding… Some days you couldn't win. Marian giggled.

Bossgond continued shouting orders. "Transfer to Alf Island through the innermost pentacle. It has remnants of Power, too. We need to get her there and started on her Tower raising *fast*, so she can use this energy before it burns her out."

She stared at the yellow banner that was Bossgond. He flapped in the breeze, agitated. She'd never seen him so disturbed, never heard him emphasize his words in normal speech. Then came a time that bent and twisted.

"This is something I don't want to miss," shouted Alexa. "We'll follow on our volarans."

Wind and fire and water. The scent of wildflowers so perfect that she wept and felt tears sizzle dry on her skin.

Her feet connected with the land and the rootedness shocked her clear to her heart. This was *her* land. Her place, forever.

The yellow waves of air approached, holding a large peacock-colored pearl. Bossgond placed the lovely pearl on her shoulder.

Hello, Marian, Tuck said, nuzzling her neck.

Tuck! She was back. She was home.

"Raise your Tower, Fifth Degree Circlet Marian Dale Harasta!" Bossgond thundered the command, brooking no denial.

Marian responded instinctively.

And it started. The first of her Power siphoned from her, coalescing into a three-dimensional image of the perfect Towers for her, and her mind cleared. She smiled. Who could have guessed?

They were square. She'd wanted square after all the round towers she'd inhabited. They weren't simple, but a Victorian fancy of what castle towers should look like. How fun. How amusing to plant this here on Amee.

Power encased her. She could do anything. She could raise these towers!

So she settled into her balance, digging her toes into the rich dirt that was nothing like the soil of Colorado. Tuck dug in, too, his claws into her shoulder.

She sorted the Power inside her. The stronger tune of Amee herself wound through Marian's blood, and she felt the energy of the land settle in her belly.

She swayed a little to catch the spray of the incoming surf on her face, distilled the Power of Water: surging, ever flexible, ever changing, yet strong enough to carve beaches and canyons. The hidden, secret, infinitely unknowable depths of the oceans flooded her with energy. She hunkered down to hold the Power. But it had blinded her, so she raised her arms, tilted her face to the sun to feel the warmth of it, of fire.

A solar flare licked her body, burned through her to mix with, then separate from the water energy. From swollen, cracked lips she said, "Wind! Air!" It whirled around her, buffeting her, and she laughed, for she could feel only the touch of the air and what she contained within herself, could not see, or hear or taste the spray of the tide on her lips. For an instant the wind brought all the dark, rich scents of Amee. Then that sense, too, vanished as a whirlwind as it spun inside her.

She thought she shrieked with joy, with the incredible Power. It tugged at her in four directions—a pleasure-pain tempting her to succumb to the elements, be torn apart in ecstasy. She danced with it, the streams of Power whirling around her in rainbow of colors, surging through her in great chords of melody so beautiful she thought she might splinter into iridescent shards.

A great tug of something else, some other Song, shuddered through her. A quiet, strong melody of love and lust and yearning. Jaquar. It was easier to remember his name than hers. Marian? Yes, she was Marian. Once of Earth and now of Amee.

And by the Power she would raise her Tower.

She screamed with laughter at the simple rhyme, but it focused her, made her concentrate, harnessing the Power—so hard, so difficult when it raged wild—shaping it, harder still—did she pant, sweat, turn bloodless with the effort? And fling it into the shape of two connected towers—like Tower Bridge of London.

Too great an endeavor for both towers and the bridge and the walkway. So the bridge shrank and Marian fell and felt the hard ground of Amee cut into her knees. And still she strove to *build,* to manifest in reality what she knew in her mind. No bridge, but instead of arches for traffic to pass through, the bottom stories were solid! She grunted with effort.

"Done!" someone shouted. "Let the Power go!"

What Power? It was all used up. Marian fell to her side, and the tiny bit remaining of the four elemental Powers trickled from her grasp into...Tuck? He'd hopped onto the ground and now bathed in the last shining remnants of her Power.

Feeling came first. Jaquar cradled her in his arms, but the Song of Amee linked her to the planet and the grass was cool against her calves. She had Towers and a world and a man.

Then she noticed the exquisite mixed fragrance of sweet grass and flowers and sea spray.

"Well now," Alexa said, and Marian could *feel* her hearing sharpen. "That's a sight I never thought to see again." Alexa chuckled.

As if Alexa's words were a spell—and they could be, couldn't they? Alexa was as strong in Power as she, though trained in a different discipline—Marian's blindness faded and overbright colors and shapes replaced it. She blinked and blinked again, and found herself staring at Alexa, who stood holding Marian's brithenwood staff and her own Jade Baton. Alexa gazed at the two Towers of Tower Bridge. They were connected with a little Victorian fancy of a walkway on the fourth level.

Marian looked at them, delighted. She never would have thought that her "perfect" image of a tower would be these fussy buildings. What a fabulous house. And Ritual room. And study. What wondrous things she could do in a place like that.

"Two," Jaquar said, and his chest rumbled against her. "Two. For you and Bossgond? Or for you and Andrew?"

Marian tried to speak, but coughed. Her throat was dry. Had she been screaming as she'd thought?

Bossgond squatted down near them, held a wineskin to her

lips. She drank gratefully, uncaring that some of the thick mead trickled down her chin.

"I thought." She met Jaquar's eyes and saw anger there—and deep hurt. That wasn't acceptable. She wanted his smile. Clearing her throat again, she said, "I thought for me and Tuck."

Jaquar's hurt flashed out of existence. He laughed. "That hamster is *prancing.*"

Tuck scrabbled up the side of her leg, danced up her thigh to her stomach. Her mouth dropped open. He was a rainbow-furred hamster. He sat back on his haunches, something large in his right cheek pouch. She had the suspicion that it was a shriveled stone heart and didn't want to contemplate that.

Tuck said, "I am pleased. But I do not need a whole Tower."

He nuzzled her neck, then hopped off her to the ground and *grew.* Marian goggled, then stared some more when he was joined by a matching foot-long rainbow-colored hamster.

Sinafin.

"We will make a little turret and take turns living here and with Alexa." Tuck came up and his tongue darted out to lick her chin. "Thank you. I shall live long and have Powerful offspring."

"Huh," she said, and tried to sit. It was beyond her strength, but Jaquar moved so she was propped in a sitting position against him. He held the wineskin now. Bossgond had risen and moved away to join everyone else in surveying the Towers.

"Perhaps," Marian whispered, "you'd like to live with me in one Tower and we could use the other for our studies?"

Jaquar shook his head.

Her stomach tightened and the mead turned sour in her mouth.

"They're square," he pointed out, "and silly looking. My masculinity might be called into question."

Bastien, Alexa's Pairling, had wandered back and now snorted. "I think they're fine Towers. If you don't want them, I bet I could convince Alexa—"

Jaquar hugged Marian tight. His heart was thumping hard, but his voice was cool. "I want them, and Marian." He glanced up at Bastien. "I'll use your worthless self as witness. I hereby formally ask Marian to Pair-bond with me in a coeurdechain."

Bastien snorted again. "You Sorcerers, always so formal. Why don't you just kiss her?"

So Jaquar did, and she felt the Song that rose between them twine them together. His total self opened to her and she responded. She tasted the true intensity and richness of life that could be found in giving and sharing love with a partner.

She broke the kiss and touched his cheek, smiling. "I look forward to exploring every aspect of our lives and our world with you."

Then she studied the people around her. To her amazement Andrew-Koz was there, swaying in the hold of a massive Swordmarshall, eyelids heavy.

She jumped up and ran to hug him. His arms came around her, but he didn't hug her back as he always had. Her heart flipped into her throat. "Andrew?"

He blinked. When he answered, his words slurred. "I think you should call me Koz." He was speaking Lladranan! Of course he knew French, and Marian had tried to teach him rudiments of the language on Earth. Did the brain have language patterns—? Her mouth dried.

"Koz?" She stepped back, and his arms fell to his side.

"Yep," he said in English, and that reassured her a little. He switched back to Lladranan. "And I think I'll live in Horseshoe Hall at the Marshalls' Castle. I'm a Chevalier now." He puffed out his chest, but it was a larger chest than he'd had and he overbalanced.

The Swordmarshall steadied him. "Easy, lad."

Koz-Andrew glanced at the Towers, then to her. "Go, Marian," he said, and the lilt when he said her name was the same, though the voice was deeper. He smiled, and somehow that was the same, too.

She grabbed his hands, which were not at all the same. "I'm your sister and I love you. I want you to be happy." She didn't want him fighting. But it was not her decision.

Marian swung her gaze to Alexa's. Koz had been a part of Alexa's household. The other Exotique winked and nodded, and Marian released a relieved breath. Alexa would watch out for him.

Koz was taller than Marian, so she stood on the balls of her feet and brushed a kiss against his cheek. "I love you."

"I love you, too," Koz said. His eyes narrowed as he looked past her to Jaquar, who came up to them and placed an arm around Marian's shoulder. "Looks like you've got a man. Don't take any crap from him."

She smiled. "I won't."

Bossgond announced, "I think I will establish a school centered around my Tower." He stood, hands on hips.

"Wonderful!" Marian said. The old Circlet needed to be more sociable. She looked at Bossgond, a grumpy old man who'd become the father she'd never had. Alexa and Bastien gazed at her, smiling, too. Sinafin and Tuck paraded around as peacocks and Marian caught Tuck's chirp.

"*I* am the boy. I have the pretty feathers. You are the girl and are a pea*hen*."

Sinafin ignored him.

Everything Marian had ever wanted was here, even though she'd never known it, could never have imagined this life. She'd been right to return. Her heart and future lay here.

On Amee she'd learned to open herself to more people than Andrew—to trust and love. Her adventure had forced her to become an integral part of a vibrant community engaged in an awesome task, instead of a distant, academic observer of life. Relationships with people, particularly these people, would be fascinating and ever-changing, expanding the knowledge of her heart and leading her to wisdom instead of mere understanding.

"You're my friends," she said.

They cheered. She curtsied.

A breeze feathered against her skin. The last, blessed lesson of the day floated over her, into her—the knowledge that she was perfect in her own unique way.

She laughed. "I won against the Master Mahlyar. *We* won against the Dark." Marian looked at her twin Towers and flung out her arms and whirled in complete freedom. They were hers. Her new home and school. But who knew what condition they might be in? Whether there would be furnishings or food? She didn't care.

She said something she'd never said impulsively before, because before it had needed to be planned, it had needed to be perfect and right and tidy. But this moment was perfect in itself, as were all moments. As she was. "Let's party at my place!"

Jaquar scooped her up and spun her around and they lifted off the ground in a rush of air.

Another perfect moment. She'd live a lifetime of perfect moments.

Shaking her head, she chuckled. That sounded very Zen. But she was an Exotique Circlet, ready to add another melodic line to the symphony that was Lladranan culture.

Marian slipped from Jaquar's arms and took his hand. She Sang her Song as she ran to her Towers, and her lover and friends and brother followed.

* * * * *

There will be another Exotique Summoned—but who, and for which Lladranan faction? Find out in 2007....

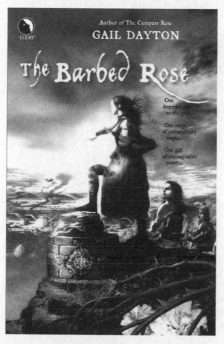

If you enjoyed what you just read,
then we've got an offer you can't resist!

Take 1 bestselling
love story FREE!

Plus get a FREE surprise gift!

Clip this page and mail it to the Reader Service®

IN U.S.A.
3010 Walden Ave.
P.O. Box 1867
Buffalo, N.Y. 14240-1867

IN CANADA
P.O. Box 609
Fort Erie, Ontario
L2A 5X3

YES! Please send me one free LUNA™ novel and my free surprise gift.
After receiving it, if I don't wish to receive any more, I can return the shipping
statement marked cancel. If I don't cancel, I will receive one brand-new novel
every month, before they're available in stores! In the U.S.A., bill me at the
bargain price of $10.99 plus 50¢ shipping & handling per book and applicable
sales tax, if any*. In Canada, bill me at the bargain price of $12.99 plus 50¢
shipping & handling per book and applicable taxes**. That's the complete price
and a savings of 10% off the cover prices—what a great deal! I understand that
accepting the free book and gift places me under no obligation ever to buy any
books. I can always return a shipment and cancel at any time. Even if I never
buy another book from LUNA, the free book and gift are mine to keep forever.

175 HDN D34K
375 HDN D34L

Name _____ (PLEASE PRINT)

Address _____ Apt.#

City _____ State/Prov. _____ Zip/Postal Code

Not valid to current LUNA™ subscribers.

Want to try another series?
Call 1-800-873-8635 or visit www.morefreebooks.com.

* Terms and prices subject to change without notice. Sales tax applicable in N.Y.
** Canadian residents will be charged applicable provincial taxes and GST.
  All orders subject to approval. Offer limited to one per household.
  ® and ™ are registered trademarks owned and used by the trademark owner and
  or its licensee.

LUNA04TR   ©2004 Harlequin Enterprises Limited

ROBIN D. OWENS has been writing longer than she cares to recall. Her fantasy/futuristic romances finally found a home at Berkley with the issuance of *HeartMate* in December 2001. She credits the telepathic cat with attitude in selling that book. Since then, *Heart Thief* was a launch book for Berkley Sensation in June 2003, *Heart Duel* was published in April 2004, and *Heart Choice* was published in July 2005. She has now moved on to shape-shifting fairies and average American women who are summoned into another world to fight monstrous evil in her LUNA Books series, beginning with *Guardian of Honor*. She is profoundly thankful to be the recipient of the 2002 Romance Writers of America RITA® Award for *HeartMate* (for Best Paranormal Romance), the 2003 Denver Area Science Fiction Association Golden Lungfish Award for Writer of the Year and the 2004 Rocky Mountain Fiction Writers' Writer of the Year.

LUNA™

www.LUNA-Books.com

LUROIBC04TRR

THE TEARS OF LUNA

A shimmering crown grows and dims and is always reborn. Luna has the power and gift to brighten dark nights and lend mystery to the shadows. She will sometimes show up on the brightest of days, but her most powerful moments are when she fills the heaven with her light. Just as the moon comes each night to caress sleeping mortals, Luna takes a special interest in lovers. Her belief in the power of romance is so strong that it is said she cries gem-like tears which linger when her light moves on. Those lucky enough to find the Tears of Luna will be blessed with passion enduring, love fulfilled and the strength to find and fight for what is theirs.

THE TEARS OF LUNA MYTH COMES ALIVE IN **A WORLD AN ARTIST CAN IMAGINE**™

Over the last year, LUNA Books and Duirwaigh Gallery presented the work of five magical artists.

After many entries, our contest to win prints of the art created by these artists and a library of LUNA novels has come to a close.

Thank you for the great enthusiasm we received and please visit our Web site for more great books and art!

A WORLD YOU CAN ONLY IMAGINE ™

LUNA™

www.LUNA-Books.com

DUIRWAIGH Gallery

www.DuirwaighGallery.com